PRESUMED DEAD

MASON CROSS

ORION

An Orion paperback

First published in Great Britain in 2018 by Orion Books
This paperback edition published in 2018 by Orion Books,
an imprint of The Orion Publishing Group Ltd,
Carmelite House, 50 Victoria Embankment,
London EC4Y 0DZ

An Hachette UK Company

10 9 8 7 6 5 4 3 2 1

A CIP catalogue record for this book
is available from the British Library.

ISBN 978 1 4091 7243 7

Typeset by Deltatype Ltd, Birkenhead, Merseyside
Printed and bound in Great Britain by Clays Ltd, Elcograf S.p.A.

www.orionbooks.co.uk

For Scarlett

PRESUMED
DEAD

APRIL 6, 2004

It was raining again, but not like it had rained on the night she had last seen her father.

This was merely a moderate downpour. Nothing that would flood the low part of the south road, or make the river burst its banks; both of which had happened over the winter. She sat in the easy chair by the window and watched as the rain fell through the branches of the big oak tree and splashed in the puddles in the yard. From the living-room window, she could see all the way down the hill. She saw the lights of the car two minutes before it got close enough to be sure that it was a sheriff's department vehicle.

She heard the creak of a floorboard and turned to see her mother standing in the doorway. She was staring out of the window as the blue-and-white patrol car reached their house and stopped. Her hand was pressed against her chest, her eyes wide.

Her mother didn't look at her. She turned back to the window, in time to see the sheriff and one of his men get out, fitting their hats on and hunching over in their black raincoats. They approached the door with expressions darker than the late afternoon sky. Time seemed to be suspended in the gap between the car doors closing and the inevitable ring of the doorbell.

Her mother's voice was almost inaudible. She had known this was coming for five months. She was resigned to it now. It didn't make it any easier to hear.

"They found him."

Present Day
Thursday

1

CARTER BLAKE

After the service, most of the mourners moved on to the gathering at Betty's house. I hung back, watching as the crowd shuffled away from her graveside. I found a spot by a tall pine tree that was far enough from any of the knots of people hugging or smoking that I wouldn't get drawn into a conversation. A white-haired man in a rumpled black suit who looked to be in his early eighties squinted at me over the rims of his glasses. He stared at me for a few seconds before shaking his head and moving on. I didn't know him, but maybe he had seen me around in the old days.

I bowed my head, which made me fit in just fine in the circumstances, and everyone else filed past without comment. I recognized a few faces: all of them older and sadder. Nobody I felt like talking to, in particular. And then I saw a familiar face. Karen Day's mother, Lauren. She looked in good health.

I hadn't been back to Ravenwood in more than twenty years. I hadn't thought much about the place in almost as long. Only one thing could have brought me back, and unfortunately that one thing had happened. I didn't intend to linger: just stay long enough to pay my respects. But it was a crisp and cloudless late-November day, and I felt an unexpected urge to hang around a little longer. Perhaps it was the funeral, perhaps it was being back in a place I had put down roots, once upon a time.

I was parked a couple of streets down from the church, and I took a circuitous route back to the car, partly to avoid the crowds, partly because it would take me past the house where I used to live.

Forty-two Hemlock Road was still there, though I knew Betty had long since moved to the small apartment where she died. The house had weathered the years well. The lawn was neatly kept, the paint job looked fresh. A shiny red kids' bicycle was lying on its side at the line where the grass met the sidewalk, its owner clearly having no cause to worry about passing thieves. There was a love seat hanging from the lilac tree out in the front yard – a new addition. When I looked closer, I could just make out a frayed, gray loop of rope curled around the thickest branch, from the tire swing I had hung there a lifetime ago. I wondered if I was the only one of Betty's kids to come back for the funeral. It had been pure chance I had happened to read about her passing. I guessed the rest of them were out there somewhere. I had never formed any lasting friendships with any of the others she fostered. The only person I ever occasionally thought about from my Ravenwood days was Karen Day – the lost girl.

I took a last look at the house and headed back down the hill toward Main Street. I was passing Dino's Diner, reaching into my pockets for the car keys when I heard a name being called. A name I hadn't gone by in twenty years.

I turned and saw Karen Day's mother, standing in the doorway of Dino's, holding the door open. Lauren Day had to be in her mid-sixties by now, but was wearing it well. Her brown hair showed only a few streaks of gray. She was slim and had a narrow face, only a few lines around her eyes. She was dressed for the occasion. Dark pants, black shoes and a white blouse. No coat, so I guessed she had come out of the diner just to see me. I turned and retraced my steps. I hesitated over the appropriate greeting then she pulled me in for a hug, kissing me lightly on the cheek.

"I thought that was you," she said. "Are you staying in town?"

I shook my head. "Just here for the funeral."

"It was a lovely service," she said. "People always say that, though, don't they?"

She was still holding the door open. "Do you have time to get a coffee?"

I hesitated, but made my mind up when I saw the hope in her eyes. What harm could it do?

We went inside and sat down in a booth by the window and I ordered a black coffee. Lauren already had a full cup of Earl Grey in front of her.

"It was good of you to come. We tried to get in touch with all of the kids, but ..."

"Hard to find some people," I said. "I saw the obituary in the *Times*."

It had been the first time I had picked up a physical newspaper in months. The previous customer had left it on the table at one of my regular breakfast places.

She smiled. "Betty wouldn't have minded. It was enough for her to know she had made some kind of difference."

"Dino isn't around anymore, huh?" I observed as my coffee was delivered. Dino — a short, rotund guy with not much hair and even less regard for service with a smile. The diner was open seven days a week, seven a.m. till nine p.m., and if he took a day off, I never knew about it.

She shook her head. "Heart attack. Ten years ago, maybe."

I wasn't surprised. "You look well," I said.

She waved away the compliment. "You're seeing me at my most presentable, dear. Weddings and funerals. So, what do you do now? Somebody said you had joined the military?"

"That was a long time ago," I said. "I work for myself now."

"Doing what?"

"Consultancy. The work varies."

"My, that's awfully vague."

I smiled. "I look for people. Usually they're the sort of people who don't want to be found. How about you?"

She took a breath and hesitated a second. "Actually, I look for people too. I've been doing what I do for a lot of years. I started it up after what happened to Karen, figured I would get the ball rolling, but it's just grown and grown."

Karen Day had been in the year above me in high school. She was tall, and had her mother's brown hair and eyes. We were friends, but not close friends. Then again, none of my friends had been all that close.

She had gone missing on the night of May 25, 1995. She had been working at the Esso station on the edge of town and left at eleven, after closing up. Nobody ever saw her alive again. Over the course of that long, hot summer, we searched for her. There were six hundred acres of woods separating Ravenwood from the next town. At first, we had teams of volunteers out there, all of us reassuring each other she would be found safe and well. The whole town searched for weeks. Gradually, it set in that if we found anything it would be a body. Little by little, the volunteers found other commitments, until there were only a few of us left. The first big storm of the fall brought her back. The coroner speculated that her killer had trapped her body under water, and that was how her corpse ended up on the riverbank.

She had been dead for months, probably since the night she disappeared. Her killer was never found.

"It's called the Missing Foundation," Lauren continued. "We have staff now, a half-dozen offices across the country. We work with families of people who go missing. We eventually found Karen, but not every family is so fortunate."

Fortunate. Some would think that an odd choice of words. I didn't.

"It sounds like important work."

She nodded. "I really think so."

We looked down at our drinks in silence for a few moments. I thought about Karen. How the whole town had gone from concern to foreboding to despair. I had gone through a different cycle. Building frustration that I couldn't find her, rage when we learned her fate. I had never really forgotten those feelings. I couldn't help but admire Lauren Day. She had channeled her own grief and sense of helplessness into something worthwhile, something that touched other lives.

"Are you able to help everyone?"

She considered. "Nothing can fill the hole in these families' lives. Nothing. But in some way, we can usually help. There's this one man I've been in contact with who—"

She hesitated. I motioned for her to go on.

"Obviously, confidentiality is important, but I don't have to tell you his name. Some of our clients, we have a relationship that lasts years. This man is one of those. His sister was taken many years ago."

"Taken?"

"They never found her body, but she was one of several people who disappeared in the same area at the same time."

She didn't have to say any more. There are at least a couple of dozen serial killers operating in the United States at any given time, according to the experts. Some of them are never caught, some of their victims are never found. I have more knowledge about this subject than I would like.

"Something happened recently that was curious," she said.

I met her eyes, realizing that perhaps there was a reason she was relating this particular story about this particular client. Maybe on some level, it was the reason we were having this conversation. She needed to talk to somebody about this case.

"You have to understand," she continued, "denial is incredibly common among these families, especially in the early days. This man never really got over his sister's disappearance, but I always thought that intellectually he knew she was never coming home. Head and heart pull you in different ways, don't they?"

"What happened?"

Lauren Day looked out at the street for a long moment.

"His sister is dead. The authorities are sure of it, and deep down I believe he had accepted it too. But then something happened."

"What?"

"He says he saw his sister. Alive."

2

CARTER BLAKE

What do you know about the Devil Mountain Killer?

Lauren Day's question came back to me that evening as I turned my key in the door of the 40th-floor apartment in Battery Park City that was my home for the moment.

I switched the coffee machine on in the kitchen, took my jacket and shoes off and sat down on the couch, looking out at the view of the Hudson that was one of the main reasons I hadn't felt the urge to move on just yet.

She was good: I didn't realize I was being recruited until it was too late. Maybe she had been doing the work she was doing so long that she could identify the right skills in someone she needed to do a job.

I had told Lauren I knew the name, but not much more than that. She gave me the potted history. The Devil Mountain Killer was the moniker given to the unidentified person or persons responsible for a series of murders and disappearances in northeast Georgia fifteen years ago. A rural, sparsely populated area, not far from the course of the Appalachian Trail.

The killer had claimed at least nine victims, with more suspected, between August 2002 and October 2003. The murders attributed to him shared the same M.O.: killed by gunshots to the head from a .38 caliber pistol. The same .38 caliber pistol. The gender balance was almost even: five men and four women. There was no evidence of ante-mortem beatings or torture, no evidence of sexual assault. These were more like dispassionate executions: a double tap to the head. As far as the investigators could work out, the killings had always taken place out in the woods. Lonely stretches of highway, remote trails. The victims were hikers or hunters or drivers passing through, who must have stopped for the wrong person. The bodies were found concealed in rivers and shallow graves in the vicinity of Devil Mountain, hence the media-friendly name.

The killer was never caught. Too often, they aren't. The killings just ceased with as little explanation as they had started. People did what they always do when there's a loose end: they speculated about what had happened. Some thought he had moved on to a new hunting ground, or gone to jail for another crime, others assumed that he had killed himself. The authorities worked along the same assumptions, looking closely at anyone from the area who fell into one of those categories. There were no similar killing sprees in nearby states that matched the pattern. They found candidates for the jail or suicide explanations: one man serving time for a stabbing in a bar fight, another for holding up a liquor store, and another who had hanged himself in the first week of November of that year. The lack of evidence left behind by the killer meant that there was frustratingly little information to work with to definitively rule any of the three in or out. Both of the imprisoned men denied involvement, and the one who killed himself hadn't left a note.

Over the years, the media and the police moved on to fresher cases. It was still technically a live investigation, but the FBI had enough active murderers to catch without expending resources on the ones who were retired or dead.

On the way home, I had stopped to buy a book on the case called *Devil Mountain: State of Fear*, by a guy called William P. Heaney, along with a Rand McNally state map of Georgia. In the middle of the book were a series of pictures showing some of the locations where bodies had been discovered. There were photographs of some of the lead investigators on the case, a couple of the suspects, and family snaps of some of the victims. I was looking at one of these.

The man Lauren Day wanted me to talk to was named David Connor, and the girl in the photograph was his sister, Adeline.

The photograph in the book showed a seventeen-year-old girl. She was pictured sitting on the hood of a red car. She wore cut-off jean shorts and a T-shirt the color of claret. She had black hair and brown eyes, and wore a thin chain around her neck with a small gold crucifix attached. Adeline Connor's wasn't one of the eight bodies that had been recovered, but the cops were sure enough of her death that she had been written up as the final official victim of the Devil Mountain Killer.

Sometimes, the bodies of victims are found years or decades later. Often, they're never recovered. What doesn't happen is them showing up alive and well. Chances were good that David Connor had seen someone who looked like his sister and had been blinded by wishful thinking. Chances were also good that any attempt to find her would be a waste of time, and worse, would reopen old wounds.

I thought about it for a long time before I picked up my phone and dialed the number Lauren Day had given me, looking at the picture of Adeline Connor as the phone rang.

"Hello?" The voice was that of a relatively young man, but with a smoker's huskiness. The tone was wary. Someone who wasn't used to his phone ringing.

"Is this David Connor?"

"Who's asking?"

"Lauren Day asked me to give you a call. My name's Carter Blake."

3

DWIGHT HAYCOX

Haycox sang the opening lines of "Mr. Brownstone" under his breath as he typed in his username and password. He sat back and sipped from his lukewarm cup of coffee and watched the status wheel circle, as though it was thinking carefully about whether to permit him access.

No new posts since your last visit.

His eyes moved to the top right corner of the screen.

Private Messages: 12 (0 new)

Nothing new. Nothing from "Bloody Bill", the user who had contacted him the week before, teasing some new information. It wasn't exactly an unusual occurrence on the boards. The type of person who logged in here liked to know more than everyone else. Often, they were fantasists; the type of people who called in to talk-radio stations boasting about knowing the *real* story. Or the type who take it a step further and confess to the police investigating the case. They were easy to filter out.

This guy was different. If it was a guy at all, username notwithstanding. Most likely it was. The profile of users of this kind of website was overwhelmingly of one kind: white, mid-twenties to middle-age, and male. Ironically, not too different from the profile of your average serial murderer. Not for the first time, Haycox wondered if that was a coincidence.

Playing the odds, and for the sake of convenience, he was happy to think of "Bill" as a he. Bill had focused on something that no one else would have had any reason to connect to the DMK case: the death of Walter Wheeler. Somehow, he knew David Connor had hired Wheeler. Bill thought there could be more to his death than met the eye. Haycox concurred, though his sources in Atlanta hadn't yet responded to his questions.

He closed the browser window and opened the file drawer in the desk. The desk had come with the apartment. It was too big for the room, but it suited his purposes. He pulled out the file and leafed through it.

Haycox had been interested in murderers for as long as he could remember. It was a big part of why he had gone into his chosen profession. Something about DMK had stuck out, though. The fact the case was unsolved was important, of course, but many of them were. Perhaps it was because he had visited the location at an impressionable age. Either way, when the position had been advertised, it had seemed too good to be true.

The copies in the file were arranged chronologically, with his own notes in the margins. They came straight from the source, much of the information unavailable in any of the websites or the books written on the case. The sheriff's department would not be pleased if they knew these copies were here, but they would never find out.

He closed the drawer and switched off the computer screen, plunging the room into full darkness. The glow from the streetlamp across the road filtered through the branches of the tree in the yard. He watched the road for a while. Nothing came past, even though this was the main route through town.

He walked through to the small kitchen and microwaved the last chili dinner from the freezer, then ate it with a beer in front of the late news. Then he took a shower and laid out his uniform for the morning. Light blue shirt, blue coat, gray hat. He ran his fingertip along the embossed letters on the badge on the sleeve. *Lake Bethany Sheriff's Department.*

If only they knew.

Friday

4

ISABELLA GREEN

The Mercer place was just off Cherry Hill Road, about a half-mile outside of the Bethany town limits. It was a wide one-story house with whitewashed wood siding. A big integrated garage took up almost half of the front, and there was a covered porch that wrapped around to the back of the building where it became a raised deck overlooking the woods behind.

Deputy Isabella Green pulled the venerable blue-and-white Crown Victoria into the rainbow-shaped concrete driveway, keeping her eyes on the door and the windows as she parked behind the white pickup out front. If anyone heard her approach, there was no outward sign. She knew from the record that Waylon Mercer was thirty-eight. Five years older than she was. At about six-one, three inches taller. Two hundred and thirty pounds: a hell of a lot heavier.

Isabella lifted her hat from the passenger seat and fitted it over her head before she opened the door. Out of habit, she reached down and patted her sidearm in its holster as she approached the house, not hurrying. She climbed the three wooden steps, hearing the wood creak beneath her, and heard a rustle. She paused and bent at the knee to look between the steps. There was a skinny black water spaniel staring up at her with moist brown eyes. The dog looked away after a moment and busied itself sniffing at the ground. Isabella straightened up and climbed up to the porch. She knocked hard on the door and stepped back. There was no sound from inside. No raised voices, no television. If it hadn't been for the pickup outside, it would look like no one was at home. She knocked again, harder this time, and heard footsteps approach. The door opened.

Mercer had wide shoulders and jet-black hair that was beginning to recede a little. He wore jeans and a white vest beneath a plaid work shirt. His belt buckle was a brass star, like a sheriff's badge in the Old West. He had been handsome in high school, and had been able to coast on that ever since.

He forced a smile.

"Deputy ... Green, right?"

Bethany was just about big enough that he could get away with pretending not to be sure of her name.

Isabella didn't return the smile. "Is your wife at home, Mr. Mercer?"

His eyes narrowed at the confirmation of why she was here. "She's not feeling well. What's this about?"

"Routine check," she said. "After the trouble you had last month."

He waited for her to say more. When she didn't, he just shrugged. "Everything's fine."

"I'm glad to hear it. Can I talk to Mrs. Mercer?"

"I said she isn't feeling well. She's sleeping."

"I heard you. I'd like you to go ask her to come out here and talk to me."

Mercer looked down at the deck, giving a little head shake, like he was amused she wasn't getting it. "She's asleep."

Isabella waited until he raised his eyes again before she spoke.

"Go wake her up, then."

The amusement drained out of Mercer's eyes and he straightened up and stepped toward her. The nightstick was clipped to the left side of Isabella's belt, the Glock 43 on the other side. Her hands didn't move to either one, not yet.

"I said she's asleep, Deputy. Now why don't you come back tomorrow? I'm sure she'll be happy to tell you the same thing I just did, since it seems that ain't good enough?"

"It ain't," she said, pronouncing the Ts hard.

His eyes moved from Isabella's to where she had parked the car. She could almost see the thought process going through his head. First, making sure she didn't have a partner with her. Then wondering if the car had a dash cam or something like that. It did, but the pickup was obscuring the line of sight. That was deliberate.

He seemed to consider it and then, without taking his eyes off her, reached behind him to close the door.

"Step out of the way, sir," she said.

Mercer took another step forward, getting in her face. He raised his voice. "Come back with a warrant. This is harassment."

She leaned in even closer, smelling juniper berries on his breath. Early for gin. Or perhaps the night before was still going on.

She lowered her voice by the same degree he had raised his. "Get out of my way, or I'm going to make you get out of it."

Before he could stop himself, he had raised his right hand and swung it toward the left side of Isabella's face. Open hand. Big mistake. Even if she had let him connect it would have been weak. But instead she ducked and punched him hard in the stomach, right above his stupid cowboy belt buckle. He folded over around her fist, and she reached for the nightstick, snapping it off her belt, bringing it up and cracking it over the back of his head while he was still bent forward. She didn't hit him hard, not enough to knock him out or anything. Just a tap on the head to remind him not to do anything else foolish.

Mercer lost his balance and sprawled on the porch, before scrambling onto all fours.

Isabella crouched down before he could get to his feet again, holding the nightstick loosely. They locked eyes. She could see he was fighting the urge to strike out again. His face was red. She shook her head. His eyes dropped.

She stowed the nightstick again and gripped him by the lapels of his shirt, hauling him up to his feet. She dusted off his shoulders and stood back.

"Try that again?" she asked, leaving her precise meaning open to interpretation.

He rubbed the back of his head and smiled, stepping out of Isabella's way and giving an exaggerated "come in" gesture.

She kept her eyes on him as she opened the door, then nodded her head to indicate he should take the lead.

The front door led into a hall with a tiled floor. At the far end, it widened out into a kitchen at the back. There were three closed doors leading off the hall: two on the left, one on the right. As Mercer stepped into the hallway, the farthest door opened.

Sally Mercer was thirty-four. She wore a blue-and-pink floral dress, and her blond hair was tied back in a ponytail. She was looking down at the carpet, and her left hand was massaging the side of her head, failing to conceal a fresh shiner.

"Everything okay?" she said in a shaky voice, without looking up.

"I told you she wasn't feeling so good," Mercer said, his

voice a little less steady now. Not so sure of himself.

Isabella stepped forward and gently took Sally's hand at the wrist, moving it down so she could get a look at the black eye. It was recent, within the last fifteen minutes. She wasn't just going on the look of the bruising to tell that, of course. That was when the neighbor had called them.

"He hit you again, sweetheart?"

Sally avoided her eyes, shook her head weakly. "I fell down."

Isabella turned back to Mercer. He was leaning back against the wall, watching the two of them coolly. She wished he would take another swing at her, but knew he wouldn't. Outside had been a mistake and he knew it.

"The sheriff told you we were going to be keeping an eye on you, Waylon," she said.

He didn't reply.

"I'm going to take Sally to get that eye looked at. Can't be too careful. You never know what domestic accidents can lead to."

She put a hand on Sally's shoulder and started walking out. Mercer didn't even look at his wife, just stared at Isabella the whole time.

As they reached the doorway, another department vehicle rounded the corner and swung into the driveway. This one was an SUV, a GMC S-15 Jimmy, also blue-and-white.

Deputy Kurt Feldman got out. Isabella was struck again by the thought that he looked more like the guy in the catalogue modeling the uniform than a real cop. His uniform was impeccably pressed, the boots spotless, the hat perfectly positioned on his head, the aviator sunglasses hiding a pair of deep blue eyes. The only thing creased on him was the brow above those sunglasses, which was knotted in concern.

A sudden, rapid barking from the far end of the house made

his head jerk to the source. Isabella looked and saw the black spaniel scampering out from under the porch, turning and then running toward her and Mrs. Mercer. She saw Feldman's hand reach to his holster and held her free hand up.

"It's okay."

The dog reached the two women and went up on its hind legs pawing at Mrs. Mercer's stomach, as though asking her not to go.

"Easy Swifty," she said.

Isabella ruffled the top of Swifty's head as its wet brown eyes glanced at its owner. The dog seemed to size Isabella up, then licked her hand.

"Swifty, get in the goddamn house."

Sally flinched. The dog obeyed Mercer's gruff voice instantly, scampering up the stairs and into the house.

Shooting a glance at Mercer, then at Isabella, Feldman spoke for the first time. "You okay?"

"She's fine," Isabella answered, though she knew her colleague wasn't asking about Mrs. Mercer.

Sometimes, she felt like Feldman treated her like an unruly child who needed to be watched like a hawk, lest she hurt herself. He had always been protective, and she assumed part of that was just him looking out for a fellow cop. Perhaps it was her imagination, but she felt like his protectiveness had stepped up a notch since her mom's health had been declining.

"Really, I just fell," Sally was saying as Isabella guided her past Feldman. He saw Mercer in the doorway and narrowed his eyes.

"Any problems here, Isabella?"

She glanced back at Mercer. He had a wary look on his face. She could probably book him for assault. A piss-poor *attempt* at assault, anyway. Feldman would swear he had witnessed it. But that wouldn't make a difference in the long run, and might actually make matters worse for Sally. Best to keep the powder dry for now and see if he learned the lesson.

She shook her head. "Not even close."

5

ISABELLA GREEN

"I know it must seem real easy to you."

Isabella watched Sally Mercer's eyes over the rim of the paper coffee cup. Or rather she watched the lids, since she had avoided looking anyone in the eye since they had gotten into the car. The bruise around her right eye was swelling up and darkening. They were in the small interview room. Table and three chairs, no windows, cinderblock walls, reinforced door, a potted fern in the corner. Isabella hated speaking to victims in here, because it always felt too much like an interrogation. But it was the nicest option they had. There was no fern in interview room one, and the chairs were bolted down.

"It seems anything but," Isabella replied. "All the same, I'd like you to consider pressing charges."

Sally put the cup down, let out a little sigh, and met Isabella's gaze for the first time. Her voice was surprisingly firm when she spoke.

"I told you it was an accident, this time."

Kurt Feldman spoke before Isabella could say anything. "You really think we buy that?"

Isabella shot him a look that told him to shut the hell up.

"Let me tell you something," he continued, oblivious to her look. "You keep having accidents, you're going to wind up dead."

"Deputy Feldman," Isabella said sharply. "Sally could use a refill on her coffee."

"Actually," Sally began, "I'm—"

"I insist."

Feldman narrowed his eyes and took the hint at last. He gave Isabella a look of mild apology and picked up the paper cup from in front of Sally Mercer before opening the door and stepping out into the corridor. The spring hinges snapped the door back and slammed it into the frame loudly. Sally jumped at the bang.

"He lacks tact," Isabella said.

The corner of Sally's mouth curled up in a half-smile.

"But he has something of a point. How long are you going to put up with this shit, Sally?"

She was silent.

"Till death do you part, that it?"

She flinched, visibly shocked that Isabella Green of all people would have chosen those words, and then dropped her gaze again.

"Trust me," Isabella said quietly, "it's overrated."

"I'm sorry," Sally said in a muted tone. There was no reason she should be, it was Isabella who had brought it up. Sally raised her gaze again and changed the subject. "How did you know to come by, at that moment?"

"Somebody called it in, heard the fight."

"There wasn't a fight."

"Sure."

"Can I go home now?"

Isabella became aware there was someone behind her. She

looked up at Feldman, standing holding the door open, the refilled cup of coffee in his hand. She hated when he did that. Everyone else in the world made a sound when they opened a door. She turned back to Sally.

"I can't change your mind about pressing charges?" she asked.

Feldman drew a breath and Isabella glanced back at him quickly. He thought better of whatever he had been about to say.

"I'd like to go home."

Feldman put the unwanted cup down on the table and stayed behind to put the recording equipment away, while Isabella walked Sally back along the corridor to the main office. It was a wide room with a reception desk, four small workspace cubicles and a big picture window. It looked more like a realtor's office than a sheriff's department. The department had a total staffing complement of eight, which was actually pretty luxurious for a jurisdiction the size of Bethany and its surroundings. Isabella knew Deputies Sam Dentz and Carl Bianchi were out in one of the cars running the afternoon patrol. Dwight Haycox was on the desk. He looked up as they emerged from the corridor.

"All done?" Haycox was twenty-two and looked younger, like he had only just started to shave. He had reddish-blond hair, and was tall, though he hid it by sitting down or leaning against things whenever possible. His pale blue eyes met Isabella's and then moved over to Sally Mercer. She was holding a hand up to hide the bruise again, making like she was scratching an itch.

"The sheriff back yet?"

Haycox turned his head to look at the closed door to McGregor's office and chewed the lid of his ballpoint pen as though he had to think hard about Isabella's question. He did that a lot, thought about everything before answering. He was fresh out of training, so perhaps this was a technique they had drummed into him. He was keen — Feldman thought he was an idiot, but Isabella didn't think so.

"Nope," he said.

That was standard. The sheriff liked to disappear for hours at a time. Perks of the top job. It wasn't like civilization was in danger of imminent collapse while the department was undermanned, of course. The morning's action was as exciting as it tended to get.

Isabella noticed Haycox had his arm over a piece of paper on his desk, as though he was shielding it. She angled her head to look at it. Before she could see anything beyond the fact it was a Xerox of an older, typed document, Haycox pulled it away and thrust it into his drawer.

"I'm just fixing the, you know... the numbers that the sheriff asked me to do."

Isabella raised an eyebrow. He blushed like a schoolkid caught with naughty pictures on his phone. She lowered her voice, so Sally couldn't overhear.

"You know, McGregor catches you doing that on duty, you'll be a dead man."

He swallowed and nodded. The sheriff was relaxed about his people maintaining hobby cases, so long as everything got done. But Isabella knew he would have a problem with the particular hobby case Haycox was looking into. Lucky for him, he had mentioned it to Isabella first. She had made sure she was the only person he mentioned it to. When he had discovered Isabella's own connection to the case, he had apologized as though the whole thing was his fault. She told him not to worry about it.

Sally cleared her throat when she saw they had finished talking and asked to use the ladies. Isabella pointed the door out while she hunted for the keys to the Crown Vic to take her back. Feldman appeared from the corridor and glanced around, seeing that Sally wasn't in the room. He put a hand on Isabella's arm and moved her to one side.

"He's gonna kill her, you know that," he said, quietly enough for Haycox not to hear. She wasn't sure why he did that, but he did it a lot.

"Not much we can do right now," she said. "Other than keep an eye on the situation."

Feldman sighed and took a seat behind the spare desk, tapping on the keyboard to wake the screen.

"Haycox," he called out, without bothering to look at the other man. "I'm sending you something over. Get it done, okay?"

She saw Haycox grimace and say nothing. Probably wondering when he would have put in enough time to tell Feldman where to go.

Sally came back out, wearing the reassuring smile that Isabella knew she had spent the last five minutes practicing in the mirror. They went out to the lot and got back into the car. She offered again to take Sally someplace else. They could fix her up with a place for the night at Benson's Cabins, or she could drive her to a relative, but Sally declined. Back home it was, then.

Waylon Mercer was waiting for them at the door, probably had been watching for the car as they started up the hill. They got out and Isabella followed a step behind Sally as she approached the house. Mercer's face showed none of the smirk or anger from before. He put a hand on Sally's shoulder as she reached him.

"You okay?" he asked, almost sounding convincing.

Sally just nodded without looking directly at him, and went inside. He looked back at Isabella and his lips tensed.

He was probably thinking about how she had slapped him down earlier, and hoping she wouldn't bring it up.

"Take very good care, Mr. Mercer. We don't want any more accidents."

His eyes didn't waver from Isabella's.

"Appreciate the concern, Deputy," he said at last. "You have a good day now."

He turned to go back inside and Isabella got back in the car. Despite Feldman's grave warning, she didn't expect any more trouble in the Mercer home tonight. Waylon was a bully and an abuser, but he wasn't an idiot. Sally had stuck to the accident story, and she would tell him that. Her presence and the fact he wasn't in handcuffs was all the proof he needed. Isabella guessed Sally had bought herself a few days of kid gloves, maybe even a week. But she knew they would be back up here sooner or later.

She twisted the key in the ignition and pulled out, wondering what the rest of the shift would bring before she knocked off. Two miles from the station, she passed David Connor, out for one of his walks. He didn't look up as the car passed him.

6

ISABELLA GREEN

When her shift finished at seven, Isabella switched the Crown Vic for her personal vehicle, a five-year-old green Chevy Impala, parked around the back of the station. It took her less than ten minutes to drive up the hill to the house she shared with her mother, on the western edge of town.

Feldman had been a little strange again this afternoon, in his manner with her. He had been more protective of her since her mom's stroke, but now that she thought about it, the change had really come after she had come home to find the two of them speaking, a couple weeks after her mom had gotten out of hospital. For a little while, she wondered if Kathleen had said something about the night their lives had changed, all those years ago. But Feldman gave no hint that they had discussed that, and she was sure he would have done.

Speaking of the past, she wondered whether Feldman knew anything about Haycox's hobby case. She hoped not. Over the years, people in Bethany had gotten used to people showing up and asking questions about what happened. This was the first time one of them had managed to inveigle himself into the damn sheriff's department, and Isabella couldn't help but admire Haycox's commitment, no matter how misguided he was. Besides, he was proving himself to be a decent cop, and he had had sense enough not to broach the subject with Feldman or McGregor or any of the other guys.

The little house she had done most of her growing up in was at the end of a line of four well-kept one-story homes on a wide, level patch of ground on the slopes of the hills west of town. She parked out front, beneath the branches of the big oak tree that had been there before she was born and would probably be here long after she was gone. She opened the front door and immediately smelled something cooking. Mary Cregg stuck her head out of the kitchen and smiled. Mary was older than Isabella's mom; in her early seventies, with white hair and a face creased with wrinkles. She had known Mary as long as she had lived in Bethany. She had lived next door since before they moved in, and had gotten on well with the family at once. Occasionally, it would catch Isabella by surprise how old she looked. She tended to think of her as eternally forty-something.

"Right on time."

"Smells amazing," Isabella said.

"Just a pot-roast. You hungry?"

"You really shouldn't have," she said, meaning it. If Mary wasn't so close by and so constantly willing to help, Isabella would have had to think about alternative arrangements for her mother by now. As it was, she knew the clock was ticking.

"Shouldn't I? You don't sound too convincing, Isabella."

"I guess I could be persuaded. But Sunday night I'm cooking for you. Where's mom?"

Mary indicated the direction of the living room, the smile fading a little. "She's tired today."

"Tired" was Mary's preferred euphemism for Kathleen Green's worse days. Ever since the stroke, there were days she was almost her old self. Other days when she got her daughter confused with somebody she had been friends with at school. Others where she seemed almost catatonic.

Kathleen was sitting in front of the TV, watching an old episode of *Quincy*, her eyes fixed on the screen. She didn't look up as Isabella entered, didn't react at all until she went over and put a hand on top of hers. She looked up and smiled. Isabella saw brief confusion in her eyes and wondered how tired she was, but then something clicked.

"Honey. Good day at work today?"

Does anybody ever truly want to know the answer to that question? Isabella knew her mom didn't, so she lied and told her it had been a wonderful day.

Kathleen nodded and looked back at the screen. Isabella sat down on the couch across from her and closed her eyes, massaging the side of her head and wondering what tomorrow was going to bring.

7

CARTER BLAKE

I was still wary of flying since the Winterlong business, so I made the journey to Georgia by road, selecting a gray Lincoln Continental from the rental company. On the Friday night, I stopped at a motel on Route 81, just south of Harrisonburg. I ate dinner in the deserted restaurant adjoining the motel and finished reading the book on the Devil Mountain Killer. It helped to put what Lauren Day had told me about her client in context.

David Connor and his sister Adeline had lived in Lake Bethany, the nearest town to Devil Mountain itself. Halloween night, 2003, she had left home after an argument with her brother. She told him she was going to stay with a friend. That was the last he or anyone had heard of her.

Most people were unaware of Adeline's disappearance at first, because that same night, another person from the town had gone missing. Arlo Green, a forty-four year old father of one, had gone for a drive and hadn't returned home. His car was found on the north road out of town, crashed into a tree. There was no sign of him. The damage to the car suggested the collision had been low-velocity, and the airbag wasn't deployed.

Meanwhile, David called the friend Adeline had gone to see a couple of days later and found she had never showed up. One person going missing without explanation didn't necessarily mean the worst, but two? A town of just three thousand people, Bethany had lost one person to the killer already: a hunter named Georgie Yorke, whose body was found the previous summer.

The story was familiar. As the weeks passed, a sense of dread set in. Everybody had theories about what had happened, nobody wanted to say it out loud. I thought back to the summer we had searched in vain for Karen Day, and felt a hollow ache in my gut.

Two months later, some cops from Kansas City came to the town and added a new wrinkle to the puzzle. They were looking for a man named Eric Salter, who had disappeared on a driving tour of the south. They had tracked him as far as Atlanta and found no trace of him or his car, a blue 1999 Ford Tempo. He had last been heard from on October 31st, just like Adeline and Arlo Green. He had been headed north. The FBI task force worked on the theory that Salter's disappearance was connected with the other two. Could their paths have crossed somehow? Could Salter himself have been the killer?

They found Salter's Ford the following April. It was buried in a ravine below one of the vertiginous curves on the road up to the start of the Devil Mountain foot trail. But this had been no accident, and he hadn't been alone.

I flicked back to the pictures bound into the center pages. One showed a crane lifting a wrecked car from a ravine.

Arlo Green's body was found in the back seat of Salter's car, only a single bullet wound to the head in his case. The front seats were empty, but the interior told a graphic story. A .38 caliber bullet was dug out from the headrest of the driver's seat, which was drenched in Salter's blood. There was blood in the passenger seat too, even more of it. It was tested and matched to Adeline Connor. It looked as though Salter had picked both Adeline and Green up, maybe at the same time, maybe not. All that was certain was someone had fired multiple shots from outside the vehicle.

Salter's mostly skeletonized remains were eventually found a mile from where the car had come to rest. It looked like he had been thrown clear when the car had plunged – or been pushed – into the ravine, and been swept along in the river. Investigators theorized that the same fate had befallen Adeline Connor. An exhaustive search of the area followed over the weeks and months that followed, but her body was never recovered. That she was dead was considered beyond doubt. The amount of blood lost alone almost guaranteed that, even before taking into consideration the sixty-foot drop into the ravine.

I closed the book and went back to my room, planning for an early night and an early start in the morning. But when I lay down on the bed, the wheels of my mind wouldn't stop turning.

Adeline Connor was dead and gone. So why did her brother think he had seen her alive and well in downtown Atlanta?

8

DWIGHT HAYCOX

"You get done with that paperwork?"

Haycox thought that Feldman always managed to sound like an angry dad whenever he spoke to him. He didn't even think he had to consciously put it on anymore. He took a second to compose a smile before looking up at Feldman. "Of course."

He located the document and handed it over. Feldman took it in a manner that approached a snatch. He examined it, then grunted a thanks and walked back toward his desk. He stopped halfway there and turned around, glancing at the clock on the wall.

"Aren't you off-duty, Haycox?"

Haycox shrugged. "Just finishing up."

Feldman shook his head. "Keen as mustard."

Haycox ignored him and finished up the edits on the report, before emailing it to McGregor, copying Isabella. McGregor was old school enough to demand a hard copy of everything, but three years of college followed by a year at the academy down in Forsyth had taught Haycox to make sure he kept an electronic trail of everything.

Except for the things he didn't want a record of, of course.

He watched Feldman as he tapped away on his keyboard, no longer paying him attention. Feldman hit the keys hard, as though using a manual typewriter, even though he was probably young enough to never have touched one. Haycox looked back at his own screen. He wanted to log in to the Brownstone account, check if there had been any other messages, but he knew he shouldn't risk it. Feldman came across as only marginally more tech-savvy than the sheriff, and Isabella already knew about his extra-curricular interests, but it was safer to maintain a complete separation. Just because no one around here would have the desire or wherewithal to interrogate his computer didn't mean no one ever would.

Feldman had pissed him off more than usual today. His attitude earlier when Isabella had been around, for a start. And then that report, which had consumed ninety minutes of his day, which Feldman could and should have written himself, had been accepted with no more than a grunt. He decided to prod the bear a little. He couldn't help it.

"So, is there some history there?"

Feldman looked up, as though surprised to see Haycox still here.

"What?"

"You and Deputy Green, I mean. Just something I picked up on."

He stared back at Haycox for so long that he started to wonder if he was ever going to speak again. Regretting the decision to say anything, he cleared his throat and looked back down at the paperwork. "Just wondered, is all," he finished lamely.

"I still haven't worked you out, son."

"I don't follow."

"Why here? I saw your file when it came in. Top five per cent of your class. You would have had no trouble getting a prime posting in Atlanta. Or someplace else, if you wanted to get farther away from home. Why here?"

It wasn't the first time someone had asked the question. Usually, they were satisfied with his explanation: that he had fallen in love with Bethany on a camping trip years ago and wanted to work here. In a way, it was kind of true. He had first encountered the stories of the Devil Mountain Killer on that long-ago boy scout trip, and they had stayed with him ever since.

"I like the town," Haycox said. "It's a great place to live."

"Remember what I told you on your first day?"

He did remember, but affected a puzzled look.

"I told you to keep your mouth shut and your ears and eyes open if you wanted to make it in this town. You remember that?"

"Sure."

"Little more of the ears and eyes," he said, indicating those points on his own head. "Little less of the mouth. Clear?"

Haycox stared back at him, not wanting to give him the satisfaction of looking as though the older man had rattled him. Instead, he got up and put his hat on.

"I'll see you tomorrow."

Feldman didn't answer, just looked back down at his keyboard. He resumed typing, harder than he needed to.

Saturday

9

CARTER BLAKE

Starting out at six a.m., I made good time on the second leg of my journey to David Connor's home town. Lake Bethany was about a half-hour south of the Tennessee state line. It was nestled in the Blue Ridge Mountains, population around three thousand. High up and isolated. Any visitors tended to be of the sort who would use it as a stopping-off point, rather than a destination: hunters, hikers, fishermen, people on driving or motorcycle tours of the South.

Devil Mountain itself was a couple of miles outside of town. Only two of the victims had been found on the trails on the mountain itself, but it wasn't hard to see why the name of this particular location had leapt out to the media when reporting on the case.

My route took me through some of the most beautiful country I had ever seen. The leaves were all but gone from the trees as winter began to settle in, and the sky was a crisp, almost arctic blue. There were only two ways to approach Lake Bethany; opposite ends of the same road. It left Route 19 to the north of Bethany, wound through town, and rejoined 19 five miles south. Aside from that, the town was a closed system.

I reached the town a little before one in the afternoon. Planning out the trip a couple of nights before, it hadn't taken me long to decide on accommodation options. The only game in town was Benson's Cabins. A knot of vacation cabins on the south-western outskirts, by the shores of the lake that gave the town its name. I took the northern exit off the highway so I could drive through the town itself on the way. The place made Ravenwood look like the big city. It had the basics, and not much else. One of everything: a general store named Andy's, a post office, a realtor, the Peach Tree Diner, Value Propane, and Jimmy's Bar. A sign indicated that the sheriff's office could be reached by turning right at the main crossroads. I expected I would be paying them a visit later.

I parked in one of the spaces outside of the general store and got out. It was cold, but the sun was high in the clear blue sky. I saw something on the sidewalk as I approached the door and stopped to examine it. It was a doodle in blue chalk showing a stick man with a sad face. Underneath it was neatly lettered: *The customer is always wrong*.

I went inside and bought a bottle of water, and asked the best way to the cabins. The guy at the counter was in his sixties, with a mane of untidy gray hair and a beard. He wore glasses with circular frameless lenses, like John Lennon's. He regarded my charcoal suit and white shirt and raised an eyebrow. Perhaps I was a little more formal than the tourists he was accustomed to. He didn't remark on it, though, and greeted me warmly. He took the cash for the water, and then came out from behind the counter and led me back to the door.

"Keep on for about a mile, then take the south road as if you're headed back toward the highway, and you'll see a sign on your right-hand side in about another half-mile. Can't miss it."

"I hope you're right."

"You hit the lake, you've gone too far."

As we finished speaking, another car pulled in. A green Chevy Impala.

"Here's trouble," the guy said in an amused tone.

The door opened and a woman got out. She was tall, maybe five-eleven, and had shoulder-length strawberry blond hair. A pair of oversize sunglasses was pushed back above her forehead. She wore a turquoise summer dress under a jean jacket. Definitely a local. She didn't look as though she had been behind the wheel for a long drive.

She smiled at the old guy and her blue eyes scanned me in a quick appraisal.

"Afternoon, Rick," she said.

"Afternoon, and a mighty fine one it is too," Rick replied.

She glanced at me and raised an eyebrow just as Rick had.

"Afternoon," I said.

She replied with a smile, then she passed between the two of us on her way into the store.

Rick repeated the directions, before going back inside to serve the woman for milk or instant coffee or cigarettes or whatever she was buying. I got back behind the wheel. I followed his directions, taking the road out of town. Before I got to the sign, a lone house up the hill from the road caught my eye. It was hulking and dark against the blue sky. It didn't exactly look like the Bates house from *Psycho*, but it had the same vibe. A little ramshackle, and definitively not inviting. I recognized it from when I had looked up David Connor's address for directions. I would be coming back this way later.

I found the turnoff from Benson's Cabins just as easily as Rick had promised, and a quarter of a mile later I was pulling into a grove in the trees where there was a horseshoe of eight identical wood buildings. Coarse gravel crunched beneath my tires. Through the trees, I could see the lake glinting in the sun. A thin black man, maybe in his sixties, maybe older, was already on his way out to greet me.

I got out of the car and caught a firm handshake before I could close the door. He was of medium height, a little hunched over, with a smoothly shaved head and a gray mustache. He wore a charcoal cardigan over a shirt and tie, and suit pants with a sharp crease in them.

"Mr. Blake?"

"That's me."

"Joseph Benson. Call me Joe. Thanks for choosing Benson's," he said with genuine warmth, as though my choice had been made after careful deliberation over several dozen promising options. "You're staying a whole week, huh?"

I nodded, and realized he probably didn't get too many customers who stayed that long at the end of the season. "Kind of open-ended," I said. "I could be staying longer, if that isn't a problem?"

"No problem at all, Mr. Blake. You just let me know what you need. Give you a hand with your bags?" he added, turning his gaze to the trunk.

"Thanks, but I'm fine," I said, opening the rear door and taking out a small suitcase.

"Traveling light," he observed.

"That's the way I like to do it," I agreed.

"Hiking, hunting, or nervous breakdown?"

I paused and looked at his stony face, which creased into a grin after a second.

"I'm just kidding with you. Though that's the reasons most folks come all the way out here." He stopped and gave me an appraising look. "You don't look like any of the three, though."

"Thanks, I think. I'm actually here to meet someone."

"Oh yeah?"

"A guy named David Connor, lives at the big house back that way?"

His features took on a serious cast for the first time, and I wondered if I had made a mistake.

"You know you're the second fella to stay here and tell me that."

"Oh yeah?"

"Best I don't say too much more," he said turning away, before thinking of something and turning back. "Word of advice though, be careful who you tell you're a friend of Connor's, okay?"

I wondered why that might be, but decided not to probe any further. After all, I would be able to make my own judgment of Mr. Connor in a short time.

"Let's get you set up with keys. I picked you out cabin eight. Best view of the lake. Same one your friend Wheeler stayed in, matter of fact."

"Wheeler?"

He let my question hang in the cool air. The look in his eyes told me I'd satisfied a question.

"Wheeler," he repeated finally. "The last guy who was here to meet David Connor."

10

CARTER BLAKE

Cabin eight was modest, but cozy. A small bedroom, bathroom, and a spacious living area and kitchen. There were French doors that led out to a covered deck with a view of the lake. There was no wind, so the surface of the water was perfectly still. Like a mirror laid flat on the ground in front of the hills on the other side.

I hadn't eaten since breakfast, and Benson recommended the food at Jimmy's Bar, but I wanted to check in with David Connor first.

By the time I drove back along the road to where I had passed his house, the sky had clouded over a little. I turned off the road and drove up a steep tree-lined path. The house towered above me, hulking and black. It looked even less inviting up close. I wondered if Connor was home. I hadn't been sure when I would arrive in Lake Bethany, so hadn't given him an ETA, only that it would be sometime today.

Connor had been suspicious at first, on the phone, as though he expected me to be a prank caller. I dropped Lauren Day's name before I said anything else, and he was immediately reassured. He told me his sister was alive, he was certain of it.

The house was an old Victorian, with siding painted a dull blue, and a steep gable roof. The windows were all shuttered. Two covered decks outside, one north-facing, the other east. A tall oak tree loomed over the building. There was a bright orange Ford Ranger pickup truck parked outside. I climbed the three steps to the east-facing deck and pushed the doorbell. An ancient, muffled chime sounded from inside. Now that I was closer, I could hear something else as well – music. Something with guitars. An interior door creaked and the music got louder. Rock music. The front door opened and David Connor was there.

Connor looked out of place, like he had been matched with the wrong house. The wrong town, too. Maybe even the wrong state.

Knocking on the door of a house like this, you expected the door to be answered by an old widow who had owned the property for six decades. Connor looked in his early thirties. He had scruffy black hair that came down almost to his shoulders, and wore jeans and a black T-shirt with the words "Little Nikita" printed on it in white capitals. He was barefoot. There was a chain around his neck and a ring on the middle finger of his left hand. He had a dazed, hung-over look to his eyes. Maybe I had woken him up.

"Campbell Blake, right?"

I held out a hand. "Carter. I prefer just Blake, though. Good to meet you."

"Likewise. Thanks for coming out here. You fly into Atlanta?"

"I drove down from New York. Seems like a nice town."

He snorted and started to say something, and then changed his mind. He turned and walked back inside. I assumed he wanted me to follow.

The door opened onto a spacious hallway with a wood floor and a wide staircase with intricately carved banisters. The air smelled faintly of pot and dirty laundry. We passed a room with an architect's desk and a big bay window. Pencil sketches and watercolor paintings adorned the wall. Mostly landscapes, but sketches of people, too. I saw a familiar face over and over. Adeline Connor, seventeen years old.

He led the way to the living room. The song finished playing and a new one started up. It sounded familiar, a rock band whose name was just on the tip of my tongue.

The living room was bare of furniture apart from a battered leather couch in front of a big screen television. The carpet was beige and stained, and there was a big rug with a Mexican design, on top of which an Xbox and a PlayStation were lined up in front of the television. There was one of those Amazon Alexa speakers, which was the source of the music.

Connor indicated the couch and I took a seat. I looked up and saw there were more paintings and sketches on the walls, some of them framed, others just pinned up. I saw Adeline's face a few more times, a sketch of Main Street, some cityscapes, and one arresting piece in the corner. It was in charcoal, most of the space taken up with a hulking silhouette of a man, just the outline of his bulk, and wild, tousled hair. The only features David had sketched in were two bright, almost demonic eyes. It reminded me a little of an *Incredible Hulk* cover from the seventies.

"I hope that one wasn't a life drawing," I said. "Who is it?"

David glanced over his shoulder and shrugged. "It's no one. It's abstract." He turned around, and before I could say anything else, moved us on to business. "Lauren said you could help me. I've uh ..." he scratched his stubble and smiled wryly, as though at a private joke. "I've had some trouble getting anywhere with this."

"It sounded like I might be able to help," I said.

"Yeah," he agreed. "Uh, Lauren wasn't sure how much you charge."

I thought about Lauren Day, about how she had devoted the last two decades of her life to helping people. I thought about the nice big payment into my account from my previous job.

"I'm here to see if I can help," I said. "No charge. Maybe I can help, maybe I can't."

He seemed to consider this. "The other guy was two hundred a day, which sounds like a lot, but he knew his stuff. I think he was really getting somewhere."

I remembered what Benson had said earlier, about how I wasn't the first.

"'The other guy,'" I repeated. "Wheeler, right?"

"Right. Did you work with him?"

I shook my head.

"Real shame, man," Connor said, looking into space.

"What happened? Lauren didn't mention anything about it."

"I didn't tell her. What was the use, right?"

He leaned back and told his fancy speaker to decrease the volume. The band faded to only just audible.

"I love this record, man. You heard it?"

"Who is it?"

"Queens of the Stone Age, *Songs For the Deaf*. Nobody listens to albums anymore, right? It's just songs all out of context. Nobody cares about the big picture."

"I know what you mean." He seemed to have forgotten all about what we were talking about. "You were going to tell me about Wheeler."

"Right. Yeah, damn, sorry about what happened."

"What happened?"

He looked confused, as though he expected me to know. "He died."

I could tell it was going to be a long conversation. "How did he die?"

"Carjacking. Down in Atlanta."

I took another drink and put the bottle down on the rug. "Why don't you tell me everything from the start?"

He sighed. "I was working down there. That's where I go in the summer. I work April to September, then I come back here."

"What do you do when you're here?"

He shrugged. "Nothing. The house is paid for, it was my parents'. And I live cheap. Working the summer gives me enough to get by until next year."

I cleared my throat. "Your sister is legally dead," I said. Ten minutes before, I would have broached the subject more gently, but I wanted to keep him on track. "She died in 2003."

"I guess I thought that too," he said. "Until I saw her."

I waited for him to continue. He was staring out of the window, out at the trees.

"Couple of months ago. Middle of September. It was about eight o'clock in the morning. I was headed back to the apartment I was staying at in Lakewood Heights, after my shift. I was on the bus. There was construction outside of Turner Field. We stopped at the lights. I was listening to music, just looking out of the window. Lot of people on the sidewalk, going to work. All of a sudden, I see her."

"You saw your sister in the crowd?"

"Yes."

"How do you know it wasn't just someone who looked like her?"

He shook his head, as though frustrated I wasn't getting it. "Not her face. I saw her talking to somebody. A guy with tattoos. She had her back to me. She was carrying a red bag, like dark red. Her hair was shorter, but somehow ... I knew it was her, right away, before she even turned around."

"You recognized her from behind, after fifteen years?" I

knew I wasn't doing a good job of hiding my skepticism.

He turned his head from the window and fixed me with a glare, daring me to disagree. "That's right. I knew it was her, like that. I knew it was Adeline. Then she turned around, and that was when I knew for sure. She recognized me."

"How do you know?"

"I saw it in her eyes. She caught my eye and just ... just flinched. She opened her mouth as if she was going to say something, but then she turned away again quickly, and the lights changed and the bus moved off."

"What happened then?"

"I got up and told the driver to let me out. He told me no way, next stop. I got in an argument with him and eventually he opened the door and told me to get the fuck off his bus."

I knew what was coming next, but I let Connor tell me it.

"We had gone a couple of blocks down the street. I ran back along the sidewalk. By the time I got to the place we had stopped, she was gone, and so was the man with the tattoos."

There was no proof, no tangible evidence that this was anything other than a hallucination or a case of mistaken identity. And yet, listening to him tell it, I could see why Lauren Day had believed his story.

"What did he look like? The guy with the tattoos."

Connor smiled, as though he had expected me to ask. He got up and picked up a large cardboard portfolio from the table. He opened it up and leafed through. I saw more pencil sketches. He stopped at one, considered, flicked forward a few sheets and held it to me. It showed a woman with shoulder length dark hair and dark eyes. It was a great likeness, assuming the person it showed existed.

"This is what Adeline looks like now."

He leafed through another couple of sheets and then handed me another sketch. This one showed a serious-looking guy with a shaved head and tattoos on his forearms. One of them was a heart tangled in barbed wire.

"This is the guy."

I examined the two pictures. "You've always been an artist?"

He glanced down at them, as though he hadn't given the matter much thought. "I like to draw."

I put them down and looked up at him. "So what did you do next? After you realized they'd gone?"

"I hung around that neighborhood for hours, looking for her. I waited until it got dark but didn't see her again. Then the next day I went to the same place and waited. I did that every day for a week."

"Did you talk to the police?"

"I talked to a lady on the phone at the FBI. Missing Persons. She said Adeline can't be considered a missing person because she's legally dead. I told her about how they never actually found a body, but ..."

"What about the cops around here?" They were next on my list to visit, but I thought it wouldn't hurt to ask what – if anything – Connor had told them already.

He smiled again. The same little smile he had given me at the door when I had said it was a nice town. "Believe me, man. I'm the last person they're interested in talking to. They don't want to hear it. They weren't happy when Mr. Wheeler went talking to them either."

I wasn't exactly surprised.

"How did you find Wheeler? He was a PI?"

He nodded. "I talked to him on the phone. Then he came to see me. I told him what I told you."

"What did he say?"

"That he would look into it. He talked to Sheriff McGregor, like I said. Even though I told him not to bother. Next day, he called me from Atlanta. He said he had a ..." he paused and thought of the exact words Wheeler had used. "A promising lead."

"He say anything specific?"

"Just that it was about the guy with the ink. Apparently it was a gang thing, and he was going to talk to somebody who might be able to point him in the right direction. I guess that's what put him in the wrong place at the wrong time."

"What happened?"

"He was stopped at lights and somebody jacked him. He was shot."

"They get the shooter?"

He shook his head. "I felt bad for him, you know? Like, he wouldn't have been there if I hadn't hired him."

"It wasn't your fault," I said.

He shrugged, like he didn't feel like arguing either way.

"How old were you? When Adeline was ... when she disappeared."

"I was eighteen."

Almost half a lifetime. And I knew he would divide his existence into before and after Adeline. I remembered what he had said about the ownership of the house, and knew the answer to my next question. I asked it anyway. "Your parents, are they still around?"

"My mom died when I was six. Dad took off a while before Adeline disappeared."

"Know where he is now?"

"Probably six feet under." He sat back on his heels and gestured around him. "Just me, now. All this time."

I looked around. A big house for one guy, all on his own. A lot of time to dwell on things.

"So what do you think, Blake?"

"I'd like to find out what Wheeler was looking into before he died. I won't lie to you, though, I think this one's a long shot. Even if the woman you saw was your sister—"

"She was my sister," he cut in, his voice hardening.

I let the rebuke hang in the air for a second and then continued. "I'm keeping an open mind about that. Even if you're right, and it was her, she could be long gone."

"She was long gone for fifteen years. Difference is I know she's out there, now. I know I can find her this time."

His words touched on something that had been at the back of my mind. "I only have one other question for you, before I get to work."

"Shoot."

"You think the woman you saw was Adeline, and what makes you sure about that, is the fact she recognized you."

He nodded firmly.

"So if she recognized you, why didn't she stick around?"

The amiable look slowly drained from his face and his eyes narrowed.

"I guess you can ask her that question when you find her, Mr. Blake."

11

CARTER BLAKE

Be careful who you tell you're a friend of Connor's.

I thought about Joe Benson's words as I drove back to the cabins. Next on my list had been speaking to the local cops. Perhaps some of the personnel who worked on the original Devil Mountain murders were still around. Benson's warning had been my first inkling that it might not be plain sailing, and from the way Connor talked about the Bethany authorities, I was less than optimistic. I had expected that, of course. Small towns have long memories. I decided to spend a little time seeing what else I could find out about Wheeler. I was pleased to find the cabin had wifi, and used it to do some digging. The news report on Wheeler's carjacking gave me a few more details.

Walter Wheeler had just filled up his tank at a gas station in Adamsville, on the west side of Atlanta. A security camera showed him paying at the counter, talking to the cashier, and then driving out.

Police were called to the intersection down the road eleven minutes later. They found Wheeler face down in the middle of the road. Somebody had shot him twice in the head and hauled him out of his car. Dead at the scene.

I checked the news reports and there were follow-up stories over the next few weeks. It seemed Wheeler's murder tied in to a rash of carjackings in the city. His case had one important difference from those other cases though: his was the only fatality. I wondered if he had fought back, caused the situation to escalate.

David Connor told me that the Atlanta PD had traveled up to interview him when they found out that Wheeler was a private investigator and that he had been working on a case for him. From the way Connor talked about it, it sounded like they were interested in him as a suspect, but I guessed they had been able to eliminate him, since it looked like the case was still unsolved.

I thought about the reason Wheeler had been there in the first place. It would be easy to dismiss David Connor's story as the wishful thinking of a family member who had never gotten closure. Without a body, it's impossible for anyone to be sure, and that uncertainty often leads to false hope.

The Devil Mountain killings had taken place between 2002 and 2003. Before social media really got started, but well after the internet had embedded itself in everyday life. For whatever reason, this case hadn't lingered in the public consciousness the way others do. There had been enough serial killings, mass shootings and terrorist attacks since then to bury it. In the wider world, it seemed few people thought much about the Devil Mountain Killer anymore.

In among the news reports about the killings, getting sparser and more brief as the years went on, I found an old discussion forum about the case. It was hosted on a site called TrueSleuths, which was still active, though there were only a handful of posts on the Devil Mountain forum in the last five years. From the web design, it looked like it had been set up as a bulletin board in the early 2000s, maybe even the late 90s, as a place for armchair sleuths to come and debate the latest media-sensation murder cases, as well as older, pre-internet cases, going back to Zodiac and Manson.

The most recent posts were from a user called "Mr. Brownstone". I had a look. The first one was a link to a news article in Virginia, speculating about a link between two murders in Lynchburg in 2004 and the unsolved case. Two hitchhikers killed on rural roads, double tap to the head, .38 caliber, an attempt to conceal the bodies. All part of the Devil Mountain Killer's signature, as "a source" had pointed out. Mr. Brownstone was skeptical. The hikers were both over sixty and had been robbed. Several of the Devil Mountain victims had been found with their wallets and jewelry untouched; robbery had not been the motive. I clicked through to the linked article and agreed with him.

It looked like superficial similarities only. At the foot of the article was a linked piece from two months later confirming his thesis. An itinerant drifter named Rodney Goggins had been tried and convicted for the murders and was currently on death row. A full confession, DNA evidence, the works. The classic motive – he just wanted the money.

I clicked back to the forum. Mr. Brownstone's next post was recent, from earlier this month.

Adeline Connor alive?

This was brand new. Nobody had commented. I clicked in, wondering what Mr. Brownstone, whoever he was, knew. There wasn't much there, just a short paragraph about Adeline, and how her body had never been discovered, and then the revelation that her brother, who had been under suspicion briefly in 2003, now believed he had seen her alive. But how the hell did he know that? Connor hadn't spoken to the media, as far as I knew.

I spent a little longer going through the posts on the forum, but found nothing to tell me who he was or where Mr. Brownstone came from. I considered posting something myself, or sending him a message, but decided to wait until I had done a little more digging. In the meantime, I had other people to speak to.

12

CARTER BLAKE

"You got an appointment?"

The question was not asked in an unfriendly tone, but all the same, the look in the young deputy's eyes told me the answer to the question ought to be yes. The metal name tag on the right breast pocket of his light blue shirt said HAYCOX. He was in his early twenties, I guessed, and tall, though he was sitting down. His fingernails were neatly clipped, and he wore an expensive-looking watch on a leather strap. It stuck out: a wristwatch was practically an eccentricity on someone of his age.

I looked around. The front office of the sheriff's office was small but neat. Pine woodwork, a gray carpet, a couple of pot plants. The kind of place where they have the time to vacuum and generally give a damn what the place looks like. The three desks in the office were uncluttered. From in the back somewhere, I could hear the sound of a radio. I looked back down at Deputy Haycox.

"No, I don't have an appointment," I admitted. "I can come back later if it isn't convenient."

He shot a glance at the back of the room. I followed his gaze and saw two doors. One marked "Private", the other "Sheriff J.M. McGregor". As we looked, I could swear I heard the volume of the radio being turned down a little. So the sheriff was in.

"What's it about?"

"I wondered if I could talk to him about David Connor."

Haycox blinked as he heard the name. "In regard to what?"

I heard a slight creak of hinges as the door opened behind me.

"It's okay, Dwight."

I turned and saw the man I assumed was Sheriff McGregor standing in the open doorway.

I estimated he was in his early sixties. He was dressed in the same uniform as Haycox: light blue shirt, navy tie and chinos. His hair was gray and neatly trimmed. His eyes were brown, and they regarded me in that way all cops do, whether they're looking at a possible DUI, a murder suspect, or a guy asking for directions: suspicious, until you give them a reason not to be.

"Sheriff McGregor?" I held my hand out.

He reached out and gripped it hard for a moment, then released it. "I happen to have five minutes. Your lucky day, I guess, Mr ..."

I considered giving him another name for a split second, and then decided against it. No reason to. Not anymore. "Blake," I said. "Carter Blake."

He took that in and then glanced at Haycox, who said nothing.

He gestured for me to go in first and followed, closing the door. The sheriff's office was like the public area, only more so: both smaller and neater. There was a desk and a computer and a swivel chair, and a wooden chair with red fabric upholstery for visitors. McGregor sat down behind his desk, reaching underneath it to turn the radio down even further, but not quite off. It was a football game he was listening to. The breathless commentary and swells of crowd noise lingered in the air, too quiet to easily make out any words.

Aside from the monitor and keyboard, there were only two items on the desk: his hat, which was gray felt with a gold trim, and an autographed baseball. There was a steel filing cabinet and a bookcase against the wall. The bottom shelves were taken up with neatly labeled binders, and the two upper shelves with books. I scanned the spines and saw the titles were mostly things like *Georgia Department of Lakes 2015–17* and *State Census 2011*. I also saw the Devil Mountain Killer book I had bought in New York. That Haycox guy outside would have been in elementary school then, but McGregor was the right age to have been around for the original investigation, assuming he hadn't moved here from elsewhere. His name didn't ring a bell from my quick reading of the book, though.

I was conscious of his eyes on me as I looked around his office. Eventually, he broke the silence.

"You mentioned David Connor out there, Mr. Blake. I assume that means you're here about Walter Wheeler."

Straight to the point. I had wondered how I would broach the subject of Wheeler, but McGregor had saved me the trouble.

"Has David Connor spoken to you about that?" I asked.

He shook his head slowly. "Connor's smarter than that. What's your interest?"

I let that one go for the moment. Again, my mind shuffled through the index of ways I could justify my presence. When dealing with law enforcement, particularly personnel that might be hostile, it's always better not to give them an excuse to shut you down right out of the gate. I opted for something like the truth.

"I'm working with an organization David Connor has been in touch with. The Missing Foundation, perhaps you've heard of it?"

"Can't say as I have."

I cleared my throat, taking care to avoid words like "we".

"The foundation works with the family members of victims of certain crimes."

"Certain crimes?"

"Specifically, people who have been abducted, or are suspected of having been murdered, but where no body has been recovered."

McGregor folded his arms and leaned forward on the desk, a thin smile on his lips. "Something told me it would be along those lines."

His tone did not promise great cooperation in my future.

"You're familiar with the case, then."

He took his time answering.

"A few weeks ago, a guy was sitting where you're sitting, asking me the same questions you're no doubt about to ask. That man is dead now."

He left a pause that seemed to demand some sort of response.

"Is that a warning?"

"This isn't amusing, Mr. Blake. You ask if I'm familiar with the case, by which I assume you *really* mean, am I familiar with the Adeline Connor murder case. I'm familiar with it, all right. I headed up the search team when we looked for her. I was there when we found Eric Salter's car."

"You believe she's dead."

"She *is* dead. That bastard got her. Even if she wasn't dead when that car went into the river, she was afterwards. No way could she have survived that, and the blood loss. Her body was swept away by the river. I hear David Connor is having trouble accepting that."

"Have you spoken to him?"

He shook his head. "I just told you no. Connor hasn't spoken to me or any member of this department in fifteen years, as far as I'm aware. Some people would say it was understandable."

"Because he was a suspect?"

"Whichever way you look at it. Either because we suspected him to begin with, or because we never caught his sister's killer." McGregor sighed and closed his eyes, massaging them with the balls of his thumb and index finger. He seemed to look ten years older, all of a sudden. "To tell you the truth, I'm not sure if David Connor has spoken to *anyone* in town for fifteen years. It beats me why he's still here. He could have sold that place and started fresh someplace else."

I didn't interrupt, but I had my own ideas about why Connor would stick around. Leaving Lake Bethany would be an admission that it was over, that he had given up.

McGregor looked out of the window at where my rented Lincoln Continental was parked in the lot. I saw him register the New York license plate, and knew he was committing the plate to memory. He looked back at me.

"So we had kind of forgotten all about Connor, in a way," he said. "The younger kids talk about him, about how he was the killer and we just couldn't prove it. He's the spooky old man in the house on the hill, and he ain't even thirty-five. And then a few weeks ago, your friend Wheeler comes in to see me, asks if I can spare the time to talk about ... about what happened fifteen years ago."

"You don't like to talk about it."

"You're very perceptive. I like you better than Wheeler already." He reached forward and picked up the autographed baseball, weighing it in his hand. "We got a lot of that back then, of course. News people coming by all the time, then amateur detectives for a little while. We kept quiet, hoping people would move on, and eventually they did. It tailed off after a few years, and I was just fine about that. Things took a long time to recover. Maybe they still haven't. The rubberneckers still come, maybe not so many, but they come. The families don't come, not like before."

I nodded. "You don't want people dragging up old memories."

"And I don't intend to encourage you to, either. So if we keep this discussion confined to David Connor and the unfortunate death of Mr. Wheeler and why I think you're wasting your time here, you and me will stay friendly."

I considered carefully.

"How much do you know about what happened to Wheeler?"

"How about you tell me what you know, and we'll see if we can take it from there."

I knew there wasn't much I could tell him that he wouldn't know already if he had taken the time to read the news report or put in a call to his colleagues in Atlanta, but I guessed he wanted to make sure the information transfer wasn't a one-way deal.

"David Connor hired him," I said. "From what you've said, I figure he went private right off the bat because he knew ..." I paused, chose my next words carefully. "He knew that coming to see you wasn't an option for what he wanted."

McGregor eyed me carefully, as though looking for an implied insult. After a minute, he motioned for me to go on.

"Connor believes that he saw his sister in Atlanta, several weeks ago. Alive."

"I'm aware that he is under that illusion, yes. Wheeler told me."

How many other people had Wheeler spoken to? Could one of them have been the guy calling himself Mr. Brownstone on the TrueSleuths forum? McGregor was waiting for me to continue.

"He tried to find her himself, with no luck. He reached

out to my friend at the Missing Foundation, like I said. They weren't able to directly help him, but they suggested hiring a private detective. That's where Wheeler came in. He was looking into Connor's story in Atlanta when he was killed."

I stopped and just looked at McGregor. I could have told him a little more than that, of course, but I had talked enough. It was over to him.

"Shame for Wheeler," McGregor said. "Like I said, I never took to the guy, but ... damn shame. You have to be careful, in an unfamiliar city, don't you? Mr. Wheeler wasn't careful enough."

"So he came and spoke to you after taking the job," I said. "Just once?"

"Definitely just once. I couldn't have helped him even if I particularly wanted to. He told me why he was here and asked a whole lot of questions."

"You didn't like the questions he asked?"

He paused and gave me that appraising look again. "I didn't like the questions, or the way he asked them. He seemed to believe Connor with no evidence. I hope you'll be a little more skeptical. He talked to me like we'd screwed up, that Adeline was alive. I told him what I told you: that she isn't. She's out there, somewhere, but not alive."

My eyes moved to the books on his shelf. The one about the Devil Mountain Killer in particular. I wondered if I was about to ask one of the questions that had gotten Wheeler kicked out.

"And what about her killer?" I asked. "Is he still out there, too?"

McGregor sighed and looked down, as though disappointed.

"The thing to remember about Bethany: trouble comes from outside. You play nice, we'll treat you nice. You cause a ruckus, you'll be run out of town faster than you can spit."

"I'm not here to cause a ruckus."

"Time's up." He turned on his swivel chair and looked out of the window. Interview over. I didn't push it.

"Thank you for your time."

I got up and opened the door, pausing when McGregor surprised me by speaking again.

"You want my advice, Blake?"

I didn't answer, fully expecting to get it regardless.

"Take a couple of days in town if you want. Bethany is a nice place. But then you should tell David Connor you're not interested in wasting your time, and you should go someplace where you can do some good."

"Again," I said, "thanks for your time."

The door swung shut behind me. Haycox looked up, pretending that he hadn't been listening to our parting exchange. I bid him a good afternoon.

As I approached the door, I saw someone coming the other way. A woman. I recognized her. It took me a second to realize it was the same woman I had seen at the convenience store earlier on. Not because she had the kind of face that was easy to forget, but because she was dressed in the same uniform Haycox and McGregor were wearing, her blond hair tied back. I opened the door and held it for her.

I saw recognition flicker in her eyes too, and she smiled quickly. "Afternoon, again."

She nodded inside the office as if to draw my attention to where I was. "Everything okay?"

"Everything's fine," I said.

I went outside and got behind the wheel, thinking about what McGregor had said. Perhaps he was right. The odds were good that Adeline Connor was dead, and that the Devil Mountain Killer was dead too. Perhaps I should just forget about the town and go home. Those were real possibilities. But I had some questions to answer first.

13

ISABELLA GREEN

"Who was that guy?"

Haycox opened his mouth to answer Isabella's question, but Sheriff McGregor beat him to the punch.

"More trouble, is who that guy is."

McGregor was standing at the window, watching as the man with the dark hair and green eyes drove off in the gray Lincoln Continental with New York plates.

"Don't tell me ..."

He nodded. "David Connor. You think he would have quit after what happened to the last one." He let out a long sigh. "I'm going to have to have a conversation with that boy."

Isabella glanced back at Haycox, who was typing something and pretending not to be interested in the discussion.

"Who's out on the road this evening?" the sheriff asked, not taking his eyes off the parking lot, even though the Continental had disappeared out of view. "Feldman?"

Isabella shook her head. "Me."

He considered for a moment. "He says his name is Carter Blake. Keep an eye out for him, make sure he doesn't make any trouble."

"Any reason you're expecting him to?"

"I hope not."

With that, the sheriff turned and went back into his office, closing the door behind him. Isabella turned to Haycox and asked him if he had finished the TC16 reports for last quarter. As he was opening his mouth to answer, she moved closer keeping her voice low. "What did he ask about?"

Haycox gave a disappointed shrug. "They went in there. I guess it was about Adeline Connor."

She sighed. "Poor girl should be left to rest in peace." Haycox colored a little at that. "Any new theories?"

Haycox smiled and looked as though he was about to say something, and then shook his head.

"What?"

"Nothing."

Isabella narrowed her eyes and stared him out.

He leaned forward, his voice conspiratorial. "Okay, I got something that looks promising. I'm talking to a guy who—"

"You know what doesn't look promising?"

"What?"

"Your future employment prospects if you don't get me those reports."

He grinned sheepishly and gave her a salute. "Yes ma'am."

Isabella turned away before she smiled. She liked that Haycox was starting to be a little more comfortable with at least one member of the department.

14

CARTER BLAKE

I took a drive out to the last place anyone reported seeing Adeline Connor alive. It was on the north road, about a mile and a half out of town. She had been spotted at a small bridge across a culvert, just before the road forked: the last stretch to route 19 in one direction, the road that wound up to the start of the Devil Mountain hiking trail in the other. She had been out in the rain with no coat. A woman named Jennifer Gorman, had been driving by. She had wanted to stop, but had been in a hurry home to relieve the babysitter. An hour later, unable to forget about seeing Adeline, she had sent her husband out to drive the road. There had been no trace of her. She came forward a couple of days later, when David Connor reported his sister missing.

The next trace of Adeline had been the blood in the car found at the bottom of the ravine. I drove out to the bridge first and got out. It wasn't much of a bridge. Just a series of wooden slats over the culvert. Water carried down from the hills trickled through the pipe on its way down to the river below. The bridge was as wide as the road, and the drop was so shallow there weren't even guardrails at the side.

I parked at the side of the road and got out. The clouds had cleared again and the sunset was glowing through the branches of the trees. The wooden slats of the bridge looked old, and I was a little nervous about driving over it. But when I stepped onto it, it was firm, stronger than it looked. I walked across the bridge, listening to the soft burbling of the water beneath me. I reached the other side and stepped back onto the blacktop, surveying the area. Woods on both sides. The road disappeared around a curve a quarter of a mile in the direction I had come, and ahead of me rose about another quarter-mile until it was obscured by the tree cover. My eye caught something and I took a couple of steps to my right to get a better view. There was a house up there. Small, clad in dark wood, with a stone chimney on one side. It looked as though it could be abandoned.

I heard the sound of an engine from far off and looked both ways, trying to work out which direction it was coming from. After a couple of seconds, a battered old Volkswagen pickup truck appeared from the direction I had come. The driver was an old man wearing a faded denim baseball cap and glasses. He had a bushy gray beard and peered through the glasses first at my car and then at me as he crossed the bridge and saw me. I smiled and raised a hand, because it seemed to be the kind of thing people do in the country. He didn't acknowledge me, just passed and sped up at the hill. He slowed as he approached the old house and swung in, the vehicle disappearing behind the structure. Not abandoned after all.

I crossed back over the bridge and got in the car. As I passed the old house, I glimpsed the man in the cap standing at his living-room window, staring out at me.

A couple of minutes later, the Lincoln's GPS told me I had reached the point I was looking for, just as I spotted a sign warning of the drop and indicating a turn in the road. I knew the location by sight, anyway. I thought back to the picture in the book, the one of Eric Salter's car being hoisted from the ravine by a crane. It had been set up on a wide shoulder at the side of the road, and there were only a few such spots in the vicinity.

There was no crash barrier, probably because the curve

was gentle, curving in a wide arc around and slightly upwards. I parked at the side of the road, framing the view through my windshield in approximately the same position as I remembered the picture. I took my phone out and called up the image, finding my position matched almost exactly to where the photographer must have stood in 2004.

The foliage on the verge had encroached into the shoulder, but aside from that not much had changed in the past fifteen years. I stood still and listened, just as I had done at the bridge. I didn't expect to find anything new at either of these scenes. The events of Halloween night 2003 were too far in the past for that. But I like to visit the important scenes of any investigation if I can. You can never pick up everything second hand, or from photographs.

I got out of the car and faced in the direction of the edge of the ravine. I was a dozen paces from the big tree at the side of the road, and therefore fifteen or sixteen paces from the edge, but you wouldn't know that from my position. I walked forward, slowing down when I got to the edge of the shoulder, and picking my way carefully through the undergrowth. Underfoot was a deep tangle of long grass and twisting weeds. I kept my eyes down, being careful not to trip. I could hear the faint sound of running water ahead and below me as I got farther in. I reached the tree and braced my right hand on it, only now seeing where the ground disappeared, less than five feet in front of me. I looked back in the direction of the road and realized why it had taken two seasons to find Salter's car. Unless there had been clear tracks, there would have been nothing to suggest anything had gone through here. A crash would have caused more damage, but Salter's car hadn't crashed. Investigation of the wreckage showed that somebody had put it in neutral and pushed it over the edge. It had been an ideal spot for both the murders and the disposal of the evidence. Opportunism, or local knowledge?

The drop was about sixty feet, a steep slope that was almost vertical. The river carved its way through a stone bed at the bottom. McGregor was right, if the occupants of the car hadn't been dead when they went over the edge, they sure as hell were when they hit the bottom.

I remembered the picture of Salter's vehicle being hoisted out of the ravine. The car had impacted front-end first; the hood compacted to half its length, the engine block driven back into the cab. The windows were all shattered and the driver's and passenger side doors had been ripped off. It was easy to see how the bodies had been carried away. Or at least one of them had, if David Connor's story was true.

Looking at the drop and thinking about the condition of the car, I found myself agreeing with Sheriff McGregor. There was no way Adeline Connor had survived the car falling into that ravine. So that left only one plausible line of enquiry.

What if she hadn't been in the car when it went over the edge?

15

DWIGHT HAYCOX

It was getting dark and Haycox was on his way home when he spotted David Connor's distinctive orange pickup truck pulling to a stop across the street in front of Andy's. He watched as Connor got out and made for the door, head down. Haycox hesitated a second, and then crossed the street. He glanced through the glass door and saw Connor at the register, and then turned around, acting like he was inspecting the front wheel of the pickup while he waited for the sound of the bell over the door as Connor exited.

"There a problem, Deputy?"

Haycox took another couple of seconds to examine the wheel and straightened up.

"Not so far as I can see."

Connor was standing in front of the doorway, a six-pack of Corona cradled in his left hand. Haycox had made a point of trying to talk to anyone with a link to the DMK case, but in the six months since he had moved to Bethany, this was the closest he had been to David Connor.

"Good to hear it," he said, moving toward the driver's door.

"We had your guy down at the station today," Haycox said.

Connor reached past and put his hand on the driver's door handle. He stared at Haycox, expressionless, waiting for him to move.

"We're just hoping he's more careful than the last guy. Wheeler, wasn't it?"

Connor broke into a grin and looked down at his feet. He dropped his hand and stepped forward, raising his eyes to meet Haycox's.

"Not bad." He glanced down at the nametag. "Haycox. How many credits do you need to complete the sheriff's mini-me course?"

Haycox cleared his throat and tried to think of a witty comeback. But Connor was already speaking again.

"Get out of my way, Deputy. I don't have time for this shit."

He reached for the handle again, and this time Haycox stepped aside. He kept his eyes on him, and watched as he pulled out into the road and made a U-turn. When he was sure Connor was out of earshot, Haycox cursed under his breath.

Ten minutes later, Haycox got a glass of water from the kitchen and sat down on the couch, slipping his tie off and unbuttoning the collar. His brain was still cycling through the three or four best comebacks to Connor's question he had come up with on the short walk back to his apartment.

He opened his laptop, selected the TrueSleuths website from the favorites bar, and logged in, humming the start of the song unconsciously.

One new discussion on the Bundy forum. Nothing new on DMK. And then he looked at his inbox.

Private messages 13(1 new)

He clicked in to read the new message.

16

CARTER BLAKE

It was later than I thought when I got back into the car. The digital clock on the dash read 17:32 when I turned the key in the ignition. Atlanta was only about a hundred miles or so from Bethany, but I wanted to wait and see it in the daylight.

I stopped a couple of minutes down the road, parking at the edge of the trail up to the old house where I had seen the old man go. I got out and approached the house on foot. It was small. There were places where the dark wood siding was patched with newer pieces, and the slates on the roof were coated by moss. There were half-shut blinds on each of the two windows flanking the front door. The pickup was still parked around the back, the front bumper sticking out slightly from behind the house. I knocked three times on his door and waited. There was a small brass nameplate reading ROUSSEL screwed into the door frame just above a sign that warned, *No hawkers, no politicians, no Jesus freaks*. I hoped I would be able to reassure Mr. Roussel I was none of the above. But there was no answer after a minute.

As I drove back toward town, I put the thought of Adeline Connor to one side, and began to think a little more about the person responsible for her death, and the people hunting him.

I had finished the true crime book on the killings before going to sleep last night. Digging into a case over a decade old is a difficult task. I had been lucky that the killings, however briefly, caught public attention. The author had interviewed several of the detectives on the task force, and had gotten access to autopsy reports and unpublished crime scene pictures. Sheriff McGregor was conspicuous by his absence.

The most frequently cited investigators were Captain Willard H. O'Neill, who had led the task force, and Sergeant Dave Correra, of the Atlanta PD. O'Neill had died in 2007, but Correra was still listed on the Atlanta PD's Homicide Department web page. I hoped he might be more willing to speak to me about the case.

Eric Salter, Arlo Green and Adeline Connor were the last official victims credited to the Devil Mountain Killer. After those killings, nothing. There had been a long, tense period as everyone waited for the next murder, but it never came. Sometimes that's the way it happens, there's no neat resolution.

As the months passed, the usual theories were floated. The killer, obviously a nut to begin with, had decided to do the world a favor and put the next bullet in his own head. Or perhaps somebody else had done it for him. The discussion forums I had skimmed on TrueSleuths and similar sites had had a strong line in conspiracy, the most popular of which was that the cops had found the killer, executed him, and covered the whole thing up for their own nefarious purposes. I thought it was amusing that they thought the police would want to avoid credit for catching a murderer.

And then, there were less hopeful scenarios. The killer hadn't stopped, he had just moved on, or perhaps gone to jail for an unrelated crime. That would mean the killings might start again someday. Perhaps that explained why this town had never fully been able to relax and put the events of 2003 behind them.

I was so deep in thought that I was taken by surprise when I saw the blue lights flash in my rearview mirror, just as I crossed back over the wooden bridge where Adeline Connor had last been seen. I saw a blue-and-white Crown Victoria fifty yards behind me, not in any hurry.

I drove the rest of the way across the bridge and pulled to a stop at the side of the road. The patrol car swung in behind me and stopped, keeping the engine running. I stayed put, kept my hands on the wheel, and sighed as I watched the driver's door of the car open in the mirror.

So Sheriff McGregor had decided I had been a little too curious. He was cutting it fine if he planned on telling me to be out of town by sundown. The sheriff didn't strike me as the type who liked to indulge clichés, but you never know.

And then I saw that it wasn't McGregor. The female cop I had seen in the store, and again this afternoon, got out of the car and fixed her hat on her head. She approached me unhurriedly. I saw the holster on her belt was unbuttoned, and her right hand hovered a couple of inches away. Force of habit, or at least I hoped so. I thought about the details of the Salter autopsy I had read in the book. Two shots to the head, close range.

I buzzed the window down as she drew level with the driver's side. The setting sun was blazing through the trees, getting in her eyes. She held her left hand over her brow so she could look straight at me. The uniform fit her well. The nameplate over her right breast said GREEN.

"Mr. Blake, right?"

"Is there a problem, Officer?"

"There doesn't have to be," she said. "Can you tell me why you're out here?"

"Just going for a drive."

She held my gaze, to let me know she knew exactly where I had been.

Then she straightened up and looked away from me, maybe just to give her eyes a rest from the glare of the sunset. She relaxed her posture a little, bringing her left hand down and threading both thumbs through the belt loops on either side.

"I probably don't have to tell you you're making Sheriff McGregor a little nervous," she said without looking back at me.

"I appreciate that," I said. "I'll try not to cause any trouble. You can tell him I'll be headed down to Atlanta tomorrow, if that helps."

"Atlanta? What for?"

"I don't know yet."

"How much is Connor paying you?"

"That's kind of between me and my client."

She bent down again and rested both arms on the sill. Her

face was close enough to mine that I could smell peppermint gum on her breath. She looked amused by my evasion, rather than pissed off.

"Fair enough. I hope you're being compensated appropriately though."

"I'm used to challenging work," I said.

"How about impossible work?"

"Everybody seems very sure of that. Except David Connor."

She nodded, but didn't say anything.

"Is this the part where you give me some friendly advice to move on?"

She looked away again and breathed out through her nose. A line appeared between her fine eyebrows, beneath the strand of blond hair that had fallen out from beneath her hat. She was making her mind up about something.

"You know what I think? I think it would be easier if I just explained to you why you're wasting time. You can buy me a coffee."

17

ISABELLA GREEN

Just from the two-minute conversation, Isabella knew Carter Blake wasn't anything like the other man who had visited a few weeks before.

That guy, Wheeler, had been a proper licensed PI. McGregor had checked that out. His bona fides were in order. Wheeler had the air of a salesman, though. The kind of guy who'll tell you whatever you want to hear for a buck. Not that Isabella had spent much time conversing with him, of course. He got off to a poor start with her, asking "Is the boss in, babe?" when she was on the desk.

Blake didn't come across that way at all. He wasn't selling anything. He hadn't pissed the sheriff off any more than he'd had to. Isabella got the impression he just wanted to do his job without causing unnecessary grief. That told her it might be worth a different approach.

She suggested to Blake that they go to Freddie's diner, out on Route 19. It wasn't that she was trying to keep their conversation secret from McGregor, exactly. Discreet would be a better word. And after all, he had asked her to keep an eye on the guy. This might save the both of them some time.

It was a ten-minute drive along the north road to the inter-section with 19, and Freddie's was a couple of miles from there. Isabella went ahead, keeping an eye on Blake's gray Continental in the rearview mirror. She pulled into the lot outside Freddie's, parking outside the long concrete building with the tin roof and the red neon sign that was missing the 'I'. The lot was almost empty, just a rusting white removal van for company. That was why she had picked this place. Blake pulled into the spot beside her and got out.

Freddie, a sixtyish gray-haired Italian whose rail-thin frame belied the calorie count of his offerings, shouted his usual good-natured greeting as they entered and gestured at her usual booth by the window. Carter Blake sat down opposite her and glanced around. His green eyes seemed to study the room like he had been told there was going to be a test at the end. His gaze lingered a second on the sole other customer, a bald guy in his forties with a long black beard, who Isabella assumed was the driver of the van outside.

She watched Blake as he looked around. He had dark

hair, was clean shaven, and those green eyes. She thought it was something about the eyes that had made her decide to handle him differently from Wheeler.

When Freddie came over, Blake looked at Isabella, waiting for her to order first.

"Usual, Freddie."

"Latte, decaf, got it."

Blake ordered a black coffee and Freddie disappeared into the back. Blake glanced at the menu in the little stand in the middle of the table.

"How's the food?"

"Like the coffee," she said. "Uninspiring. I like this place because it's quiet."

He seemed to accept that this was an obvious attraction. "So you were going to tell me why I'm wasting my time."

"You first," she said. "How'd you get involved in this? You know what happened to the other guy, right?"

"Yeah. I'll try to be more careful than Wheeler was." He hesitated a second, and then spoke again. "Somebody put me in touch with David Connor. She's a friend of mine, from an organization that works with ..." he searched for the right phrase "... families of the missing. She told me his story, and asked if I would come and see if I could help him."

"You're a private investigator? Like Wheeler?"

"Not exactly. I'm kind of a consultant, but I'm pretty good at finding people."

"What sort of people?"

"People who don't want to be found."

"I do a little of that myself," she said. "Sounds like a dangerous profession."

"It has its ups and downs."

"I bet. So what makes you think Connor isn't imagining this whole thing?"

"I haven't ruled that out. My friend believes him, though, and she has a lot of experience working with people in his situation. She knows all about false hope and denial. She seemed to think Connor was different."

"And what do you think?"

"Like I said, jury's out. But if I had to choose ... yeah. I think he's telling the truth. The truth as he knows it, anyway. I think he believes the person he saw was his sister."

"Even though she's dead."

"The body was never recovered."

"She's dead. Her blood was all over Eric Salter's car. Too much blood. Both Salter and—" she hesitated a little before she said the name. She could see Blake's eyes register the half-second pause. "Both of the other victims were killed instantly. She wasn't the only body they never found." Isabella looked out the window and pointed at the white ash trees across the road. "It's all woods from there to South Carolina," she said. "There are trails, sure, but there are places out there no one's ever set foot. Plenty of places for bodies to end up. It's not like in the big city where all you have to do is check a few dumpsters. Out here, sometimes sure enough has to be enough."

"And it's enough for you?"

She nodded. "Enough for me, enough for the county coroner. Adeline Connor is dead, it's in the books."

He considered it. "How long have you been on the job?"

She smiled coldly. "I'm too young to have worked the case, so how can I be sure? Is that it?"

"I didn't mean that, I'm just interested. You're from Bethany?"

"Almost all my life. We moved here when I was six. We lived in Atlanta before that. My dad didn't like the city, said it was no place to raise a family." As she repeated the words she had heard her father say so many times, she couldn't help but think of the irony. What had happened here a few years later had demonstrated that there was no such thing as a safe place.

"You were around when the killings were happening then," Blake said. "You would be what, early teens?"

"Not bad. I was sixteen."

Blake didn't miss a beat. "Only a year younger than Adeline was."

"That's right," she said.

He considered for a moment. "Did you know her, back then?"

"Not well. I saw her around in high school. I was the year below though, so ..."

"How about David?"

"Same. I didn't know him well or anything. Different years, and you know how it is, we moved in different circles."

"He wasn't one of the popular kids?"

"What makes you think I was?"

Blake thought about it. "You have good people skills. That's why we're having this conversation, isn't it?"

Isabella sighed. "David was a little odd, even back then. A stoner. I think he played bass in a band, or drums or something. It was a weird family set-up. His mom had died years before, and his dad left them a few months before the murder. I guess David was the only one left to take care of her. No wonder he took it so hard."

"What happened to his dad?"

She stopped and considered. Jake Connor had been known as a drunk and a jerk around town, but she had only crossed him once. She had ridden to the gas station on her bike to get candy, must have been about eight or nine. When she came back outside, she saw that Connor had collided with her bike on his way out. The front wheel was warped out of shape, and Connor was examining his bumper for damage. She remembered the anger in his eyes when he looked up and saw her, asking what the hell she was doing, leaving this piece of shit here.

She had just turned and run, back into the kiosk. He had made to follow her, then got back in his car and drove away. Isabella never forgot the look in his eyes, though, like he was only just restraining himself from hitting a scared little girl. It reminded her a lot of the look in Waylon Mercer's eyes.

"He just upped and left," she said. "He wasn't missed."

Blake thought about it. "I heard David was a suspect for a while."

"I don't know how seriously they looked at him. But yes, there was gossip. You know how small towns are, and high school kids. He went from being a little odd to being a real outcast. Everybody was wondering if this kid was the killer everybody was looking for."

"Did you wonder that?"

She shook her head. "I didn't think so. Still don't."

Isabella watched Blake's eyes as he took a drink of his coffee. She wondered if she had really expected to persuade him he was wasting his time.

"He hasn't been carrying around this idea that she's been alive all this time," Blake said. "He stuck around Bethany for fifteen years, and from what you've told me, it wasn't for the social connections. He was still looking for her, right?"

Isabella wondered if Connor had told Blake this, and doubted it. He had worked it out himself. Good instincts. She hadn't exchanged more than a couple of words with Connor in years. But everybody knew what he was doing on those hikes in the winter, when the leaves and the foliage died back.

"Yeah, that's what he was doing."

"But he was looking for her body. That means he had accepted she was dead. He just wanted to find her and lay her to rest. But now he believes he saw her."

Isabella gave him a skeptical look, waiting for him to acknowledge how foolish it sounded. He met her gaze and said nothing.

"So what do you do now?"

"I'm going to go to Atlanta, see if I can do better than Wheeler."

She had to respond to that with a grim smile. "If you return with a pulse, I'll consider it mission accomplished."

"That's usually my baseline."

She finished the last of her latte and glanced out of the window at where their cars were parked. It was getting dark now, and she had spent more than enough time talking to Blake. She still had to drop the car back at the station and get back in time to look in on her mom.

She wasn't exactly sure why she had gone out of her way to talk to him. Something in his eyes maybe. She hadn't gone looking for it, but Blake was the first person outside of Bethany who she had exchanged more than two sentences with in months. He seemed to sense a change in her. Perhaps she had let something show in her expression when she looked out of the window.

"Before you go," he said, "can I ask you a question?"

18

Deputy Green's eyes narrowed. The distant, almost sad expression that had appeared on her face vanished and was replaced with the more familiar look of suspicion. I think they teach that look to trainee cops on their first day. Guaranteed to stir a guilty conscience.

"Ask away."

"Was Arlo Green your father?"

"Yes."

I hadn't made the connection until the moment she had paused when talking about the other victims in the car. She had avoided saying his name, or more likely, "my dad".

"I'm sorry."

"Why? You didn't kill him. It was a long time ago. And at least we had a body to bury."

I considered carefully before I asked the next question. If I thought it was going to upset her, I would have held my tongue, but she had been so matter of fact about her father's murder that I went ahead. Because I really wanted her take.

"What do you think happened to the killer?"

She straightened a little in her seat and looked back at me. "The killer is as dead as Adeline Connor."

"You seem pretty sure of that."

She didn't blink. No doubt in her eyes. "Cop's instinct. Or maybe just looking at the evidence. Between nine and twelve murders in the space of eighteen months, and then nothing since."

"It doesn't mean he's dead," I said.

She smiled, but this time without any of the warmth.

"You're going to tell me the Devil Mountain Killer isn't dead either now? Is this your next job after you find Adeline Connor? Maybe you want to find Elvis first though, I mean I'd love to see him in concert."

"I have no idea," I said. "That's why I asked you."

"Well, now you know."

"What if he's locked up? What if he moved somewhere else?"

"If he went to jail for something unrelated, it would probably be something minor, and we would have had more killings a year or two later. If he went somewhere else, we would know about it."

"You're talking about the MO. The .38 caliber double tap."

"Yes. The killer was very consistent. Even if he changed weapons, which would make him unusual, there was nothing else with that kind of signature. And people were waiting. Obviously, I wasn't on the job back then, but ..."

She closed her eyes, as though summoning the sense of what it was like to live here fifteen years back.

"It's hard to explain. A small town like this – we lost three of our own. Adeline, my dad, and a guy named Georgie Yorke the previous year. When this kind of thing happens in a city, I suppose people just get on with it. They don't think about it the way they don't think about muggings, or hit and runs, or poison gas attacks on the subway. But Bethany has a population of three thousand. Three people murdered out of that population has a ripple effect. Everybody's affected. And because the perp was still out there, it was even worse. People were speculating it could have been somebody from Bethany. We were waiting. We waited years. We would have known."

"So what do you think happened to him?"

"I think whoever it was walked out into the woods where no one would find him and killed himself. One more mystery. And good riddance." And then she thought of something. "But maybe you're asking the wrong member of the Bethany Sheriff's Department."

"You mean McGregor ..."

She shook her head. "Not McGregor. Haycox has a real bee in his bonnet about the case. He keeps it on the down low, though." She stopped as though she had said more than she had intended to.

I thought back to the other cop I had seen at the station. He was young, quite a bit younger than Green.

"The rookie? Did he grow up here too?"

"No, he moved here last year. He knows all the theories, though. I was inside his apartment once, he has all the books."

"What does McGregor think about this little hobby?"

"I think Haycox is being very careful not to let him find out."

"But he told you."

"People tell me things."

I nodded, wondering if he had confided in her despite the fact she was related to one of the victims, or because of it.

"I haven't talked you out of this, have I?"

I shook my head. "Not at all. You've given me a lot to think about."

She sighed. "Do me one favor, okay? Keep out of trouble while you're here."

"I'll do my best."

The corner of her mouth twitched as she registered that that wasn't a promise. "It was interesting talking to you. Y'all have a nice trip tomorrow."

"Wait a second," I said. I reached into my pocket and took out a blank business card. I wrote my cell number on it. "In case you need to get hold of me."

She examined the card for a second before taking it. "Girl could get the wrong idea. I suppose you'd like my number too, huh?"

I shot her a puzzled look. "You changed it from 911?"

She smiled, got up and put her hat back on. She walked to the door without looking back. I reached for my wallet and realized she had trapped a bill under her coffee cup without me seeing, even though I hadn't looked away.

I stayed at the table as she got into the blue-and-white cruiser and pulled out of the lot, wondering if Deputy Green might prove to be a bigger problem than any of her colleagues down the line.

19

CARTER BLAKE

After I watched Green drive off, I decided to go back around to Bethany the long way, heading down Route 19 and taking the exit that led back around into town from the south. I kept going past the road to Benson's Cabins, deciding to go into town to get something to eat. As I approached the turn for the winding hill up to David Connor's house, I saw strong headlight beams pointed out of the entrance way.

I slowed and watched as Connor's orange pickup appeared out of the drive and turned left onto the road, passing by me a couple of moments later. I made a snap decision and quickly turned the car in the road, heading after him. As far as I was aware, the only thing on that road before the intersection with Route 19 was Benson's place. Was Connor coming to talk to me? Perhaps there was something he had forgotten to tell me earlier. But then he passed the sign for Benson's Cabins without slowing.

Without quite knowing why I was doing it, I slowed down until he rounded the next bend, then switched my headlights off and sped up again. I kept within a couple of hundred yards of him; ready to switch my lights back on as soon as I saw a car coming in the other direction. I didn't want Connor to know I was following him, but I also didn't relish the idea of a head-on collision with a semi.

But there was no oncoming traffic. It looked like nobody was driving into Bethany this time of the evening. The road narrowed and I could see there was a drop on my left hand side. I kept the car as far over from the edge as I could. I kept Connor's taillights in view, trusting them to show me the turns ahead. And then the lights winked out as he rounded a corner, and everything was black. I slowed down and focused on keeping the steering wheel steady. I risked turning the running lights on, which gave me just enough illumination to see the road ahead. The next curve was about fifty yards away. I advanced slowly and got ready to cut the lights as I got around the corner, hoping he would still be in view.

Connor's car had disappeared.

I went to full lights, then high beams. The road extended in a long straight section. He couldn't have covered the distance that quickly at the forty or so miles an hour he'd consistently been doing. Had he spotted me? Waited until he was out of sight and then floored it, in the knowledge I would have to take the turn slowly?

And then out of the corner of my eye, I saw his taillights. But they were off to the side, through the trees. I cut my own lights again and backed up. There was a narrow road leading into the woods. Almost obscured by the trees was an old, rusted sign.

DEAD END – NO THRU TRAFFIC

There was nothing else to indicate where the road led. I saw the brake lights of the pickup flash as he slowed for an obstruction, and then slowly drive on.

I waited and then followed. It wasn't a dirt road, but it evidently hadn't been resurfaced for years. It was bumpy and rutted, weeds sprouting up from potholes everywhere. I wondered how far into the woods the road went.

I had lost Connor's taillights, so I risked turning my running lights on again. I saw something glinting in them a hundred yards away. As I approached, I realized it was a sheet of metal lain across the road. No, across a gap in the road. It was a bridge about twenty feet long, spanning a stream. The bridge looked a lot newer than the road. I stopped and got out.

It was a temporary bridge, like they use on construction sites, and the military uses in the field. Flat-packed, easily transportable: the IKEA approach. I wondered if the bridge would take the weight of the car; but given Connor had passed this way in his considerably heavier vehicle, I already knew the answer. And then I heard music, and knew I could go the rest of the way on foot.

After walking for a couple of minutes, I crested a rise and saw that the road ended in a wide clearing on the shores of the lake. There was a house there. It was big and old, almost a mansion. It was three stories high, with a steep roof. I could see broken windows and places where the roof had caved in. There was an old barn or storage building next to it. The house was in darkness, the only light from the headlights of David Connor's pickup truck, parked out front. There was a raised deck around the house that turned into a long jetty out onto the lake. Connor had turned up the music from his car. Some hard rock song that I didn't recognize. He was sitting at the end of the jetty, looking out at the water.

I thought about walking down there and telling him I had followed him from the house, but I decided against it. I didn't particularly want to confess that I had tailed him, but that wasn't what held me back. It was something about his posture out there. It would be like interrupting someone meditating, or praying.

I turned and headed back across the temporary bridge to where I had left the car. I could talk to David Connor after I had been to Atlanta. Maybe by then I would have some of the answers he was looking for.

20

DWIGHT HAYCOX

Devil Mountain wasn't one of the very highest peaks in the area, but all the same, Haycox didn't exactly relish the idea of climbing it alone in the dark. It would make more sense to wait until daylight, but he was curious to see if his contact was on the level.

This time, Bloody Bill had left a number to call. It had

been answered by a man with a strong Georgia accent. A little too strong. Like it was being exaggerated. He said he had been reading Haycox's posts and was interested in his theories. He refused to answer when asked for his real name, of course, but said he had grown up in the area years before and moved away in the seventies. He had followed the Devil Mountain Killer case with interest, and had recently been reminded of it. He said there was a shelter on one of the old trails that he had never seen mentioned in any of the books or articles, and wondered if it had been searched as part of the original investigation.

Haycox had never seen a reference to a shelter. He dug out the trail atlas from 1968 he had picked up a year ago in a second-hand bookstore in Macon and leafed through to the section showing Devil Mountain. The new trail had already been routed by the time of printing, but the older one was still indicated on the map. It wasn't on newer editions. It looked like a shorter, but steeper route to the summit. Sure enough, there was a little triangle indicating a shelter, half-way between the point where the old trail diverged from the new and the summit.

He compared it with a more up-to-date trail map, and then with Google Maps. It didn't appear on either. The old trail had been erased from the record. Switching to Google Earth, he could see no sign of it, but that wasn't surprising if it had been untended for fifty years or so. It was only by careful comparison with the '68 map that he was able to focus in on the spot to see something that looked like it could be a small building.

Haycox had climbed Devil Mountain twice before, when he first came to Bethany, and in the spring just after he had transferred in. Both times in temperate weather during daylight hours. Tonight, he felt the November chill even through an overcoat and gloves. His breath came out in clouds, lit up by the beam from his flashlight as he ascended into the mountains.

He heard things moving in the darkness of the woods all the way up the initial slope. Every once in a while, something would make a big enough noise that he would sweep the beam around, occasionally catching the glint of a pair of animal eyes, more often nothing at all. There hadn't been a bear sighted this close to Bethany in forty years, but he took little comfort from that statistic. He was relieved when he emerged from the tree line and onto a barren patch of slope. The clear sky hung above him, the stars so bright after the darkness of the woods that he was able to turn off the flashlight and still see the path.

He stopped for a rest at a point where he could see Bethany below him. It looked deserted, but for the lights. Like a battery-lit town built into a model railroad. He glanced down at his geolocation device, sure he must have missed the coordinates, and found that he was almost on top of the divergence point. Two minutes later, he found it. Beyond a line of thick bushes, he found the slender trace of an old track, almost completely overgrown. It led into another stand of trees. He pointed the flashlight at the trail, took a deep breath, and headed back into the woods.

21

CARTER BLAKE

I turned back onto the main road and drove toward Lake Bethany, the rumble in my stomach reminding me I had skipped lunch. There didn't seem to be much in the way of options in town. The little coffee shop was closed, and although Joe Benson had offered to fix me a sandwich whenever I needed, I decided to try out the bar at the far end of Main Street.

Jimmy's Bar & Grill was a big, beat-up shack that somebody had slapped some neon on in the last few years in lieu of a real makeover. It was a one-story building with wood siding and a roof that sloped gently upwards. A flag hung limp in the still air above the sign that said JIMMY'S in red and advertised BEER, MUSIC, BAR-B-Q in smaller, green letters. I parked the car and went inside.

It was busier than the coffee place out on the highway had been, but not by much, even though it was Saturday night. Two women sat at the bar, conversing animatedly. A guy in jeans and a Stetson with a bushy gray mustache was stretched over a pool table in the corner, lining up for a bank shot. There was no one else with him. On the other side, behind the bar was a skinny kid of college age wearing a black T-shirt that looked at least one size too big for him. He was polishing the glasses that were suspended from the apron above the bar.

There was a jukebox in the corner; one of those things that's got up to look like a real 1950s wax-spinner, but is basically just a gigantic plastic iPod under the façade. The choice of music was okay at least. Creedence Clearwater Revival, 'Have You Ever Seen the Rain'.

The cowboy looked up, gave me the once-over, and then looked back at the table and nailed his bank shot. The ladies at the bar and the bartender didn't register my entry. The music didn't stop. I crossed the wooden floor, which was worn, chipped and in need of a coat of varnish, and took a seat in a booth by the picture window where I could see the road and where my car was parked. I ordered a steak when the guy from the bar came over and introduced himself as Jason. I noticed the two women at the bar had spotted the newbie and were whispering in hushed tones as they took turns to examine me. I might as well have been wearing a sign that said 'out-of-towner'.

I turned my head to the window, remembering why I'm more comfortable working in places where I can blend in a little more. Perhaps a change of wardrobe would be sensible, although I might not take it as far as a Stetson. As I looked out at the lot, a pickup pulled in. I could tell it was as alien to this place as I was. A shiny black Toyota Sequoia, last year's model. Probably the best part of fifty thousand bucks. The modest coat of dirt on the sills looked fresh. The two guys who got out were out-of-towners too.

One of them was broad and tall, over six feet. The other was maybe six or eight inches shorter, but even wider. They were dressed for a hunting trip. Boots, camouflage pants and down vests over olive shirts. They wore matching camo baseball caps, too. The taller one had a full beard; the shorter one was playing catch-up with a couple of day's growth. His cap had the word "Jeff" stitched above the brim. I didn't know if it was some kind of logo, or if he just needed help remembering his name. They had parked a couple of spaces down from where I was, and close enough for me to see the New Jersey plates on the rear.

The two of them exchanged a few words while looking at the place, and then started walking toward the door. "Jeff" led the way, eyeing the place suspiciously as though he was a soldier approaching an enemy encampment. They took a table near the bar and hollered for Jason's attention.

He was on his way back out to me with my beer and waved at them to let them know he had seen them.

"In your own time, jag-off," the one with the beard said, loud enough for both me and Jason to hear. With his back to them he rolled his eyes. I gave him a supportive shrug and accepted the beer. The guy with the Stetson potted the last ball and headed for the door, shooting a suspicious look at the two men.

I decided I had spent long enough people-watching and turned my attention back to the local map I had bought in the general store. One of the pictures bound into the center pages of the Devil Mountain book I had bought was a schematic detailing where the different bodies had been found, and on what dates. I took out a sharpie and plotted the discovery sites as accurately as I could onto the more detailed map of the area. When I had finished, I had eight black dots, all within a ten-mile radius of Devil Mountain.

I knew there were probably more dots in the same area, invisible on this map. Unmarked graves. The ones who had never been discovered. One more for the killer, if Isabella Green and the sheriff were right.

I barely noticed when Jason arrived with my steak. He set it down at the side of the table as I moved the map over, and told me to enjoy it. I straightened the map and went over the body dump locations as I started to eat, not really paying attention to the food.

It wasn't difficult to see why suspicion had fallen on the population of Lake Bethany. It wasn't just that three of the victims had been from the town; it was the fact that it was the only settlement of any size that fell within the circle of the killings. I didn't think that necessarily meant anything. In general, it's true that serial killers like to prey somewhere they know, and often that's close to where they live. A killer operating within a city will often live within the circle defined by the primary crime scenes or dump spots. But when it comes to wild, rural areas like the country around Bethany, a frequent visitor like a hiker, hunter or fisherman can easily have as good or better knowledge of the terrain than somebody who's lived there their whole life.

From everything I had read and heard so far about the manhunt in 2002 to 2003, the authorities had agreed with me. There had only been one temporary suspect from Bethany, and that had been because Connor was a figure viewed with suspicion, related to one of the victims, and who admitted arguing with her beforehand.

I thought about the hour I had spent with David Connor that afternoon. I could see why he was something of an outcast around town, and got the feeling that would have been true even if his sister hadn't been killed. But I had to agree with Green: he didn't seem like a killer. Then again, I've been wrong before.

I looked up at a yelled "Hey", and saw that the shorter man I had seen earlier – the one with "Jeff" on his hat – had moved over to the bar and was crowding the two women who were talking. From the body language of the three, it looked like Jeff had started to get a little too friendly and his attentions had been rebuffed.

Instinctively, I started to rise out of my chair, and then I gripped the side of the table and stayed put, keeping my eyes on the two women and Jeff, and reminding myself of the warning Sheriff McGregor had given me.

Trouble comes from outside. You play nice, we'll treat you nice. You cause a ruckus, you'll be run out of town faster than you can spit.

Jason, the bartender, was tentatively approaching from his side of the bar, asking if there was a problem. Jeff's head snapped around, but before he could say anything, the brunette was holding a hand up.

"It's fine, Jase. We're just leaving anyhow."

Jeff shrugged as though it was her loss and swaggered back to his table, shooting Jason a wary glance on the way. The two women gathered up their bags, slipped their coats on and made their way out. One of them gave me a mildly reproachful look. I wasn't even slightly bothered. Nobody got hurt, and I didn't have to do anything. Win win. Neither Jeff nor the one with the beard said anything to them as they left. Jason turned away and busied himself with some kind of paperwork on the other side of the bar.

I relaxed my grip on the table. I finished eating, keeping the two men in the corner of my eye.

Ten minutes later, as I was leaving cash and gathering up my reading material, I was thinking that Sheriff McGregor's little motto about trouble coming from outside had been proved right. A scrape as a chair was thrust back and a yelled "What did you say to me, boy?" made me look up from what I was doing. I hadn't seen what sparked it off. Perhaps Jason had forgotten one of the side dishes, or brought Coors instead of Bud. Either way, Jeff was on his feet, leaning into Jason's face, as the latter shrank back, one arm held loosely up across his chest. Jason said something in reply, too quietly for me to catch it from across the room and over the sound of Neil Young on the jukebox. I heard Jeff's rebuttal, though.

"Are you shitting me, you goddamned queer?"

Jeff was getting in Jason's face, moving forward as he shrank back. Jeff glanced down at his friend, who was sitting back in his chair with his arms folded. There was a serious look on his face, but I could see amusement behind his eyes. The international look of the bully's best friend.

Jeff reached out and grabbed the front of Jason's shirt, gathering it in his fist and drawing him closer. At that point, I wondered if they even remembered there was someone else in the bar.

"We're not paying for this shit."

Jason was breathing hard, looked as though he was trying to work out what to say. And then he cast a desperate glance in my direction. That made my mind up.

"Is there a problem?"

Jeff's head snapped around. Looked me up and down as I approached. He blinked, seemed to have trouble evaluating how much of a threat I presented. I could see his beady little blue eyes struggling with the calculation. If I had been as slight or as young as Jason, or a female, he wouldn't have been worried. But I was a little taller than him and in reasonable shape, so it wasn't quite that simple. Jeff still had one important advantage: backup. He shot his friend a meaningful glance. The one with the beard stood up immediately and turned to face me, the mild amusement gone from his eyes.

"No problem that's any of your business, asshole," Jeff said.

"It just looked like you were having some sort of problem, that's all. The sort of problem that can be fixed by you paying your bill and leaving." I finished with a friendly smile as I held unblinking eye contact.

Jeff smirked and he and his friend exchanged a glance. He turned his gaze to me again and seemed to size me up, before looking at Jason, who had taken advantage of my interruption to move back a couple of steps.

"What is this? You his boyfriend or something?"

I said nothing. I kept the smile on my face. I studied his eyes and knew exactly what was coming next.

Jeff didn't disappoint. He lunged for me and stopped halfway, expecting me to start. I didn't flinch. Close up, I saw his eyes take on a slightly desperate look. I saw a bead of sweat run down the side of his forehead.

The one with the beard clamped a gentle hand over Jeff's shoulder. He spoke without averting his eyes from me. "You heard the man," he said. "Let's go outside."

Jeff took a step back, then another, then a third. He turned and walked toward the exit. The one with the beard followed, stopping at the door to give me a look before he stepped through it. I sighed. It had been a while since I had had to be involved in this kind of nonsense.

"Hey, thanks man," Jason said when the door closed.

"I take it those two aren't regulars."

He shook his head. "Fuckin' weekend hunters. Never seen them before and I hope I won't again. You better wait in here while I call the cops."

I held a hand up. "Better not."

He paused with a hand on the phone that was attached to the wall. "They're waiting for you out there," he said. "They're going to kick your ass."

I took my jacket off and handed it to Jason.

"Give me two minutes to have a word with them."

He looked unconvinced, but took his hand away from the phone.

I followed in the direction Jeff and the Beard had gone.

Before I pushed the door open I could see that Jason's instincts had been astute. They were both waiting for me outside, positioned at diagonals in either direction from the door. Jeff on the left, Beard on the right.

"You're going to be sorry, you prick," Jeff started as he moved toward me. He had started the confrontation with me, so presumably he felt honor-bound to take the first swing, in the safe knowledge that the Beard had his back. I watched his hands and was ready when he swung at me with a right. I caught his fist in my left palm and tensed my arm, stopping his forward motion. Then I relaxed it and he came forward a little. I planted my right hand square in the center of his chest and pushed him back, hard.

The movement took him by surprise, exactly as it was supposed to. It thrust him backwards three or four steps until he lost his balance and fell on his ass in the dirt. By the time he had taken his second involuntary step back, I was already on the offensive. I didn't wait for the Beard to react, and anyway, I knew he would give Jeff some time to fail before he jumped in. Beard presented a different proposition, which meant different technique. He had a couple of inches and fifty pounds on me, so he wasn't going to be a literal pushover like his friend.

I bent my head and tackled his midsection, knocking the air out of his lungs and bringing him down as he was thinking about getting his hands up to defend himself. He flailed about and started to get up on one knee. I grabbed his head and smashed it with moderate force against the wooden guardrail on the deck. Not hard enough to cause a concussion or knock him out, just with enough emphasis to discourage him. If everybody stayed out of the hospital, it would be better for all concerned.

Jeff was still getting to his feet, his jaw hanging half-open in disbelief as he watched things unfold a little differently to what he had planned.

I took a step back and smoothed the arms of my shirt down, keeping them both in my field of vision.

"Time to quit while you're ahead," I said. "I don't know you, you don't know me, and I'm happy to forget this ever happened. Get in your car."

Jeff blinked. He looked convinced. I switched my focus to Beard and saw he had greater reserves of pride to bruise. He wasn't about to give up. Shit.

As I was bracing for him to rush me, strong beams of white light swung over the three of us and I heard an engine and the scrape of tires on the gravel. The three of us looked up to see a blue-and-white SUV swing into the lot. I relaxed and took a step back from the other two.

A tall male cop got out. I squinted against the headlights and saw it wasn't the sheriff, or the younger one. I wondered if Jason had changed his mind and decided to call anyway, then decided the cop had gotten here too quickly. More likely he had just been passing.

"What's going on here, gentlemen?"

As he got closer, I read his nametag in the neon light from the sign: FELDMAN. He was about forty, six-feet, a hundred-and-eighty pounds with no sign of flab. He was eyeing the other two. Jeff was picking himself up, the Beard was bracing himself against the guardrail. I was very glad I hadn't broken his nose, now. Feldman turned his attention to me, putting together what had just happened. He was looking at my hands, to see if there was anything in them. I held my arms out from my body a little, palms open so he could see I wasn't carrying anything.

"Nothing, Deputy. No problem at all."

He gave me a long stare, then looked back at the other two. "That right?"

Jeff's eyes stared into mine, wanting me to understand how mad he was. I couldn't care less. I wouldn't be here tomorrow and in all likelihood, neither would these two jackasses. I responded with another smile. That made him scrunch his features up like he was trying to hold himself back from launching himself at me again, but I knew it was for show. They weren't going to do anything in front of a cop.

"That's right," he said, not looking away from me. "There's no problem, Deputy."

Feldman shined the beam of his flashlight into Beard's face. He flinched and lifted his hand to shield his eyes.

"What about you? Why were you on the ground?"

"I slipped."

"You slipped."

None of us said anything. After a minute, Feldman shook his head and sighed. "I'll let you get on your way then. You two first."

Beard and Jeff walked back to their shiny pickup, a little of the swagger returning. Jeff shot me another of his looks. I ignored it. As they got in and reversed out of the spot, Feldman took a second to read their license plate, before he clicked the flashlight off and walked across to me. The taillights of the pickup had disappeared by the time he spoke.

"Mr. Blake, isn't it?" There was a phony-looking smile on his face. I guessed word had gotten around about me after my visit to the department.

"That's right."

The smile faded and the fake warmth seeped out of his tone. "Watch your step."

"How do you mean?"

He cast his eyes over the wood railing, the one I had bounced Beard's face off a couple of minutes before. "Easy to make a mistake, like that gentleman." His eyes found mine. "You could get hurt."

22

DWIGHT HAYCOX

The shelter was a stone structure, still reasonably intact. About ten feet square, with a wood and slate roof and a doorway open to the elements. Inside there was a wooden bench on each wall, a dirt floor and a blackened alcove that bore witness to long-ago fires. There was a burnt beer can in the ash. When he picked it up and turned it to the light, Haycox could just make out the ghost of an old Coors logo on it.

Discarding the can and kneeling down, he played the beam of his flashlight under the benches. Nothing beneath the first one, only a pile of magazines beneath the next. No – not just a pile of magazines. There was a small canvas pouch there too.

Feeling a chill that was nothing to do with the cold of the night, he reached under the bench. The sleeve of his coat caught on one of the supports and he had to tug it back to get it free. The shape and weight of what was in the pouch was exactly what he expected.

He straightened up and carefully opened the pouch on top of the bench. He drew it back over the object, being careful not to touch it.

A Smith & Wesson .38 revolver.

23

CARTER BLAKE

I got back to Benson's Cabins at nine. The encounter with the two hunters had been the last thing I needed. The bartender would back me up, but I didn't think that would make much difference. Deputy Feldman would be only too happy to report back to Sheriff McGregor that his instincts about my potential for troublemaking had been right.

The approach from Deputy Green had been unexpected, though, and I was still working out how I felt about it. Maybe McGregor had told her to keep an eye on the enemy. Good cop, bad cop was the oldest trick in the book after all. So why did I instinctively believe she was on the level? If it was an act, it was a very good one. She wasn't overly friendly, she wasn't too eager to be helpful. I thought about what she had said about growing up in the town, experiencing the case as a civilian, and then as a family member of a victim. Perhaps, despite what she had said, a part of her wanted to go digging. Perhaps she saw me as an excuse to do that. And then there was Haycox, quietly looking into the Devil Mountain Killer under his boss's nose.

I got out the map I had marked up in the bar and laid it across the small desk in front of the window that looked out on the lake. Eight spots on the map. Twelve suspected victims. David Connor was certain that one of those names should be taken off the list.

I grabbed another map from my backpack, this one was a roadmap of the southern states. I traced my finger from Bethany down Route 19 to Atlanta. A hundred miles, give or take. If I left at eight, I could be there by ten. I had had an educational day in Bethany, but I didn't want to wear out my welcome all at once. It was time to pick up the trail a little farther south.

24

DWIGHT HAYCOX

It was impossible to tell from looking at the gun how old it was. It could have been bought yesterday, or it could have lain here for years. All of a sudden, he became very conscious of the silence. The gusts of wind had died down. He reached for his own gun and drew it, holding it beside his flashlight as he stepped outside and flashed it around the plateau where the shelter sat. He let out a breath and went back inside to examine the gun, making sure to face the doorway as he did so.

He took out a pen and inserted it in the muzzle, lifting it up so he could inspect the cylinders. It wasn't loaded, unless there was one in the chamber. He sniffed the barrel. The faintest hint of gunpowder. So faint that he could not be certain it was not his imagination.

He sighed and used the pen to drop the gun back in the pouch, cinching it and holding it by the end so as not to smear any prints.

So Bloody Bill just happened to remember an old shelter that everyone else had forgotten about, and there just happened to be a gun stashed here. A gun that was of the same kind used by the Devil Mountain Killer? All of a sudden,

Haycox felt very alone up here, on the mountain in the dark.

He had been stupid, to come out here alone. It hadn't felt so different from the other hikes he had made, some of them at night. But this *was* different, because somebody had told him where to look. Somebody had put him where they wanted him, and nobody else in the world knew where he was. Up until now, this had all been history. A fascinating diversion. Now it was starting to seem all too current.

He retraced his steps along the old trail, being careful to avoid the fifty-foot sheer drop next to the shelter. He back-tracked down the steep slope and around to where it rejoined the path. He kept his flashlight in his left hand and his eyes wide open. He kept his right hand close to his holster, when he wasn't using it for balance or to clear branches from the path. It took him less time to descend back to the tree line, and the creatures in the wood seemed to be less disturbed by his passage on the return trip. He was in sight of the gravel lot at the base of the trail when he heard something moving behind him. Haycox fumbled for his gun, keeping the flashlight trained on the woods, and had barely gotten it clear of the holster when a figure stepped out onto the trail.

He flinched and dropped the flashlight without thinking to grip the gun with two hands. His finger tightened on the trigger.

"Sheriff's Department," he called out. "Identify yourself."

The flashlight had fallen so that its beam illuminated a pair of dirty boots and blue jeans, but nothing higher than the knees. The rest of the figure was silhouetted against the gap in the trees.

The figure raised its hands, slowly. Haycox tried to focus on the hands. It was difficult to see if he was holding anything.

He was going to have to get closer.

Sunday

25

CARTER BLAKE

Joe Benson rustled me up a hearty southern breakfast that would have fed four hungry people. Bacon, fried eggs, hash browns, grits, lots of black coffee. He piled a smaller serving onto his own plate and I asked if he was going to join me.

"Don't mind if I do," he said, pulling out a chair on the opposite side of the big wooden table in the cabin that functioned as a communal kitchen-cum-mess hall. The table would seat ten comfortably, and there were a couple of others the same size, their legs folded up and leaned against the wall, next to stacked-up chairs.

"Must be a lot busier in the summer," I said, looking at the extra tables and chairs.

"I wish," he chuckled. "What are your plans for today?"

"I'm going to Atlanta," I said. "I might be back tonight, might stay over, if that's okay with you."

"You paid for the cabin, up to you when you sleep in it." He took a forkful of food and chewed thoughtfully. "I hear you got yourself in a little trouble last night."

"News travels fast here."

"You better believe it."

"And what's the town gossip saying?"

"They're all talking about what you're here for, for a start." He looked at me pointedly, not feeling the need to elaborate on that. "And it seems you got in a bar fight last night. Although looking at you, I guess you came come out on top."

"It really wasn't a fight," I said. "Just a minor disagreement."

"Well, so long as you stick to disagreeing with out-of-towners, I reckon you'll be okay."

"I hope so," I said, refilling my cup. "I spoke to Deputy Green yesterday, as well as the sheriff. She seems okay."

Benson smiled. "Most guys think she's okay. Okay to look at, that is." He gestured the tip of his fork at me reprovingly. "Some of them regret trying it on with her."

"I was meaning she seemed like a good cop. Conscientious."

"A good cop who happens to be easy on the eye, though," he said with a note of amusement.

Easy on the eye and easy to talk to. There was no point denying that. I had found myself thinking about Deputy Green a little ever since our conversation, and I had to admit that might not be entirely to do with this case.

"She told me her dad was one of the Devil Mountain Killer's victims," I said.

His expression changed and he nodded sadly. "So I hear. Although, like I said . . ."

"People don't like to talk about it," I finished.

He pointed the end of his fork at me as though to say, *Spot on.*

"Anyway, she doesn't need any more grief."

"I'm not planning on giving her any."

"That's good."

We ate in silence for a couple of minutes.

"So what's in Atlanta?" Joe asked.

"That's what I'm going there to find out."

"Mr. Wheeler was killed in Atlanta."

"So they tell me."

He waited for me to elaborate, and when I didn't, he moved on. "A lot of people around here think Connor sent him on a wild goose chase. They think he's doing the same to you. I hope he's paying you well."

"Everybody seems to be certain he's delusional. That Adeline Connor is dead. What do you think?"

"Me?" He shrugged, as though he had never considered he might have an opinion. "It was all before my time. I mean, I moved here in '06, and the whole thing was still an open wound at that time. Asking around about this subject the way you're doing would have gotten you a frosty welcome back then." He saw a flicker of a smile at the corner of my mouth and pointed his fork at me again. "You ain't seen nothin' if you think it's bad now. Things have healed a little. But I guess people don't like the scab being picked at."

"Some people can't help picking at scabs," I said. "It's in their nature."

"You asked me what I think. I think anything's possible. But sometimes the simplest explanation is the right one. That she's dead, and Connor is fooling himself."

"It doesn't do any harm to test the simple explanation a little, though."

"That's where you may be wrong, Blake," he said. His eyes took on a faraway look. "Sometimes it can do a lot of harm."

I walked back across the gravel lot to my cabin and packed the few things I would need into a small backpack. A change of clothes, some cash and David Connor's sketches of the two people he had seen in September: the woman he thought was Adeline, and the man with the tattoo.

The last thing I did was to take a pack of pencil leads from my case. I placed one in the hinge of the door, where it would break soundlessly if someone opened it. I was turning away when a vase of plastic lilies on a table beside the door caught my cyc. Only it wasn't really a vase, it was a glass jug. After a second's consideration, I took out the flowers and hung the jug on the door handle, before leaving by the French doors at the back. Overkill, even for me. But then again, there are some towns where you can't be too careful.

I reached the city limits of Atlanta a little before noon. The spot where Walter Wheeler had been killed was on the west side of town, where the 285 intersected with the 20. The gas station he had stopped at was just up the road from the intersection where his body had been found. I pulled into the forecourt and parked by one of the pumps. The tank was down to below a quarter full anyway, so I took the opportunity to fill up.

The attendant was a teenage girl, probably not much older than Adeline Connor had been when she disappeared. She sat behind the counter with a bored expression on her face, seeming to stare right through me. She had blond hair with a streak of turquoise dye through it which looked out of place with the red polyester uniform top.

I paid with cash as usual, and she made change and handed it back to me without meeting my eyes, as though the action hadn't roused her out of sleep mode. Bored and going through the motions: a good sign.

"I wonder if you could help me," I said, cutting her off as she recited the amount of change and told me to have a good day.

Her green eyes snapped into focus at the deviation from the script and she smiled. "Sure, what's up?"

"I'm looking for some information about the shooting a few weeks back, did you hear about that?"

She nodded quickly. "Oh yeah. Did you know the guy came in here *right before it happened*?"

"You were on shift when it happened?"

Headshake. "I was here in the morning when the cops came by. I saw them all set up down there on my way in, wondered what had happened. I guessed some kind of accident. That's a really bad intersection, people jump the lights all the time. One time I saw a car go straight into the side of a bus."

"I'll make sure I look both ways. So did the police speak to you?"

"They asked me a bunch of questions and then they talked to Brenda."

"Brenda?"

"My manager. They took our security footage." She pointed at the small camera that was mounted on top of the display cabinet behind her, aiming directly at my face. "I don't think it did them much good though. Hey, did they get the guy? Are you with them? The police I mean?"

"No," I said. "The man who was killed was working for my client, and I was just wondering what happened."

"Oh, okay. Well it was a carjacking. Did you know the guy?"

"Only by reputation."

"Well, I'm sorry. It's tough when someone you work with dies. Roberto, the guy who was on weekend nights here? I mean, he didn't die, but he had some really bad infection. He was in the hospital. Maybe he did die actually, he never came back."

I steered her back to the death I was interested in. "So who was working when Mr. Wheeler came in that night?"

"That was Mal."

"Did Mal speak to the police too?"

"Yes, but he couldn't tell them any more than what was on the tape. The guy came in, paid for gas and bought a bottle of Mountain Dew and a pack of Twinkies, said goodnight and then he was gone." She stopped and thought about it. "Isn't that wild? You can be buying Twinkies one minute and dead the next."

"It's wild," I agreed. I took out the sketches David Connor had made of Adeline and the man with the tattoos and placed them on the counter. "You recognize either of these two people, by any chance?"

She didn't, but she did like the guy's tattoo.

Five minutes later I found the intersection where Walter Wheeler had been shot. There was a warehouse on one side of the street, a gravel lot with a hamburger stand on the other side, looking directly onto the set of traffic lights where it had happened. I pulled into the lot and got out, taking a look at the scene. There were no cameras in range, and the shooting had happened at night with no witnesses, so the investigators had had to piece together what had happened from Wheeler's last known location and where his body had been found. A gang of kids had come by about a half hour after Wheeler had left the gas station and found his body lying half on the sidewalk, half on the road at the set of lights. After looking very closely at the kids and ruling them out, the Atlanta PD had decided Wheeler's death was probably exactly what it looked like: a heat-of-the-moment homicide carried out in the commission of a carjacking.

The simplest explanation is the best. I was hearing that a lot lately.

Wheeler's car had turned up a hell of a lot faster than Eric Salter's had done in Bethany. It had been found six hours later, burned out behind a furniture wholesaler.

The investigation was still open, but this long after that

fact it was unlikely it would ever be closed unless somebody confessed, or somebody who knew something cut a deal. I knew that by now, weeks later, it would be on the back burner. There would be no great pressure on the homicide team to go the extra mile, not when there were undoubtedly fresher cases to work. Wheeler had strayed into a bad part of town and gotten unlucky. It happens.

So why did something not sit right with me about it?

Perhaps it was the fresh memory of the scene where Salter's car had been found yesterday. The circumstances of Wheeler's death: a vehicle, night-time, a stranger, a shooting death. The echoes were hard to ignore.

The light was at green and traffic was moving freely through the intersection. Even at this time of day, it wasn't a busy road. It was easy to believe there had been no witnesses after dark. A good spot for a carjacking, if the perpetrator had even put that much thought into it.

I turned away from the road and walked up toward the hamburger stand. The guy in the window was watching me as I approached. He had bushy curly black hair and a little mustache. He was overweight, his beefy arms folded on the counter. There was a tattoo of a grinning skull with a bullet between its teeth on one of them.

"Afternoon," I said. He tipped a finger to the side of his forehead to acknowledge me and straightened up a little. I ordered a cheeseburger and a soda.

He turned away from me and started arranging the components on the griddle: a patty, some chopped onions. He took a pre-sliced bun from a plastic bag full of them and rested it beside the griddle, ready to heat it when the burger was almost ready. He turned back to me, and looked past me to the intersection. "You here about the shooting?"

I didn't say anything, just gave him a questioning look.

"You were staring right at the spot where they found the body. Nothing to see now."

I glanced back at the road. "Did you see anything then?"

He shook his head. "Close at ten. Excitement was all over by the morning. You know the guy or something?"

"No, but we had the same client."

"That right?"

"Yeah. As a matter of fact, I'm in town to finish his job."

"What's that?"

"Looking for someone."

"You a cop?"

"No. This was more of a family thing."

"Gotcha."

He folded his arms again and I saw the grinning skull again. It gave me an idea.

"I like the tattoo. You get it done locally?"

"If Baghdad counts as local."

"No kidding," I said. "When were you there?"

His eyes narrowed. "Iraqi Freedom, '03 to '04. You were there?"

"Mosul, later on."

"Infantry?"

"Not exactly."

He grinned knowingly and shook his head. "One of those."

I reached into my jacket and took out Connor's sketch of the tattoo. I unfolded it and showed him.

"Since you're a man who knows his ink, you ever see one like this before?" I thought about giving him the sketch of the face as well but stopped myself, deciding it would be better to let him focus on the image.

He took the sheet of paper from my hand. He paused to brush a sprinkling of corn dust out of the way with the side of his big right hand, and put it down on the brushed steel surface of the counter, smoothing out the folds.

"Nice lines. This done from life?"

"Memory."

"Your work?"

I shook my head. "My client."

"He's talented."

He stared at it for a while and then passed it back to me. "I would remember that if I had seen it, you're right."

I folded it and put it back in my jacket. "That's okay, it was a long shot. But maybe you can still help me. If somebody was looking to get a design like this done around here, where would he go?"

He turned back to the griddle before answering, his internal culinary clock alerting him to a more important matter. He flipped the burger over and added a slice of cheese, then scooped the onions onto the bottom of the bun, added salad, the burger, and finally the lid of the bun. He wrapped it in foil and handed it to me with a napkin.

"Terry's on Peachtree Street, or Ink Spot down by Ormewood Park."

I thanked the big man and went back to the car and ate quickly, facing the spot Walter Wheeler had breathed his last.

It was still a long shot, based on a long chain of ifs.

If the girl Connor had seen had really been Adeline. If she knew the guy with the tattoo. If he had gotten it done in Atlanta. If it had been recent enough that anyone would remember at the tattoo shop. A lot of ifs. I reached into the back and took my laptop out of the bag. I brought up the map of Atlanta, onto which I had plotted the various points I wanted to check out. There were four of them: the gas station, the intersection where I was currently, the place

Connor had seen Adeline, and the address of the Atlanta PD's Homicide division.

I looked up the two tattoo places the guy at the burger stand had mentioned and added them to the list.

26

ISABELLA GREEN

Isabella awoke at five-thirty, though not by choice.

She didn't generally dream, not since the counseling when she was younger. The counsellor's name had been Caroline. Caroline had been nice. Eager to help, and easy to fool into thinking she was doing so.

On the occasion she did dream, or could remember it at any rate, it tended to be an unpleasant experience. So it was this time. She started awake in a cold sweat. It was raining outside. Not raining hard, though, not as hard as that night.

She gave up on sleep and went for her usual morning run early, trying to force the visuals to the back of her mind as her feet pounded the road. Blood, rain, a mangled car. Her father's casket at the funeral. On normal days, when she slept through until her alarm, she detested losing a half hour in bed. But the routine of running every day was important to her. Had been for years, but even more so recently. On the rare occasions she missed a morning run, she felt tense and angry all day.

After she got home and showered, she got into her car and drove down the hill to the station. There wasn't even the light traffic Bethany got on weekdays, so she had time to pick up a bagel and a decaf latte at the Peach Tree and still make it to the station at five minutes to seven, parking in the empty spot beside one of the department cars.

The sun still wasn't up yet. The clocks had gone back at the start of November, and the darkness in the morning was still new enough to be a novelty. Isabella knew she would hate it by January. She sipped the last of the coffee and thought about which route she would take for the morning patrol. One thing she knew for sure, she would be avoiding the Devil Mountain road after that dream.

She put the images from her dream in the locked box and thought about something else instead. Carter Blake. She didn't know what it was about him. It certainly wasn't that he reminded her of Dan, her ex of a couple of years.

Blake was different from Dan, in temperament as well as physically. He had the air of knowing exactly what he was doing, but at the same time not taking life too seriously. He had a slighter build than Dan, but there was a grace to the way he moved, like each muscle was perfectly calibrated.

Isabella hadn't intended to talk to him for as long as she had, but once they had gotten started, it was so easy to keep talking. Hell, he had even talked her halfway into the possibility that David Connor's bullshit story was worth looking into. If she didn't know better, she would be curious about exactly what Connor had seen down in Atlanta herself. Scratch that – she already *was* curious.

Blake had planned to go there today. Isabella switched the coffee cup to her right hand and looked at her watch. If he had left early, he would be there by now.

27

CARTER BLAKE

Detective Correra, the surviving investigator from the Devil Mountain taskforce in 2002 to 2003 was still working. I found his name in several news reports relating to homicide investigations. He hadn't investigated the Wheeler killing, but there were a lot of other cases he had closed since 2003. He was based at Atlanta PD's Zone 5 office, about eight miles east of the place Wheeler had been killed. On the way, I made a stop at a coffee shop down the street called Bean & Berry.

Correra's office was small, and looked out on a busy urban plaza. There was a desk and two chairs. There were a couple of framed certificates from the City of Atlanta on the wall, flanking a wedding picture of a younger Correra and the woman I assumed was his wife.

Correra had an amused look on his face as he closed the door behind us. He was black, slim, in his fifties, with close-cropped hair and glasses. He wore a dark suit with a tie that was a dull gold color.

"I would tell you you've asked for the wrong detective out there, but I don't think you did. You're not just here to talk about Wheeler."

"Good guess." I put the box of pastries I had brought down on the desk and offered him one of the go-cup coffees. He raised an eyebrow and took it from me, nodding approvingly after a sip.

"You make a better impression than Wheeler did, I'll give you that. But I'm not telling you anything about the case. This buys you five minutes of my time, and maybe a little more politeness in my inevitable refusal to bend over and let you pillage our records."

"Then Wheeler came by to see you?"

"He did. You're another PI?" He opened the box, perused the options, and selected a cinnamon whirl. "You looking into Wheeler, or Wheeler's case?"

"A little of both, I guess." I held a hand out. "Carter Blake. I'm not a PI."

He transferred the cinnamon whirl to his other hand and shook. "I like you more already. What's your story?"

"I'm a locating consultant." I hate that term, but it sounds almost like a real job. "Wheeler's client hired me."

"'Locating consultant,'" he repeated, enunciating each syllable.

"I find people who don't want to be found."

"Sounds like a PI."

"When did Wheeler come to see you?"

"The day he died. Now, I don't mean to speak ill of the dead, but ..."

"He was kind of a jerk?"

"That's right. It wouldn't surprise me if that was what got him killed."

"How much did he tell you about the job?"

"Not a lot. He said he was looking for somebody and it was related to Devil Mountain. I still get this every so often. More when an anniversary comes around, but I guess nothing really goes away on the internet these days. Most of them don't get past the front desk."

"I'm honored."

"I was feeling generous today. And hungry." He sat back and cast his mind back a few weeks. "Wheeler was cagey, all he wanted to do was ask questions. It took me a couple of minutes to work out he was different from the usual amateur investigators."

"Because he wasn't looking for the killer," I said.

Correra said nothing.

"He was looking for one of the victims. Adeline Connor. The last one. They never found her remains, but she was declared dead along with Eric Salter and Arlo Green."

"I remember her. Makes it worse, when you don't find them."

"Adeline's brother is my client. He thinks she's still alive."

He shook his head. "Just because they don't find a body doesn't mean they're not dead."

"How certain were you?"

"As certain as you can be without a body."

I sat back in the chair and considered. Wheeler had really misjudged this guy. He had told him nothing, and that was the exact wrong way to go about getting any sort of cooperation from a cop like Correra. So I took the opposite approach.

I talked him through everything I knew. How Connor had seen what he thought was his sister one day, and become obsessed with finding her. I told him that the local cops in Bethany were even less keen than he was to dig up old bones. I gave him my take: I didn't believe Connor was delusional or blinded by grief. From talking to people who knew him, he had been as sure as everyone else that his sister was dead, right up until he saw her. That certainty was enough to convince me that it was worth looking into.

Correra was sitting back in his seat. He had finished the pastry and his fingers were steepled under his chin. "I guess anything's possible," he said. "Maybe Wheeler would have told me some of this if I hadn't kicked him out." He looked down at the legal pad on which he had been scribbling the occasional note as I talked. "So he thinks he saw her more than two months ago, from the window of a moving bus, outside of Turner Field, talking to a guy with a tattoo." He raised his eyes from the page. "That's not a lot to go on. Even for a person locator."

I produced the sketches. First the portraits of Adeline and the mystery man, then the close-up of the tattoo. "How about this?"

He examined it. "Better. If this is accurate."

"He has a good eye. I'm going to try some of the local shops. I was recommended Terry's or Ink Spot."

"Not a bad idea. I have a better one, though."

I took a donut from the box and took a bite out of it. "I was hoping you might."

Correra told me to go get a coffee and he would meet me when he had something. I took out a blank card, wrote my cell number on it and gave it to him. In contrast to Deputy Green, he took it without comment. I didn't know how long it would be before he called me, so I took a drive down to the place David Connor had apparently seen his sister.

I looked up at the brick and glass entrance to the stadium itself. Turner Field had originally been built for the Olympics in '96 and reconfigured for baseball. I watched the pedestrians move past in varying states of hurry. None of them looked much like Adeline Connor. The radio was tuned to news, but all they were talking about was the president's latest outburst of unpresidential language, so I zapped through a few more stations until I found one playing a Hold Steady song. I was listening to the lyrics about that first night when my phone lit up with a withheld number. It was Correra. He told me he had knocked off for the day, but I could buy him a drink on his way home if I liked.

Twenty minutes later, we were in a booth in the back of a bar called Damon's. I paid for the drinks: a Coors Light for him, a Coca Cola for me, since I was in the birthplace of the drink.

"Gotta love the modern world," Correra said, opening up his laptop. "This is pretty new. Came out of Michigan State University. Biometric tattoo recognition technology. It's not perfect, and if a design isn't in the system, you won't find it. By the way, Blake, I hope I don't need to tell you—"

"That this is all off the record?" I smiled. I had known a lot of cops, and Correra wasn't the type to take a bribe. If he was, it would have cost a hell of a lot more than a box of pastries and a schooner of Coors Light. He was helping me because he liked me. That, and something else. He was curious about the problem, too. He didn't necessarily believe that Adeline was alive, but it was intriguing enough for him to want to find out more.

"That's right. We never had this conversation."

"Understood."

He turned the laptop screen around. There was a picture of a man's left arm, photographed under harsh neon light. The rest of him was cropped out in the picture, but the tattoo looked like a pretty good match for the drawing David Connor had made. Hearts and barbed wire.

"Looks promising," I said. I looked up at Correra. His expression told me it wasn't as promising as I thought.

"What? They forgot to take a name?"

He shook his head.

"There are three hundred guys in the metropolitan area with this tattoo? What?"

"There's a name. And only one name. Only problem is, the name also shows up on a homicide from a few weeks ago."

It took me a second for the full meaning of Correra's words to hit me. "Somebody killed him?"

He nodded. "Gang related, apparently. I've read the file, I would have said that too before I talked to you. Now? Now I'm not so sure."

28

CARTER BLAKE

I once read a magazine article about a guy who was struck by lightning seven times. The odds against that are something like ten million to one. Impressive, in its way. But I thought that the odds of two people related to a missing persons case being killed in the same city in the same twenty-four-hour span in unrelated homicides had longer odds than that.

Correra gave me some more details. The tattooed man's name had been Vincent González. Twenty-seven years old, of Puerto Rican heritage, but born and raised in South Atlanta. Since the age of thirteen he had been in and out of juvie and the state pen, most recently on a possession bust. That last arrest had been when his tattoo had been photographed and added to the Atlanta PD's database, part of a new program tying in with nationwide work by the FBI. He had been found dead in his apartment on the morning of Sunday September 30th. The day after Wheeler had been killed. González had been tied to a chair. He showed signs of a beating and he had been finished off with a knife. Throat cut. A different method to Wheeler's killing, but that didn't mean it wasn't the same guy. González's apartment building was a busy place according to the report, comings and goings all night. A blade was a lot quieter than a gun.

A witness statement had been taken from a Miss Theresa Kiffin, 26, resident of the same block. She was an acquaintance of González. I suggested trying our luck with her, to see if she knew the brunette he had been talking to.

Correra knew which of his colleagues was handling the Wheeler case. He had to look up the González case, and found it was being investigated by somebody different.

"I'm going to need you to talk to them both," he said. "No reason to connect these cases, on paper, but you just gave us a big reason to connect them."

"Sounds reasonable," I said. "Why don't you ask them to call me, and in the meantime, we can see what we can find out about González."

Correra went outside for a cigarette while he made some calls. I waited in the booth, thinking about the past couple of hours. I had tugged on a couple of loose threads and had unwound a completely different mystery from the one I had come here to investigate. It looked like I had uncovered a hidden link between two seemingly-unconnected murders, but I wasn't a whole lot closer to finding the woman David Connor thought was his long-lost sister.

My phone buzzed on the table and I answered it, even though the number was private.

A familiar female voice. "It's Deputy Green, we spoke yesterday."

I smiled at the fact she thought there was a need to remind me. "Good afternoon Deputy, good to hear from you."

She answered my unspoken question right away.

"I'm calling for a couple of reasons. You said you might be headed to Atlanta today."

"I'm here," I said. "Drove down this morning."

"You find your ghost yet?"

"I'm working on it. Couple of interesting developments."

"Oh yes?" She sounded curious, despite herself.

"What's the other thing?"

"I'm sorry?"

"You said you were calling for a couple of reasons."

"Oh, the other thing was I believe you had some kind of altercation last night."

"I wouldn't call it an altercation, exactly."

"You wouldn't?"

"A slight disagreement, resolved amicably by the time your co-worker showed up. Deputy Furman, was it?"

"Feldman. I thought I told you to be careful."

"If you talk to the bartender, he should be able to reassure you."

"Already did. Jason says the other guys started it. You were lucky they were out-of-towners too. That kind of shit goes down with a local, it won't matter who started it. It'll go against you. Hard."

"That doesn't sound entirely fair."

"Because it isn't. I'm just telling you the way it is." She paused, and I knew she was still curious about what I had found it Atlanta. "So tell me how you're getting on."

I hesitated a moment, and decided to give her something. "I got a promising lead on a guy David Connor saw with Adeline."

"With the person he *thinks* was Adeline."

"The only problem was, the guy is dead."

If she was startled by that, it didn't show in her reaction. "Bad break."

"For him, especially. He was killed within twenty-four hours of Wheeler."

"You're kidding me."

"I'm not."

"Same cause of death?"

"No, the other guy was killed with a blade, Wheeler was shot. But I don't think this is any coincidence."

"You need to go to the Atlanta PD right now. I can—"

As though it had been choreographed, Correra entered by the door, replacing his phone in his hip pocket as he came back toward the booth.

"Way ahead of you. They're looking at both cases now, trying to establish the link."

"And what about you?"

"I have a couple of other loose ends to chase down."

"I think you should be careful. If the same person killed Wheeler and this other guy, it's because they were related to ... to whatever you're looking into."

"The thought had crossed my mind," I said. "I'll try not to become number three."

29

CARTER BLAKE

"Pretty."

Theresa Kiffin, neighbor of the late Vincent González, was staring at David Connor's sketch of Adeline appraisingly, but unfortunately for us, not in a way that suggested she recognized the subject. Correra and I were standing at the doorway of her one-bed apartment in Adair Park. In the room beyond her I could see a boy of about twelve with cropped hair lounging on an armchair, staring at a sitcom playing on an out-of-sight television.

Theresa was skinny, with wispy blond hair that was almost white, and wore a lime-green tank top and ripped jeans. She didn't seem to be too broken up over González's recent death, but looking at the far-away focus of her gray eyes, I found it hard to believe she would get broken up about many things.

"Know who she is?" Correra asked.

"Should I?"

Correra rolled his eyes. We had already explained we were looking for a woman who may have been a friend or acquaintance of Vincent González, her dear departed drinking buddy. Clearly Theresa was struggling to make the connection.

"This is the woman we were talking about," Correra prompted.

"What's her name?"

"We don't know that. Could be Adeline, something like that."

She shook her head. "She's out of Vinnie's league," she said, adding quickly, "God rest his soul, I mean."

"She wouldn't necessarily be his girlfriend."

"Vinnie had a lotta girlfriends. None who looked like this." She handed the sketch back. "What's this about?"

"We're trying to locate her. She may have information about Vinnie's murder. She was seen talking to him outside Turner Field a few weeks back."

She shook her head. "Sorry."

I tried to recall David Connor's description. "The woman was carrying a red bag. Dark red, like maroon or burgundy."

"Sor ..." she began again and then something flared in her eyes. "Like a big insulated pack?"

Correra glanced at me for direction.

"Could be," I said. I hadn't pressed Connor on this detail. It had seemed incidental.

She was forming a shape with her hands. "About this big? Yeah, that explains it."

"Are you going to tell us?" Correra asked after a wait.

"What's it worth?"

"Depends what you tell us."

"Okay, the bag means she's a Zoomr delivery girl."

"What?"

"You know, Zoomr. Vinnie always got food delivered to him. There's an app."

"They delivered to him in the middle of the street?"

"Sure. There's an app."

I took my phone out and quickly keyed it in. The logo was a stylized burgundy Z. No E in the name, obviously. I tapped to download the app as Correra continued questioning Theresa Kiffin.

"How did they know he would be there?"

"I told you, there's an app, he ordered, they delivered to him."

Correra looked at me. "There's an app," I said.

He gave a long sigh. "Millennials. Okay, where does this food come from?"

"It depends. They have a whole bunch of places they pick up from, they're a whatcha-call-it, third party supplier."

I decided to take over before Correra blew his top. "Any-place in particular Vinnie liked to order from?"

"Sure. Always a burrito. He liked Bank Street Burritos and Mexicana Grill."

I looked down at my phone. The Zoomr app had finished downloading. Both establishments were listed, along with the office of the company, which happened to be a couple of blocks from Correra's building.

Correra shrugged, as though coming round to the idea. "Do they deliver pastries?"

She looked puzzled at the question. "I don't know."

Correra's phone rang as we left Kiffin and headed back down the stairs. It was his wife, asking why he wasn't home for dinner yet. He turned away from me and I heard him deliver an apology with a good-humored tone that said both parties were used to their roles in calls like this. Correra hung up.

"I was making it home in time today, before you showed up."

He suggested that he should take the Zoomr company office, since he might have more luck with a request to look at employment records. He took one of the copies of Connor's drawing and told me to call him in an hour.

30

CARTER BLAKE

The redheaded woman serving at Mexicana Grill recognized the woman in the picture, which was great. Unfortunately, she hadn't seen her in weeks, and suggested she might have moved on to a different job.

Bank Street Burritos, a mile south, was getting busy ahead of the evening rush. I went in and took my place at the end of the line at the counter. There were a few tables, but most of the customers were perched on stools at the window. Nobody looked anything like Adeline Connor. I took Connor's sketch out and glanced at it again, ready to show it to the guy behind the counter.

And then I noticed the woman at the head of the line had dark hair. She wore jeans and a black leather jacket over a white blouse. She was a brunette, slim, five-seven, late twenties or early thirties. The right physical attributes, the right age. I froze. She collected her order, something wrapped up to go, and then stood aside to let the next person in line order. She was putting her change in her purse and looking down as she turned around.

I didn't take my eyes off her. And then she looked up. She didn't catch my eye, but I had a full view of her face now. I glanced down at the sketch, back up again. It was her.

She slung the purse over her shoulder and headed toward the exit. Her path took her within touching distance. I quickly turned the sketch over and lowered my eyes as she passed.

I heard the little bell on the door chime as she opened it and stepped out onto the street. I angled my eyes a little to look out the window as I counted to ten. She didn't go past, so she had gone the other way.

I turned right out of the door and scanned the people on the sidewalk until I saw the black leather jacket and the strap of the purse over her shoulder.

I followed, keeping ten paces behind her, weaving between the oncoming pedestrians and making sure not to take my eyes from her. She walked three blocks north, never looking back once. Then she looked left and right and jaywalked between the traffic to the opposite side of the road. She appeared to be heading into a big glass-and-steel building with a sign identifying it as the Philips Arena. Below was a smaller sign indicating "MARTA Entry": the city's rapid transit system.

I glanced both ways and followed her across the road, ignoring the blare of a bus's horn as I made the other side and followed her through a set of doors. We descended a long escalator into the station. I had to let her out of my sight briefly to buy a ticket at the automatic machine, and then hurried through the turnstile.

There was a train at the platform and the door alarm was already sounding. I ran for the nearest set of doors and just made it as they closed on me, sticking for a second, and then just letting me through. As the train moved away, I looked around the car. It was busy. Everybody was following the universal public transportation etiquette: eyes down, don't talk to anybody. People of all shapes and sizes, all ages and races, were staring down at phones and books and newspapers. I didn't see the woman with dark hair. I was in the rearmost car. I walked back toward the door into the next one, swinging between the support posts and smiling politely as other passengers grudgingly moved out of my way.

She wasn't in the next car either. I started to wonder if I had missed her on the platform somehow. I recalled the mental snapshot I had taken as I descended the escalator. No, the platform had been empty apart from four or five people. Had she noticed me following? Doubled-back just to lose me? I didn't think so, but if she had, it was as smooth a counter-surveillance move as I had ever seen, particularly as there had only been one entrance and exit to the station. The train exited the tunnel, flooding the car with bright sunlight.

And then I saw her. Standing at the far end of the last car, holding one of the posts with one hand, the other resting on her purse, holding it around the front in a safety position that was probably unconscious. I took a standing position at the first set of doors and kept her in the corner of my vision.

She got off at King Memorial station. I waited for a couple of people to get off ahead of me and followed her onto the platform. This station was elevated, and I followed her down three flights of stairs to street level. I emerged into a quieter neighborhood. Lots of residential buildings, narrower sidewalks, not so many stores, not so many people. I hung back, considering what I would do if she went into one of the houses or apartments. I could wait for her to go in and then ring the buzzer, or approach her while she hunted for her keys at the door. Neither was ideal. She walked two blocks and turned a corner, then crossed the road and entered a public park. Still not looking back. If she was aware of the tail, she knew how to hide it. A minute later, she stopped at a long bench in front of a pond and sat down. She unwrapped the burrito and took a bite out of it. With her free hand, she reached into her bag and took out a small tablet device.

After consideration, I decided I probably wouldn't get a better opportunity to get close to her without freaking her out. I walked over and sat on the opposite side of the bench. She glanced at me, gave a polite smile, and shifted her bag a little closer, before looking down at her tablet.

I looked out at the ducks on the pond while I considered my opening gambit. "Excuse me, but have you been missing, presumed dead for the last fifteen years by any chance?" Perhaps not. I was still working out what to say when she turned and spoke to me.

"This might sound weird, but you look just like the guy I'm looking for."

31

CARTER BLAKE

"Excuse me?" I said, wondering if I had misheard.

But no, there was no mistake. She was looking straight at me, smiling.

"I said you look like just the guy I'm looking for." She held the tablet up so I could see the screen. "How's your stock portfolio?"

I opened my mouth to say something, but nothing came out.

"I'm sorry. That's an awful intro, isn't it? They make us do that. I think half of the people think I'm a nut, the other half assume I'm hitting on them. I'm Jane."

I took the hand she was offering and shook it. "Is that part of the opener too?" I asked. "If so it's good, very disarming."

She smiled but admitted to nothing. "Honestly, this is a really good deal. Have you invested in futures before?"

"I can't say that I have. I tend to live in the moment."

"Very good. Well, I can get you signed up today, right here. Twenty minutes, no hassle. Risk level is completely up to you, but you know what they say, courage conquers."

"Courage conquers," I repeated. "I think I've heard that before. You sell people stock options in the park?"

"The digital economy. Versatile, agile. No office space."

"What's the company called?"

"Honorific. Based right here in Atlanta, so you're shopping local. You're not a local though, are you?"

I shook my head. "Just visiting. Here on business."

Now we were talking I had a perfect excuse to study her features. I was ninety, maybe ninety-five per cent sure she was the person in David Connor's sketch, but all that proved was that he had seen her. It didn't mean she was who he hoped she was. I thought about the yearbook photo and the other pictures of Adeline I had seen at her brother's house. Result? Inconclusive. The hair and eyes were right. She definitely *could* be the same person, but fifteen years is a long time.

"What business are you in?" she asked.

I made a decision and threw a line out, to see if I got a bite. "I look for missing people."

She raised an eyebrow, interested. Not surprised or taken aback, which was a bad sign. If she was Adeline and knew someone might come looking for her, that should have given her a moment's pause. "You mean you're with the police?"

"Freelance."

She considered this, seemed to realize there was something more behind this conversation than she had thought. "So if you're here on business, who are you looking for?"

I turned my eyes to the screen. There were lines of names and dollar amounts that meant nothing to me.

"I'll tell you what," I said. "I'll buy one of your ... options if you let me ask you a few questions."

Her expression gave way to confusion. "Okay, I don't know how I could help you, but ..."

"The person I'm looking for looks a lot like you."

She grinned. "You stole my line."

"I'm serious."

She withdrew a little, the smile slowly vanishing. "Listen, if this is some kind of ..."

I took out two pictures from my pocket and laid them flat on the bench. The sketch and the yearbook picture. I turned them around so she could see them. She stared at them for a moment and looked up at me, expectantly.

"This is who I'm looking for."

"Who is she?"

"Is she you?"

She looked at them again. "She looks a lot like me. It's kind of freaky, actually. But no, that's not me." Her eyes met mine again. "Who is she?"

I held her gaze for a long moment. She didn't blink. I couldn't read her. Her eyes were like slate.

She laughed and looked away. "This is definitely my weirdest sale. No offense."

"Her name is, or was, Adeline Connor. Does that ring a bell?"

She shook her head. "Never heard of her."

"She'd be thirty-two years old now, comes from a town called Lake Bethany."

"I'm only twenty-nine, but thank you." She shrugged. "I'm from California."

I didn't say anything.

"I've been here for five years, ever since college."

Hair, eyes, bone structure, it all fit. This was David Connor's sketch come to life, and a dead ringer for an older version of the girl in the yearbook photo. In an ideal world, she would have had some kind of unique birthmark that could have made it certain either way.

She sighed and her voice changed a little as she tossed the sales demeanor out of the window. "Not that I owe you an explanation or anything, but here." She dug in her purse and produced her driver's license. I scanned the details.

Jane Violet Graham, twenty-nine like she had said. Address here in Atlanta.

"I was born in Orinda, California. Date of birth 4/22/88.

My mom and dad were Brad and Louise Graham. You want me to give them a call? I think dad videotaped the birth, so . . ."

"Where did you go to school?"

She blinked. "Dean Elementary, then Morgan High. Do you want to see my freakin' prom photos?"

I had found who I was looking for. This was the woman David Connor had seen, and I understood exactly why he had thought she was his sister. The only problem was, she wasn't Adeline.

I looked away. "I'm sorry."

She looked down at the pictures again, her tone softening a little. "I mean, yeah I can see the resemblance." And then it sharpened up again. "Hey," she said, her brow creasing as she came to a realization. "You didn't just happen to sit next to me, did you?"

I shook my head. "I'm afraid you're not the only one who has to approach a customer carefully."

"How did you find me?"

"I followed you from the burrito place."

"You what?" She recoiled, pulling her tablet back toward her as though she was worried I would try to wrestle it away from her. "What gives you the right to do that?"

"Rights don't come into it, it's my job. Just like you sell stock options to people who don't really need it."

"I don't like people following me."

"That's fine, you won't have to worry about it after this."

"And how did you even find me there? First time I've been in in weeks."

I gave her the short version, figuring I owed her some explanation. A man was looking for his sister, had seen somebody who was most likely her here in Atlanta, and had tried to find her to no avail, hence bringing in professional help. I left out the details about what had happened to the original professional who had come looking for her. I told her about the man with the tattoos, and how we had worked out she worked for Zoomr.

She thought about it. "Oh yeah, that guy was a regular. Never tipped. I quit Zoomr a couple weeks ago – the Honorific thing pays better. So where do you think your client's sister has gone?"

I considered before answering. There was no reason not to, she could just look up the name on the internet.

"She's probably dead," I said. "Murdered, a long time ago. They never found the body."

Her eyes dropped to the sketch again and she touched a finger to the side of the face. "Jesus."

My phone buzzed. I took it out and looked at the screen. It was Correra. I put it back in my pocket, I could call him back later. When I looked back at the woman with the dark hair who looked so like Adeline Connor, she had composed herself again.

"Well?" she asked. Her eyes held mine, unblinking. No trace of artifice. She was asking if I had anything else to ask. I didn't.

"I'm sorry to have troubled you with this, really," I said.

She slid the tablet back into her bag and looked up at me. "It's okay, you were right. You did what you had to."

"I appreciate you understanding."

"What will you do now?"

"Go back to my client and give him the bad news," I said. "Nothing else to do." As I said the words, I knew that wasn't entirely true. Apparently, I had answered the question I had come here to ask, but in doing so I had opened up a whole new set of questions, questions that would need a closer look. Like who exactly had killed Wheeler and González?

She stood up. "I hope your client can find some peace, now he knows she's really gone."

"Me too."

32

CARTER BLAKE

I took the train back to downtown and walked to where I had parked my car. When I got there, I took my phone out and called Detective Correra to let him know I had found the woman I was looking for ... and that she wasn't the woman I was looking for. He was sympathetic, but unsurprised. He had already spoken to Zoomr and confirmed her story. Jane Graham, no longer in their employ. Correra said he would talk to the detectives on the Wheeler and González cases, and they would probably give me a call later.

"Who knows? Maybe it really is a coincidence," he said.

Halfway back to Lake Bethany on US 19, I stopped at a gas station. After I filled the tank, I bought a machine coffee at the kiosk and leaned against the hood of the Lincoln as I watched the traffic pass by north and south. Since leaving Atlanta, I had ignored two calls, both from David Connor. I had already decided the bad news should be delivered in person.

The break had been a good idea. I would have driven straight through otherwise, without taking time to unpack what had happened over the previous few hours. David Connor had seen somebody who had a very good re- semblance to his dead sister. As a direct or indirect result of that incident, two people were now dead: Walt Wheeler and the man with the tattoos.

Conclusion? Maybe somebody didn't like the fact that anyone was looking for Adeline, even though it had turned out to be a wild goose chase. Detective Correra might be able to chalk it up to a coincidence, but I wasn't so sure.

And then something else occurred to me. The whole time since I had first heard of David Connor, I had regarded Adeline Connor as the focus. But what if she wasn't the focus? Maybe the problem was not that someone was looking into Adeline Connor. Maybe it was that someone was looking into the person responsible for her death.

I flinched as the driver of a big truck leaned on his horn. I looked up and saw him waving at the attendant in the gas station as he passed. The attendant returned the gesture with an exaggerated, sweeping salute.

Wheeler had been murdered; of that there was no doubt. Killed in a carjacking. Those types of murders are overwhelmingly of one kind, and it's hardly a unique method of killing. Something like eleven thousand people die in shootings every year. That's thirty a day. A couple of people had probably been shot somewhere while I was drinking my coffee. The point was, that method of killing hadn't stuck out one bit: to me, or to anyone else.

But that was a matter of context. In one context, a carjacking, it was entirely typical. Lone man, stopped at traffic lights at night in a rough part of a city with which he was not familiar. Shot and killed. Tragic, but an everyday occurrence, literally.

I tried putting it in another context. An investigator looking for someone presumed to be the victim of a serial murderer. Killed in the process of his investigations. Killed in the same way as the victims of the serial murderer.

Night-time, relatively quiet location, two shots to the head.

All of a sudden, I started to think that somebody might have an even greater stake in ensuring the past wasn't dug up than Sheriff McGregor and the tourist industry of Lake Bethany. Somebody who had been quiet for a long time.

I got back into the car. The sun was already almost down, and I had fifty miles still to go. I wanted to speak to David Connor tonight.

33

ISABELLA GREEN

So much for Sunday. Isabella had driven by Waylon and Sally Mercer's house again in the late afternoon, and had managed to catch Sally alone this time. Waylon had gone out for the day, she said, without giving any more detail. She said things had been fine since yesterday, and this time Isabella believed her. She said he was always calm for a while after a big blow-up. Isabella wasn't surprised. Waylon knew he was pushing his luck and that it would give her great pleasure to throw his ass in a cell for the night. And so he would behave himself for a while. It wouldn't last.

Waylon Mercer arrived in his truck as Isabella was leaving. In contrast to Friday, he was charm personified. Even went so far as to apologize about the "misunderstanding" the other day. Isabella didn't say anything to him, just got back into the car. As she was pulling out, she saw Swifty the dog run out to greet him like a damn hero.

She had left her phone in the car, but there were no

messages. Haycox was supposed to have called in by now. He was on twilight shift; seven till midnight. The department didn't have a night shift, per se. Each deputy was designated on call one night a week, but Isabella could count on the fingers of one hand how often she had been woken up in her ten years. Trouble wasn't unheard of in Bethany, but it tended to happen on a predictable schedule. Saturday nights, last night being a case in point. Or the start of hunting season. That made her think about the two hunters who had started the trouble at Jimmy's. She wondered if Blake would be staying over in Atlanta, and where those loose ends he had mentioned would take him.

Isabella headed along the north road and, before she could change her mind, took the fork that led up to Devil Mountain. She felt her heart rate quicken as she approached the wide turn in the road, the one that skirted the drop down to the ravine. She pulled in at the side and stared ahead at the trees and the invisible drop beyond. Before joining the department, she had avoided coming anywhere near this spot for years, after that night. Even now, she tended to speed up whenever she needed to pass this way, to avert her eyes from the spot where her father had ...

She put it out of her mind. Shut it down and locked it in a box. Caroline the counselor thought she had taught her that trick, but she had been doing it for years before.

When she became a cop, she had no choice but to get over it and use this road. During the summer, it was a hotspot for teenagers necking and smoking weed, so between March and September it got two visits a night on the twilight shift. There were no teenagers, or anybody else here right now. Isabella took out her phone and called Haycox again. It rang out. It wasn't like him. Perhaps he had left it at home and was at the station already. She closed her eyes and focused on her breathing. When it had returned to normal, she made a turn and headed back down the road, trying not to think about the locked box at the back of her mind.

It was seven-fifteen when Isabella unlocked the door of the station and found the office empty and in darkness. No messages on the desk, and the place was freezing, so she knew Haycox hadn't been in and out. She called his cell again, and then his home phone. No answer.

There was a procedure for a no-show, just like there was a procedure for those rare night calls. There was a procedure for everything. In the event someone didn't report for duty on time, and didn't call in, the sheriff was to be notified immediately. Only that would mean dropping Haycox in it. Isabella sat back in the chair and pondered what to do. Haycox lived in an apartment just off Main Street, not far from Feldman.

Feldman wasn't answering his home phone either. She had better luck with his cell.

"Everything okay?" he answered, in lieu of a hello. The two of them got on fine, but they weren't in the habit of exchanging social calls, so Isabella wasn't surprised he assumed something was wrong.

"Nothing major. Where are you?"

"Just heading back home, five minutes away."

"Can you stop by Haycox's house?"

"Has that little jerk forgotten he's on duty?"

She let out a sigh. She wasn't sure of the source of Feldman's animosity for Haycox. He had been riding him since the day he started work. She had wondered if it was some sort of hazing thing. Like he was skeptical if Haycox was made of the right stuff. She kept waiting for Feldman to decide the kid had earned his respect, but it had been almost a year now. Haycox was occasionally clumsy, but he worked hard.

He was conscientious about applying the rules equitably in a way that sometimes acted against his interests in a small town like this. Isabella knew Sheriff McGregor had had a word with Feldman about it, and things had calmed down a little. But Feldman clearly hadn't gotten over it completely.

"I'm getting a little worried," she said. "He isn't answering his phone."

"I'm almost there, call you back."

Two minutes later, he called back as promised.

"No sign of him, place is in darkness."

"His car there?"

"Nope."

A mystery. Maybe there had been some sort of family emergency. His folks lived in Macon, so perhaps he had had to go there at short notice and forgotten to call.

"Listen, I hate to ask, but ..."

"But you need somebody to cover Haycox." He made an effort to sound grumpy, but she knew he was going to volunteer anyway. Feldman usually tried to help her out, and she had an inkling of why that was. She usually made an effort not to take advantage, but ...

"I wouldn't ask normally, but I'm having dinner with my mother tonight."

"It's okay, Isabella. How's your mom doing?"

"The same," she said. "I really appreciate this, Kurt."

He gave a weary sigh. "It's no problem. Give me twenty minutes to hop in the shower and I'll let you get away."

She hung up, closed her eyes and rubbed her finger against her temple, hoping it would soothe the headache. Mission accomplished: she had covered Haycox's back for a little while longer. She was starting to worry about Haycox though. About more than a minor disciplinary.

Her eyes snapped open when she heard the door open.

Sheriff McGregor was in the doorway, looking pointedly at the empty seat behind Haycox's desk. He turned to look at Isabella questioningly.

So much for mission accomplished.

34

CARTER BLAKE

Night had fallen by the time I turned off Route 19 and onto the south road that would take me through the thick woods toward Lake Bethany. On the way, I passed the trail out to the old ruined house I had followed David to the other day, and then the entrance to Benson's. Both were dead ends, like all of the roads in this town.

The single light was still burning in the upstairs window of David Connor's house as I pulled the car up the curving drive. A slim figure appeared at the window, just a black outline against the light. I parked and got out. When I looked up, Connor was still at the window. I raised my hand in a hello, but he didn't move to respond. A moment later, he turned and vanished.

I climbed the stairs up to the deck, and by the time I got to the door it was swinging inward. David Connor looked out at me, his eyes wide and expectant.

"Did you find her?"

"Let's go inside," I said.

Five minutes later, I was sitting on the patched leather couch as David Connor paced back and forward on the rug. There was a loose board by the window which creaked every time he passed that way on his circuit of the room. He kept running the fingers of his right hand through his hair, pushing it back.

"You let her go, man. That was her."

"She looked a lot like her," I said. "I was halfway convinced myself. But it wasn't Adeline."

He blinked a few times, and then turned his head away from me. I thought he was about to start pacing again, but he pivoted and collapsed in the big easy chair, the fingers of both hands threading through his hair now as his hands framed his face. He looked like a math undergrad struggling with a complex equation.

"That doesn't make any sense," he said quietly, to himself rather than me.

"I know it feels that way," I said. "But sometimes, people are just gone. Sometimes you can't find them."

He looked up at me, eyes focusing in on me as though he had just remembered he wasn't alone.

"That's not what I meant. Wheeler told me he was close."

"Wheeler never spoke to her," I said. "If he had, he would have told you the same thing. Her name is Jane, not Adeline. She's from California. She showed me ID."

"That can be faked," he said.

"You're right. I suppose it could be faked. But why would she do that?"

He didn't answer.

"Sometimes the simplest explanation is the right one. Even if it's the explanation you least want to be true."

"It doesn't make any sense," he said again.

"David ..." I began. "I have some other questions for you, based on some other things I found out when I was down there."

"Other things?"

"First of all, do you know if Wheeler was expecting any trouble when he went down there? Did he have any enemies that he mentioned?"

He looked confused. "It was a carjacking, I told you."

"Right, the local police agree that's what it looked like."

"What do you mean 'what it looked like'?"

"You ever hear of a guy named Vincent González?"

He shook his head. "Should I have?"

"He's the tattooed man."

Connor's voice was urgent again. "Did you talk to him?"

"He wasn't taking questions. Somebody cut his throat the day after Wheeler was murdered."

Connor's eyes narrowed, but he didn't say anything. I left a long silence as I tried to read his expression. Something about his eyes triggered a memory and I realized what it was. Jane Graham had had the same hard-to-read gaze. It was disconcerting, and suddenly I was a little less sure of what I had told Connor.

I got up and walked to the window, looking out at the night. The ash trees enclosed the house on three sides. A cocoon of darkness. I put a hand to the glass to block the interior light so I could look out at the driveway and Connor's shiny orange pickup truck.

He got up and crossed the floor to where I was, not hurrying. He held eye contact the whole time. Those dark eyes that gave nothing away.

"Wheeler is dead and the tattooed man is dead."

"That's right."

"And you still think there's nothing there? That she wasn't Adeline?"

"I didn't say there was nothing there. But it isn't what you want it to be. You're right, I don't think it's a coincidence, but right now you are the only person I know of who links Wheeler and Vincent González."

"And Adeline."

I let that one go. "I think the same person killed them. I want to know why. I was hoping you might have an idea."

He looked out of the window at the dark again. "What you said about the simplest explanation being the right one. The cops thought that back when Adeline disappeared, you know that?"

"I know they looked at you."

"What do you think? Is it always the simplest explanation?"

I thought about it. "No. Not in my experience."

"I want to go to Atlanta. Take me to see her."

"I can't do that," I said. "But I want to know what happened to Wheeler and González."

"Why? That's not the job."

"It's not the job, but if I don't try to find out what happened, it'll eat away at me. I don't like not knowing."

He understood that, at least. I could read that much in his eyes.

"And if I'm right, there's a killer out there who's getting away with it. I don't like that either."

35

CARTER BLAKE

After leaving Connor's place I took out my phone with the intention of calling Deputy Green. I changed my mind after a second, thinking it might be better to talk in person. I drove back into town, turned right off Main Street and a minute later I was at the sheriff's office.

I parked outside, and before I had time to get my seatbelt off, I saw Sheriff McGregor at the door. I knew this wouldn't be good. I got out and approached. He nodded as though he had expected no better and leaned on the door frame, his arms folded.

"Back so soon," he observed.

"I went to Atlanta today," I said, still considering whether I wanted to tell McGregor about what I had found. He had made it clear I was about as welcome as an outbreak of measles, but he had knowledge I needed. He was someone who knew David Connor, had spoken to Wheeler, and had worked the Devil Mountain case back in the day. The look on his face was not promising.

"I know where you went," he said.

That meant either Joe Benson or Deputy Green had told him where I was headed. Or perhaps he had spoken to Connor, but I doubted that. My money was on Green.

"I also know where you were last night."

So that was what it was. The incident with the two idiots at Jimmy's Bar. I had already forgotten about it. I should have known it would make more of an impression on the sheriff.

"I don't know how much of the background you know, but—"

"You do this job long enough, you learn to judge people by what happens, not *how* it happened. I thought after our little talk you understood that we don't take kindly to people coming in and stirring up trouble."

"If you talk to Jason at the bar, he'll tell you I didn't stir up anything."

"We don't take kindly to people stirring up trouble," he repeated, as though I hadn't spoken, "whether that takes the form of a bar fight, or trouble of a more insidious nature."

All right, so that was it. It wasn't really to do with the two guys last night.

"You find anything down there in the city, Blake? You turn up that dead girl?"

"Nothing to report," I said.

"That's a damned shame. If you had listened to me, you could have saved yourself a trip."

"I appreciate your concern, but I think it was worthwhile."

He raised an eyebrow. "I told you this was a dead end, Blake. No need for you to stick around wasting your time."

"I don't think my time's wasted at all. I'm getting to spend some time in your beautiful town, meet lots of interesting people."

The sheriff took his eyes from me for the first time since I had gotten out of the car and raised them to the road that led back to Main Street. "Don't stay too long. We're a friendly town, but a fella can outstay his welcome pretty quick. If he's not careful."

"Thank you for the advice. I'll be careful."

He looked back at me and straightened up, taking his weight off the door frame. He walked four paces toward me, stopping midway between my car and the building.

"To be clear, we're going to be watching you. You pull any more bullshit like last night – no matter the *background* – and I'll have to think about getting a little more official. Do you understand me?"

I nodded. There wasn't much room for misinterpretation.

"And one other thing."

"Yes?"

"Stay away from Deputy Green." He stared at me for a moment, as though to make sure I knew he meant it. "I don't want you bothering her."

With that, he turned and walked back to the office, shutting the door firmly behind him. That parting shot had caught me by surprise. The rest of it had been standard procedure straight out of the small-town lawman's book of intimidation. But the last thing had been different. His tone had been different when he said it. Like that part wasn't just the usual spiel, like he was worried about Green.

As I drove back out to the cabins I thought about why that could be. She didn't strike me as the fragile type. Not at all. But perhaps her history was just one more reason McGregor didn't want the past disturbed.

There was no sign of Joe when I got back to the cabins. I let myself in by the French door around the back and checked for signs of entry. Nothing looked disturbed, the vase was still hanging on the door handle, and the pencil lead I had placed in the hinge was unbroken. I undressed and hung my suit up in the closet. I remembered the looks I had gotten in the bar the previous night, and decided a more casual mode of dress might be in order from here on in.

I got into the shower and stood under it for a long time. I thought about the two dead men in Atlanta, about the woman who looked just like my missing person, about how she'd convinced me I was wrong. Then I thought about the way David Connor's certainty had made me doubt everything all over again. After all, driver's license aside, I hadn't seen anything to prove he was wrong, just I hadn't seen anything to prove he was right.

Deputy Green was still on my mind. Why had she made the effort to reach out to me, when the rest of the department had been about as welcoming as a Stasi squad? I thought about our conversation the previous evening, going back over the information she had given me, the little snapshots of the town's history. After a while I realized that I wasn't just remembering her words. I was remembering the way she kept her eyes on me when she moved her head to toss a stray lock of blond hair out of her eyes. Her crooked smile when she found something I had said amusing.

I slammed the shower onto cold.

The sheriff wanted to protect her from something. Perhaps it wasn't about her father. Maybe he was suspicious on her behalf of male attention in general, maybe me in particular. I stepped out of the shower, dried off and wrapped the towel around my waist. The blinds were open on my window, and when I stepped out of the bathroom I saw Deputy Green parking her civilian car outside.

Our eyes met, and she looked away, obviously not expecting to see me in a towel. I threw on a T-shirt and jeans and went out the back way, coming around to meet her at the front door. She was waiting outside, her hand on the wooden guard rail, looking out at the lake.

It was a cold, clear night. The stars and a crescent moon were reflected in the inky blackness of the lake beyond the pines.

"Beautiful view," she said. "In the daytime, I mean."

"Makes you want to stick around," I agreed.

She turned to face me. "How was the city?"

"Actually, I was hoping we could talk about that."

She seemed to think about the offer. "Did you eat yet?"

I shook my head. "I tried Jimmy's last night. I don't feel the urge to go back."

"I thought you might say that," she said. She turned and walked back down the stairs toward the car, digging her keys out of her pocket. "Come on."

If Jimmy's was out, I wondered where she was going to suggest. The diner on Route 19 again, I guessed. "Where?"

"Your lucky day, Blake. It's not every man I'll take to meet my mom."

36

CARTER BLAKE

We took Green's car. She drove fast, but with precision.

Her mother had been ailing following a stroke, she explained. She was still able to do most things for herself, but Green didn't like her to be alone at night.

At one point on the drive, Green slowed the car and I realized she had spotted something on the road ahead. A pair of pinpoints of light in the dark. She slowed to a stop and flashed her lights.

"Come on, curious."

As I watched, the pinpoints blinked, and then a deer stepped out into the field of the lights. It paused a second to stare at us, and then darted across the road and into the woods.

She watched it go, and tapped her hands on the wheel, thinking.

"About four years ago a stockbroker from Connecticut driving a Maserati hit a deer on this road going at eighty."

I winced.

"Yeah. Have fun cleaning that up. Double fatality. The deer and the asshole driving." She turned to look at me. "Decapitated."

"The deer or the driver?"

"The driver."

I settled back into my seat, grateful that Deputy Green seemed to be a careful driver so far. She shifted into drive again and pulled away. I kept my eyes on the side of the road, looking for more eyes reflecting back the headlights. A couple of minutes later she took a turn off the main road and we started ascending a hill. We passed through a thick avenue of trees and then it cleared on one side and I could see a valley and the black outline of Devil Mountain against the stars.

Green's mother's house was at the top of a long, lazy hill, grouped with three other houses in an enclave with a big oak tree out front. It was more modern than David Connor's place, looked like it had been built in the eighties. It was a wide, low building. There was a porch out front from which hung a string of fairy lights. The lights were all on. Green parked outside and we got out.

"This is where you grew up?"

She nodded, though she was looking back at the view, rather than the house. "We moved here when I was six. I loved it from the first time I saw it."

Green's mother was slightly younger than I had expected,

perhaps only in her late fifties. She greeted us at the door, smiling at Green and giving her a kiss on her cheek before turning her eyes to mc.

"Who's the gentleman?"

Her accent was subtly different from Green's and I guessed she had come from farther north originally. She was very slim, with gray hair tied back in a tight bun, wearing a green dress with some kind of Celtic pattern on it.

Green looked back at me. "Not a gentleman, just another troublemaker I picked up on the mean streets of Bethany. Mom, this is Carter Blake. He's visiting town."

I stretched out my hand and she shook it. "Pleased to meet you, I'm Kathleen."

She stepped aside and gestured at the open door. I entered the house, making sure to ignore the questioning look Kathleen gave her daughter when she thought I wasn't looking. It was neat, but lived-in. There was a grandfather clock at the far end of the hall, the ticking sound audible from the door. She led me past a series of pictures showing a stern-looking man with Green's blond hair and blue eyes. In some of them, he was posing with a younger Kathleen, and Green as a child. In others, he wore hunting garb.

"That's dad," she said, unnecessarily. "Everybody says I take after him."

She indicated a picture of the two of them in the woods, her cradling a Remington 700 that was almost as big as she was.

"I bet you handled yourself okay in second grade," I said.

"Mom disapproved. Said I was too young. I don't think she would have kicked up a fuss if I'd been a boy."

"You still hunt?"

She shook her head. "Grew out of it, I guess. How about you?"

"Only things on two legs."

Dinner was roast chicken with broccoli, carrots and sweet potato. We ate and made conversation. Green hadn't said anything beforehand about avoiding sensitive topics, but I knew the drill by now. Anyway, it tends to be bad form to bring up murder over dinner. I spoke a little bit about working on a project here and in Atlanta and deflected things back to talk about the town. If Green hadn't told me of Kathleen's condition, I might not have picked up that there was anything wrong. She occasionally forgot words and got details wrong, but for the most part she was just fine. She was occasionally indiscreet about Green's childhood and teenage years, but that was hardly an unusual parental trait.

When she went through to the kitchen, muttering about fetching something, Green leaned over and whispered.

"This is a very good day."

"She's quite a woman," I said.

"I think it's been really good for her, having somebody new to impress."

After dessert, Kathleen excused herself and went to bed. Green took a beer and a bottle of water from the refrigerator. She handed me the beer and we sat down on the couch.

"She seems really proud of you," I said.

Green thought about it. "She is, I think. When she remembers to be."

"What was the diagnosis?"

"It's called Cadasil syndrome. It's an acronym for a lot of long words I've never been able to memorize. Long story short, there's no treatment, and it's downhill from here."

I started to say, "I'm sorry" again and stopped myself.

She took a drink of her water. "What happened in Atlanta? Fill me in."

I told her about Atlanta. Detective Correra. The tattooed

man. How I had started to think Wheeler had been targeted, rather than the victim of a random attack. Finding the girl Connor had seen; the girl he thought was his sister.

"You break it to him yet?"

"Of course."

"Let me guess, he didn't accept it?"

I made a noncommittal noise.

"You think they're connected somehow? Wheeler and the tattoo guy?"

I hesitated. I had a good feeling about Green, both as a cop and ... more than that. But I had known her just over a day. I didn't know if I could trust her with my suspicions. I played for time instead of making a decision.

"You said you had something on your mind earlier. What was it?"

She looked puzzled for a second, and then remembered what it was. "Oh. It's nothing really. Certainly nothing compared to the day you've had. It's Deputy Haycox."

I remembered the young guy in the station. The one with the Devil Mountain Killer hobby. "What about him?"

"He didn't show up for work today. It isn't like him."

"Does he have family out of town?"

"Macon. That's what I came up with too. Maybe it was a family emergency, and for some reason he hasn't gotten around to calling yet. I'm sure he's absolutely fine. Although he won't be once Sheriff McGregor gets his hands on him."

I was watching her. She looked like someone trying to talk herself into feeling better.

"What's wrong?"

"Tell the truth, I was only a little worried until I talked to you. Now I have a very good idea that somebody targeted Wheeler and the tattooed guy. Somebody who may have a connection to Bethany. And Atlanta isn't so far away."

Atlanta isn't so far away. As she spoke the words, I put some of the pieces together in a new formation. Could Haycox have something to do with the two deaths?

But Green wasn't thinking along those lines at all, I realized. Quite the opposite.

Her eyes found mine. She put her bottle of water down on the coffee table, as though she had just remembered she was holding it.

"I'm sure we'll hear from him tomorrow," she said. "If not ... will you help me take a look for him? Since it's what you do, and all."

"Sure."

"How did you get into that line of work, anyway?"

"By accident," I said. "I found out it's what I'm good at."

She decided not to press further, perhaps too tired for an interrogation. She took another sip of the water, thinking. "The person who killed Wheeler and the other guy. You're thinking it could be the Devil Mountain Killer, aren't you?"

It was the first time anyone in Bethany had directly referred to the person she had correctly assumed I was thinking about. Most people talked about "What happened", or maybe "Him". No one had used the name in front of me until this moment. Just then, we heard a muffled roll of thunder outside. Before it tailed off, the pitter-patter of raindrops picked up the tune on the roof. I waited for her to continue.

"You said somebody doesn't want anybody looking into Adeline Connor's murder. Or into the past generally. Two dead in Atlanta."

"González was stabbed, but Wheeler was shot. Two to the head."

She shook her head firmly. "You're wrong."

"I didn't say anything."

"You didn't have to, but you're wrong. The Devil Mountain Killer is as dead as Adeline Connor."

"You seem pretty sure of that."

"The killer is gone, Blake. Maybe he died, maybe he's sitting in a cell somewhere for some other murder. But he's long gone. If the same person really did kill Wheeler and the other guy, this is something new."

The grandfather clock in the hall chimed softly, and I realized it was later than I had thought. I counted eleven chimes. It was as though a spell had been broken.

"I should go," I said.

She opened her mouth as though she wanted to say more, but then nodded. "I'll get the keys."

On the drive back, we didn't speak until Green had made it almost halfway back to the cabins. It had started raining for real just as we were leaving, and the downpour had intensified. She kept her eyes on the road and the needle under forty-five on the winding road. I had forgotten all about deer and reckless Maserati drivers.

"It was a bad time."

I looked over at her, but she kept her eyes on the road.

"I know what you think. Little backwoods town, they don't like to hang out the dirty laundry. Keep up the pretense that nothing has ever gone wrong in good ol' Lake Bethany, Georgia. And part of it is that. Have you ever lived anyplace like this Blake?"

I thought about Ravenwood, the town I had had cause to visit recently for the first time in twenty years. Not so different in size, and yet very different in other ways.

"Once," I said. "For a while."

"A while. Then you can't understand. For a lot of people here, Bethany is the world. Back in '03, we were living in dreamland. Like, everybody knew bad things happened out there in the world, but not in this little bubble. And then it was like ... it was like a curse. The first body was found here, and the last."

I understood what she was saying. It was like the killer hadn't just taken lives, he had taken the soul of the town itself.

"Things never really got back to normal after that. You never forget seeing the fear in your neighbors' eyes. It changes things. Everything."

As she said that, her eyes shifted from the road for the first time and met mine. There was a curious blankness in them, as though she was reliving those dark days in her youth.

"You must have been afraid too."

"That's the funniest thing. I never felt afraid. Even after what happened to my dad. I can't tell you why."

We reached the cabins and she dimmed the lights to avoid waking up Joe, if he had turned in already.

"Thank you for dinner," I said.

She made a dismissive gesture. "Thank you, you did me a favor. I'm just sorry things got ... maybe we could do something again."

"Sure," I said. I got out and shut the door. Green backed out, turned in the road and drove away without looking at me again.

I stood in the darkness, in the shelter of the porch, looking out at the black void of the lake, thinking about everything Green had said. I unlocked the door of my cabin and my hand was tightening on the handle when I remembered the little trap I had set. I circled around the back of the cabin and entered via the French doors.

The vase wasn't hanging on the door handle any more. There was an even semicircle of broken glass on the tile floor at the door. I held my breath and listened. Far across the lake, a nocturnal bird called out. I moved across the room to the light switch and turned it on. I checked the kitchen, the bedroom, the bathroom. I approached the door, kicked some of the glass out of the way. Perhaps a gust of wind through the cabin had dislodged it. I examined the hinge, and decided no gust of wind could have snapped the pencil lead.

I stepped back and looked at the shards of glass. From the pattern, it looked like the door had been opened three inches, and then closed again as the vase smashed. Could it have been Joe Benson? Perhaps he had come in with fresh towels or something.

Except that the cabins were serviced weekly, on a Wednesday. Probably not at night, either. And Joe would certainly have cleared up the glass, and probably left me a note.

It wasn't a large cabin, and I hadn't left much in it. It took less than twenty minutes for me to be satisfied that nothing had been taken, and nothing had been left. Perhaps whoever had opened the door had run when they heard the breaking glass. I checked the locks again and put a chair under the front door handle.

It had been a long day, but I ignored the lure of bed for a few more minutes. I opened my laptop and searched for Jane Graham's hometown. Apparently, Orinda had been voted one of the top twenty places to raise a family in California. I recalled what else she had said about her childhood and looked up the local schools. Dean Elementary was there. Morgana High was close by.

I sat back in the chair and thought about the woman with the dark hair as the rain clattered down on the roof of the cabin. All thoughts of the broken vase and the evening with

Green gone from my mind. I doubted a school would release information on old students over the phone, but perhaps there would be a yearbook somewhere. Not that that would conclusively prove anything, either. I switched screen and composed an email to a company called Honorific.

After that, I called it a night. I didn't dream. I slept right through until the banging on the door woke me.

Monday

37

CARTER BLAKE

"Open up, Blake, we know you're in there."

The sun was streaming through the gap in the curtains. I rubbed sleep out of my eyes and took a second to remind myself where I was, knowing that whoever was banging on the door at dawn probably didn't have good news to impart. I went over to the window and peered through the gap. There was a sheriff's department SUV outside. Deputy Feldman was watching the back porch, his gun drawn.

"Open up, Sheriff's Department."

I recognized McGregor's voice and walked to the front door. Before I put my hand on the door handle I spoke out loudly to let him know what I was doing. I knew there was a gun drawn on one of my potential exits, it was likely there was one on the front door too. If I absolutely have to get shot someday, I don't want it to be accidental.

I was right. McGregor had his gun out and pointed at my bare torso as I opened the door. I raised my hands carefully. Across the lot, I saw Joe Benson standing in the doorway of his house, in a robe and slippers. The expression on his face was impossible to read.

"All right, I promise not to swipe the towels."

"Very quick with the humor, Blake. For a guy looking at twenty-five to life, best case."

Feldman drove me in the department SUV, while McGregor followed in the Crown Vic. On the ten-minute drive from the cabins back into town, he kept tight-lipped. The closest he came to communication was a long stare as he watched the sheriff guide me into the back of the car. My hands were cuffed behind me, which wasn't the most comfortable position, but I knew my complaints would fall on deaf ears. As would questions, so I didn't give Feldman the satisfaction of getting to tell me to shut up.

I had plenty of them, of course. Starting with who was dead, and what made the cops think I had killed them. Even in the South, they don't hand out "twenty-five to life, best case" for something minor. I noticed that Isabella Green was nowhere to be seen, and I sure as hell hoped it wasn't her. Neither was Deputy Haycox. I remembered Green's concern last night. He hadn't shown up for his shift, and it wasn't like him. So maybe it was Haycox who was dead. But what made them think I had done it? And did it have anything to do with the fact somebody had tried to break into my cabin last night?

Fifteen minutes later, I was in the interview room at the back of the Bethany sheriff's office. It was a rectangular box, about ten feet long by seven feet wide by seven feet high. There was no window, just a big sheet of mirrored glass through which I could be observed from the adjoining room. The walls were cinderblock. The door had a wood veneer, but I knew it was reinforced from the weighty clunk noise as it had swung back into place.

They kept me waiting a while, maybe half an hour. It was hard to be exact, because there was no clock, and they had confiscated my phone and my watch, along with my belt and shoelaces. An over-precaution. I didn't think I was going to be able to hang myself from the light fitting, which was a dirty yellow Plexiglass dome screwed to the ceiling.

Eventually, I heard voices outside. Both male. McGregor and Feldman, I thought. And then the loud clack noise of the lock being disengaged, and the heavy door swung outwards. McGregor was there, Feldman a step behind him. He waited for me to speak, but I just sat back in the bolted-to-the-floor chair and kept my eyes on his.

After a minute, he nodded at Feldman to dismiss him. Feldman hesitated a second, and stepped back, closing the door and locking it.

"Am I under arrest?"

"All in good time. I suppose you'll be wanting a lawyer."

"Most likely," I agreed. "Unless you want to clear this mistake up quickly so you can find your murderer."

McGregor smiled thinly. "I'm looking right at him. And who said anything about murder?"

"Is Green okay?" I asked.

He looked like he was going to stonewall again, but then thought better of it. "Deputy Green is fine. Why do you ask?"

I leaned forward. "Look, I'll make you a deal. I could shut up and wait for a lawyer, and you would waste all day being very pleased with yourself until you find out you've got the wrong guy. Or you could tell me what the hell this is about and I can help you."

"If you want to make a confession, I'm all ears, but we'll need to get recording equipment in here."

"All right, you can at least start by telling me who I'm supposed to have killed."

He didn't speak. The little smile stayed on his mouth. I couldn't tell if he really thought I had done whatever it was, or if he had an open mind but was enjoying watching me squirm, regardless.

Something about the sheriff's demeanor, and Feldman's, had made me start to suspect I was mistaken about the victim. It couldn't have been Haycox. They were treating me too nicely.

They hadn't exactly been polite to me since the knock on my door, and I spent the last hour being shoved, ignored and barked at, but that was nothing out of the ordinary. I hadn't been roughed up, not really. Neither Feldman nor McGregor had looked close to losing control and screaming at me, or throwing a punch. Neither of them seemed inordinately upset that a human being had, apparently, been killed. If it had been Haycox, a brother in blue, the last hour would have been a whole lot less pleasant for me. For the same reason, I knew McGregor was telling the truth, and it wasn't Green either.

Then who?

I knew it would be pointless playing twenty questions with McGregor, so I ran through the previous two days, working out who I had come into contact with in Bethany. I already knew Joe Benson was alive, because I had seen him back at the cabins. Green and Haycox I had ruled out. David Connor, perhaps? That would make sense. It would explain why they had immediately focused on me, since he was my client. And then I remembered I had come across others in Bethany.

In Bethany, but not *from* Bethany.

38

ISABELLA GREEN

Isabella was thinking about Haycox as her feet pounded the sidewalk, her breath puffing out wispy clouds in the cold morning air. Still nothing. His parents had finally gotten in touch. They had been out of town, and there wasn't a cell number for them on record, but when they called back, they said they hadn't heard from him since last week. Now Isabella was even more worried, and she had worried them.

She ran one of her short routes, down by the school, along Main Street and back up the hill, because it would take her past Haycox's place. He lived in a one-bed apartment on the second floor of a building at the corner of Main and Lavigne. Wherever he had been all yesterday, surely he would be back by now. She jogged up the stairs and knocked on his door. Nothing. She tried his phone for the twentieth time. Still going straight to voicemail. She considered knocking on the door downstairs, but Haycox's neighbor was a nice old lady in her eighties. If she had any helpful information, it could wait a couple of hours.

Isabella leaned on the railing and looked across Haycox's yard and up into the woods on the slope behind his house, thinking about what she had said to Blake. There was a whole lot of out there, out there. She had hoped the run would do its usual job, draining out some of her tension and the anxiety. It hadn't.

Her phone rang and she reached into her pocket, hoping it would be Haycox. It wasn't, it was Feldman. But why was he calling so early?

"Where are you?"

"Out for a run," she said, noting that the tone of his voice confirmed this wasn't a social call. "What's happened?"

"We have two gunshot victims up on Slateford Pass. Both dead."

"*What?*"

"I need you to go up there and meet Dentz. I'm . . . we're following up."

Part of her wanted to ask him what exactly he was following up, and why he sounded so cagey about it. But the rest of her was already calculating how long it would take to run home and get changed.

39

CARTER BLAKE

I put my hands flat on the table and looked across the table at Sheriff McGregor. "The two guys at the bar the other night. Which one of them got himself killed?"

"Both of them got themselves killed, as I think you well know."

"I didn't do it."

"I've heard that before."

"Where's Deputy Green?"

His eyes narrowed and I could see my continued interest in Green's whereabouts was irritating him. "She's outside of this little room, and therefore that's my business. Your business is what happens in here."

I sighed. "Aren't you going to ask me some questions?

Establish if I have an alibi, that sort of thing? I know you haven't had many murders here lately, but presumably you've seen the process on TV."

He didn't blink at the barb. "If you want to waive your right to representation and proceed to formal questioning, that can be arranged."

I thought about it. The smart play is, always ask for a lawyer. If anyone else was in this situation asking me for advice, that's the first thing I would tell them to do.

But in my exact situation, I wasn't sure. McGregor really seemed to believe he had his man. The simplest explanation strikes again. A pair of strangers and a lone stranger come into town on the same day. They have a fight. A day later, the pair are dead. He had no idea that somebody else with a connection to Bethany might be in a mood for killing.

I thought about it for a minute. I knew I could call a firm in New York I had dealt with in the past, and assuming someone was available, an attorney could be here within hours. But that would mean wasting a lot of time. I made my mind up. There was no way they could pin the murders on me without evidence, and I knew there would be no evidence, because I was innocent. I didn't plan on being influenced by McGregor's no doubt formidable interrogation techniques to the point where I would sign a false confession, and if it came to it, I could always make my phone call later on.

"I don't need a lawyer. Show me where to sign," I said.

40

ISABELLA GREEN

The bodies of the two hunters were laid out ten yards apart in front of their black Toyota. At the precise midpoint between them, were two rifles, two wallets, a wristwatch, a baseball cap, and two cell phones. It was orderly, thoughtful: a neat little pile of the dead men's personal effects, as though they had been sorted and were awaiting return to the owners who would never again need them. Isabella was staring at the pile, her mind full of competing emotions. She was so lost in thought that she started when Sam Dentz patted her on the upper arm.

"Sorry Isabella. First homicide, right?"

Dentz was a little shorter than she was, and stocky in build. He had dark hair that was starting to recede a little. He had less time in the department than she did, but he seemed to feel some need to protect her from the nastier parts of the job.

She shook her head. "Just thinking."

"It gets easier. If you want you can go sit in the car. Get a deep breath and so forth."

Isabella shot him a sidelong glare, knowing he probably wouldn't get that message either. "I'm fine," she said flatly.

The rain started to fall harder and Dentz pulled up the hood on his raincoat. Isabella didn't bother. Her hair was already wet.

Bethany wasn't a big enough town to have its own forensic or autopsy facilities, of course, so they had waited for the coroner investigator from Blairsville. He had gotten delayed thanks to his van failing to start, but had arrived now, and was processing the bodies before transport to the morgue. He'd already been able to estimate a narrower-than-usual time of death, because it hadn't rained until eleven o'clock last night, and the ground beneath the bodies was bone dry.

The two men were dressed in hunting gear. IDs said they were Jeffrey J. Friedrickson and Thomas Allen Leonard, both of New Jersey. Friedrickson was dressed in woodland army fatigues, and a canvas baseball cap with the word "Jeff" stitched into it. Leonard wore jeans and an expensive-looking outdoorsman jacket. Both were wearing the recommended safety gear for hunting: orange hi-vis vests, to make it real easy not to mistake them for a deer. A preliminary check on the system threw up a ten-year-old assault conviction for Friedrickson and a couple of DUIs for Leonard, nothing that warranted the death penalty. And that was definitely what this was. Somebody had hunted these men down and executed them. Just like . . .

Isabella shivered. She put the thought back in the locked box and turned the key.

She tried to blank her mind entirely, as she went down on one knee to examine the wounds. Both men had been killed with gunshots to the head. Double-tap in both cases, just like Walter Wheeler in Atlanta. Friedrickson had been shot in the back of the skull. The middle finger on his left hand was missing, which suggested one of the bullets had passed through on its way in. She stood up and looked over at Leonard's body, ten feet away. Two in the head for him, too, although only one of them looked close range. While Friedrickson's body was slumped over, his was sprawled face down, as though he had been upright when he was killed.

"Fella did this doesn't screw around," Dentz said, looking

down at the first corpse. "How do you suppose it went down?"

Isabella closed her eyes. Saw the scene as clearly as a movie. It wasn't difficult to do; the hard part was switching it off. Two kneeling figures, trembling, maybe begging. Bang. One down. The second reacts predictably. Bang. Two down. Bang. Bang. Just to make sure. She opened her eyes.

"This guy died first," she said, indicating Friedrickson. "The perp made them kneel. I guess up until the point he pulled the trigger, they were still kidding themselves that they had a way out of this. When this one saw his friend's brains in the dirt, he tried to run. Too late."

Dentz smirked, but looked impressed. "You're a little too good at this stuff."

She looked back down at the wounds. Classic double-tap. Military style. And familiar in more ways than one. But Isabella knew it couldn't be. She looked over at Dentz and realized that he hadn't used the name yet. He hadn't mentioned anything about it. The Devil Mountain Killer had been before his time, but it wasn't like he was unaware of the killings, or their MO. Surely it couldn't be that he hadn't drawn the connection.

He must have seen something in the way she was looking at him and read her mind.

"Just like before, isn't it?"

He didn't seem to find that too disturbing, and Isabella wondered why. "You think we have a copycat?" she asked.

He looked confused. "No, I mean I guess it's just coincidence that he killed them that way. Maybe he didn't know."

"Maybe who didn't know?"

"The perp. That Blake guy."

Her brain took a second to process what Dentz had just said. "What?"

"I thought you knew. Feldman didn't tell you?"

Feldman had told her nothing, only that there were two dead men up in the hills, and could she take over the scene until the CI got here. He didn't say anything about a suspect, let alone that it was Blake.

"Where is he?"

"Take it easy. I don't know, down at the station, I guess. You don't know about this? Feldman broke up a fight between Blake and these two Saturday night. Looks like he decided to finish it off later."

Isabella looked at the dry grass beneath where Friedrickson had lain. "You sure about that TOD?" she asked the coroner investigator.

He took a couple of seconds to respond, taking his time to finish a note he was writing down. Eventually he looked up. "Normally we would have a wider window, but because of the rainfall, we know it had to have happened before eleven o'clock, which means between nine and eleven last night."

"What gives?"

She ignored Dentz's question and walked to the pile of personal effects. "Okay if I go ahead and bag the phones?" she asked the CI.

He shrugged. "As long as you're careful. I don't think these guys will mind."

Isabella stretched on a pair of surgical gloves and took a couple of small, clear plastic evidence bags from her pack. She lifted the nearest cell phone by the top corner, careful not to smudge any prints. The screen awoke. No pin. Sloppy, but maybe it could give them a head start. She held it by the top corner, hovering just above the second bag, and then asked it a question.

"Okay Google ... where have I been today?"

Dentz looked at Isabella as though she was in the initial

stages of a nervous breakdown, but the coroner investigator gave her a sly grin as he realized what she was doing.

Google thought about it for a couple of seconds, and then came back with a map listing the locations the phone had been over the last twenty-four hours. It looked like the owner had been pretty active until ten-twenty-six last night, when he reached this spot, and never moved again.

"McGregor's got the wrong guy," she said.

"What makes you so sure?"

"Because Blake has an alibi."

41

ISABELLA GREEN

The sheriff folded his arms and sat back in his chair, looking back at Isabella through half-lidded eyes.

"What can I do for you, Isabella?"

With an effort, she suppressed the urge to ask why the hell no one had told her Blake was in custody. She suspected she would be better off asking Feldman, in any case. He was the one who had called her without divulging that particular piece of information, after all.

"Dentz said you're holding Blake for the murders."

"He's correct."

"Any particular reason, other than what happened on Saturday?"

"Do you have a better suspect?"

"Did you find a weapon on him?"

"No, but I'm sure he would have been careful to hide it somewhere. It'll turn up."

"GSR on his hands?"

"He had plenty of time to wash them."

"Did you ask him where he was last night?"

McGregor sighed, as though he had been expecting this. "He said he wanted to talk to you before he answered that one. Why would that be, Isabella?"

"You can wipe that look off your face, Jim. You're right, I'm his alibi. We had dinner with my mom. She can alibi him too, if you catch her in a lucid moment."

He shook his head. "Are you saying you can alibi him . . ." he paused meaningfully before the last two words, ". . . all night?"

"Not that it's any of your business, but that's not what I'm saying. I drove him back to the cabins after dinner, got there about eleven-thirty."

"Then he had plenty of time to go back out there, find those two men and shoot them."

She shook her head. "Look at the preliminary scene report from the coroner. The rain started at around eleven o'clock. The grass was dry underneath those two bodies, which means they had to have been killed before that. Nine at the earliest, he says. And that would be an outside possibility. I was with Blake from eight. That's consistent with the data from their cell phones – they were moving around until just before ten-thirty, and then they stayed put. That's your time of death, at which point Carter Blake was five miles away helping me stack the dishwasher."

McGregor's face lost the knowing look. Isabella was grateful for that. She knew that with anyone else, he would have maintained the poker face.

"You've seen the PSR already?"

"And got it from the horse's mouth. The CI said there's no way those men died before nine. Blake couldn't have done it."

McGregor pinched his chin between the thumb and index finger of his right hand. It was a tick he always had when considering new information. If Isabella was reading him right, it didn't look like this information had come as a complete shock. She wondered if Blake had halfway convinced him of his innocence already, even without telling him who he had been with.

"Could someone have messed with the data on the phones?"

"I called in a request to AT&T on my way down here. They'll tell me if their records match. I think they will."

He nodded, pleased at her thoroughness, if not her conclusion. She pressed him.

"So you have no gun. You have no GSR on your suspect's hands, and you have a circumstantial motive at best. Now you have an alibi that shows he couldn't have killed these men. That is, if my word is good enough for you."

"Shit," he said after a moment.

"Shit indeed. Because whoever did this is still out there."

Isabella didn't add what else she was thinking. This guy still being on the loose was just the start of their problems. Blake wasn't the killer, and therefore this crime did not have the easily explainable motive of a bar fight escalating into murder. The two men had been killed out in the woods, with two shots to the head, and now there was no apparent motive. That meant Dentz's theory was a live possibility.

If the ballistics came back showing a .38 was used, then there was a good chance they had a Devil Mountain copycat on their hands.

42

CARTER BLAKE

I guessed I had been sitting in the cell for a couple of hours when I heard the footsteps approaching. The door opened and I looked up, expecting to see McGregor. It wasn't him.

"I thought I warned you to stay out of trouble."

Isabella Green's expression was neutral, but there was just enough wry amusement in her voice to tell me that my situation was improving.

"Did you talk to McGregor?"

She nodded. "Lucky for you it didn't start raining until after those two men were killed last night. Otherwise you would be sitting in here until a better suspect came along. And sometimes, one never does."

McGregor and Feldman joined her at the door, both giving me matching hard stares.

"You're letting me go?" I asked. It was almost a rhetorical question. It sounded like Green had given me my alibi, and in any case the evidence against me was so thin it could barely even be called circumstantial. You could just about make the case for motive, and that would be it. A half-decent lawyer would have had me out on the street within hours, but I could see that cooperating, along with Deputy Green's help, had very probably saved us all those hours.

He nodded reluctantly. "You can go."

I stayed put, because the way he delivered those three words had me expecting a "but".

"But I'd like you to stay around town for the next few days. Or at least be contactable."

"That's a switch," I said, glancing at Green. She didn't smile.

"Come on, McGregor. You never thought I did it, did you?"

McGregor shifted uncomfortably. Beside him, Feldman glared at me. I got the feeling at least one of them had been pretty sure I was guilty. Or at least really wanted me to be.

"I'd like to keep you around," McGregor continued, without answering my question, "because whatever happened to those men, you were the last man to see them alive that we know of. Aside from their killer."

"Not exactly," I said. "Deputy Feldman here saw them at the same time. The bartender, too."

"Neither of us got into a fight with them," Feldman said. Then, addressing McGregor, "No need to be hasty here, we can keep this prick until tomorrow morning."

McGregor's eyes shifted away from mine for the first time, and the look he gave Feldman was a wordless rebuke. It said, *If I want your advice, I'll ask for it.* Green diplomatically examined her shoes. I cleared my throat and spoke.

"I'd like to help."

All three looked back at me again. McGregor looked curious. Feldman's mouth opened, and then he thought better and closed it again.

"That's good to hear, Blake," McGregor said. "Leave your number. We'll be in touch."

"That's not what I meant. I have some expertise in this area and I'd like to offer it."

Green looked back down at the ground. I understood. She had already positioned herself a little too close to me. She wanted us to argue this out with no input from her, whatever her opinion on it.

"Your ... 'expertise' is in missing persons, Blake. That

right?" McGregor said. "These two men are a lot of things, but they ain't missing. We know exactly where they are: on a slab waiting for the cutter."

"Sometimes missing means dead," I said. Out of the corner of my eye, I saw Green flinch at that, and remembered there was a missing person still to be accounted for: Deputy Haycox. I ignored that for the moment and kept speaking. "If I can take a look at the crime scene, maybe I'll think of something helpful. Besides, this way you get to keep an eye on me."

McGregor considered it. I could tell Feldman wasn't happy, but he had shot his bolt too early. After a few seconds, McGregor turned to Green. "Speak to you for a moment?"

The two of them stepped outside the cell, leaving Feldman and me alone. He waited a moment, and then stepped in front of the door and closed it behind him, keeping his eyes on me all the while.

"Looks like you'll be leaving us a little earlier than planned," he said.

"No need to apologize. Could have happened to anyone."

He stepped forward and I wondered what he was going to do. Provoke me into doing something that would extend my stay, perhaps. I stood up and crossed my arms.

"I want you out of town, today," he said.

"The sheriff doesn't seem to agree."

"We'll find you if we need to, trust me," he said, bringing his face to within six inches of mine. He was so close I could hazard a guess at his brand of toothpaste.

"How about we wait until the boss comes back?" I said.

Feldman took a second to think about that, and then he raised his hand and slammed it hard against the wall, right beside my head. With an effort, I didn't blink.

"I'll be watching you every second until you leave this town." He moved his hand down and took a handful of my shirt collar. "Oh and one other thing."

"What's that?"

He lowered his voice to a whisper and leaned in to speak directly into my ear. "Stay the fuck away from Isabella."

The door opened and Feldman drew back, patting my shirt back into shape where he had grabbed it.

"Deputy Feldman, is there a problem?"

He looked back at McGregor, who was standing in the doorway with his hands braced on his hips.

"I don't think so, Sheriff. Not anymore."

McGregor waited for Feldman to leave, and then approached me. He gave me an expectant look, as though waiting for me to say something about my exchange with Feldman. When I didn't say anything, he nodded.

"After due consideration, I've decided you have a point. I don't know how much help you're going to be. Directly. But why not? Deputy Green will be keeping you company. You two seem to have gotten to know each other already."

McGregor stepped aside, leaving a wide-open doorway in front of me. Something told me to forget everything I had just said, walk out of that doorway, get into my car and drive away from Bethany.

But I didn't do that.

I couldn't do that.

43

ISABELLA GREEN

Isabella could have killed McGregor for that bullshit. Apart from anything else, she knew it would piss Feldman off even more, and that would come back to bite somebody later. Most likely Isabella herself. She was so preoccupied thinking about it that she almost forgot there was anyone else in the car with her until Blake spoke.

"Thank you."

"For what?" she glanced over at him. He wasn't looking at her, instead staring ahead at the road.

"For getting me out. I don't think McGregor was in the mood for letting me go before he had to. Whether he thought I had done it or not."

She didn't reply to that. He was dead-on, though. Instead, she asked, "What did Feldman say to you, when we left you two alone?"

"He asked me to stay away from you, as a matter of fact."

"What?"

"Well, I say 'asked'. It may have involved the phrase 'stay the fuck away from'."

Isabella felt herself color, and was immediately furious at Feldman. She would have to talk to him. The truth was she had had to talk to him for a long time, but had always found excuses to put it off. Seeming to sense her discomfort, Blake changed the subject.

"How did you know I didn't do it?"

She glanced over at him before answering. "I didn't, at first."

Now he was looking at her.

"Don't give me that innocent look. If you're asking if I think you're capable of killing someone, then the answer's yes."

"You think I would kill those two idiots?"

"Maybe not. But anyway, I'm a cop. That means I think everyone is guilty until proven innocent, don't take it personally. Sometimes a killer doesn't look like a killer."

"What convinced you?"

"Evidence. It started raining at eleven last night. The ground was dry under the bodies, so you were with me when they were shot. Cell phone data backs it up. They were shot when we were eating dinner."

"Then I guess you were right," he said after a pause.

"How do you mean?"

"When you said it was my lucky day, yesterday."

It took them twenty minutes to drive back out to Slateford Pass. The coroner's van was long gone, the deep impressions of its tires in the mud at the side of the road. Isabella parked up and the two of them got out. The rain had collected in the channels made by the wheels. She remembered the shiny black shoes Blake had been wearing along with his suit when he visited the station and glanced down at his feet. He had changed to brown leather walking boots, quickly re-laced after the laces had been returned to him on checkout from the Bethany SD Motel.

Blake saw her regarding his footwear and waited for the verdict. "Better?"

"Good call," she said, making sure to sound as bored as possible. When she had first met Blake, he looked so at home in a suit that it was hard to picture him in more casual clothes, but he looked good in jeans and boots and a work shirt. The fresh stubble helped with that. Isabella guessed the sheriff hadn't felt like waiting around for him to shave before he arrested him. By the evening, she would be able to take him to Jimmy's Bar and he wouldn't stick out at all among the locals.

She turned her attention to the scene. If you knew where to look, you could see where the long grass had been flattened where the bodies had fallen, but otherwise there was nothing to see but evidence flags planted to indicate the positions of the bodies and the other items. She would be making a return trip when the rain stopped to see if anything had been missed, but she doubted it. She thought about Haycox and how he would kick himself for missing this: what would be his first homicide, quite apart from the potential link to a case he was fascinated with. And then she felt another pang of worry. With each hour that passed, the feeling only got more intense.

Blake was surveying the scene. Isabella thought about listing their findings so far, but held off, waiting to see what he thought. His first question wasn't one she expected.

"What were their names?"

It took her a second to recall them. "Jeffrey Friedrickson and Thomas Leonard. IDs say they were both from Jersey. Tourists."

"I thought they were hunters."

"So did they. Doesn't mean they weren't tourists."

"Did they have their guns with them?"

She indicated the flag in the middle of the clearing. "Brownings. A .223 and a .270. Placed right over there."

"Placed?"

She reached into her pocket for her phone. The crime scene photographer would have gotten better shots, but Isabella always took a few for her own reference. She cycled back to the first in the series and handed the phone to Blake. He took his time swiping through, looking up and frequently changing his position to align with the shot he was looking at. When he was finished, he handed the phone back.

"What do you think?" she asked him.

"They were caught off guard, that's for sure. Either of them get a shot off before the guns were taken from them?"

Isabella could tell he was thinking about the way the guns had been neatly placed on the ground, between the positions of the bodies. She shook her head.

"Somebody got the drop on them," he continued. "That takes confidence. Two men with guns. Two men we know were not averse to a little confrontation. That means they believed their killer had the upper hand, which could mean there was more than one of them. The killer, or killers, made them kneel. Executed the big one, then the other one as he tried to run. Whoever it is is a decent shot. Point blank is one thing, hitting a moving target with a head shot takes skill."

"Not bad," Isabella said, taking care not to sound impressed.

"You have the caliber yet?"

Her eyes were on the flag where Leonard's body had lain. She looked up at him before she answered. "You mean do I think it was a .38?"

He looked back at her, waiting for her to go on.

"This isn't that, Blake. I told you ..."

"You told me the Devil Mountain Killer is dead. How sure are you about that?"

"Sure."

"And this is just a coincidence?" He shook his head. "I think whoever did this is sending you a message."

An involuntary chill swept through Isabella. "What do you mean?" She heard a catch in her voice and wondered if Blake would notice it.

"Not you personally. 'You' as in the department. This is about what happened back then."

She sighed. "Do you know why I really let you come out here?"

He considered the question. "Because David Connor is my client."

"You're right. I don't want you to say a damn thing to anyone else about this, and that includes McGregor, but if those slugs come back as .38 caliber, then I don't think this is a coincidence. I don't think it's the killer risen from the grave, mind you, but I don't think it's a coincidence."

Blake held her gaze for a while and then looked back down at the ground where the two hunters had fallen.

"Okay," he said after a minute. "Let's go talk to David Connor."

44

CARTER BLAKE

Connor was expecting us. By the time Green's patrol car reached the top of the steep, winding drive up to his house, he was waiting at the doorway, his arms folded. He was wearing knee-length khaki shorts and a white T-shirt, with no logo this time. His eyes were locked on the driver at first, but when he looked at who was in the passenger side, he looked taken aback.

"What are you doing with her?" he said as I got out. Before I could answer, he looked at Green. "The sheriff forget to ask me something? Like where I was when Abe Lincoln was shot?"

I exchanged a glance with Green. So McGregor had beaten us to the punch. Strange that he had kept Green out of the loop, or maybe not so strange, since he had assigned her to babysitting me.

Green stepped forward and stopped at the bottom of the steps, her hand on the guard rail. "Can we come in, David?"

Connor looked at me again, the wariness changing to resignation. "Let's get it over with."

He led us inside, directing us into a kitchen at the back of the ground floor this time. There was a big rough wood square table, six feet on a side. No tablecloth. I got the impression he didn't host many dinner parties. There were four wood-backed chairs around the table. He sat down at the far end, not saying anything, just staring at me.

I got the idea we would be waiting a long time for him to ask us to take a seat, so I pulled the nearest chair to me out and sat down on Connor's right. Green followed suit, on the opposite side from me. She took out her notebook and a pen and laid them side-by-side on the tabletop.

"I assume you know what I'm going to ask you about," she said.

Connor didn't take his eyes off me. "McGregor and his right-hand-man left ten minutes ago. They wanted to know where I was last night."

Since he was still here in his kitchen, I guessed that whatever answer he had given had been satisfactory. Or at any rate, it hadn't given them reason to take him in.

"What did you tell them?"

He switched his gaze to Green for a moment, then looked back at me.

"Why are you here?"

I considered carefully. "Because they asked me the same questions before they got to you, David. Sounds like they were a little more polite with you."

He didn't look surprised at that piece of information. "I told them where I was. Where I always am: here."

"Okay," Green said. "Anybody with you at the time?"

"No."

Which meant they hadn't been able to rule him in or out. But I guessed McGregor had decided one hasty arrest was enough for one day. "How much do you know about what happened?" I asked.

"Two out-of-towners were shot, that's all McGregor told me. I said I hadn't come across them. Funny thing was, after they asked where I was, all they wanted to talk about was you, and what you were doing for me."

Green's eyes met mine. So McGregor was thinking along the same lines. That it might not be a coincidence; the murders coming right after Connor started hiring people to dig up the past.

"Because you're Blake's client, right?" Green asked. She had put her notebook away.

He snorted. "Not anymore. Mr. Blake here thinks I'm nuts, don't you?" He smiled at me, with all the warmth of a deep freeze.

I remembered Jane Graham's dark hair and brown eyes, how she was an almost perfect match for Adeline Connor. And I had seen her from up close.

"I don't think you're nuts at all. The person you saw in Atlanta looked—"

"It was her."

"Your sister is dead, David," Green said gently. "I'm really sorry. But Blake's right."

Was I? I wasn't sure about anything in this case, anymore.

Connor just shook his head and looked down at the table.

Green continued. "We think all this could be related in some way, though. There are certain similarities between the murders last night and the ..." she caught herself and took a second to think about her wording. "And the MO used fifteen years ago."

"Just say his name."

Connor was looking down at the table. His hands had formed into fists.

"I don't—" Green began.

Connor's head jerked up. "Say his fucking name! The Devil Mountain Killer. That's who you think it is. You think he's come back. You think I woke him up."

Green didn't flinch at the outburst. She waited for Connor to finish, and then straightened in her chair. "I don't think that, and I don't think McGregor does either," she said. "Yes, there are similarities. So much of what happened fifteen years ago is in the public record. Everybody who knows how to google knows pretty much everything we know from 2003. Could this be a coincidence? Sure. But if it isn't, it's a copycat, not a ghost."

Connor stared at her as she spoke.

"And you think I'm the copycat?"

She met his gaze. "I don't know what to think, David. If you didn't do anything last night, I guess you don't have to worry about anything."

Green stopped the car as soon as we got out of Connor's driveway and called McGregor.

"I just spoke to David Connor," she said. I heard a pause on the other end and McGregor's voice replying.

"I guess great minds think alike. Any word from Haycox?"

Her eyes closed as McGregor answered in the negative.

"We have to find him, Sheriff." She paused and listened to him. "If that were true, we'd have heard from him by now. I think we need to get some volunteers and start beating the bushes." Another pause. "But Sheriff . . . Understood."

She hung up and looked out of the windshield at the house. "It's not like him. Haycox I mean."

"You've tried everything, right?"

She nodded. "I mean I was worried last night, but ever since we found those hunters . . ."

I had exchanged only a few words with Haycox, but I was starting to become almost as concerned about his whereabouts as Green was, though perhaps for different reasons. An intense interest in the DMK case. Access to files nobody else could see. Someone who held the authority to get people to do what he wanted. Somebody trained in firearms, probably able to hit a moving target with a headshot.

"You're right," I said. "We need to find him."

45

CARTER BLAKE

On the way to Dwight Haycox's place, Green told me that McGregor had vetoed her request to organize teams of volunteers from the town to help with the search. I understood why: there was a killer out there. The last thing McGregor wanted to do was to send teams of civilians wandering around in the woods. Instead, he had authorized Green to go looking, and promised to put Dentz on it as well. With a double murder on his hands, that was all of the manpower he could spare.

I knew what Green was thinking. She had been worried before. Ever since the discovery of the bodies, I could tell she was fighting the inbuilt law enforcement pessimism about what we were looking for. I wondered if she had considered that there was more than one negative outcome possible on this search. We had two dead bodies and one missing person. Sometimes that's a closed loop.

From our brief interaction, it was jarring to imagine Haycox cold-bloodedly executing two strangers. But then you never really know. A killer doesn't always look like a killer, as Green had said a short while ago.

Haycox's apartment was the upper half of a two-story building. Green knocked hard on the door. She told me she had come by in the morning, and Feldman had tried last night. For a third time, the knock went unanswered. I started sizing up the door, wondering how easy it would be to break down, when Green produced a key.

"The spare, from his desk at work," she explained.

She inserted it into the lock and the door swung open. There was a short entrance hall with four doors leading off: living room, kitchen, bathroom, bedroom. Just the basics. There was a small alcove to the immediate left of the door, with room for a pair of black boots and an upright vacuum cleaner. We opened each door in turn and examined the four rooms. It didn't take us long to search the place. Haycox kept the apartment almost as neat as his desk. It wasn't *perfectly* tidy, though, which told us something. There was unopened mail on the kitchen table, the trash in the kitchen was half-full, and there was fruit and milk and half of a chicken casserole in a Tupperware container in the refrigerator. It told us Haycox hadn't planned on going anywhere for an extended period. The bed was made and there was a pair of sneakers neatly positioned underneath it.

"His uniform isn't here," Green said, seeming to read the thought I was having at that moment. I looked up to see her standing by the bedroom closet, running a hand through the hanging shirts.

"He wouldn't leave it at the station?" I asked.

"No, we wear the uniform to and from work. Tight budget, remember? It's not like we have shower and gym facilities down there."

"Okay, so wherever he is, he has his uniform. That means either he didn't go home after his shift, or he put his uniform on when he wasn't on duty."

"More likely the former," she said. "Damn it."

I understood what she meant. If Haycox hadn't gone home after his shift, it meant he had been missing for longer than we had thought. Since Saturday evening.

In the living room, there was a desk with four drawers, two on either side. When we looked through them, we realized this was where Haycox was keeping his hobby case. Devil Mountain newspaper clippings, notes, a copy of the book I had.

"Weird," Green said. "I thought there was more than this."

It looked like enough to me. There was a map on the desk, marked up similarly to the one I had. Only there was an extra spot marked on this one, in blue ink instead of the red used for the eight body locations.

"What's wrong?" Isabella asked.

"Too many bodies," I said. Green looked at it, then saw what I meant. She pointed at the odd one out in blue. It was a location on Devil Mountain itself, way off the path.

"What does this mean?" she asked, as though talking to herself. "Does he think that's another body dump location? One that was never found?"

I tapped on his computer to wake the screen. It asked for a password. Green considered and then started typing.

"He got me to log on to his emails at work once when his phone was out. If we're lucky he uses the same ... bingo."

We exchanged a smile. That's the thing about passwords. You need so many of them these days that most people recycle them.

She opened his emails and found nothing. Then tried opening a browser and looking at recent items. The first URL that came up was familiar.

"TrueSleuths," I said quietly.

"What's TrueSleuths?"

I didn't answer, I was too busy looking to see if he was logged in and what his username was. It didn't come as a surprise.

"He's Mr. Brownstone."

Green looked at me, waiting for me to explain.

"I looked at this a couple of days ago. It's a site where people go to talk about unsolved crimes. Haycox seems to be quite the history buff."

"Check his DMs," Green said.

I clicked into his profile and found direct messages. There were a number of them from other would-be sleuths, either fulsomely praising or abusively criticizing his work. And one, sent Saturday, that had been opened and read. It was from a user calling himself Bloody Bill.

Got some more thoughts on DMK you might be interested in.

There was a cell phone number. Without speaking, Green took out her phone and dialed it. It went straight to a message saying the number wasn't operational. Not even the option to leave a voicemail.

"I'll see if we can link this to a name," she said, not sounding hopeful.

I was looking at the map again. The road that terminated at the start of the trail up Devil Mountain was the one I had driven on Saturday. The one that passed the spot above the ravine where Green's father's car had been found all those years ago. I remembered the little house on that road and asked Green about the old man who lived there.

"Roland Roussel? Kind of a hermit. Makes David Connor look like the life of the party."

"I saw him at the window the other day, just before you pulled me over. I knocked on his door to see if I could talk to him, but he didn't answer, even though he knew I had seen him in there."

"Sounds like old Roussel."

We left the computer and gave the rest of the place a once-over. The apartment was so small that it didn't take long to check thoroughly. If Haycox didn't show up soon, I knew the next people to visit this place would be a forensic team. As we were heading back to the front door, I saw the boots and the vacuum cleaner and looked down at Green's feet. Same boots.

"What?"

"How many pairs of those do you have?"

"Just one pair, till they wear out," she said slowly as she saw where I was going. "Tight budget."

I followed Green as she hurried back to the bedroom closet. She pushed the shirts on the hanger back to expose the wall of the closet. There was a small chest of drawers in the corner, leaving about a square foot of space in front. Green kneeled down and examined it. I watched as she trailed her finger across the linoleum on the bottom of the closet, through a fine dust. I looked closer. Not dust, dried mud.

Green looked up at me. "Wherever he went, he took his walking boots."

"Let's go," I said.

Before we left, we gave the backyard a once-over, going around the side of the building. Like the apartment, there wasn't much to see. Just a square patch of grass and a six-foot wood fence which had been recently painted. As we made our way back out to the street, the door on the ground floor opened. A lady in her seventies or eighties appeared, holding it part-way open. She had fluffy white hair and wore a wool sweater with a red scarf coiled around her neck. She peered at us through big glasses, and it seemed to take her a few moments to decide who we were, and then she opened the door wider and stepped out.

"Any sign of him, Deputy?"

Green shook her head. "I'm afraid not, Mrs. Adams. You already spoke to Sheriff McGregor, I understand."

"That's right. I told him I hadn't seen him since Saturday morning." She glanced behind her as though expecting a crowd to be forming, and then stepped closer to Green, giving me a suspicious look. "You don't think ... *he* could have gotten him, do you?"

"'He?'" repeated Green, although it was obvious she knew what the old woman meant.

She hesitated, as though not wanting to come right out with it. "The killer."

"If you're talking about the two gentlemen who died last night, we still don't know what happened there," Green said. "Unless you can tell me different, Mrs. Adams."

Mrs. Adams looked around, as though concerned she would be overheard, and then leaned in.

"You want my advice, go talk to the Connor boy."

46

ISABELLA GREEN

The gravel lot at the foot of the Devil Mountain hiking trail was on the regular patrol routes, and therefore Isabella had driven past Roland Roussel's place three times a week, but she hadn't thought of the old man in a long time. Part of that was the effort of not thinking about what had happened to her father on that road back in 2003, of course.

She pulled off the Devil Mountain road onto the single-lane track that branched off to Roussel's place. The house seemed to blend into its surroundings, as though it was being slowly reclaimed by the woods. His old pickup truck was parked outside: a blue Volkswagen, looking like the rust was the only thing holding it together. She had never been this close to the house itself. Roussel was another of those Bethany natives who had been around forever, part of the wallpaper. Isabella had given him a warning a couple years back for driving his heap with a broken taillight. He had just listened carefully, nodded, and driven off when she told him to be on his way. She didn't think anybody in town knew him any better than that, to be honest. The sheriff had told her he was a veteran, but not of which war. Vietnam, probably, or maybe Korea.

He didn't answer on the first knock. Blake stepped back to get a better look at the windows. She knocked harder. "Mr. Roussel? It's the Sheriff's Department."

She heard a scrape of something inside, like somebody pushing back a chair on a wood floor. A minute or so later, the door opened a crack.

She had seen the old man around town all her childhood, but always from a distance. Up close, Isabella decided Roland Roussel could definitely have served in Korea. Hell, maybe even World War II. He was thin, with white hair and a bushy beard that covered most of his face, leaving a little space for his watery brown eyes and long nose. He glanced over at Blake, then looked at her expectantly.

"How are you today, Mr. Roussel?"

"What's this about?"

"Can we come in?"

Roussel grunted and turned away from the door, leaving it open. Blake and Isabella exchanged a glance, and followed. He led them down the short hall. Old newspapers and magazines were carefully stacked along one side, like a second wall, built out of newsprint. He showed them into a living room with barely more floor space. Every surface of the 1960s furniture was covered with books and magazines and unopened mail and knickknacks. The place had a musty smell, like an attic. That was exactly what it felt like, an attic. Only someone lived in it.

"We're looking for someone, but I'd appreciate it if you could keep it under your hat for the moment."

Roussel stared back at Isabella, his face almost totally blank, with a hint of mild irritation. She knew the request was redundant, because she and Blake were probably the first two human beings Roland Roussel had spoken to this year, but she wanted to be careful. She had never had to investigate the disappearance of another cop before, and it felt a little odd. Like a lawyer representing her brother or something.

"His name is Dwight Haycox. He's a deputy, like me."

"You're the only cop I've seen today," he said, his eyes shifting meaningfully to Blake, conspicuously un-uniformed.

Blake was examining a framed picture on the wall. Some kind of military crest with a dragon, above the words *37th Armor*, and a motto that was too small to make out. Blake turned to Roussel, a preoccupied expression on his face.

"Sorry, I'm Carter Blake," he said, offering his hand.

Roussel examined it, and then shook it loosely. "I saw you the other day, down on the road."

"That's right," Blake said. "I tried knocking on your door, but I guess you didn't hear me."

Roussel looked back at Isabella. "What's this about?"

"I told you, we're looking for Deputy Haycox. He might have come by this way, just wondered if you had seen him."

"When I saw him looking about, down there ..."

Blake spoke before Isabella had the chance to say anything. "I'm in town on a different matter, I'm just helping out with this."

"A different matter?"

"I'm working for David Connor. Looking into the disappearance of his sister, Adeline."

At the sound of the name, Roussel seemed to forget all about Isabella, fixing Blake with a cold stare.

"She's dead. Died a long time ago."

"You lived here back then?" Blake asked, ignoring the finality in Roussel's tone. "Did you see anything that night? The car going over the edge must have made a lot of noise."

Roussel glanced at Isabella before he spoke. She kept her face completely straight, as though Blake were discussing the weather. Roussel may have been a hermit, but he knew whose daughter she was.

He shook his head. "Some deputies came by a few days after she disappeared. I hadn't seen her. Nobody knew she went over the edge down there for months."

Blake stared back at him, a polite intensity in his gaze,

and Isabella suddenly realized he would make a very good cop.

It certainly made Roussel uncomfortable. He averted his eyes from Blake and turned back to her. "Are we done? I'm a busy man."

They left Roussel and walked back out to the car.

"Worth the detour?" she asked Blake.

He didn't answer, just shrugged noncommittally. Despite their current objective, she knew he was still thinking about his other case. He couldn't help it, like he had caught the Adeline bug from David Connor. They got back into the car and Isabella drove the rest of the way up the road, until they got to the wide plateau where the road terminated in the circular gravel lot. There was a four-foot-high wooden post that marked the start of the Devil Mountain foot trail. Had Haycox come this way? Maybe they would be finding out soon.

They got out of the car and Isabella popped the trunk of the Crown Vic. She pulled out the small canvas backpack and itemized the contents. Flashlight, bottled water, energy bars.

"Be prepared," Blake commented.

She allowed herself a small smile. "Being a cop out here is about twenty per cent boy scout."

"I was never a scout."

Isabella looked over at the start of the trail, then turned back to Blake, looking him up and down. "How fit are you?"

"I think I can manage it."

She gave him a skeptical glance. Before she could say anything, her phone buzzed.

It was McGregor. Isabella told him where they were headed, and that Haycox's walking boots had been gone. She didn't mention the map, or the discussion forum on his computer. She asked if Dentz had had any luck. McGregor hesitated before answering.

"Actually, I reassigned him. I've got him surveilling David Connor's house."

She thought about pressing him on that. Did he have another reason to believe Connor could have been involved in the killings? A reason beyond the apparent link to what happened to his sister? She decided that conversation could wait until they had checked out the extra point on Haycox's map. From the sounds of things, she was the only one looking for Haycox now.

"So I'm on my own, then," she said, unable to keep the irritation out of her voice.

"Not quite. Mr. Blake's helping you, isn't he?"

Isabella hung up and stared at the blank screen as she thought. McGregor knew fine well Blake hadn't killed the two hunters. She didn't know if he really suspected David Connor had either. But all the same, he was making sure the both of them were being watched.

47

CARTER BLAKE

The trail took us up at a steep incline. The path was covered in shale rock, occasionally with short bridges whenever we crossed a stream. We made quick progress, scanning the edges of the path as we walked. There was no point lingering. If we found evidence Haycox had been here, it would have to be on the trail, or very close to it.

The woods on either side were thick, dark and secretive even though it was a clear, frosty day and the sun was high. Light filtered through over the path but the canopy in the woods shut out the light, making it a perpetual twilight.

I stopped and took a drink from the water bottle Green had given me, wiping a sheen of sweat from my brow. I caught an amused glance from Green. She looked as though her heart rate was the same as it would be when she was lying on the couch watching a movie. I was in reasonable shape, but it was city shape. It was a long time since I had climbed a mountain.

"You realize this could all be a coincidence," Green said after we had been walking for a while. "Haycox could be fine. Those two hunters could have pissed off the wrong guy, the way they did with you. Maybe none of it has anything to do with the fact David Connor asked you to come and look for his sister."

"It could be," I said. "But you're only thinking about Bethany. It would have to be a coincidence that Wheeler and González were killed too."

We passed only a handful of other climbers on the route. It was late in the season, and Green told me that a couple of months earlier, we would be waiting in line at some segments of the trail, but the time of year combined with the cold snap the previous week had cut the numbers down. I counted a dozen other hikers in total as we ascended the two-and-a-half-thousand feet. Green stopped each of them and showed them Haycox's picture, asking if they had seen him. All of them did the same thing: stared at Haycox's smiling face and then shook their heads and told us they hoped we would find him.

We kept going, kept our eyes at the sides of the paths. I

thought about what was beyond the reach of our sight, out in the woods.

After a while, we came to a place where a narrow path forked off from the main one, barely visible beneath the undergrowth. Green checked the map. We were close to where Haycox had put another pin on the map. The branch off the main trail was much narrower, much older. There was a wooden sign recommending climbers keep to the main path. We took the road less traveled.

The small path snaked off into the woods, almost blocked off by thorn bushes at one point, and then we had to climb over a felled tree on the other side. After that it became wider and flatter. Ten minutes off the main track, there was a sheer cliff wall, forty or fifty feet high, and a trail that wound off into the woods at its base. Green checked the map and looked up at the point where the cliff plateaued.

"Up there."

I looked up at the cliff wall. I could see the first few hand-holds I would pick.

"Looks doable."

Green shook her head. "Or we could just follow the trail." She indicated on the map that it wound around for a quarter of a mile before circling back up at a gentler gradient.

The trail wound around the cliff until it became a steep slope instead of a vertical. After around twenty minutes, the path forked, hair-pinned and stretched upward at a steep climb.

A little later we were level with the top of the cliff, an almost flat plateau about fifty feet wide before the steep slope up toward the summit. There were tall, spindly trees all around, and a clearing. In the middle of the clearing was an old stone shelter. It wasn't much bigger than a shed, with an empty doorway and a slate roof that was sagging but still intact.

Green was staring at it like it was a suspicious suitcase left in the middle of a train station concourse.

"Did you know this was here?" I asked.

"No. Never been up this way before."

She drew her gun and approached the shelter. I kept pace with her, watching the shelter and listening for any sign of life. But maybe a sign of life wasn't what either of us was worried about.

We drew level with the doorway. There was a musty, damp smell from within. Green let out a slow breath as we saw the shelter was empty. There was an uneven dirt floor, and two benches on either side. I saw an old, crumbling pile of magazines underneath one. I leafed through them. Just some old *National Geographic*s and *TV Guide*s. If this had been the hideout of a killer, I would have expected more extreme reading material.

I wondered if Haycox had made it this far on Saturday night. I wondered if there had been anyone waiting for him.

Green had holstered her gun and was crouching in the opposite corner, examining something on the ground. She picked it up and showed it to me. It was a button. Wordlessly, she moved it beside the one on the cuff of her uniform. It was a perfect match.

"We know he was here. So where did he go?"

The secondary path finished at the shelter and the slope was too steep to climb, so we retraced our steps back down and around the cliff, circling back to the main track. When we got to the fallen-down tree fifty yards from the intersection point, Green stopped and rummaged in her pack. She took a bottle of water out and sat down on the tree, taking a long drink. She still hadn't broken a sweat. When we were driving up to the trail, she had mentioned she ran three or four miles before work every morning, without fail. It was clearly working for her. She offered the bottle to me and I took a drink.

"You're changing your mind, aren't you?"

"About what?" I asked.

"About Adeline. David Connor's convinced you again, hasn't he? You think there's something there."

I didn't answer, because I wasn't quite sure what the answer was myself. There was a gap in the trees that meant we could see part of Bethany in the foothills, looking tiny from a couple thousand feet up. Roland Roussel's little house was down there somewhere, too. Something about that house had bothered me, but I couldn't put my finger on it yet.

"Not a bad view, huh?" Green said. "It'll be better from the top."

"Oh great, more climbing."

A grin broke out on her face and then vanished just as quickly, as she remembered why we were here. She got to her feet again and put the bottle back in the pack. "Let's get a move-on."

"This is the worst part," I said. "The not knowing."

She nodded. "You must do this a lot," she said.

She thought I was talking about my job. Before I had time to think about it, I shook my head. "When I was sixteen, one of the girls from school disappeared. We didn't find her body for months."

She glanced over at me, her expression saying I had just answered the question she asked me the other night, about how I got into this line of work. And now I thought about it, maybe it went some way toward explaining why I couldn't let David Connor's problem go, either. She had opened her mouth to say something when we heard a whisper of movement in the trees.

I snapped my head around to look in the direction of the sound. Green's gun was in her hand. We looked straight ahead and a second later there was another rustle of leaves and a sleek gray fox emerged from the bushes beneath a stand of trees. It regarded us both curiously for a second and then darted off into the woods. It had only stuck around for a moment, but long enough to get a good look at it.

I glanced at Green. "Did you see that?"

She didn't reply, but the way she had turned pale gave me my answer. There had been a reddish smear around the animal's muzzle.

We advanced toward the spot in the bushes from where the fox had emerged. The smell hit us first. It wasn't too bad, still the early stages of decomposition, but it was un-mistakable. A second later I heard Green's breath catch in her throat and I saw it.

A mound of loose earth, a partially gnawed left forearm and hand protruding from the dirt. The fingernails were neatly clipped, and I could see a wristwatch on a leather strap.

Tuesday

48

ISABELLA GREEN

Isabella forced herself to go faster and harder than she could ever remember on the morning run. Last night's dreams had been worse than the previous night. Much worse. Rain and blood and the wreck of Eric Salter's car had featured prominently. She knew that it was working this case that had brought all of this to the surface, but it seemed like it was getting harder and harder to keep everything in the locked box.

She kept thinking about the last conversation with Blake, before McGregor and Feldman arrived at the scene.

You're asking me to withhold information? Maybe important information?

She had done as he'd asked, though. And now she was wondering if she should remedy that, tell McGregor everything.

She ran flat out until her lungs were burning, and then slowed down a little, but forced herself to keep going at a steady pace. Eventually, she collapsed against the oak in front of her house with a stitch that felt like it would be terminal. She survived, though. An hour later, she was showered and dressed and sitting across the desk from McGregor in his office.

She felt his eyes on her as she scanned through the

reports: autopsies, scene of crime, ballistics. Taken together, they told a very clear story. Same perpetrator, same weapon. It looked as though Haycox had been killed late Saturday night. Almost a full day before the two hunters. All of them had been shot in the head at close range by a .38 caliber pistol. *Just like the gun—*

She cut that thought off like she was hitting the snooze button on her alarm clock. Funny thing about snooze buttons, though. All they do is postpone the inevitable.

There was a TV crew setting up outside the station. McGregor was going to be on the local news in ten minutes. The two hunters had barely made the radio news bulletins. Haycox's murder had drawn a lot more attention. She knew this crew would be the first of many. Soon, it wouldn't just be local media, either. She remembered what it had been like in 2003. Television and print journalists from across the country had camped out for weeks, waiting patiently for the next body to show up, or the next hitchhiker to disappear.

McGregor picked up the first file on the pile and waved it at Isabella. "You able to vouch for Blake's whereabouts between eleven p.m. Saturday and five a.m. Sunday as well?"

She looked up from the report she was reading. Haycox's autopsy. She didn't need to say anything, the look she gave him said it all. He didn't even have the flimsy justification of Blake having a tussle with the victim this time around. If he really wanted to pull him in again, he was going to need something a lot better than that. Besides, Isabella had a feeling another suspect had displaced Blake on McGregor's list.

He dropped his eyes from hers and raised a hand. It was as close to an apology as she was going to get. "All right, I know. But this all started when Blake showed up."

"It didn't start with Blake," she corrected him. "What about Wheeler?"

"How is that related to this?"

Isabella considered whether to tell McGregor about what else Blake had uncovered in Atlanta, and decided against. She didn't have to. Based on what they had here, a green-as-grass rookie would draw the connection with the Devil Mountain killings, and she knew the only reason McGregor wasn't admitting to it was because he actively did not want to.

"Because it's an unexplained gunshot homicide, perpetrator still at large. Just like Friedrickson and Leonard. Just like Haycox. And they all visited Bethany right before they died. I think you're right, Sheriff. This is happening now for a reason. But it wasn't Blake who started it, it was David Connor seeing his si—" She stopped as McGregor looked up at her sharply, and qualified the statement. "*Thinking* he saw his sister."

McGregor thought it over. "Say you have a point. What does that mean? Why does that son-of-a-bitch's delusion mean people are getting killed all of a sudden?"

Just then, the phone on McGregor's desk rang. He kept eye contact with Isabella as he picked it up and answered. And then he forgot all about her.

"*What?* Well I suggest you goddam well find out where." A pause. "I'll be there in ten."

He slammed the phone down and sighed heavily.

"That idiot Dentz went into the woods to take a piss. He didn't see any change when he came back. A half hour later he gets a little worried he hasn't seen any movement at all in Connor's house. He knocked on the door and there was no answer. Connor's pickup is gone from the garage."

"He'll be back," she said. "Besides, he knows you're watching him. Even if . . ."

"What?" he asked when she didn't finish.

"I don't think Connor did this, Sheriff. This is someone else."

"Someone else. Great."

He sat down and took a drink from his mug of coffee, grimacing when he realized it was cold.

"What are you going to say to them?" she asked, looking out at the shiny television van parked outside.

"Well, all we can do is tell people to be safe. We're looking for this guy, and we just have to hope we're there next time he goes hunting."

"All we can do?" she repeated, before she could stop herself.

He stared at her, as though daring her to challenge him. She stared right back at him. McGregor had intimidated the shit out of her when she was younger. First as an authority figure, then as a boss. But that had been a long time ago. In for a penny, in for a pound, she decided. She would have to bring this up sooner or later, or hope that Feldman did.

"Kind of dancing around the elephant in the room here, aren't we?"

"I don't follow."

"Come on. Head shots. .38 caliber rounds. The woods. A connection to David Connor's dead sister."

"It's not that," he said flatly. "That's history."

"What about the possessions of the victims? Left out by the bodies."

He seemed to stiffen. "What do you know about that?"

"I know it's what you held back from the press, Sheriff. People know wallets and jewelry were untouched on the intact victims, that robbery wasn't a motive. But they didn't know they were carefully placed like that at some of the scenes."

"Good point. And how could you know that, for that matter? You weren't with us back then."

"Haycox told me. You knew he was into this case big time, right? It's why he asked for this posting. He knew a lot of things about the case fifteen years ago, and unfortunately, we can't ask him any questions about it."

McGregor said nothing.

"The killer's gone, Sheriff, I know that. This is somebody new. But it's not a coincidence, not at all. I think we need to talk to the FBI."

"Absolutely not."

"I don't see why—"

"We're not having this conversation. That was then, this is now, and we handle this ourselves. Only way it can be."

"Sheriff, at the very least this is a serial we're talking about now. Three dead here, and maybe whoever's responsible killed Wheeler too. We should be talking to them."

"Technically you're wrong, Deputy Green. Three dead in two incidents doesn't mean the FBI gets to waltz in here. And I intend to catch this bastard before he bags any more."

"I just think we should explore our options."

"And I will decide how and when we do that. Is that clear?"

She didn't reply. On one level, she understood his reluctance. He had been at the center of one of these circuses before, and she hadn't. She was a cop, though, and she knew exactly why cops didn't like calling in the feds.

But on the other hand, she knew they needed help. No matter how much the sheriff didn't want there to be a connection to what happened before – no matter how much *she* didn't want it – she knew there had to be one. Whoever was killing people wasn't the Devil Mountain Killer, but he seemed to be a fan. There would be more bodies to come, of that she was certain.

"You've had a rough couple of days, Isabella," McGregor said after a few moments. The use of her first name suggested he was trying to sound concerned, but his tone suggested anything but.

"I told you I was fine."

He stared back at her, like he was evaluating her somehow. "Just let me know if you need any more time, that's all I'm saying. A talk with someone, even."

"I'm fine."

He paused, waiting for her to say something else. When she didn't, he continued. "So we're clear on everything. We find this guy ourselves. And we can start by finding out where the hell David Connor has gotten to."

"Clear," Isabella said.

She turned and walked out to the car. She was crystal clear on exactly what the sheriff had meant with that little expression of concern, which was actually a threat. The help they needed wouldn't be coming from the FBI, at least not until McGregor's hand was forced. But that didn't mean there was no help at all.

She got in the car, turned the key in the ignition and turned out into the road. When she reached Jimmy's, she pulled into the lot and left the engine running. She scrolled through recent calls on her phone, hitting redial when she found the one she was looking for.

Carter Blake's voice answered, saying her name.

"You have time to talk?"

49

CARTER BLAKE

Green's Crown Vic pulled up outside the cabin just as Sheriff McGregor finished talking to the reporter on TV, tersely explaining that it was an ongoing investigation and he couldn't comment in detail on that, and certainly wasn't going to comment on any wild speculation about links to historic cases. I wasn't giving it my full attention. I was looking at an email on my phone.

Thank you for getting in touch with Honorific. We'd like to help you return the bracelet to its owner, but I've checked and we don't appear to have a Jane Graham on our payroll. Could you have heard the name wrong?

The email I had sent them had been intended to provide a means of establishing contact, or tell me that "Jane Graham" had lied about where she worked. Now I had my answer. I wondered if the address on her license was just as fake. Had she spotted me following her? Spun the whole story on the spot?

I put the phone down on the coffee table and let Green in. We went out on the back deck of the cabin and Green filled me in on her morning so far. To no one's surprise, preliminary indications suggested the same person was responsible for all three murders. I was pleasantly surprised to hear I wouldn't be spending more time in the cells unless anything changed. More worrying, David Connor had slipped his surveillance. Green told me her instinct was they needed to talk to the FBI. I concurred. So why wasn't it happening?

She bit her bottom lip and shook her head. "McGregor.

He's got a bug up his ass about keeping this in-house. He says we don't need any outside help. I think he's wrong."

"So go over his head."

"No can do."

"Why not?"

There was a flash of irritation in her eyes. "Because I say so. He's still the sheriff. We do it his way until I can convince him otherwise."

"Or until the next couple of dead bodies convinces him otherwise," I said.

She glared at me again and then looked out at the lake. I knew that that wasn't disagreement.

"Did you tell them about the shelter?" I asked.

She shook her head without looking back at me. Seemed like she wasn't proud of it.

"That's good," I said. "I don't think we can trust anyone."

She turned to me. "What do you mean by that?"

I thought she knew exactly what I meant. Our discovery last night conclusively ruled Haycox out of being the killer. That didn't mean I was ready to rule out everyone wearing the uniform. I weighed it up. I had to trust somebody. It might as well be the one person I knew couldn't have killed the two hunters on Sunday night.

"I think we should be very careful about who we talk to," I said slowly.

Her eyes narrowed, waiting for me to continue.

"Somebody tried to break in here on Sunday night, while we were having dinner. The night the hunters were killed."

"What makes you think that?"

I told her about the pencil lead and the broken vase. She came back with the same rational explanations I had considered the other night. I batted them away the same ways. I had talked to Joe Benson and he said he had heard breaking glass. There was no one around when he came out to investigate.

"The thing is," I concluded, "that was only a little worrying Sunday night. It was a *lot* worrying when McGregor and Feldman showed up at my door Monday morning looking for a murderer."

"You think somebody wanted to frame you for the killings?"

I nodded. "And we can't rule out that someone being a cop. That's why I think we need to play some cards close to our chests. If Connor's hiding out there, I think we need to be the ones to find him."

Her lips were pursed together. I could tell she didn't want to hear this, but she couldn't dismiss it out of hand, either.

"So are we going to check out the shelter or not?"

"It's an idea," I said. "But it'll take us a while to get up there. What if he headed out of town, as in really out of town?"

"Beauty of only having one road in and one road out," she said. "McGregor has men on the exits of the north and south roads, and Connor's vehicle is pretty damn conspicuous."

All of a sudden, I had a good idea of where he might have gone. Green saw it in my expression.

"What is it?"

We left the cabin and got in the car. I told her about the other night as she drove back toward the south road. How I had tailed Connor to the old house out in the woods. She looked confused. "The old Marion House?"

"Big old gothic place?" I asked. "Looks like a set on a slasher movie? It's just off the road, about a mile or two from here."

"I haven't been out there since ... for a long time. Every small town has somewhere the teenagers go to drink, that was where we went in Bethany. I went to a couple of parties, Connor did too."

I thought back to our conversation the other night. "You said you knew him back then, but not well, right?"

"Everybody around here knows everybody to some extent, sure. If I saw him walking along the street I knew his name and whose brother he was and where he lived. But no, I didn't *know him* know him."

"You never talked to him?"

She shrugged. "I met him at a couple of parties, I guess. Before Adeline went missing. Maybe a couple of conversations." She thought back. "I don't want to sound conceited or anything, but I think he might have liked me."

"But that wasn't exactly unusual back in high school. Boys liking you."

She glanced at me, a suspicious look like she was wondering if that was a line. It wasn't, just the truth. "Small town. You look halfway presentable and you'll get some attention."

I said nothing, because what I wanted to say was that she would have gotten attention in a town of three thousand or a town of three million, and that really *would* have sounded like a line. The fact it was true didn't change that.

"So you had a couple of conversations."

She nodded. "This would have been the summer before Adeline disappeared. After that, he was the one getting the attention. Though a different kind of attention. *The brother of that poor girl*, you know? He was all alone, I think a lot of people wanted to mother him at first. I got that too, of course, because my dad ..." She closed her eyes and started again. "I played along though, went to the counseling sessions, thanked people when they stopped by to check Mom and I were okay. David didn't play the game. He pushed them away. Started getting into trouble. Fights, drunkenness."

"Understandable."

"Completely understandable," she agreed. "But you know what places like this are like. Or maybe you don't. People want to help, but if you turn that down, you're the bad guy. And then it got worse."

"The cops started looking at him for the killings."

"He didn't help himself. Truth was he stuck out before it all happened. Long hair, stoner, listens to metal. This was 2003 by the calendar, but we have a time difference in Bethany. In some ways it's 1953, you know what I mean?"

I did. A familiar story. High-profile case, no good leads, the authorities under pressure to nail somebody. You start to look at the misfits, the oddballs. David Connor fit the bill, and even more so because he was a relation to one of the victims.

"But he was ruled out," I said. "No way it was him, right?"

"No way." She sounded certain. The same way she sounded when she said the 2003 killer was dead.

"What happened to his folks?" I asked. I knew they were both gone by the time Adeline had disappeared, but not the circumstances.

"Their mom died years before. I don't know exactly when, but I guess when Adeline was a baby. Their dad had kind of a reputation as a drunk and a bully. People were surprised when he disappeared too, but only because he had stuck around that long. I don't think he was what you would call a positive role model."

"When did he leave?"

"Maybe six months before what happened to Adeline. David was eighteen, so I guess as far as the authorities were concerned, they were all growed-up and somebody else's problem."

We were approaching the turnoff into the woods. I told

Green to slow down. I wondered about Connor's motivations in skipping surveillance. There could be any number of reasons he would want to do that.

"You don't think he killed the people back in 2003," I asked. "What about now?"

Before she could answer, Green's phone rang. She pulled over to the side of the road. She checked the screen, raised an eyebrow and answered.

"Feldman?"

A pause, and then a sharp intake of breath.

"Where?"

She listened, her mouth half-open in shock.

"I'll be there in ten minutes."

She hung up and looked at me. "They just found Roland Roussel dead. And David Connor's pickup was spotted driving away from the scene."

50

ISABELLA GREEN

They forgot about the turnoff to the Marion house. Isabella made the return trip into town at twice the speed. She filled Blake in on what Feldman had told her during the phone call on the way.

Roussel had been found shot to death behind the wheel of his car about two miles outside of town, on the north road. A member of the public had called it in, but had either been too distraught to give his name, or hadn't wanted to. The caller said he saw an orange pickup truck driving fast and so erratically it nearly hit him. About a mile farther along the road, he had come upon a beat-up blue Volkswagen pickup parked at the side of the road with blood all over the windshield.

"Caller was anonymous?" Blake asked.

"Let's focus on the shooting," Isabella said. "How many bright orange pickups do you think there are around here?"

Blake didn't answer. He didn't say anything. Didn't have to. She knew what he was thinking. It was all a little too neat.

The most direct route to the scene was through town, but Isabella knew the lights on Main Street would slow them down this time of day. She took a right onto the old track that ran parallel with the main road. It was barely a single lane, and turned into dirt and mud for a mile-long section, but it would bring them back out on the other side.

They made it there in five minutes.

Isabella saw Dentz first. He was manning the barricade: three sawhorses across the road with a sign marking the long diversion to 19 via the south road. Roussel's pickup was parked at the side of the road. There wasn't a lot of room, so the rear bumper was sticking out into the road a little.

Two of the other deputies were standing by the car, both with drawn faces.

"Four in two days," Isabella said, mostly to herself. McGregor couldn't hold out without calling in the feds much longer, surely. It would be out of his hands. "Stay in the car," she told Blake.

He nodded, looking ahead at the Volkswagen. Isabella got out and approached, ignoring Dentz's greeting. There was a bullet hole in the driver's side of the windshield, difficult to see with all the blood sprayed all over the inside. A male victim, head on the steering wheel. Gray hair, dark blue raincoat. She hunched down to confirm what she already knew: it was Roussel. As she circled the car she saw there was a lot of blood on the side window too, even though it was rolled halfway down.

This time she didn't need to close her eyes to see the movie start to unfold. Roussel's eyes, narrowed in suspicion, then widening in fear. The recoil of the gun. The bullet finding glass and then flesh and bone.

She was grateful when Sheriff McGregor's voice snapped her out of it. "You made it here fast."

"You get ahold of the caller yet?"

McGregor shook his head. "We'll find him. Priority right now is snagging Connor before he kills somebody else. If he knows he was ID'd at the scene, there's no telling what he'll do. I have Feldman back in town in case he decides to go postal. Jerry and Carl are still watching the exits onto 19 – full roadblock now. I have an APB out for Connor's vehicle with state."

"The caller ID'd him?" Isabella repeated, surprised. "He described Connor?" If things had gone down the way the caller described, that would be very unlikely. At the point he saw the truck driving erratically, he had no reason to suppose the driver was fleeing the scene of a murder. You see a car driving toward you, you get out of the way, you don't waste time looking at the driver.

McGregor shook his head and confirmed her suspicion. "Carl took the call. He didn't get time to ask him about the driver before he hung up. You know a lot of other orange pickup trucks in this town?"

Isabella grimaced as her own words were thrown back at her. But it didn't mean they weren't right.

"What's he doing here?" McGregor said, eyeing Carter

Blake. For the first time, there was something in his voice that said he wanted something. Something other than to see the back of Blake.

"As a matter of fact," Isabella said, "he was going to help me look for his client."

McGregor paused, seemed to be weighing something up in his mind.

"Let me ask you a question."

"The answer's yes, Sheriff. He can help us."

He bit his bottom lip as though he was surveying a tricky repair job and turned his head to look at Blake. Isabella glanced back at the car. Blake was watching as the two of them talked, his face completely impassive, as though he were stuck in traffic and daydreaming. She didn't doubt he knew exactly what they were discussing.

"That wasn't what I was going to ask."

"It wasn't?"

"It wasn't the only thing I was going to ask. The other part was, do you think we can trust him?"

She flinched inwardly, thinking about what Blake had said earlier. About how they needed to be careful about who they talked to. She was starting to question a lot of people now. Blake wasn't one of them.

"Yeah. Yes, I do."

"Then let's stop wasting time."

51

CARTER BLAKE

Before Sheriff MacGregor even looked at me, I knew that the parameters of my job had changed from a couple of days before. I had come to town to see David Connor as a client, and now he had turned into my quarry.

That wasn't to say I was ready to believe he was guilty yet, but I had to admit the evidence was piling up. The timing of the new killings, for one. The fact he had been one of only a handful of people who would have known Wheeler had been in Atlanta, and why. And a witness seeing an orange pickup truck driving away from the scene? That was one of two things: damning, or a little too convenient.

There was another thing, too. If I was right about where Connor had gone, it was mostly down to a lucky break on my part. McGregor's people might not need luck. They knew the area better than me, and the old house was likely on their radar. Maybe it was one of the boltholes on Feldman's list to check. With one of their own lying on a slab, tempers were frayed. If the Bethany sheriff's department found Connor before I did, his life expectancy might drop significantly.

McGregor signaled to me to get out of the car. I obliged and approached the Volkswagen, where he and Green were standing. I took the opportunity to take a closer look at the bloody windshield and the body slumped over the wheel before I met McGregor's stare. Why had Roussel been targeted? I couldn't shake the feeling that it had something to do with our visit.

"What you said the other day," McGregor said. "You're

good at finding people who don't want to be found."

"It's a living."

"You might have noticed we have ..." he paused and glanced at the body behind the glass, "... a situation here. There'll be time for working out the rights and wrongs later, but right now I need to do one thing."

"Keep people safe," I said.

"Exactly. I don't know what your usual fee is, but—"

"We can talk about that later."

"You'll help us, then?" He practically issued the question through clenched teeth.

"Yes. I don't know if David Connor had anything to do with this, but I think we'll make progress either way by talking to him."

"Okay," McGregor said, seeming satisfied with that. He looked back at Green, who gave him a nod. "So what do you need? Obviously we're covering the bases. APB out for Connor's jeep with state. I have a request in for a location on his phone. Feldman is in town, and I have another couple of men at Connor's house."

"What about the driver who spotted him?"

"We'll find him."

"All right," I said. McGregor's delivery was prickly, his gray eyes watching me carefully, like he was waiting for me to point out what he had missed. He hadn't missed anything. He was doing a good job. "I assume you'll want to search Connor's place once the warrant comes through."

"Already came through. I spoke to Judge Chalmers on my way out here."

"Fast work," I said.

"So?"

"So you're doing everything right," I said. "Ordinarily, you wouldn't need me."

"Ordinarily?"

"There are a limited number of roads he can take, which you've got eyes on. Only one road in, one out. You've got somebody watching the town in case he comes back, you've got people at his house. It's a waiting game. Only problem is, if he's running from you, he probably knows all of that already. And he won't stay on the roads."

McGregor sighed. "And as you've probably noticed, we have a shitload of off-road around these parts."

"There's an old ruined house on the shore of the lake," I said. "There's a road branching off the south road that takes you down there. You know it?"

"The Marion house?" McGregor asked, glancing at Green. She kept her face straight, not letting on that this wasn't new information to her.

"I haven't thought about that place in years," he continued. "It used to be a hangout for teenagers until the curfew. A flash flood took the bridge down in '04. After that, it seemed to drop off the party circuit. Jimmy's and the old cabins were easier options."

"I went to a couple of parties there, before the curfew," Green said. "I never liked it. It was a creepy place. Everybody said it was haunted."

McGregor looked doubtful. "You have a reason to believe that's where he's gone?"

"I followed him down there on Saturday," I said. "He didn't know I was there. You said the bridge was out?"

"Yes, washed away. Probably lasted fifty years past its natural life by then, too."

"Not anymore. There's a new bridge."

McGregor sucked his teeth. "I'd need to pull Feldman from his post to go down there. Half-hour round trip, even if the bridge is back up."

I shook my head and looked at Green. "The two of us will go. It'll help if I'm there to talk to him."

Green opened her mouth to protest. I pre-empted her.

"I don't mind hanging back. But if I'm right, I want to be there. How else can you use me?"

McGregor touched Green on the arm. They turned away from me and walked a few steps, going into a brief huddle. When they turned around, McGregor beckoned me over.

"Okay Blake, it's worth a shot. Thanks. But let Deputy Green approach first, clear? If Connor turns up there, he may not be pleased to see either of you."

52

ISABELLA GREEN

As Isabella drove, an on-the-hour news bulletin told her and Blake — and everyone else in the world — that another person had been found shot to death in Lake Bethany, and the authorities were on the lookout for a suspect named David Connor. They gave his description and last-known whereabouts, and warned he was not to be approached.

Blake sighed. "There goes the element of surprise, if we had it to begin with."

Isabella bristled a little. "It was the right thing to do. Like you said, the priority is to keep people safe."

They were approaching the turnoff for the old road down to the Marion house when they saw another vehicle up ahead of them. It was Feldman, moving fast. How the hell had he gotten out here so fast? Out of the corner of her eye,

Isabella saw Blake glance over at her. She said nothing.

They followed Feldman's car onto the old road. It was rutted and overgrown. Isabella hadn't been down this way since the old bridge came down, and that had been way before she had gotten her license. Even the sign warning of a dead end looked like an artefact from centuries past. She slowed as they approached the gully and she saw that Blake was right: there was a bridge. A twenty-foot-long metal temporary bridge had been erected to join the road. Isabella could still see some of the remains of the old bridge supports beneath. She expected Feldman to stop and inspect it, but he just drove straight ahead, barely slowing. She held her breath, but Feldman's SUV glided over it with no trouble. They followed.

The Marion house appeared out of the woods like a specter, its gray walls and irregular lines blending it in with the woods. It was so familiar, and yet so strange seeing it in the present. Like a fragment of a dream that had somehow come to life.

It was just as Isabella remembered it. The broken windows, the old barn at the side, the strange, asymmetrical tower on the east side. Feldman hadn't beaten them by much; he was getting out of the car, his gun drawn. There was no sign of Connor's orange pickup.

Feldman stayed put, waiting for Isabella to catch up. She brought the car around in a circle, so they were facing back the way they had come. Blake popped his seatbelt as they rolled to a stop, reaching for the door handle.

Isabella put a hand on his arm. "Remember what McGregor said. You're an observer."

Reluctantly, he settled back into the seat. "All right. Be careful."

"I can handle David Connor."

"I was more worried about Deputy Feldman."

She didn't respond to that. She reached for the keys, and it was Blake's turn to put a hand on her arm. She turned to look at him. Stupidly aware, given the situation, that they seemed to be touching each other a lot. She opened her mouth to tell him to forget it, if he was thinking about insisting on coming.

"Leave the radio on? Just in case anything else comes up."

A fair enough compromise. Isabella left the keys in the ignition and got out. Feldman waited for her to approach, keeping his eyes on the windows and his gun ready.

"What's he doing here?" he hissed under his breath, not looking away from the house.

"If we find Connor here, it's because he gave us a helping hand. How did you get here so fast?"

He didn't answer, focusing all his attention on the front door as the two of them approached the house. The glass in the windows was long gone. The door was closed over, but Isabella expected it was unlocked. No one owned the place, and there was nothing to steal. She unholstered her own gun and clicked the safety off, but kept it pointed at the ground. She glanced at Feldman's Glock. "Take it easy," she said. "We still don't know for sure."

"Better to be judged by twelve than carried by six."

Isabella bit her lip to stop herself from responding. She didn't know whether Feldman was acting out because he didn't like Blake; or if it was just that spending time with Blake had left her with less patience for his standard bullshit. Isabella knew one thing: McGregor's sensible directions aside, she knew which one of these guys she would rather be going through this door with.

The two of them reached the door. She resisted the impulse to look back at Blake, fifty yards away in the car.

She reached out and turned the handle. The door swung inwards. Both of them kept a step back from their respective sides of the doorway, out of the potential line of fire.

"Sheriff's Department," she called out into the darkness of the abandoned house. "Anybody in there, make yourself known to us."

Isabella's voice disappeared into the dark and was absorbed by the house. She looked at Feldman. He raised his eyebrows.

She spoke again. "If anyone is in there, come on out slowly. We don't want anybody getting hurt, okay?"

They waited another ten seconds.

"I'll go first," Feldman said at last.

Without waiting for an acknowledgment, he stepped over the threshold. Isabella followed. The hallway was long and stripped to the bare floorboards. Here and there, there was a gap in the boards, exposing the cellar below. There was a smell of stale smoke, as though somebody had lit a fire in here recently. The two of them picked their way forwards, approaching the stairs.

As Feldman put his boot on the first step, Isabella heard a roar from outside as a powerful engine revved to life.

She ran the way they had come, stepping carefully to avoid the gaps in the floor. Feldman caught up, and the two of them almost collided as they made it back to the doorway simultaneously. They made it outside in time to see David Connor's orange pickup truck smash through the rotting wood doors at the front of the old barn.

Isabella leapt down the stairs, keeping her eyes on the truck as it approached. She got her gun up and aimed it at the windshield. She saw David Connor's face. His eyes were looking right through her. As she was opening her mouth to yell at him to stop, she heard three reports from above her, with answering cracks as the bullets smashed into the pickup. Two in the windshield right by the driver, the third smashing one of the lights on the roll bar. She looked up to see Feldman at the door, calmly adjusting his aim as the pickup passed by.

"What are you—"

Her shout distracted him. His fourth shot was way off, clipping the tailgate of the pickup. It flew past them. The wheels caught the surface of the approach road, skidded, recovered, and then straightened out. The pickup accelerated quickly, headed back toward the bridge and the south road. Connor had been lucky not to be hit by one of Feldman's first two shots. Feldman hadn't been shooting for the tires. Those were kill shots. Isabella took aim at the tires and squeezed off another couple of rounds, knowing it was useless at this range.

"I had him!" Feldman yelled angrily.

She turned to look at him. She didn't know what she was going to say, because in the next second they were both distracted by the sound of a second engine as her own car roared onto the road in pursuit, Blake behind the wheel.

"Come on," she said, not bothering to look back as she holstered her gun and ran toward Feldman's car. She got in the driver's seat, his keys were in the ignition, too. She started it up and threw it into reverse as Feldman caught up and scrambled in the passenger side. She hit the siren with her left hand as she yanked the wheel around and floored the gas, following Blake, following Connor.

"I had him," he said again quietly.

Isabella didn't respond, too busy processing the last fifteen seconds or so. Radio, my ass. Blake had been expecting this.

53

CARTER BLAKE

Rule one of vehicular pursuits: don't get into a drag race with somebody who knows the road better than you.

The narrow road through the woods was roughly finished and dotted with potholes, every one of them magnified tenfold at the speed I was taking them. The suspension complained and every indent in the ground registered with a painful thump as I drove, keeping the tailgate of the pickup in view. Connor's vehicle was built with this kind of terrain in mind. Green's Crown Vic was no fragile little city car, but it was struggling. Connor hit the temp bridge fast, the end nearest me jolting off the ground as he came off the other side. I didn't slow, felt it sway as I passed over it.

I was grateful when we hit the asphalt of the main road only having lost a few hundred yards on Connor. Out here, the Crown Vic's 4.6 liter V8 gave me the advantage. I floored the gas pedal, closing the gap.

I focused on the taillights of his car, trying to close out any other consideration than keeping him in sight and keeping my own car on the road. My mind was turning faster than the car's revs. That was David Connor driving, all right. No doubt about it, I had seen him clearly as he passed within feet of me. I had been lucky Green had parked in a position that didn't require turning around. She and Feldman would lose valuable seconds getting his car backed up. They would be calling it in as they drove, maybe alerting whoever was on the south roadblock. Only they didn't know what I knew, that he had turned left instead of right, headed for

Bethany rather than the highway. He knew there would be no way out by car. His best chance was to ditch his pickup and then flee into the woods. We had already found one of his boltholes, maybe he had more. Like the old shelter on Devil Mountain.

If he wasn't the killer, why was he running? I had to admit he looked guilty as hell. The road straightened out and I started to close the gap. Two hundred yards, a hundred. Connor's brake lights lit up as he slowed for a tight bend, and I had to feather my own brakes to keep from running into the back of him. A tanker truck appeared from out of the bend. I caught a flash of the driver's startled eyes as the two oncoming vehicles swerved out in his lane before tucking back in with a second to spare. I heard a distorted blast of the horn as he passed us, missing Connor's pickup by inches. Another bend up ahead, this one skirting a sheer drop into a ravine.

The brake lights flashed again, and then he was speeding up out of the curve. The road straightened out again for a quarter-mile. Clear, for now.

I shifted down to fourth, floored the pedal and swung out into the left lane, drawing level with the driver's side of the pickup. Connor was looking straight ahead. If he was even aware of me, he didn't show it. I leaned on the horn. He glanced at me, back at the road. A couple hundred yards to the next curve. Steep upward slope on our right hand side. I jerked the wheel to the right and slammed into him. The weight disparity worked in his favor now. The pickup jolted and swerved a little, but he kept it on the road. I started to steer in again, watching Connor's face. And then I saw his eyes widen. I looked ahead, saw a green truck emerging from the curve, less than a hundred yards away. There was no time to brake, nowhere to go.

The calculations rushed through my mind. Head-on collision at a combined speed of over a hundred miles an hour, or a plunge down the ravine. Neither felt like an attractive option.

And then Connor's orange pickup vanished from alongside me. Without processing what had happened, I yanked the wheel to the right and slipped into the space he had been. The green truck flashed by.

I hit the curve and it kept curving, a hairpin bend. I slammed my foot down on the brake to stop from flying off the edge. The back wheels slewed around and I straightened up and leaned in on the brake. As soon as I could see the road ahead was clear I risked a glance in the mirror and saw Connor aiming to overtake. I braked the rest of the way and swung across the road, blocking his path.

He slowed, and then picked up speed again, slamming into the side of Green's Crown Vic and rocking it a little forwards, making a little more space in the road, but not yet enough to get past. I shifted into reverse and closed the gap. He backed up and revved the engine, no doubt calculating how much distance and speed he would need to knock me out of the way. He was unlucky on the location. The road had gradually narrowed over the last mile, so that even though I had stopped diagonally rather than horizontal to the road, there was barely a foot of clearance on either side. With time and perseverance, he would probably be able to shunt me out of the way. But time was on my side. I heard the sound of a siren on the road behind us. Still distant, but getting louder.

I turned so I could make eye contact with him. The blank look I had seen earlier had gone, he was pissed now. He eased off the gas and glared at me. I decided to take a chance.

I opened the door and got out of the car, palms up,

watching Connor's hands on the wheel. He made no move to shift them.

"You're making a mistake," I called out.

I knew Connor heard me. His window was rolled down and he was looking right at me, but he didn't answer. He gunned the engine again. I glanced at the position of my car. He wouldn't be able to shunt it easily, but I thought it was a good sign that he had stopped trying.

I heard another siren in the distance, coming from ahead of us. Feldman and Green had called in backup.

"It's over. They have to bring you in dead or alive. I would rather you were alive."

"Why the fuck would you care?"

"Because you're my client. It's bad for business to let a client get himself killed."

The siren got closer and Feldman's cruiser appeared at the bend, slamming on the brakes when he saw the two cars blocking the road.

Connor's hands dropped from the wheel. I approached, putting myself in between him and Feldman's car. I hoped that would make him less likely to shoot. Then again, given his attitude, maybe I should have been the one hiding behind Connor.

We had less than five seconds before things were taken out of my hands. I looked Connor in the eye.

"Was it you, David? I need to know before they take you in."

He didn't answer. His eyes were watching Feldman and Green as they scrambled out of either side of the car, guns drawn. Feldman's face was red: exertion or rage or a blend of the two.

I looked back at David, ignoring Feldman's shouts for me

to get the hell out of the way. His eyes met mine. He shook his head.

"David?" Green's voice.

"David, I'm going to need you to get out of the vehicle and lie down on the ground with your hands behind your head."

I turned to look at her. She was standing a couple of paces in front of Feldman, who had his gun pointed straight at Connor's head. The muzzle didn't waver, but his eyes kept moving. From his target, to Green, to me, back to the target.

I took a step back. "I think you better do what she says."

54

ISABELLA GREEN

"If you didn't do anything, why did you run?"

David Connor straightened a little in the interview room's chair. He looked at Isabella Green for a full ten seconds before he answered. Then he said simply, "I didn't run."

"There are a couple of good dents in the side of my car that say different."

He was looking in good shape, all things considered. Despite the high speed chase, despite being shot at a couple of times, despite the fact he was being held on suspicion of several murders, he was entirely unruffled. His shoulder-length hair was tied back in a ponytail. He wore a clean gray T-shirt and jeans. He had been booked and fingerprinted and swabs of his hands had been taken to check for gunshot residue. The only visible mark on him was a shaving cut that looked a couple of days old. Isabella had the feeling that wouldn't be the case if it had been Feldman who had caught him, instead of Blake.

She glanced behind her at the two-way mirror, knowing Blake was there watching. He had done exactly what McGregor had asked him to, found his target and helped us to bring him in. He had used a department vehicle without authorization in order to do so, but neither she, nor even Feldman, were in a hurry to mention that detail to anyone, since that would entail explaining exactly how they had almost let their suspect slip through their fingers.

Blake had pressed hard to be allowed in on the interview, redoubling his efforts when Connor waived his right to a lawyer, but McGregor had stonewalled. They owed him for catching Connor, though, so the compromise was he got to observe from outside along with Feldman. Who hadn't been best pleased to lose out on a spot in the room himself, naturally.

Connor's eyes flicked to McGregor's. The sheriff had stayed quiet so far. It was a technique he and Isabella had developed without ever really discussing it, during the interrogations they had handled together thus far. Not so much "good cop, bad cop" as "talkative cop, taciturn cop". It had the same effect, achieved with a little more subtlety.

"I heard on the radio you were looking for me for those murders. I know what happens when the cops find someone they like for something like this."

Isabella sat back in the chair. "I don't know, why don't you tell me?"

"I have a better idea, why don't you count the bullet holes in my car?"

McGregor glanced at Isabella, waiting for her response.

She wanted to drag Feldman in here and let him take that one, but she didn't.

"You were a suspect fleeing from armed deputies."

"Something tells me I wouldn't have done any better staying still for him."

"Connor, I know you feel like people have it in for you. But can't you see how it looks? If the GSR tests come back negative, if we don't find any evidence you were at the scene, maybe we'll start to believe you. Why cause trouble for yourself?"

He turned his eyes to the ceiling and sighed, in the manner of one tired of explaining himself to idiots.

"Maybe I should get a lawyer," David said.

"That's your decision, David," McGregor said. "If you've got something to hide, that's your best option. But if not, maybe we can clear it up quickly."

"You really think so?"

McGregor nodded. "We have a lot of questions, David, as you can imagine. Why don't we start with where were you this morning between seven and ten?"

Connor turned his gaze on McGregor sharply. "Aren't you tired of this shit?"

"Tired of what shit?"

"Me. Again. We went through all of this bullshit fifteen years ago when Adeline disappeared."

Isabella thought it was interesting that he had raised that already. She wondered what Blake was making of it, resisting the sudden urge to turn again and look back at the two-way mirror.

McGregor didn't respond to that, just folded his arms and looked Connor in the eye. The message was clear. He wasn't going to repeat his question. She thought about asking it again, decided that would not please her boss. After a minute or so, Connor sighed and held his hands up.

"I went for a drive. Got sick of your guy sitting outside my house. Then I went down to the Marion place. Next thing I know, I hear on the radio I'm a wanted man, and I'm getting shot at."

"Where did you go driving? What time did you get to the Marion place?" she shot back, watching him to see if he thought about the answers.

"Around. I drove up to the mountain road and back, then I went for breakfast."

"You were up at the Devil Mountain road? Near Roland Roussel's house?"

"I guess." He didn't blink at the name of the victim; didn't seem to register why this would be important.

"Where did you get breakfast?"

"Freddie's. Maybe a quarter to eight."

That was all verifiable, which was good. Freddie's would be quiet at that time on a Tuesday morning. It was after the early morning rush and before lunch got going. They would know Connor by sight. Isabella didn't get the feeling he was making it up, but if he was it would be a stupid lie, as it was so easily checked.

"Who served you?"

"Kelly. You want to know how I had my eggs?"

McGregor leaned forward. "Ycah."

Connor shot him a look full of contempt. "Over easy. With bacon and grits."

"So that takes us up to eight-thirty, perhaps," Isabella said. "You went straight to the Marion house from there?"

He nodded.

"Through town, or around by the south road?"

"South road."

"Anybody see you?"

"Maybe. How should I know? I wasn't expecting to have to account for my whereabouts. Not until I found out you had decided I was the goddamn Devil Mountain Killer."

It was like somebody had sucked the air out of the room. Sheriff McGregor wasn't the flinching type, but he shifted a little in his seat as Connor spoke the name.

After a long moment, McGregor broke the silence. "Who said anything about him?"

He said the word "him" in a strange way, almost like a believer talking about God.

"Come on," Connor said. "You're either the dumbest cop in the history of dumb cops or you know what's happening here. Maybe it's him, maybe it's not him, but this is all about what happened in 2003."

Isabella suppressed a shiver and glanced at McGregor. His face gave little away, other than a slight reddening to his cheeks. She wanted to talk to Connor about this, of course. This and more. Like the fact the killings had only begun after he reopened the wounds of his sister's disappearance. But first things first. First, they had to establish whether Connor was really in the frame for the murder this morning. Although nothing he had yet said ruled him out, she was becoming less and less sure they had their man.

"We could go off on tangents all day, David. Let's focus on you. Did you leave the Marion house between getting there and us showing up?"

He considered the question, then shook his head.

"Any reason someone would think they saw you on the north road around eight-fifty this morning?"

He looked puzzled for the first time, like this was the first question he hadn't expected. "Why would I be there? It's all the way across ..." and then a light came on in his eyes as he worked it out. "That's where you found the victim."

"You were identified driving away from the scene, Connor. You want to explain that, seeing as how you were all the way across town in your version?"

He rolled his eyes. "I'll explain it easily."

"Yeah?"

"Yeah. The explanation is, that's total *bullshit*."

"Not my information."

"Well, get the source of your information in here and tell him to pick me out of a lineup."

Isabella looked at McGregor out of the corner of her eye. His face was expressionless. "Maybe we'll do that." He got up and looked at Isabella, signaling for her to follow suit. "We're going to leave you alone for a while, David. We have a lot of paperwork before we move this forward, as I'm sure you'll understand. Take the time to have a think over things. It's in your interest to be as forthcoming as possible with us, remember that."

McGregor rapped on the door. Dentz appeared and escorted Connor back to the cell. They watched until they had turned the corner and the double doors had closed behind them. Isabella gave McGregor a look that said, "What now?" He said nothing, opened the door to the anteroom where Blake and Feldman were observing.

Except Blake was alone.

"Feldman went to take a call," Blake said. "Only been gone a couple of minutes."

"What did you make of that?" McGregor asked Blake, the hint of a rueful smile on his lips.

"Same as you, if I had to guess. Worst of both worlds. Nothing to incriminate him, nothing to exonerate him. Unless you come up with that anonymous caller."

The tone of Blake's voice said they might have more luck

tracking down the Loch Ness Monster. If McGregor noticed, he didn't let on.

"Do I need to ask what you think? About whether he killed Roussel this morning, I mean, let's leave everything else to the side for now."

Blake shook his head. "He didn't do it. And the only real reason he's here is because of an anonymous call, added to the fact he made himself look guilty by running. You're damned lucky Feldman missed him."

McGregor listened, expressionless, and then turned to Isabella.

"And you?"

She addressed Blake. "Do you mind if the sheriff and I talk in private for a moment?"

"He can stay," McGregor said, before Blake had a chance to answer. "I think we both know what you're going to say anyway."

She shrugged. "I agree with Blake. I don't think he's our man. Should we keep him under arrest? Absolutely. But we should be back out there, making sure."

"You might want to reconsider that, Isabella."

She turned to see Feldman at the door. He had a habit of just appearing. She hated it. There was a weird look on his face. Like he wanted to be looking satisfied with the knowledge he had and they didn't, but something about what he had learned had disturbed him. Like he hadn't entirely been expecting it.

"What's up?" McGregor prompted.

Feldman gave Blake a suspicious glance before continuing.

"That was Bianchi down at Connor's house. They found something."

"Something?"

"A body."

55

CARTER BLAKE

"A body." The two words echoed in my ears as Green and I drove up the hill toward David Connor's house.

Green and McGregor had looked as surprised as me. McGregor had sent men up to the house to search it looking for evidence in the killing of Roussel or the other three. Perhaps he thought they would even turn up a weapon, if they were lucky.

But a body? I didn't think anyone had been expecting that.

As we rounded the last corner on the steep approach to the house, I saw three Bethany cops were outside the house. Specifically, they were grouped around the deck at the front. A big, dark brown dog on its leash was pacing around, held back by one of the cops. The other two were on their knees, looking under the deck.

Green let out a long sigh as she pulled the car in. She saw my questioning look and waved at the house.

"You ever have one of those days where you're drowning in work, and then something bigger than all the things you were worrying about comes along and blows everything else out of the water?"

"Maybe a couple of times a month."

"I didn't think Connor did it. It wasn't just the funny tipoff, it was ..." she let the pause hang in the air. "I didn't think it was him."

"Maybe it still isn't."

She unbuckled her seatbelt and stopped to look back at

me as she put her hand on the door handle. "You think this is all a big misunderstanding, that it? They've mistaken a dead cat or a raccoon for a dead body up there?"

"No. But I think we should keep doing what we're doing. Looking closely at everything."

We got out and approached the house. The cop holding the dog's leash called out a greeting to Green, then moved his eyes meaningfully from her to me. He looked old enough to be pushing retirement, and his gut hung over his belt.

"He's with me, Jerry," she said distractedly. "We recognize the vic? Somebody local?"

The deputy she had called Jerry shrugged. "I don't know, these guys all look the same to me, know what I mean?"

He stepped aside and in a second we saw what he meant.

The victim looked the same to him because eventually all of us look the same, after enough time. Beneath the deck was a partially excavated grave. They had dug down three or four feet and exposed the skull and upper torso of an adult human skeleton.

"We were all set to toss the house after we got the warrant. We didn't even make it to the front door before Lucifer started barking up a storm. We let him go and he started digging right over there. We picked up a couple of shovels and helped him out and ..." he gestured at the remains, the skull grinning out at us from the shade beneath the porch.

"Coroner?" Green asked, as she crouched down at the edge of the porch.

"On his way over. Told us not to dig anymore."

She nodded.

"David Connor admit to killing the others yet, Isabella?"

"No. Not yet." She said it absently, her mind elsewhere. Jerry didn't notice the dismissal, kept talking quickly.

"Looking pretty likely now, I guess. I mean, this means

the sick bastard has been doing it for a long time. That body has to have been under here for years."

Green wasn't listening. She was staring intently at the skull, as though she expected it to turn to her and start talking.

"Isabella?"

She straightened up and looked around her, as though coming out of a hypnotic trance. She looked up at the open front door.

"You search the place yet?"

Jerry grimaced. "Started. Kind of got a little distracted by this, to tell you the truth. Why, you think there's more in there?"

She shook her head and walked up the stairs. I followed her. She walked down the hall, ignoring the cop who looked up from inspecting the underside of the couch as we passed by the door to the dining room and went straight into the kitchen.

"Are you okay?" I asked.

She said nothing. Moved with increased urgency to the sink and turned the faucet on hard. She cupped her hands beneath the water and splashed it over her face. She leaned over the sink and I saw her throat spasm, like she was going to be sick. She fought it back, gripped the edge of the sink, and then shivered. I handed her a towel that had been hung over the back of one of the chairs. She took it and dried her face.

"Sorry," she said.

"What's the matter? I'm guessing it's not your first time seeing a body, so ..."

She grimaced. "You know how old that body looks, Blake?"

I answered carefully. "Difficult to tell. Decomp rate

depends on a lot of factors. Could be a hundred years, could be six months."

She shook her head. "Or fifteen years. And that means someone is ... it means. Jesus."

She wasn't looking for an answer from me, that much I knew. Which was just as well, because I didn't have the first idea of what to tell her. Had Connor killed the people over the last few days? Wheeler too? Had it been him all along, and he had somehow faked his alibi fifteen years ago? By any objective measure, it wasn't looking good for my client. But if he was the killer, why draw attention to himself by stirring up the past?

We sat across from each other at the table for a long time. I heard more footsteps in the house, as the other cops started searching the rooms.

"Let's go talk to him again," I said.

"While you're at it, you could ask him about this."

We turned around to see the cop Green had addressed as Jerry, standing in the door clutching a large transparent evidence bag.

Inside was a wood-handled Smith & Wesson .38 Special.

56

CARTER BLAKE

A half hour later, I was back where I had been a couple of hours before. Behind the glass, watching Deputy Green and Sheriff McGregor sitting at one side of the table, while David Connor sat in handcuffs across from them. A manila file folder lay on the table by McGregor's right hand. He had carefully squared it up with the right angle of the corner.

Before anyone spoke, I could see there was something different about Connor this time. Where he had been bewildered, gradually moving into anger before, he seemed calmer now. Maybe he knew something was up. Or perhaps he had seen it in the eyes of his interrogators.

He shifted his gaze to look at the mirrored glass, and I had the eerie sensation he was looking right through it and into my eyes. I studied his gaze, seeing ... what? I wasn't sure, but something had definitely changed.

"We've had some developments, David."

Connor looked back at the sheriff and blinked, waiting for him to continue.

"We've found another body." Another pause. Once again, Connor refused to take the bait.

"Do you know where we found it?" Again, no response, if you didn't count the ripple below his Adam's apple as he swallowed. It was at that moment I came to a firm realization: he knew, all right.

McGregor and Green exchanged a glance. McGregor pushed his chair back and got up. He leaned across the table, putting both palms flat down, his fingers within inches of Connor's cuffed hands.

"I think you know exactly where we found it. Who is it, David? Who did you bury down there?"

Nothing.

The sheriff sighed and reached for the manila folder. He flipped it open and began producing color printouts of the first round of crime scene photographs taken at Connor's house, before the coroner investigators had arrived to carry out the painstaking task of completing the excavation. Or exhumation, to be exact.

"This is your house, correct?" He waited a beat for an acknowledgment, and then carried on. "This is your porch. This is the decomposed body you buried underneath it. When did you do it, David? How many more people are buried under your house?"

Connor's eyes shifted from the photograph. He looked at Green, who seemed to be playing the silent partner this time.

"Don't look at her," McGregor said. "She can't help you. Look at me. Tell me who you killed."

Connor chose to obey the first part of the instruction, closing his eyes.

"Who is it, David?"

He kept his eyes closed and murmured something. I could see his lips move, but no sound. Evidently it was too quiet for the people in the room, too.

"What was that?" McGregor asked.

Connor opened his eyes and stared back at him. "I want a lawyer now."

McGregor stared back at him. I wondered if he was calculating whether he could get away with asking anything else. I didn't think he would. It was an unambiguous declaration.

Instead, he nodded and got out of his chair, glaring at Connor. "I bet you do."

Green got up and banged on the door. A couple of seconds later, it was opened and Deputy Dentz arrived to take Connor away.

Green and McGregor walked to the opposite corner of the room and spoke in hushed voices. I looked at the empty chair where Connor had sat, trying to work out what the hell had just happened. I had been so sure he wasn't responsible. But the David Connor sitting in that chair this time had seemed like a different man from the scared, surly, pissed-off guy from earlier. It was all the difference in the world. The difference between an innocent man worried about being railroaded, to a guilty one realizing he was in trouble.

I knew his guilt wasn't outside the bounds of possibility, either. Psychopaths are great liars. They can fool people. They can fool lie detectors.

But in that case, why had he done such a poor job of concealing his emotions when he knew they had found the body under the porch? A psychopath wouldn't have broken a sweat. He would have known that a body found beneath your house, damning as it may seem, is still circumstantial evidence. They still have to prove you put that body there. A psychopath would have bluffed it out. Maybe that was what he was doing.

No, despite everything, I still thought I was right. On the evidence of those last two interviews, I had two conclusions. Conclusion one: he probably didn't kill the hunters or Haycox or Roussel. Conclusion two: he may well have killed the person buried beneath his house.

I knocked on the glass to get Green and McGregor's attention. They turned and looked in my direction, seeing only their own reflections. They both looked startled to be reminded there was someone back here. I've spent a little more time than I would like in rooms like that, and it's surprisingly easy to forget you're being watched, even though everybody knows what's behind the mirror.

I watched them exit the room by the reinforced door, and a second later, the door to the anteroom opened.

"What?"

"I need five minutes with him."

Green shook her head. "No can do, you heard him."

"I heard him say he wants a lawyer. He didn't say anything about not wanting to talk to me. Ask him."

McGregor chewed his lower lip. "It'll take some time to get a lawyer out here, even if he's going with a PD. What did you have in mind?"

"Just give me five minutes."

57

CARTER BLAKE

David Connor looked up as I entered his cell. I waited for the door to close behind me.

"Thanks for agreeing to talk to me."

"I didn't kill those people, Mr. Blake, you have to believe me."

I leaned back against the wall. "None of them? You didn't kill anyone?"

His head jerked up and his eyes burned into me, shocked, questioning. Definitely not a psychopath. He was easier to read than a Times Square billboard.

"You know what they're going to be thinking?" I asked. "That it's Adeline. That would be neat, it would explain why you thought you saw her in Atlanta. Like her body underneath the house was crying out to you, making the guilt overwhelming, like something out of an Edgar Allan Poe story."

"She isn't dead," he said quietly. For the first time in a couple of hours, I thought about the email from Honorific again. The email that proved nothing, just opened up another question.

I waited for him to say something else. When he didn't oblige, I tried a different tack.

"Why did you let me past? Back there when I was chasing you."

He looked confused for a second, and then remembered what I was referring to. The moment when he may just have saved my life by allowing me to pull ahead of him, losing the chance to escape at the same time. He waved a hand dismissively, as though not fully realizing what he had done. "There was no room on the road, had to let you in."

"Well, thanks."

He sighed and looked down at the floor.

"Whose body is it, David?"

"You couldn't understand."

"Try me."

"It's all or nothing with these bastards. You think they'll be satisfied with that? They'll pin it all on me. This week, fifteen years ago, everything."

I sat down beside him. "I believe you. You don't have to tell me anything right now. Who's your lawyer?"

"A guy named Edward Brown. Used to live here but he moved to Gainesville. He helped out on my parents' estate."

"You trust him?"

"Yeah."

"When he gets here, tell him everything."

58

McGregor and Green were waiting for me outside the cell. McGregor turned the key in the lock and took a look through the peephole to confirm his prisoner was still there before he turned to me.

"I don't suppose there's any point in asking if he confessed?" McGregor asked.

I shook my head. "He's waiting for his lawyer."

McGregor nodded. "Then I guess we all are. As well as ballistics results on whether the gun we found at his house is the same one that killed Roussel and Haycox and the others. Meantime, I'm heading back up to the house."

"I'll come too," Green said quickly.

"Why don't you go home, Isabella? I'll need you in the morning."

"But ..."

"See you in the morning," he said, fixing her with a look that quietened her. McGregor went outside and got in the car. Dentz took a seat in front of the door that led to the cell and the interrogation rooms.

"Hey, if you really want, I'll swap with you," Dentz said.

She ignored him and beckoned me outside.

"What do you think?"

I considered. "Right now, I'm thinking we should get something to eat."

"Are you serious?"

"Never been more serious. Have you had anything to eat since breakfast?"

254

Green sighed in frustration. "I should be out there at the house."

"No point. The forensics guys will do their thing, you'll get an update in the morning when you're fresh and ready to get to work. I hate to say it, but McGregor's right."

"What if they find something else? What if there are more bodies?"

"Then they'll call you."

She stopped and considered, that little line appearing between her eyebrows again. I pressed my advantage.

"Come on, dinner's on me this time."

We got into Green's personal car, which was parked outside the station. We headed up the hill to her mother's house so she could check in on her, as well as change out of her uniform. Green pulled into the driveway and parked under the big oak tree. She stayed in her seat when she had turned the engine off, looking ahead out of the windshield, as though she was staring right through the trunk of the oak.

"I don't think Connor killed Haycox and the others."

I looked over at her, surprised. Not that she had come to the same conclusion as me, but that she was ready to say it out loud. I waited for her to continue.

"I've been thinking about the Roussel shooting. What struck you about the scene? The position of the car?"

I thought back to earlier in the day. I had to concentrate. A lot had happened since then.

"He was pulled over on the shoulder, slumped over the wheel."

"That's right. Pulled over. He stopped the car before he was shot; it didn't happen while he was driving."

I started to see where she was going, but let her get to it.

"We think maybe Haycox could have been killed by

someone he trusted. But old Roland? He didn't trust anyone. You know what that means?"

I said nothing, waited for her to go on.

"It means he had a good reason to pull over. Just like Haycox had a good reason to go out on the mountain at night. Just like the hunters had a good reason to lay down their guns." She turned to me. "I think you're right, is what I'm saying. I think you're right, goddammit. I think it could have been one of us."

"How well do you know them?" I asked. "The other cops?" I had only spoken to McGregor and Feldman, and I couldn't honestly say my feelings on either would make me objective.

"Most of them pretty well. Haycox was the newest. I can't imagine any of them ..."

"I know," I said. "All we can do is keep our eyes open, and our cards close to our chests, until we know more. Whoever it is wants us to think we have our man. Let's not give him any reason to think different."

We got out and went into the house. Her mother was in her chair in the living room, watching an episode of *Columbo*. Kathleen Green showed no signs of remembering me from two nights ago, and told me it was very nice to meet me when I introduced myself again. As soon as she got past the pleasantries, she smiled and turned back to the television. It was the one with Robert Vaughn on board a cruise ship. It was weird to see Peter Falk in short sleeves and no raincoat.

"He always gets his man, doesn't he?" she said, without looking away from the screen.

"He has an advantage," I said.

"Yes?"

"He always knows who did it."

"He certainly knows people," she agreed.

I thought again about the email I had received from Honorific just before Green had shown up. With all the excitement of the past few hours, Adeline Connor had seemed like a side issue. But the reply to my enquiry had confirmed a nagging suspicion. Either the woman calling herself Jane Graham had lied to me about her real name, or she had lied to the company when they hired her. What reason would she have to do either? If it involved a convincingly faked driver's license, it had to be something important.

Green appeared after a couple of minutes, but the transformation made it look like she had spent an hour in wardrobe with a retinue of staff. She had swapped the uniform for a blue dress with a subtle white polka dot pattern. Her blond hair had been unleashed from the tight bun and hung around her neck in a wavy style from the day's compression. She looked five years younger, less uptight. She grabbed a leather jacket from a hook in the hall and looked at me.

"You ready?"

I got up and smiled at Mrs. Green, who reciprocated.

"Lovely to meet your new gentleman, Isabella. He's very charming."

Green gave me an embarrassed look and bent to kiss her mother on the forehead. "Mary is coming over at about seven o'clock. Don't wait up."

59

CARTER BLAKE

Jimmy's Bar was busier than it had been the other night. Most of the tables were occupied, and there were small knots of people standing at the bar. There were a lot of cars in the lot. After a moment, I worked out why. The stage at the far end was set up with equipment. Green saw me looking in the direction of the stage.

"Band night."

"Who's the band?"

She shrugged. "Whoever it is, it'll be blues rock."

"Could be a lot worse," I said.

"That all depends on the band, doesn't it?"

We took a booth in the far corner, in the end of the bar farthest from the stage, and consequently less busy.

Jason, the bartender from the other night approached with a couple of menus, smiling at Green and then widening his smile when he saw me and Green together.

"You guys eating?"

Green told him we were and he laid the menus down on the table.

"Thanks again for the other night. You hear about what happened to those jerks?" He turned to Green. "Hear you got David Connor for it."

Green reached out and opened her menu pointedly. "Off-duty, Jason."

His face crumpled into embarrassment. "I'm sorry, Deputy. I mean Isabella. Get you some drinks?"

I looked over at her, waiting for direction.

"Oh, I don't drink. But you go ahead. Lime and soda for me."

I remembered back at her mom's house, how she had offered me a beer and gotten herself a bottle of water. At the time I assumed she was just conscientious about drink driving. I ordered a beer and Jason told us he would give us a second to have a look at the menu.

"Sorry," she said. "Alcohol and me don't mix. It's an impulse control thing."

"You don't have to apologize. It's not weird not to drink."

"You really aren't from these parts, huh? I'm the only person in this town I know who doesn't," she said. "I don't know. I feel like I need to keep a clear head. I'm not in AA or anything. It's just, sometimes you know that if you start something you might not be able to stop."

We held each other's eyes for a moment. Then we both looked down at our menus.

When Jason came back, we ordered two cheeseburgers. Green sipped her drink through her straw, her blue eyes studying me.

"What did Connor tell you, really?"

"He didn't tell me anything I didn't already know."

She opened her mouth to say something but stopped and closed her eyes as she was interrupted by a shriek of feedback from the stage. When it had abated, she opened them again.

"What makes you think he didn't kill Haycox and the others?"

"You questioned him twice, and you can't have missed it. There was a difference between the first and second times."

"You never know for sure in this job, Blake. But you do get to trust your instincts."

"And?"

"And the first time I would have said he was innocent. Like you said. Circumstantial evidence, a vanishing anonymous tipper, and a history with the department that leads ..." she paused and considered how to word it. "*Some of my co-workers* to approach things with preconceptions."

"McGregor or Feldman?"

"Both. But mostly Feldman." The line appeared between her eyebrows again. "Don't give me that look. He's a good cop, and a good guy."

I wasn't convinced by either of those assertions. "What about the second time?"

"Guilty. Or he has something to feel guilty about, anyway."

I nodded agreement. "Different body language, different tone, asking for a lawyer. Like night and day, like two different people."

She bit the corner of her bottom lip. "It's not just that, though. It's too convenient, finding the gun like that. And the anonymous caller, they couldn't locate him. The number's a burner."

Nothing surprising there. But I sensed there was more. "What?" I prompted.

"The number it came from ... it's the same number we saw in Haycox's private messages."

We stared at each other across the table, both knowing what this meant. The same person who had lured Haycox to his death had called in the tip on Connor. And perhaps the only reason he had felt safe to use the same phone, was because we had withheld that detail from anyone else. Which meant it could be someone close to the investigation.

The band was taking the stage to a restrained cheer from the audience. I guessed things would get a little more raucous a few more rounds into the evening.

"He knows what he's doing," Green said after a minute, still looking at the band.

"The killer?"

"Yes. And he knows things. That part with the hunters, where the rifles and the wallets and the phones were positioned? That was never released to the public."

She looked away from the band and closed her eyes, and I wondered if she was visualizing the crime scenes, or the acts of murder themselves. "He's cold, professional. Like you said, sending a message." She opened her eyes again. "I mean, I still think it *could* have been David, but ..."

"But the crimes don't fit with his personality at all."

She shook her head. "McGregor would say that's irrelevant. He'd say look at the evidence. I know that's not enough."

"You would make a good profiler," I said. It had occurred to me before, watching her work, observing the quietly intuitive way she made her deductions.

"People have told me that." She shrugged and took a drink. "That, or I would make a good murderer."

I smiled.

"You're not a good influence," Green continued.

"How so?"

"Encouraging shop talk when off-duty. We're supposed to be taking a break."

"You're right. You can't be full on all the time. You have to give your brain space to work everything through."

She nodded. "My mind gets stuck on a track sometimes. The counselor I went to after my dad was killed advised me to do just that, take breaks even when it feels like there's no time. Maybe she was right."

The band struck up a tune that sounded familiar. They were a four-piece, mostly with lots of facial hair and denim.

The singer had a mane of black hair and a mustache that would have looked at home in 1973. When he started singing, I recognized the lyrics. The singer was doing a passable Mick Jagger, singing about how he used to love her, but that it was all over now.

Green sang along with the tail end of the chorus and smiled at me. "You're a Stones fan?"

"Big time."

"Beatles too?"

"Sure. But any Stones album with Mick Taylor beats anything the Beatles put out."

She scowled and formed her lips into an "ooh" shape. "Beatles vs. Stones. That's a real cats versus dogs question, isn't it?"

"How about you?"

"Cats, and Beatles."

"Half right."

"Yes, you are."

The food arrived and we ate unhurriedly, in between long bouts of conversation. We were far enough from the band that we could talk. The band was pretty good. Mostly sixties and seventies rock and country covers, the occasional number they had written themselves, which the singer always introduced with an apologetic mumble. I switched to coffee after I had finished my beer.

We were interrupted as we finished eating by a woman in her early twenties slamming her folded arms down on our table and bending down to examine the two of us. She had curly dark hair and red lip gloss, wore a black dress with a plunging neckline.

"Y'all having a good night?" Her eyes shone with tipsiness, but she hadn't had enough to slur her words or make her eyes lose focus. Friendly drunk, not wasted.

"We are, thank you," I said. Green caught my eye and smiled.

She looked from me to Green and back. "Are you two on a date?"

"No," we both said quickly and as one.

The band abruptly finished their number, underlining the awkward silence. A big college kid wearing jeans and a CBGB T-shirt approached, a long-suffering look on his face.

"Cindy, don't bother these people," his tone said he was regretting being designated driver tonight.

I waved a hand to show it was okay. "She's fine, just making sure everyone's having a good time."

The guitarist started up the opening chords of another song I half-recognized, an old White Stripes song I thought, and Cindy's eyes widened in delight. "Oh my God, I love this!" Before Green could move her hand away, Cindy grabbed it in both hands and tugged her from her seat. "You have to come dance."

"I ... that is ..." Green began, looking more perturbed than at any time I had seen her in the last couple of days.

"Come on, everybody else is," she said, inclining her head toward the dance floor. She was right. Aside from the four of us and Jason the bartender, everyone was on the floor.

"Cindy ..." the boyfriend began.

Green shot me an embarrassed look that suggested, *Want to get this over with?*

"Why not?" I said.

The song was almost over by the time we made it to the floor. They followed it up with a Free song, and then Cindy tugged her boyfriend away in the direction of the bar, winking at Green when she thought she was out of my line of sight.

I watched them depart the dance floor, and then my breath

caught in my throat when I saw them pass a brunette at the bar. The hair, the profile, looked just like Adeline Connor. Then she turned her face in my direction, and the spell was broken. Nothing like her.

"You okay?" Green yelled over the music.

I nodded. The Free song ended in feedback which segued into the gentle strumming of an acoustic as the lights went down. Another Stones song, one of the best. The dancers paired off and moved closer together. Green and I observed them, hesitantly, before she moved in closer with a wry smile. "'Wild Horses', they must know you're a fan."

We moved close to one another, swaying to the melody. They sounded a little more influenced by the Gram Parsons version. With a sense of irony, I remembered our conversation about the importance of a break, of loosening up to optimize one's thought process. At that moment I could barely remember the name of my client. Green leaned close to my ear and spoke softly.

"Tell the truth: is this what you thought you'd be doing tonight when you woke up this morning?"

When the band finished, I settled the check and we went outside and got back into Green's Chevy. We didn't speak on the drive back to the cabins. The night was cold, but Green had the window wound down halfway. The air smelled of pine and wet leaves.

When we pulled into the lot out front of the circle of cabins, I saw my own car was there, but no others. Joe Benson's cold streak was continuing. His own cabin was in darkness, and I realized it was later than I thought. Green pulled to a stop in front of my cabin, the engine running. We looked at each other.

"Thanks," she said. "I think I needed that. To switch off for a while."

"Did it work? Your head feel clearer?"

She considered and shook her head. "Not so much."

We both smiled and there was another silence. We had barely had a pause in conversation in the bar, but when we stepped outside, it had been like breaking a spell. She bit the edge of her bottom lip lightly, the way she always did when she was thinking about something.

"So," I said. "I guess I'll see you in the morning."

"The morning," she agreed. "I'll see you then."

I don't know which of us moved first. Her, or me, or both of us simultaneously. There wasn't time to dwell on it. Our lips met and suddenly my hand was in her hair, hers was on the back of my head, pulling me in.

She turned the engine off and we got out on either side and circled around, meeting in front of the hood. We kissed again and she backed toward the door to the cabin, pulling me by the lapels of my jacket until her back was against the door. I fumbled my door key out and unlocked it on the third attempt. She let out a surprised yelp and grinned as the door suddenly gave way behind her.

We stumbled into the hallway and crashed through the door into the bedroom. She pulled her jacket off and dropped it on the floor. Turning her attention to me, she ran both hands up the front of my chest, pulling my shirt out, and then started to unbutton it as we kissed again. We shed the rest of our clothes in short, efficient bursts, with long bouts of kissing in between, and then I lifted her up and laid her down on the bed.

"You've wanted to do this all evening, right?" she whispered.

I shook my head. "No."

"No?"

"I've wanted to do this since you pulled me over two days ago."

"Probably just as well you held off," she said, kissing me again. "This is not an appropriate way to introduce yourself to an officer of the law."

And then there was no more time or breath for talking.

When it was over, we lay still in the dark, her left arm and her leg still tangled around me, the bedclothes partly on us, mostly spilling onto the floor. I stared at the ceiling and listened to the sounds of the birds on the lake as I got my breath back.

"I could use a cigarette," she breathed.

"You smoke?"

She shook her head. "Never started. Knew I wouldn't be able to stop."

We lay in silence for a while longer. I thought about me and her, how this had been unplanned and inevitable all at the same time. I wondered if we should have started, and if we would be able to stop.

"What's this?" she asked, running a fingertip over the scar on the side of my stomach.

"A bad memory."

She nodded understanding, and asked nothing else. "You think it'll be okay tonight?" she said after a while. Her voice sounded sleepy. "It feels like I'm sleeping on duty."

"If it helps, I'm sure we can find some way to keep you awake."

She punched my upper chest lightly and I could see the outline of her lips in the darkness as they curved into a smile.

"If we're right and Connor's not the guy," I continued, "I think whoever it really is has to lie low for now. Otherwise there will be more questions raised about Connor's guilt, and there are enough of those already. We'll be ready for him tomorrow."

"Okay," she said.

"We should get some sleep," I said.

"Absolutely," she agreed.

"What are you doing?"

"Want me to stop?"

"Nah. I've always thought sleep is overrated, don't you think?"

60

CARTER BLAKE

Two hours later, Isabella Green was sleeping deeply, her chest rising and falling where it rested against my arm. I was still staring at the ceiling. The occasional hoots of the owls and tiny splashes on the lake were the only sounds other than our breathing.

I had started to doze off after the second time, the dopamine haze hitting me like a tranquilizer. But then I had thought of something that had snapped me all the way awake, and I hadn't been able to sleep since. A two-word phrase that confirmed what I'd been thinking.

Courage conquers.

Adeline was alive.

She was alive, and somehow, she was the key to everything. I knew McGregor and Feldman thought that Adeline was important too, but they were wrong about why. They believed that David Connor thinking he had seen his dead sister was important. Maybe it was the trigger, maybe it was a symptom. Either way, the man who had faded into the background of the town was suddenly making lots of noise about something everyone else wanted to forget about. And then people started dying.

The first guy he hired to look into it, for a start. Then Vincent González. Then the hunters, then Haycox, then Roussel. All killed within days, most of them with the same MO of the Devil Mountain Killer. Maybe McGregor and his men thought there was a possibility Connor was the 2003 killer, but they were certain he was behind the current series of killings.

Devil's advocate. What if they were right? David killed everyone. Or at least the victims in this decade.

The body under the house only reinforced that theory. If David hadn't killed the person under the house, then he had to be the unluckiest guy in the world, to mount up so much circumstantial evidence.

But did it really reinforce the theory, or did it undermine it? If Connor had snapped and started murdering people, then why was the body beneath his house so old? Even if it didn't date back as far as 2003, it would suggest he had gone a long time between that murder and the new ones.

So that left two possibilities, in the scenario where he was the sole killer. Possibility one: he had been incredibly careful about choosing and disposing of his victims over the ensuing years, before suddenly casting caution to the wind and leaving them where they could be found, presumably because the illusion of seeing Adeline had sent him off the deep end. Possibility two: he had killed once, years ago, and then been dormant for a decade or more, before the Adeline spark had set him off again.

It was possible. The standard pattern of a serial killer is to keep killing, leaving shorter gaps between victims, taking greater risks, until they are captured or something else happens. Gaps in killings are often explained by a stint in jail, or travel elsewhere. Such a gap in killings matching up to the movements of a suspect is often what helps to identify them. But David Connor hadn't been to jail, and from what I had been told, hadn't left Bethany for any long period. He had spent summers working in Atlanta, yes, but there hadn't been any unsolved series of linked homicides in that area; at least none that I was aware of. But nonetheless, it was possible.

There were examples of killers who had inexplicably stopped for a period of years. The Green River Killer, the Grim Sleeper. Those were just the ones we knew about. The FBI has hundreds of unsolved serial investigations on its books. In a lot of those cases, the suspects died or went to jail or moved away. But it's likely that some of them just ... stopped. Kicked the habit. No one knows why they started, no one knows why they stopped. That's one of the reasons they were never caught.

So the theory that David Connor was the perpetrator of the current murders, or even that he was the newly returned Devil Mountain Killer wasn't out of the question. I could understand why McGregor thought he had his man. It was seductive in its neatness.

But if Connor had been the killer in 2003, he would have had to be incredibly smart or incredibly lucky to escape the scrutiny placed on him as a suspect. It wouldn't be impossible, but it would be unlikely that he would stick around town, behaving himself for fifteen years and only springing back into action now. And that was what it all came back to: why now?

Then there was what Green and I had spoken about. He had been convincing when questioned on the recent murders, rattled when the body was discovered. I knew that meant something, and the fact Green had picked up on it too only reinforced the instinct.

Who was the body beneath the house?

It could be anyone, I supposed. But again, statistics suggested a possibility that was more likely than not. If you murder someone, it's usually a close relation. Your spouse. Your child. Your parent.

Connor's mother had died when he was a child. I knew if I made a phone call or two I could get a birth date and a death date. There would be a death certificate, listing cause of death. Maybe even a grave we could go and visit. But Connor's father had no firm date for the end of his life. He had left his teenage children. It was in character, so nobody questioned it. They just sighed and felt sympathy for his abandoned offspring, barely more than kids. All we knew for sure was that Jake Connor had vanished more than fifteen years before, and had never been heard from again. Now there was an unidentified body found beneath his house. A body that could certainly be fifteen years old.

Adeline was the key. If the body under the house was her father, she would know why.

I started dozing off again. I could drive down to Atlanta in the morning, hope that Jane Graham was secure enough in her deception that she hadn't moved on.

As I started to feel the pull of sleep, Isabella Green screamed.

61

ISABELLA GREEN

I'm walking through the woods, on the ridge above the lake. I'm quietly humming a tune to myself; the chorus of a song I heard on the radio: about going home and not being scared. I know Momma will be worried about me, out here alone in the twilight.

It's the best time of day, though. The sun sinking below the trees on the other side of the lake, turning the sky into blood-red and orange. I have to keep my eyes jammed into slits as long as I'm facing west, and then the trail curves around to the north and now the sun is out of my eyes and it's like a cool, blessed relief. The woods turn into blues and greens and the afterimage of the sun overlays everything like a brand. I feel and hear the twigs crack under my feet and I know I must be the only person to come this way in days.

And just as suddenly, I know I'm wrong.

The girl has her back to me. She's taller than me, and skinny. She's wearing a black dress with no sleeves. And then I realize it's her who's humming the tune. She's singing it softly, saying she's not scared. I catch my breath and stop in my tracks. For some reason, it's really important that she doesn't know I'm here.

But I know it's too late when she speaks to me.

"You shouldn't be here."

I stumble over my words, manage to get out: "I'm ... I'm just leaving."

"It's too late for that."

I want to turn around, but my feet are planted to the ground, just like one of the tall ash trees. The sky has clouded over and the rain is starting to fall.

Adeline Connor turns around to face me. She looks normal, and I don't know why that surprises me. And then she smiles and the blood starts dripping from her mouth and from her wide-open eyes.

And then my feet aren't planted anymore and I turn and run back along the path. I can hear her breathing like she's next to my ear but I don't dare turn around to see if she's gaining. And then I slam into something hard, at waist level. I look down and it's a blue Ford Tempo. It's all crushed up in front and there's blood all over the windshield and then I—

"I said, are you okay?"

Blake was leaning over Isabella, his hand on her shoulder where he had been gripping her to pull her out of the nightmare. It was still dark. Isabella could only just make out his face, the shadows in the hollows of his eyes. She moved his hand from her shoulder and took a second to reorient herself.

"What was it?" Concern, but also curiosity in his voice.

"I saw Adeline Connor. She was young. I was too, I think, and—" she stopped herself there. Blake shouldn't know the rest of it. Not ever.

Her eyes were adjusting to the dark. She saw his mouth open, like he was about to say something, and then he changed his mind. Instead, he reached over and brushed the hair out of her eyes, where it had been pasted by the sheen of cold sweat on her forehead.

"Try to get some sleep," he said.

She smiled to herself in the darkness, knowing that it was a ridiculous suggestion. She didn't sleep, not after a dream like that. But then he shifted position and she settled into the crook of his arm. Her ear was against his chest, and she could hear the beat of his heart. Steady and strong. Like the beat of the song she was humming in the dream.

I'm not scared.

And before she knew it, it was morning and the light was streaming through the window, and the bed was empty.

Wednesday

62

CARTER BLAKE

When the room began to get light around seven, I slipped out of bed, being careful not to wake Green. She was lying on her side, her right arm tucked beneath her head, a lock of her blond hair covering one eye. Even in her sleep, I could make out the little line between her eyebrows, as though she was concentrating on something.

When I got out of the shower, she was awake. She was sitting on the edge of the bed, looking at the screen of her phone.

"They haven't found anything else at the house," she said, no surprise in her tone.

"I don't think they will."

She looked up at me. "I'm heading up there just now. Maybe it would be a good idea if ..."

"If we didn't go there together?" I smiled.

She gave me a relieved look. "Thanks. Listen, I don't want you to think I want to hide this. Last night was great."

"That's an understatement."

"But maybe we should keep it quiet."

"Very sensible. In fact, I'm going to head back down to the city today."

The line between her brows appeared again. An unspoken question.

"I'm going back to look for Adeline."

She blinked. "Adeline is dead."

"I'm not so sure now."

I laid it all out for her as I pulled my clothes on. The slow-burn suspicions that had begun to build in the back of my mind almost from the moment I had left Jane Graham in Atlanta. The email from Honorific. The two words she had said – *courage conquers* – that just might have given the game away. When I got to my theory about who was under Connor's house, she nodded, as though she had come to the same conclusion, but she let me continue until I had finished.

"If it's really her, if you can still find her ... what makes you think it'll be different this time?"

"Because on balance, I believed her last time. She fooled me. And she was able to do that because she's spent a decade and a half making sure she believes it herself. It's like she's made herself into a new person by sheer force of will."

Green stared at me for a long moment, her expression impossible to read.

"Okay," she said finally. "It's worth a shot. But Blake?"

"Yes?"

"Try not to be long."

I leaned down and she stretched her body to meet me halfway for a long kiss.

"You won't even know I'm gone."

She smiled, and then it faded. I saw in her expression an echo of the way she had looked right after the nightmare.

"I don't mean just for that," she said. "This isn't over, is it? No matter what anyone thinks."

I shook my head. "I'll call you as soon as I have something."

I put my jacket on and grabbed my car keys as Green

watched me thoughtfully. I paused at the door and we exchanged a look. Without breaking eye contact, she stood up, letting the sheets fall from her body, and walked naked across the room to me.

"Hurry back."

Outside, the sun was peeking above the trees on the far side of the lake. I unlocked the car and was opening the door when I heard my name called.

I turned around to see Feldman standing twenty feet from me, his hands braced on his sides, the right one a couple of inches above his holster. I looked around for his car. I didn't see it. He hadn't wanted us to hear him.

"What are you doing here?" I asked.

He took his time with the response. "I live here. You don't." He turned his gaze to where Green's car was parked, and then shot a brief glance at the window of my cabin, where the light was burning behind the curtains. "I thought I told you to stay away from Isabella."

I pushed the driver's door closed and walked over to where Feldman stood, taking my time. He watched me approach. His hands didn't move, but I saw the muscles in his upper arms stiffening. I stopped two feet from him. His lips pulled into a smirk, but his eyes were utterly mirthless.

"What?" he said. A challenge.

I looked him up and down, then looked around us at the deserted lot and the lake beyond the trees.

"I'm just wondering why you think ... whatever this is, is more important than a multiple murder case."

"Already caught the murderer, Blake."

"You really believe it too, don't you?"

He looked away and broadened the smirk, as though wishing he had his buddies here to get a load of this guy. Then he took a step forward and leaned in toward me.

"You really want to fuck with me? Out here?"

He reached for his gun. It was almost out of the holster when we heard Green's voice.

"Feldman!"

He froze. The two of us kept our eyes on each other. Then he took a step back, letting gravity pull the pistol back into its leather holster with the soft noise of the air being displaced. He turned his head.

She was standing at the door of the cabin, wearing a white terrycloth robe. Feldman's jaw tensed.

"What are you doing here?" she called out. Trying to sound natural, but I knew she had just seen what was about to happen.

"We'll talk later," he said. He shot me a look that was heavy with portent and turned on his heel, walking back toward the approach road.

Green watched me as I walked back to the car. I paused when I had gotten the door open again and held up my hand in a wave goodbye. She didn't return the wave.

63

CARTER BLAKE

I was reluctant to leave Green after the confrontation with Feldman. But I knew she could more than handle herself. Besides, it wasn't her Feldman was angry at. The reverse of anger, if I read the signals correctly. No, all things considered, getting out of town for a while was the best thing I could have done.

Two hours after I reached Atlanta, I found myself standing on the sidewalk outside a two-story concrete apartment complex. A significant downgrade from the previous address I had visited. I was about to try the buzzer when the door opened and the woman who called herself Jane Graham emerged from within, looking down at her bag as she put her keys into it. She flinched as I cleared my throat.

"Jane, wasn't it?"

She looked up.

"Shit."

"Nice to see you too."

"What the hell do you want from me? I told you, I'm not this girl, okay?"

"You were very convincing. I guess you've had fifteen years to practice. You've probably convinced yourself. Nice background work, too. You made a slight slip on the name of the high school in Orinda though. *Morgana*, not Morgan. Only one letter difference, but nobody forgets the name of their high school."

She looked up at the apartment building. A radio was blasting from an open window. A heated argument between two male voices from another.

"I liked your other place better."

She folded her arms and glared at me. "How the hell did you— I mean what are you, a stalker?"

"The super at your last place, the address on your license, claimed you didn't leave a forwarding address. Fifty bucks later, his memory improved."

She rolled her eyes. "Bobby, that son of a ..."

"How about a deal?" I offered. "Five minutes of your time, and if you still want me to go away, I'll leave you alone for good this time. Promise."

"Or what?"

"Or you can skip out on this place too, find yourself an even shittier apartment in a different city. Whatever it is you do when someone asks too many questions."

She seemed to consider it. Then she reached into her purse.

"I have a counter offer."

"I'm listening."

She pulled her hand out. There was nothing in it, but she had rearranged her fingers into a familiar configuration.

"Fuck off."

She pushed past me, heading back out to the sidewalk

"Adeline," I called after her. She didn't break stride. "They've arrested David. Unless you can help him, they're going to put him on trial for five murders."

Adeline watched as I sipped my coffee in the greasy spoon on the corner of her block. Her own cup lay untouched, even though she had already ruined it with four spoons of sugar. Finally, she had admitted who she was. She had sensed I had been following her; used the Honorific thing to sound me out. She had been pretty confident that her feigned annoyance and fictional childhood memories and fake driver's license had satisfied me. And they had, for a while.

"So is David ... okay?"

"He's in a cell, and most of the Bethany Sheriff's Department think he killed four people in cold blood this week. Some of them even think they've caught the Devil Mountain Killer after all this time."

She looked down at the table, and I remembered who I was speaking to and felt a twinge of guilt. Her abrasive attitude had made me forget the circumstances of her disappearance.

"I'm sorry."

"It's okay. I've never really talked about it with anyone."

"How did you get away from him, back then?"

She shrugged. "Luck. I've always been lucky. My dad used to say if I fell in the lake I'd come out with my pockets full of fish."

"You want to talk about what happened that night?"

"No. Maybe. I mean ..." she laughed. "I've never tried."

I waited for her to continue.

"The news reports got it about right. I was hitching. Only I was planning to head north, to New York, not to Atlanta. I thought I was going to have to walk all the way to the highway when I saw lights on the road. I was soaked to the skin. I stepped out to make sure I got the driver's attention. I wasn't thinking clearly anyway, and in the rain, I didn't hear the other car."

"The second car was Arlo Green's?"

"Yeah. He came around the corner fast, had to swerve to avoid hitting me. He almost went into the other guy, but he missed it and hit a tree. The other driver, the one in the blue car stopped. I didn't know him but I recognized Mr. Green from town. I thought they would be mad that I had caused the accident, but they were both just shaken up and glad everyone was okay.

"The guy in the blue car said he would take us to get help. Mr. Green said they should drive me home, but I convinced them to take me as far as the highway. I told him David hit me, and I couldn't go back there. He offered to let me stay at his place for the night, but I said no, and that I had friends coming to get me. The other one told me his name was Eric. I don't know if they totally believed me, but Eric agreed to take me out to the rest stop on 19. There was a Foo Fighters song on the radio, I remember he was telling me he saw them in some tiny venue before they were huge. He wasn't listening to Mr. Green when he tried to direct him, and took the wrong road. We ended up on the road up to the mountain. Mr. Green was telling him where there was a place to turn. And then we saw somebody by the side of the road."

She closed her eyes, and I knew she was picturing the images from that rainy night a decade and a half in the past.

"It was ... well, I guess you know who it was."

"What did he look like?"

She thought about it for a second. "Hard to tell in the dark and the rain. Average height, I guess. Thin. A blue raincoat with a hood over his face. He slowed the car down. We didn't discuss it, I guess we both assumed it was somebody who had broken down or ... I mean we didn't even think about ..."

She was breathing faster. She was tearing strips off the napkin she had been holding.

"Eric rolled his window down to ask if he needed help. That was when he got shot."

"You need menus?"

We both looked up sharply at the bespectacled waitress, who had appeared silently beside us. The tired eyes and vacant smile told me she hadn't been listening in. Adeline looked down at her hands again.

"No, thank you," I said. The waitress moved away, but made a point to look pensively at the three vacant tables still left. The place was filling up fast, it was almost lunchtime.

"Who do they think David killed?" Adeline asked quietly when she had gone, without looking up at me.

I wanted to know more about the night she disappeared, but my instinct was to let her tell it in her own time. Besides, if I was right, it was all related.

"You didn't seem to be surprised when I told you about that," I said. She didn't respond, so I answered her question.

"Four people have been killed in Bethany over the last few days. There are similarities with what happened before. They found a gun at David's house."

She shook her head. "It wasn't him."

Adeline raised her eyes to meet mine again. She didn't say anything, but I had a feeling she already knew what I was going to say.

"They found something else at his house, too. A body, buried underneath the deck."

Adeline closed her eyes and let out the breath she had been holding.

"It's your father, isn't it?"

She opened her eyes. She glanced around the diner. Two of the three remaining tables were gone.

"Do you have a car?" she said finally.

"Yes."

"I'll tell you the rest on the way."

64

ISABELLA GREEN

McGregor studied Isabella, waiting for her reaction. He had just told her the ballistics tests had been completed, and the .38 found at David Connor's house was the same weapon used to kill Jeffrey Friedrickson, Thomas Leonard, Dwight Haycox and Roland Roussel.

"You understand what this means?"

She knew exactly what it meant. "Yes, sir."

He nodded. "We're charging him for all four murders."

"And the FBI?"

"They've been in touch. I politely declined their offer of help. I'm headed back up to the house in an hour or so, if you want to come along?"

She opened her mouth and then shut it. McGregor watched her, looking satisfied when she didn't object.

"What about Blake? Is he still around?"

She shook her head, and McGregor looked back down at the report.

"Sir ..."

He looked up, as though surprised to find her still in his office.

"I just wondered, when you went out to talk to Connor on Monday after we released Blake. What did you talk to him about?"

He watched her carefully. "Why do you ask?"

"Did he seem ..."

"Seem what? Like somebody who had just killed a couple of people?" McGregor shrugged. "We asked him his whereabouts when the hunters were killed, if he had been speaking to Blake. It wasn't a long visit. We didn't really have any reason to zero in on him at that point. He had no connection to the two victims."

"Sure, okay."

"Is there anything else?"

She shook her head.

McGregor cleared his throat. "Feldman came to me earlier on."

"Oh yes?" she kept her voice even.

McGregor hesitated a moment, and she wondered why he was bringing this up. And whether he would have done if she hadn't started asking about his brief interview with Connor. "Blake helped us out yesterday, no doubt about that."

"I sense a 'but', Sheriff."

"You can tell me I'm sticking my nose in where it doesn't belong, of course ..."

"I appreciate you giving me that latitude, Sheriff."

His brow furrowed. "Blake is not good news. And I don't think it's in anyone's interests if he sticks around after today. Least of all yours."

Isabella turned away without taking the sheriff up on his offer. She and Blake could talk about that if and when he came back from Atlanta. In the meantime, she needed to know why McGregor was so resistant to bring in help from outside. He seemed to be absolutely determined to keep everything contained within the town limits. If he had his man, perhaps that would be fine. But if not ...

The nagging headache she had had all week seemed to be gaining in intensity. She drove out around the west loop of the town, slowing as she passed the Mercer place. The drapes were closed, Mercer's jeep wasn't in the drive. She wondered if Sally was there, probably tensing up as she heard a car approach, relaxing a little when she realized it wasn't going to stop. She drove up the hill to her mom's house. That tune from the dream was still stuck in her head; it was driving her crazy. She let herself in. Kathleen was napping in the chair in front of a movie on TCM. Anthony Perkins in *Psycho II*, no doubt cut to ribbons for daytime audiences. Isabella adjusted the blanket which had fallen off her and went outside and sat under the big oak tree. She placed her hand flat on the ground and closed her eyes, trying to block out the throbbing in her head.

Who the hell was doing this? It was starting to feel personal. Like someone was stomping around the room, getting closer and closer to the fragile house of cards Isabella had built up again since the night ...

The echoes from 2003 were impossible to ignore, and not just the ones everyone knew about. Who was doing it?

Maybe Blake was wrong about Connor's innocence, maybe they had been suckered in by a calculating killer who was also a great actor. The murder weapon being found in his house suggested that quite neatly.

But maybe he was right. Maybe David Connor wasn't guilty of killing Friedrickson, Leonard, Haycox and Roussel. In that case, there was only one other reason the weapon would be found at his house. Somebody planted it there. And only one kind of person could have done that in this town.

65

CARTER BLAKE

North, back to Bethany again. The blue sky of the morning had given way to gray clouds. Light rain hit the windshield in that frustrating rhythm that's pitched exactly between two speeds of the wipers.

"Are you sure about this?"

Adeline Connor had one arm on the window sill. She had donned a pair of sunglasses from her bag, but hadn't removed them when the sky clouded over. She was staring out at the trees at the side of the road as they flashed by. She hadn't spoken since we had got in the car. I had figured she needed some time to collect her thoughts, but it had been a while now, and I was starting to think we'd get all the way back to Bethany without exchanging another word. Besides, I was interested in the answer.

She spoke without looking away from the window.

"You have to go home sometime, ain't that a saying?"

Maybe it was my imagination, but I thought her accent was getting a little more southern as we got closer to her hometown. She had dropped a lot of things about her act.

"'You can't go home again' is the saying," I said. "Thomas Wolfe said it. And you better believe it's going to be true today."

She sighed and turned her head from her window so she was looking straight ahead, which was progress.

"My father was a piece of shit, did David tell you that?"

"Not in those exact words, but I got that impression. From him and from other people I talked to."

I was concentrating on overtaking a truck, so I didn't actually see her roll her eyes. I just heard it in her voice. "Jesus, small towns. What did *other people* say?"

I passed the cab of the truck and pulled back into the lane before I answered.

"That he was a drunk, and probably a wife-beater when your mom was alive. That he abandoned you both, and he did you a favor when he did."

"He would have, eventually," she said. "Left us, I mean."

"What happened?"

"He was pretty much what people told you he was. I mean ... shit, it could have been worse. I think we had it easy compared to some of the stories I've heard. He would ignore us most of the time. Normally he was a docile drunk. He would drink a couple of six-packs of Old Milwaukee in front of the game until he passed out in his easy chair. I would throw a blanket over him sometimes. Maybe once every couple of weeks he got the dosage wrong and it would make him mean instead of sleepy. He would get rough if you looked at him the wrong way. David got it worse. Usually it was nothing serious, shoving, cussin' you out, getting in your face, you know what I mean?"

"A bully."

"Just that," she said. "As I got older, I pitied him, more than anything else. I think he saw it in my eyes once, made one of them black."

She paused and I felt no need to fill the silence. She was right. Bad as it was, there were worse stories of abuse. But too many small mundane, soul-destroying stories just like this one.

"Must have been ..." she paused to think about it. "April of that year. I was at one of my friends' houses. I got back late and David was all beat up. I knew Dad had done it, but it looked like he had gone further than before. I was expecting it, sooner or later. Used to be he'd get mean every few weeks. Lately it had been a couple times a week. David had cuts, a black eye, his hand was bandaged up. Dad had thrown a bottle at his head hard enough that it broke when he put his hand up. Dad was nowhere to be seen. That was the night he left town, as far as everybody was concerned."

"What did David say about it?"

"He said he had gotten home and Dad was in one of his moods. Something stupid. He thought somebody had eaten one of his microwave dinners. They started out with words and moved on to fists. Thing is, I was worried about David. I don't know what he's like now, but he was skinny then, and my dad had sixty pounds on him, easy. He could have snapped him in half.

"I took him into the bathroom and got him cleaned up and tried to calm him down. He was shaking, crying. He told me Dad had taken the car and gone. I believed him." She looked over at me, to see if I was going to say anything. I let her keep talking.

"I think he would have told me. I guess he ... I don't know, he wanted to protect me. Eighteen months older than me, and like I said I could have taken him in a fight, but he always did the protective big brother thing." She laughed at the absurdity of it and pushed her hair back. "God knows where he got that from, it sure wasn't the old man."

"I'm sure you would have done the same for him."

"I wouldn't. I didn't. He was better than I deserved."

"Seems to me like you're doing it now."

She didn't say anything for a while, and I wondered if that was as much of the story as she was going to tell me. There was a gap in the clouds and the sun stabbed through at us.

"The night it happened ... it was *that* night. Halloween. I remember it had been raining all day. It was the first big rain of the fall. David was at work. I was alone in the house. It had been six months since Dad had left, and I had loved every day of it. It was the happiest I had been since ... well, since ever. We had made the place pretty homely. I was thinking how lucky we were that he had finally gone, that we could start living. I always knew I would leave town soon as I graduated high school, maybe even go to college. But it was nice to have a little practice at being grown-ups, you know? David and me, we got on great, maybe for the first time. It just felt like ..." she scrunched up her face, thinking about how to explain it. "It was like your whole life you've been carrying a weight, and not realizing, and when you set it down you suddenly realize, my God, this is what it's like for normal people. This is what life is like."

She smiled at the irony, and I knew she was getting to the punchline.

"I thought it would be nice to get a fire going in the stove. Dad used to do it before the drinking got really bad. I had never so much as lit a campfire before, but I thought what the hell? I was learning so much in those days. So much.

"I grabbed my jacket and held it up over my head and I ran out to the woodshed in the rain. There was that great smell, when it rains after a long dry spell. It was late in the day and it was really dark when I got inside the door. There was power out there, but the bulb had been out for a couple of years and nobody had replaced it. Still on our to-do list. I knew there was a shutter on the window at the far end, so I climbed my way through the junk, trying not to fall over anything. That's when I noticed the smell.

"I told myself later that I thought it was a dead cat or something, but I don't think that's true. I think I knew right then. Maybe I always knew. I saw there was a big shape stuffed behind the shelving unit at the far end. Wrapped up in something. I leaned over to open the blind.

"David had wrapped him in a couple of shower curtains and taped it up, I guess he was planning to move it at some point. The tape had come unstuck at the top and it wasn't properly sealed up, that was where the smell was getting out."

Adeline's tone had changed as she talked. As the content of her story had gotten more and more troubling, her voice had adjusted in the opposite direction. She no longer sounded shaky or on the verge of crying. She was talking like someone relating a boring report at a sales meeting for the third time that day; or a woman under hypnosis. Her voice was level, matter-of-fact. She sounded younger, too.

"I knew exactly what it was. *Who* it was. But for some reason, I had to look anyway. I bent down and I pulled at the opening at the top. I didn't want to touch it. There was blood or ... or something on the inside. I felt it sticking as I pulled it back. His face was wrong. I mean, it didn't look like a person. More like a waxwork of a person. There was this ... dent in the top of his head. Right here." She indicated the spot on her own forehead absently. "There was all this sticky blood around it, his hair was matted with it.

"All of a sudden, I had to throw up. I backed away and turned around. I tripped over something, fell down. I started crawling, just knowing I had to get out of there, out into the rain, the air. I made it to the door and got up on my knees and that was when I saw him."

"David?"

She nodded. "He was standing by the back door. He had come home, found I wasn't in the house, and knew where I had gone. We just stood there looking at each other for what felt like forever. I guess seeing him shocked the urge to puke right out of me. He came across the yard to me, holding his hand out. He was saying my name. Saying other things. I couldn't hear him. It was like after a really loud noise goes off, that ringing in your ear. He was holding out his hands. I just started yelling at him. I don't even remember what. I wasn't thinking. All I knew was it wasn't enough to get out of the woodshed. It was all around me. I had to get away."

She stopped and stared ahead. We passed the first sign we had seen listing Lake Bethany as a destination. Fifty miles.

"Do you remember what you did next?"

"Kind of. Next thing I knew, I was on the north road with my thumb out, and Mr. Green's car had crashed. I keep wondering. If I hadn't been out there, maybe they wouldn't have been at the wrong place for ..."

"Someone would have been," I said. "It's not your fault."

She raised her eyebrows, as though she could understand why I said that, but it didn't mean she had to believe it.

"You probably want to know how I got away, huh?"

"Yes."

"I don't remember exactly what happened. Like I said, my mind was still back in the woodshed. I was barely listening to the driver's conversation. First thing I really paid attention to was him getting shot in the face. I saw the gun swinging around to point at me. I never saw his face, he had a hood up and his face was in shadow. I just remember the muzzle looked so wide. His fingers were thin, almost delicate-looking. I think I tried to get out of the other door, I remember getting the seatbelt off, and my hand was on the door lever, then there was another bang."

She ran her right hand up her left arm and pushed the sleeve of her T-shirt back to reveal the edge of what looked like a large patch of scar tissue on her shoulder. It was pink and mottled.

"I didn't feel anything. I guess I was knocked out, or in shock or something. Only I wasn't unconscious. I remember feeling wetness on myself, and thinking was it still raining. Then feeling everything rocking about, like I was on a boat. And then there was a big dip, like going over the edge on a rollercoaster, and all of a sudden I was outside and looking up at the sky. But the rocking had stopped, and that was all I cared about so I just drifted off."

"You must have gotten the door open a little way without the killer noticing," I said.

She nodded. "I suppose so. I mean, that's the way it had to have happened. I pieced it all together later, when I was better. I got the seatbelt undone and the door was open a little, so when the car went over the edge, I must have been thrown out."

"Who found you?"

Her brow furrowed. "Who said anyone did?"

"You lost a lot of blood. Enough for them to assume you

couldn't have survived out there with a wound that bad, even if it wasn't a headshot."

"He told me I was lucky. That was the first thing he said when I woke up. I remember it clear as day. I was in agony, no painkillers. I knew that my brother had killed my father and I had just been shot, and this guy was telling me I was lucky. Sure, time to buy a lottery ticket, right? But he was right. The way I fell kept pressure on the wound. And him happening by like that ..."

She tailed off, as though suddenly remembering she was talking out loud. Perhaps revealing more than she thought she should. I thought I could fill in the blanks myself. The more I had thought about the circumstances of her disappearance, the more I knew somebody had to have helped her. Not just because of the blood loss, but because it's difficult for anyone to disappear completely. Much less a scared, wounded teenager who's never spent any time away from home.

"The man who helped you," I said. "It was Roland Roussel, wasn't it?"

Her head snapped around, as though I had woken her from a daydream.

"What makes you say that?" Her voice was suddenly on edge, her eyes narrowed behind the sunglasses. The defenses were back up.

"Adeline," I said gently. "He's one of the people who was killed. He died yesterday."

She put a hand to her mouth. When she didn't say anything else, I continued.

"He didn't tell me, if that's what you're thinking. I put it together. Somebody had to have helped you, and that person was either somebody not from Bethany, or somebody from town who's kept it quiet all these years. Odds were it was the latter. There was only one person more of an outsider in Bethany than your brother, and that's Roland Roussel."

She was still looking at me with suspicion, her mouth a thin line.

"But that wasn't what confirmed it. You did that yourself. *Courage conquers*."

Her mouth opened and then closed. She knew immediately the mistake she had made.

"I knew it sounded familiar when you said it the other day. I couldn't work out why, though. It isn't an expression in regular use, certainly not for someone your age. It's a motto. The motto of the 37th Armored Regiment, specifically. But you know that, since you read it off the crest hanging on Roland Roussel's wall."

She turned her head and looked out of the window again. After a minute, she started talking again. "I don't remember him finding me. I was all the way unconscious by that time, even though it can't have been long. He thought it was an accident at first. Saw the car at the bottom of the ravine. He climbed down to it, went right by me without seeing. After he saw the other two were dead he came right back up, said he would have passed me by again if he hadn't seen my arm sticking out of the bushes. He tried to wake me up, when that didn't work he wrapped my arm up in his shirt and hauled me back up to his truck. He got me back to his place. He had been planning to take me to the hospital as soon as he got me patched up."

"He was a veteran," I said. "I guess the training stayed with him. He didn't call an ambulance?"

"No phone. First couple of days, he couldn't leave me. He kept saying that from time to time, 'courage conquers'. I didn't know where it came from. He expected somebody to come by, and no one ever did. I found out later they didn't start looking for me for a couple days. By the time I was well enough for him to leave me, I begged him not to.

"He asked me what happened and I told him. Not about why I was running, just the attack. I made him swear not to tell he had found me."

"He was taking a big risk. If the cops had searched the place ..."

"We were careful. And lucky that David didn't report me missing for a couple of days. Everybody was busy looking for Mr. Green instead. I rested up a few days and I helped him clean up with bleach. On the way to the house I had been in the flatbed, so we could just hose it down. We burned the clothes I was in and the sheets from the bed."

There was only one question left: "Why?"

"Lucky. Like I said, at first that seemed like a ridiculous concept, but over the next few days, I knew it was true. Nobody else got away from the killer. It was like I had been given a new life. I thought it was better for me and better for David if I never walked back out of those woods."

I didn't say anything. Maybe something else gave me away.

"You're thinking I'm a selfish bitch."

"No, I'm thinking I understand completely. But David never got over it. You don't owe anybody else anything, but ..."

"But I owe him." She nodded. "That's why I'm going back."

66

ISABELLA GREEN

Isabella drove back down the hill to town. Before she reached the turn for the station, she turned into Adams Street and then pulled into the alley running behind Main Street, parking behind the dumpsters out back of the Peach Tree. She checked her watch and waited ten minutes, until she saw the sheriff's car flash past the mouth of the alley. He was on his way back up to the Connor house, like he'd told her.

The more time that passed, the more she believed Blake was right. The gun matching the killings only made her more certain. The person behind these new killings was someone on the inside. But who? She knew all of her colleagues well enough, but if life had taught her anything, it was that everyone conceals a part of themselves. The truth was, it was all too easy to accept that one of the other cops had killed these people.

Out of the department, she had the closest working relationships with Feldman, Dentz and Sheriff McGregor. Start with them. The soft, civilian side of her wanted to start listing all the reasons why these men couldn't possibly have committed coldblooded murder: Feldman had his rough edges, but he had shown her a caring and gentle side since her mother's stroke. McGregor had been her mentor, and a good cop for thirty years. Dentz ... well, Dentz was harmless. Literally. She didn't think he'd have the organizational skills to carry something like this out, never mind the resolve.

The professional side of her dismissed those rationalizations out of hand. Any of them could have done it. Any of them could be hiding their true nature behind a mask carefully constructed over a lifetime.

So look at the evidence. Who could physically have done it?

The only person she could rule out for the four killings in Bethany was Carter Blake, because she had been with him when the two hunters were killed. The more she thought about it, the more she decided that it was an opportunistic attempt to frame him. But why? Because he was a troublesome outsider, or because someone had a personal problem with him? The latter suggested Feldman. But Feldman wasn't in charge. Feldman hadn't been the one to veto the involvement of the FBI or anyone else.

She moved into the station and checked the corridor and the interview rooms to make sure she was alone, then she locked the front door. McGregor's office was also locked, which was unusual. But the master key was in the lockbox by the door, and she had a key for that.

She opened the door. She ignored the computer. Unlike with Haycox, she had no idea of the sheriff's password, but she didn't need it for what she wanted to check. She went to the filing cabinet and tried the top drawer. It was locked, but she wouldn't need a master key for this. She took two paperclips from the sheriff's desk tidy and straightened one of them out, bent the other one into an L shape. She inserted the two clips into the lock at the top and bottom. She twisted the top clip until she heard a click and the top drawer sprang open.

Not for the first time, she was grateful for McGregor's fastidious approach to paperwork. She found the file section she was looking for in the third drawer. The fact that none of the men could be ruled out for any of the Bethany killings was neither here nor there — each could have been accomplished quickly, with minimal travel time. The killings of Walter Wheeler and Vincent González back in September were a different matter. Someone would have had to drive all the way to Atlanta and back, not counting the time it took to find and kill the two men.

She had thought about this before, and couldn't remember for certain what she had been doing on the date in question, September 29th, never mind anyone else. It hadn't been long after her mother's stroke, and the days had blended into one another. She had a feeling that Saturday had been one of her days off. But the shift allocation would tell her that.

There was one sheet per week, listing shift patterns. She leafed through to September, looking for the week beginning the 24th. The 3rd, 10th, 17th were there. 1st October was there.

The sheet for the week of the 24th was missing.

Her head snapped up from the file as she heard a key in the front door of the station.

Hurriedly, she slipped the file back into the cabinet and slid the drawer back in. it wouldn't close fully, she must have stuck the locking mechanism, but she had no time to fix it now. She pushed the drawer as far as it would go and moved to the door. As she reached it, she saw she was too late.

"What the hell are you doing?"

Kurt Feldman was standing in the doorway, his hand halfway to his holster before he realized it was Green. He relaxed a little, but his eyes took on a suspicious glint.

Isabella tried to keep her voice unperturbed. "I just came by to pick up my house keys. I think I left them ..."

"In McGregor's office?" he asked sharply.

"Yeah, I was in there earlier."

He stepped forward, trying to see past her. "Is Blake in there?"

She had time to step out of his way before he barged past her. He glanced around the room, satisfying himself that Blake wasn't hiding under the desk.

Feldman stepped out of the office and looked at her, and for a second she felt a chill. It wasn't just the unpleasant frisson of a confrontation with someone you know and usually get on with, either. It was more like the feeling when a stranger accosts you on a street at night. Her brain was telling her there was nothing to worry about, just a little heated exchange. But her gut was telling her to make a decision: put some distance between the two of them, or get ready to defend herself.

"I have no idea where Blake is, as it happens, Kurt," she said, her voice hardening. She was almost grateful for the impetus to get off the back foot.

He seemed to sense her unease, and physically pulled back, looking away from her.

When this was all over, they would have to have a talk. Perhaps Feldman was guilty of nothing more than an unrequited attraction to her, but it was starting to become a big problem. The next thing he said caught her off guard. She had been expecting him to say something about her or Blake.

"You don't think Connor's guilty, do you?"

She considered before answering. Was this a trick question? Did he know she had been snooping in the office? After a moment, she shrugged. "I have an open mind. Just want to make sure we don't miss anything, just because it looks open and shut."

He nodded as though he knew exactly what she didn't want to miss.

He looked straight ahead out of the window to the empty lot out front. Then he turned his eyes to the empty chair behind the desk. "How much do you really know about him?"

"About Connor?"

"About Jim McGregor."

Again, she considered her words carefully. "I know he's a great cop. Nobody knows this town better than him."

Feldman paused. He looked away from her before he spoke. "He wasn't around when any of them were killed, you notice that?"

"We don't know exactly when Haycox was killed."

"We know he was killed by somebody he didn't think he had any reason to fear," Feldman said. "That fits with Connor, sure. But it would also fit another cop."

She felt her mouth go dry. "What are you saying?"

"Same thing you were thinking. The reason you came down here, I'm betting."

Isabella opened her mouth to deny it, and closed it.

"And then there's Roussel," Feldman continued. "Maybe David Connor picked him at random ... or maybe someone killed him because they knew you and Blake had talked to him."

Isabella looked away from him and took a few seconds to decide what to say next. "You're right, Feldman. I think it's him. I don't know why yet, but I think it's the sheriff." She told him about the way McGregor had resisted every one of her efforts to call in outside support. About how she had come to the same conclusion about it having to be a cop.

Feldman nodded after she had spoken. "You know what? I'm not even saying I want to do anything about it. Everything seems to fit David Connor, and maybe I'm just fine with that." He turned to look at her. "All I'm saying is, be careful."

Just then, her phone buzzed in her pocket, jarring them both out of the moment. It was Blake.

"Where are you?" he asked. It sounded like he was in a car.

"Where else?"

"I'm about thirty miles away. Can I meet you at the cabin at Benson's?"

"Sure," Isabella said breezily, pressing the phone close to her ear to seal as much of the sound in as possible.

"Is somebody else with you?"

"I think that sounds right."

"Don't bring them with you."

She looked at Feldman, who was studying her face.

"Makes sense, talk to you later."

"It was Blake," she said as she hung up. "He's gone to Atlanta, wanted to speak to them about Wheeler again, I guess."

Just then, another ringtone sounded, not hers. Feldman reached into his pocket and took his cell out, examining the screen. "It's the sheriff. He wants me to come up to the Connor house."

67

CARTER BLAKE

The hairs stood up on my arms as I saw the roadblock. A blue-and-white Bethany Sheriff's Department Crown Victoria, parked at a diagonal on the road, a sawhorse blocking the rest of the road. The older cop manning this one; the one

Green had called Jerry. I knew there would be another on the north road. Green hadn't mentioned anything about this.

"What's happening?" Adeline asked, no fear in her voice, just puzzlement.

"Keep the sunglasses on," I said. "Don't say anything unless he talks to you."

I pulled to a stop and rolled down the window.

"Back so soon," Jerry said evenly.

"Sheriff McGregor decide I'm not welcome anymore?" I said, trying to make it sound like a joke, rather than the genuine question it was.

"You're in luck. I'm not stopping anybody coming in." Slight emphasis on "in".

I raised my eyebrows in a question and he just smiled in dismissal, giving the briefest glance to my passenger. "Be careful, now."

He moved the sawhorse and gave me a thumbs-up as I drove past. I watched in the rearview as he replaced the barrier and took up position looking back down the road.

"What was that about?" Adeline said when we had rounded the corner.

"The sheriff has put the cork in the bottle," I said, wondering why he had done that.

Green was waiting for us when we pulled into the lot at Benson's. She looked uneasy as I got out. It seemed like she was deliberately avoiding looking through the windshield at the person in the passenger seat.

"Are you okay?" I asked as I got out.

"Feldman told McGregor about you and me."

"I'm sorry if I've made your life more difficult," I said.

She shook her head. "It's not you who decided to be an asshole about it." She didn't look away from me, but inclined her head in the direction of the car. "It's really her?"

"Why don't you ask her yourself?"

Adeline Connor opened the door and got out, her gaze nervously on Green as she straightened up.

I looked from her to Green. I had expected her to be surprised, and I knew she would have to see to believe. What I didn't expect was for her to turn white.

"I'm sorry," Adeline said. "I was scared."

"You ..." Green began. "I ... Everybody thought you were ..."

"Dead, I know. I didn't plan it, it just kind of ... developed."

"But you ran with it," Green said, coldly.

Adeline's gaze dropped to the floor.

Green closed her own eyes and seemed to be steeling herself. Then she took two steps toward Adeline. Gently, she reached out and touched the underside of her chin, raising her head up so they were eyeball to eyeball. She spoke clearly and calmly.

"Do you remember? Who shot you?"

Adeline stared back at her for a long time, then she shook her head.

"I didn't see him. It was dark. I thought I was ..." she grimaced as she realized the irony of what she was saying. "I really thought I was dead. Maybe that was why I went with it."

Green held Adeline's gaze for even longer. I wondered what was going through her head. It was as though she thought she could read the other woman's eyes like an exposure on a piece of film. Like she could reach back through the years and see the face of the killer. And then she took a step away and trained her blue eyes on me, and I got the experience of being on the receiving end. It was like being scanned.

"I think I have some catching up to do," she said.

We went inside and Adeline started talking. She was a little more concise this time, more confident in recalling the memories, but nothing changed about her story. Finding the body of her father, running into the night, being picked up by Salter and Green's father. When she started relating the shooting, Green closed her eyes, as though focusing purely on Adeline's words.

"I'm sorry," she said, when Adeline finished.

Adeline shifted in her chair uncomfortably. "Don't be, it wasn't your fault."

"The killings stopped after that," Green said.

"I know. I read about it in the news."

"Of course you did."

I cleared my throat, and the two women looked up as one, as though each of them was remembering for the first time that I was here.

"Can I talk to you for a second?"

Adeline stared at me until she worked out she was being excused, and then moved to the back of the room with an embarrassed smile.

"The gun they found at David Connor's place ..." I began.

"It's a match," she replied. "It's the weapon that killed the four men this week."

I had expected as much. I had been sure Connor was being framed, but the fact it was the same gun meant he was being framed by the killer.

"Game over for Connor, then," I said, giving it just the hint of a questioning tone. Green didn't blink.

"It isn't him," she said. "But the gun matches, so whoever put it there is the killer. And that gives us a very short list of suspects."

She spoke quickly. She told me about her clandestine

visit to the sheriff's office. What she had found in the filing cabinet, or to be exact, what she *hadn't* found. And then she told me about Feldman coming by, and what they had talked about. Everything they had talked about.

After that, we both knew what our next move had to be.

68

CARTER BLAKE

The house was on the opposite side of town from Benson's. It was almost as far apart as two places could be within the town limits, as if the two locations were at either end of a diagonal line drawn from the southwest corner to the northeast.

Green told me about the conversation with McGregor, and how she had come to the same conclusion I had. If David Connor wasn't the killer, then there was only one other explanation for the murder weapon being found at his place. There were only two people who could credibly have planted the gun without raising suspicion: McGregor or Feldman. She told me how Feldman had seemed to read her mind when she sounded him out, telling her he had suspicions of his own.

I parked at the bottom of the street and approached the house on foot. The street was on a steep hill, leading up to a single house at the top which backed onto the woods. It looked a lot like the other houses in the street: one level, wood siding, a big front yard. On the side of the house was a driveway and a garage. There was no car out front.

The yard was neat. The exterior of the house was neat

too, the paintwork looked new, the gutters and the slates on the roof straight and clean. The windows at the front all had venetian blinds, most of the way closed.

I opened the gate and approached, watching the windows for a hint of movement behind those three-quarter-shut blinds. There was no doorbell, just a knocker above a brass nameplate. I raised it and let it drop. There was no answer the first time, so I waited a second and dropped it again.

I stepped back and glanced at the garage. Maybe the car was in there, maybe not. I looked at the windows with their blinds. Maybe someone was in there, maybe not.

There was a path leading around the side of the house to the backyard. I glanced behind me to check the street was still deserted, and walked around the side. It opened onto a patch of grass bounded by six-foot wood fencing. The branches of the ash trees on the slope behind the house hung over the fence.

There were drapes on the windows at this side instead of blinds, but no more sign of life. I reached out and tried the back door handle. It was locked, of course. Cops tend not to be careless about household security, and this one struck me as less careless than most. There was a gap at the corner of the window nearest the door. I crouched and put my eye to it. It was an office. A desk pushed up to the far wall, some bookcases, a file drawer, a map on the wall. I squinted and shifted my position to get a better view of the map. Something about it looked familiar. It was like looking at a Rorschach blot. It took a few seconds for the patterns I was looking at to coalesce into a meaningful configuration, but once they did, I could see nothing else.

I stepped away from the window and considered. I went back to the side path and glanced down it. I could see all the way down the street from this position. Still empty. No people, no sounds of cars. With any luck, the owner of the house wouldn't be back for a while.

I took my pick set out of my wallet and selected one that ought to do the job, knowing if the owner was cautious enough to have a burglar alarm it would have to be a quick visit. Even if he did, I didn't need long. I slipped the pick into the lock. Twisted one way, then the other, until I felt the tumblers click. I pushed the handle down and the door swung open onto a small kitchen. No alarm. No audible one, at least. The owner might well have other ways to check for intruders, but I could worry about that later.

The kitchen led into a hallway, and the door to the office was right across. That door was locked, too. An interior lock, so even less of a challenge than the main door. In five seconds I had it open. I moved to the desk and the map that hung above it.

I was right. The map showed the town and its surroundings. It was large, scale two inches to a mile. There were pins in it, and that was what had created the familiar pattern. The positions of the Devil Mountain Killer's victims from 2002 and '03 were marked out with blue pins. The four killings from this week in yellow pins.

There was a small pile of paper on the desk. I leafed through it and found a one-sheet criminal record check for Jeffrey Friedrickson. The printout had the date and time it was printed on the bottom right hand corner: Sunday 25th at 17:22. Before the hunters had been killed. Not necessarily incriminating in itself, but . . .

I tried the desk drawers. These weren't locked.

Everything in them was related to the 2002-03 killings. News clippings, copies of police reports, maps. I pictured him working late, running off copies of the relevant files when everybody had gone home. There were four notebooks too, every page used. I leafed through them. Same subject. Same neat handwriting. Notes, mind maps, diagrams. I saw familiar names. It reminded me of what I had seen at Haycox's place, but there was so much more material here. David Connor, Roland Roussel, Isabella Green. The file with the Isabella Green material was thicker: clippings from the time when her father had been killed, of course, but also pictures that looked as though they had been taken recently, and without her knowledge. Was Green the next target?

I felt an urge to get out of there and head back to the cabins. I gave myself another thirty seconds. I put the Green file aside and opened the bottom drawer. There was a space where something the size of a gun could fit. I pulled it out as far as it could go and found the clincher. A box, part full, of ammunition. .38 caliber ammunition.

There was a notebook next to it with a battered brown leather cover. I picked it up and leafed through. The handwriting was different from the other notes. I skipped to the last pages with writing on them. The name Vincent González, along with his address in Atlanta. It was Wheeler's notebook.

That was when I heard the creak of a floorboard behind me. I spun around in time to see Sheriff Jim McGregor standing in the doorway, his gun drawn.

69

ISABELLA GREEN

Isabella hadn't suffered a hangover in years, but the way she remembered it was pretty close to the way she was feeling as she looked at the ghost in the kitchen. Nausea in the pit of her stomach, a dark, oppressive cloud in her head, a general sense of things being unpleasantly detached. She stood by the door of the small kitchen in Blake's cabin while Adeline fussed about looking for cups, taking far longer than she needed to. Isabella watched her as she moved around, avoiding her gaze. Her dark hair tumbled around her shoulders, often swinging in front of her eyes, to be swept back by an absent flick of her hand.

The way she explained it, it all made sense. The open door, the escape from the car, the way the bullet had been just short of a fatal wound. The big unanswered question, the one which had led to everyone assuming what had happened to her, was solved by old man Roussel. Adeline couldn't have survived, bleeding bad and in shock, all by herself in the woods. And she hadn't. She had help. And Roussel had kept his secret for fifteen years, taking it to the grave with him. She knew now that she and Blake had unwittingly signed his death warrant.

But still, watching her move around the kitchen as big as life was a disconcerting experience. It was like Isabella's eyes hadn't quite caught up with the new information. Like she was staring at some kind of visual effect, wondering how they made it so *real*.

"Do you, uh ... do you have to do that?" she asked, turning to face Isabella for the first time.

"Do what?"

"Stare at me like that."

Isabella shrugged a mild apology and looked away. "You're going to have to get used to that, Adeline."

"When can we go and see him?"

"David?"

She nodded.

"He's safe where he is, don't worry about that."

She finished pouring the coffee and reached for the milk carton, holding it up questioningly. Isabella shook her head and she handed over the mug. Isabella thanked her and took a sip. She tried to think about everything else she needed to focus on. Like why the sheriff had closed the roads without telling her.

"Blake said you think David killed these people."

"He said I think that?"

"Sorry, I mean you as in," she paused and indicated Isabella's uniform. "You."

"David isn't exactly making life easy for himself on that score," she replied. "By refusing to talk ... well, you can guess how it looks."

"Will he be sent to prison?"

"Even if your story checks out, and even if you can convince him to talk, I don't think he's going to be looking at a slap on the wrist because he only committed one murder, Adeline."

"It wasn't a murder though, was it? You remember what my dad was like?"

Isabella saw the image of Jake Connor in front of her at the gas station, asking her what the goddamn hell she thought she was doing parking her bike so close to his truck. The way his eyes had lingered on her bare knees as he shouted.

"It's not a murder if it's self-defense," Adeline continued.

"We're a long way from establishing that," Isabella said.

"How much longer do you think Blake will be, then?"

"He'll call soon." She and Blake had decided one of them needed to keep watch on Adeline, while the other confirmed their theory. Could it really be right? Isabella had known him, worked alongside him for years. It didn't seem possible that he was a killer. But then you can never really know anyone, not really.

"You don't think it was him, though, not back then."

Adeline took a sip, the mug hiding her face. Her eyes stared at Isabella over the rim.

"No I don't," Isabella said. "That killer is gone for good."

"What makes you so certain?"

A knock on the door.

"Wait here. Do not come out."

Closing the kitchen door behind her, Isabella reached for her holster and pulled her gun out, keeping to the side of the hallway as she approached the front door. There was a slim window next to the door. She could see the shadow of someone reasonably tall. Blake? She opened it a crack, keeping her gun out of sight. It was Feldman. He had changed into civilian clothes, his personal vehicle, a black Ford SUV was parked outside.

"I thought you were with the sheriff?"

He angled his head, trying to look past her. Isabella was glad she had closed the kitchen door.

Feldman shook his head. "He didn't need me after all. Can I come in? I think we should talk some more about this."

Isabella hesitated, realizing she was already making herself unnecessarily suspicious. She wanted to ask him how he knew she would be here. Could he have followed her after she left the station? But if she told him he couldn't come in, it would only make him more suspicious.

"Sure." She opened the door wider and he stepped inside.

"You know he's got Jerry and Carl closing down the north and south? He say anything to you about that?"

She shook her head, and indicated the door into the main sitting area, standing in front of the kitchen door to bar his way. He glanced at the door, and she wondered if he sensed she was hiding something.

"Your mom keeping okay?"

"Good days and bad days."

He nodded.

"So. You wanted to talk about the sheriff."

He smiled. "Why don't you get us a coffee, first?"

She hesitated again.

"Okay."

Isabella got up and turned to the kitchen.

"I'm sorry, Isabella. I didn't want this."

She turned just as something hard slammed into her face, and then her ears were ringing and she was falling, and then nothing.

70

CARTER BLAKE

"I gave you a lot of leeway, Blake. Maybe it didn't seem like it to you, but I did. Do you mind telling me why I shouldn't be throwing your ass in a cell for breaking and entering?"

McGregor stepped across the threshold of Feldman's house, keeping the gun pointed at me.

"The fact that you're asking the question is why. You didn't come here for me, did you? You came to talk to Feldman. You know it's him."

He said nothing, but gave me a look that said he was waiting for more.

"Check out the room back there. He's obsessed with the Devil Mountain case."

"Doesn't prove anything. A hobby case, we all have them."

"This isn't that. He has .38 caliber ammunition in his drawer. The gun isn't there, but you know why that is. He planted it at Connor's house after killing Roussel. That's how he beat us to the Marion place, he was in the area already."

McGregor kept his face straight, but I saw something in his eyes that told me he wanted me to continue.

"There's a file on one of the hunters. He checked them out before he killed them. He has Wheeler's notebook – he had to have taken it from his car the night he was killed."

The sheriff closed his eyes, and I knew this didn't come as a surprise. I was only confirming the worst.

"It had to be you or him who planted the gun at David Connor's house. He realized Green knew that, so he tried to make her suspect you instead. Only he slipped up. He told her why Roussel was killed; because we talked to him. The only problem was, Green never told any of you that."

McGregor sighed and lowered his gun at last. "Isabella called in a request to the phone company to confirm the cell records of the hunters. They only called us back this lunchtime. They were confused at first, because they had a duplicate request on the system. Only it wasn't a duplicate request. It was called in on Sunday afternoon, before

Friedrickson and Leonard were killed. Somebody was tracking them. Whoever it was gave Haycox's name, but it can't have been him because he was already dead. Green had an alibi because she was *your* alibi. It had to be him, but I just didn't know why, until now. I told him I wanted to meet him at the Connor house. I was going to confront him, but he never showed. And if he isn't here ..."

He took out his cell phone, dialing Green's number. As it rang out, he started to look concerned.

"Come on," he said, turning and running out to the car, leaving Feldman's door wide open.

71

ISABELLA GREEN

I don't want to get up. I'm underneath the big oak tree and I'm looking up at the sun and the blue sky through the branches and it's so peaceful and so beautiful. Why do you want me to get up, Momma?

There's a ringing in my ears and I want whoever it is to turn off that darn noise, but then I realize it's my head that's making the ringing. It hurts, there's a kind of throbbing on the right side of my head. I want to touch it but I'm so tired and I don't think I can summon the effort to move my hand. Momma's shaking me, telling me to get up. When she leans over me I can see she's wearing that blue check dress, the one that makes her look so pretty. She says I can have one just like it for my birthday if I like. Something's wrong with her eyes, though. She looks scared, and I wonder what she could be afraid of. Why would I make her scared?

There's something wrong with her voice too. It's all deep, almost like a man's voice. And then I realize it is *a man's voice.*

"Green, can you hear me?"

Isabella's mother's face and the sun and the sky and the tree branches faded away as her eyelids blinked open, and then she was looking up at a ceiling and a familiar face. It took a moment for it to come back to her.

"Blake, what ...?"

And then she saw McGregor and the kitchen and she remembered everything.

"Shit, is Adeline ...?"

Blake shook his head. "Gone."

McGregor was looking down at her with a concerned expression. "We think he followed you out here, and saw Blake arrive with Adeline. I closed the roads. Carl Bianchi saw Feldman's car headed toward him on the north road, but he never made it as far as the block. He's trapped, if he's still in the car. Or he's on foot."

"Okay," Blake said. "We know two good things. The first one is that Adeline is probably alive."

"Why so?" McGregor asked.

"Because if he was going to kill her right away, we would have found her body here."

"What's the second thing?"

"I think I know where he's going."

Isabella thought she knew what he meant: the shelter on the mountain. She touched a finger to the throbbing pain on the side of her head and felt wetness. Blood on her hands. What had the son of a bitch hit her with?

In answer to her unspoken question, Blake reached out of her field of view and held up an old telephone. Feldman had hit her hard enough that the plastic base was cracked.

"Are you okay?" Blake asked, studying her eyes. Isabella knew it wasn't a romantic gesture; he was looking for evidence of head trauma.

She didn't answer immediately. Instead she allowed Blake and McGregor to help her to her feet and tried standing on two feet. No dizziness, no nausea, no vision problems. Just the devil's own headache. She spotted her gun on the floor beneath the hall table. She took three steps forward in a straight line, bent, picked it up, straightened up, and slid it back into the holster on her belt. A good enough diagnostic test of her motor functions.

"I'm fine. Let's go find them."

72

CARTER BLAKE

McGregor took us back to the station and unlocked the door to the storeroom that served as the armory. Before he opened the door, he paused with his hand on the handle and turned around.

"This isn't exactly standard operating procedure. I could get in a lot of trouble involving you. I should be calling in the feds and sitting tight."

"But you're going to do it anyway," I said. "Because by the time they get here it'll be too late. This is the only way we have a chance to get Adeline back alive."

McGregor shook his head. "Idiot. I should have called them before now."

"Why didn't you?"

He couldn't meet my eyes, only now allowing himself to admit how badly he'd gotten it wrong. "Part of me suspected all along it could be one of us. I wanted to keep this ..." He shifted his gaze to Green. "Are you okay?"

I turned around to look at her. I could see why he was concerned. She seemed paler than she had been, a distant look in her eye.

"I'm fine, Sheriff. Just can't believe it." Her tone was flat, like she was only saying what she was expected to say.

McGregor looked like he was making an effort to think of something reassuring to say, and then gave up trying. I guessed he had been in this line of work long enough to know what people are capable of. Even people you think you know well.

McGregor opened the door to a small storeroom about ten feet by fifteen, lined on either side by metal racks. They held rifles and sidearms and boxes marked with evidence tags. There were cardboard boxes and stacks of flares and a pile of gloves. McGregor picked out three Kevlar vests and tossed them to us. Then he picked out three Winchester rifles with scopes.

"Not the first time we've had to go after a runner out there. Feldman calls these hunting trips," McGregor said. "It's been a while. Never thought he would be the guy we were hunting."

McGregor went down to the far end of the storeroom to get ammunition for the Winchesters. Green was studying the straps on my vest, checking they were in place. She looked up at me. "You think we can find him?"

"No doubt in my mind," I said. "And none in his. That

might be the only reason he has a hostage. He knows we'll find him."

"You ready for this?"

"Sure."

"Something told me you'd say that." The corner of her mouth curved into a smile, and then immediately straightened as she heard the noise of the door opening in the front office. She reached for her gun and held it up, two hands on the grip as she approached the storeroom door. I heard footsteps inside the room on the other side.

"Who's there?" Green called out.

I heard the footsteps stop, but no one said anything. Green nudged the door open and stepped out into the main reception area.

I heard a gasp, followed by, "Shit! It's me, put that down."

I followed Green out to see Deputy Dentz, reaching for the sky.

"What are you doing here?" McGregor had joined me at the door, a box of ammo in each hand.

"Jerry called me to tell me what happened. I figured you would be going after Kurt. Wanted to be there when you brought him in."

McGregor looked at him for a while, taking his time to make his mind up. Then he exchanged a glance with Green, and a quicker, more perfunctory glance with me.

"More the merrier." He tossed Dentz one of the Winchesters. Dentz reached for it with both hands, fumbled a little, and recovered, looking back up at us with a pleased expression on his face once he had both hands gripping the gun.

When the four of us had finished gathering the equipment for the hunting trip, McGregor indicated the rifle I was carrying. "Blake, that's for self-defense, understood?"

"Always is," I said.

"Green, Dentz, I don't need to tell you I want to take Feldman alive if we can do it. Not just because he's one of us, either. Right now he's the only man on God's green Earth who can tell us what the hell's been going on in this town. He might make it difficult. Desperate men, up against the wall ... they often do. Don't let him."

"Yes, Sheriff," Dentz said quickly.

The sheriff looked at me. I nodded agreement.

Finally, he turned to Isabella.

"Got it?"

She nodded after a moment. "It needs to be me," she said. "I might be able to talk him down." Then she turned away, leading the way out to the car.

None of us spoke much. We rode in the same vehicle, McGregor's jeep. McGregor cracked the driver's side window open to let in the air, and though it would still be daylight for another hour, the air was colder than it had been.

I was in the back seat with Dentz, who had a fine sheen of sweat on his upper lip despite the coolness of the air. He gripped his rifle and kept his eyes on the trees passing by outside, as though he were entering Viet Cong territory, expecting an ambush anytime now. I knew he had never been in a war, but I had, and it did feel a little similar. Going into hostile territory, tooled up and braced for the unexpected. Green was in the passenger seat, one arm on the sill, watching the road ahead.

McGregor reached for his radio as we approached the fork in the road, raising his man on the north roadblock.

"Carl, any sign of him?"

"Negative on that, Sheriff."

"Keep 'em peeled."

We took the fork off the north road. A minute later we passed the spot where Eric Salter's car had gone off the road, and started to climb. Suddenly, we hit a layer of mist, as though the mountain had snagged a cloud and the trees had drawn it down to earth. Visibility dropped as we climbed, fifty yards, thirty. I knew Roland Roussel's house wasn't far from the road, but I saw no sign of it. McGregor hit the lights, which didn't do much good.

McGregor started muttering under his breath, and I knew he was losing his bearings. All we could see now was twenty feet of road ahead and the dark perpendiculars of the nearest trees through the mist. Dentz had started breathing quickly through his nose, like a nervous air passenger trying to ride out turbulence. I knew we would reach the end of the road soon: the gravel plateau at the foot of the Devil Mountain trail. Green had rolled down her window and was trying to discern what she could from the shapes moving by at a slower and slower pace at the side of the road.

"Wait," she called out.

McGregor leaned on the brakes. We were only doing twenty, so it was an immediate stop.

"Back up."

He shifted into reverse without saying anything and guided the jeep ten yards back down the track, watching Green for instruction.

She held up a palm. "Here."

McGregor pulled the handbrake on and we sat in place, on a forty-five degree slope, staring out of Green's side, looking for what she had seen. The mist had turned to fog now, visibility dropping by the minute.

Dentz's eyes shifted from his window, to the side of Green's face he could see, to me.

"What the fuck?"

Green reached down into her footwell and fumbled with the pack, not taking her eyes off whatever she had seen. Her hand came out with a flashlight. She flicked it on and a powerful beam shone into the gray and was lost. She played it over the trunks of the trees until she found the position she wanted and held it.

"There."

I saw something red glint beyond the shapes of the first trees. Some sort of reflective material, like on a car's lights.

I got out, McGregor and Green following suit. I cradled the Winchester, slipping the safety off. I stepped off the road and between the trees, taking my little bubble of visibility with me. I kept the spot where I had seen the reflector in sight until it got clearer, and then formed into a more distinct shape. A car. A black Ford Explorer, covered with branches. Even without the fog, it would have been tough to spot if Green hadn't seen it.

Thinking about Afghanistan again. The Sulaiman Mountains. There had been fog then too. The Taliban had been out there, like ghosts. That made me think about one word: ambush.

"Eyes open," I called out to the three behind me, not bothering to keep the tone out of my voice that made it an order, and not caring if McGregor got bent out of shape about it.

I kept my focus on the car, not neglecting the shapes in my peripheral vision. The black, irregular shapes of the trees loomed in and out of focus, hiding who knew what. I listened for the sounds that would give away a waiting predator committing to making his move.

I reached the car and used the barrel of the rifle to clear some of the branches from the windows. I glanced behind me to reassure me that McGregor and Green were watching my back, and then risked bending down to look inside.

Empty. No bodies, no blood.

I looked up, seeing Green and McGregor's expectant eyes. Dentz had his back to us, looking back toward the dull black shape of McGregor's jeep. I shook my head.

Sheriff McGregor looked like he was letting out a breath he'd been holding for a while.

"Least we know we're on the right track. Unless this is a bluff."

"I don't think it can be," I said. Nowhere to go from here. Nowhere except up.

We turned to look at the ground rising up until it was lost in the fog. The rest of Devil Mountain was up there, holding its secrets tightly.

73

ISABELLA GREEN

The climb got steeper as the four of them advanced, the Devil Mountain trail winding east and then west in wide, lazy ribbons, now that the gradient was too steep to go straight ahead. How often had Isabella climbed the mountain? A half dozen times, maybe? First time had been with her dad, a couple of years after the family moved here. She must have been eight or nine. He had teased her about needing so many breaks, but she could tell he was proud of her. She made it all the way to the top that time. It was July, last week of summer vacation. She remembered the sky was beautiful when they made the summit. Late afternoon, just turning into evening. The long wispy lines of the clouds starting to turn from white to orange and red. A day that couldn't be more different from this one, in every way.

Half a dozen ascents. Not many, considering the mountain had hung over her all these years. But enough to know the trail. They were about a third of the way to the top. Forty minutes' climb on a clear day. The old shelter she and Blake had found two days before was halfway between them and the summit. But knowing the trail wasn't enough, in circumstances like these. The fog made it tough to orient yourself, concealed hidden dangers. It would conceal them from Feldman, if he was up there, but that worked both ways. She knew the path, but that didn't mean she knew what lay ahead of them.

Blake walked alongside Isabella, his eyes always moving, scanning the ground and the trees ahead. McGregor and Dentz were four paces behind them. Dentz would occasionally mutter a curse as his ankle turned on a loose stone. These men were like the path: knowable, but not predictable when the circumstances changed. Blake seemed different on the ascent. He had been capable, confident ever since she had met him. It had been the quality that had most attracted her to him, if she was being honest. He had been deferential with it, careful not to step on any toes he didn't have to step on. But that sense of him holding back had vanished. The tone of his voice, the way his suggestions sounded like orders, even his posture said one thing: he was in charge, no matter what it said on McGregor's badge.

McGregor was another one. He was a good cop, but this trip was uncharted territory. Desperate times called for desperate measures. Feldman was one of the sheriff's own. She knew the betrayal would be breaking him up inside under that taciturn exterior. A wolf in the fold. You never really know anyone. Maybe not even yourself. Maybe *especially* not yourself.

They came to the place where the older path branched off; the one that led to the shelter. She knew Feldman had been up there, since he had used it to lure Haycox to his death. But thanks to Blake, he didn't know that *they* knew. The landscape was unrecognizable from the other day, and this was a part of the trail she didn't know well. The ground to their right began to get steeper and the trees became denser around them. Isabella was trying to work out how far they were from the cliff face below the shelter when she felt Blake's hand on her arm. She turned to look at him, hearing the footsteps of the other two stop behind them.

"He knows we're coming," he said quietly.

"How do you know?" she asked. She had come to the same conclusion. He wanted them to come, or wanted her to come, at least.

Blake was looking away from the path, directly up the steep slope up into the fog. Visibility was down to less than twenty feet.

"I heard something," he said, his voice a whisper.

None of them spoke, each straining to hear another hint of what Blake might have heard. The fog seemed to dampen the usual woodland noises. No birds chirping, no squirrels moving through branches, nothing.

And then something.

"Get down," Blake said sharply, pushing on Isabella's shoulder. She bent at the knees at the same instant she heard the tiny crack of a rifle bullet breaking the sound barrier, a split second before she heard the report of the rifle itself ring out.

With sick inevitability, a third sound followed. A sound all too familiar. The sound of someone screaming out in pain.

74

CARTER BLAKE

Out of the corner of my eye I saw Dentz drop like a felled tree, clutching a hand somewhere between the top of his vest and his neck. I didn't turn to look, I was too busy dropping to the ground and focusing on the place I had seen the muzzle flash. The same approximate location I had heard the soft click of a bolt being drawn back a matter of seconds before.

I estimated Feldman was less than thirty feet above us. Close enough for him to make out four targets moving through the fog. It might already be too late for Dentz, I thought, but I hoped the remaining targets had changed position enough to be more of a challenge. And the thing that's guaranteed to make a target harder to hit is when it's shooting back at you. A challenge I was only too eager to supply.

I braced the stock of the rifle against my shoulder and fired three shots in a straight line: one to the left of the flash, one to the right, one dead center in case he was overconfident enough not to have moved. I nestled in behind the trunk of the tree I had sheltered behind and glanced across at Green. She was fine, but looking across at where McGregor and Dentz were behind another tree. McGregor was keeping pressure on a wound in Dentz's neck, just above the vest. I could hear a muffled moan under a hissing noise as Dentz gritted his teeth to avoid giving away their position. I waited for another shot.

"How far is the shelter?" I whispered.

"Quarter of a mile, maybe?" she guessed.

"Not by the most direct route," I said after a moment.

She glanced back at me, looking like she was checking if I was serious. "Can you make it?"

"I think so," I said. "As long as you keep him busy."

She reached down to her hip and withdrew her handgun; a Glock 43. Without taking her eyes off the hillside she held it up and then tossed it to me. I caught it and tucked it into my belt.

Green lifted her own rifle and fired another couple of times blind. We listened, both holding our breaths. There was nothing but Dentz's hyperventilating, and McGregor's whispered reassurances that he was going to be all right. And then there was a rustle from the trees above us, and I knew Feldman was on the move.

75

CARTER BLAKE

I waited for the next burst of fire from Green and McGregor and took off down the trail at a run, keeping low. In a couple of minutes, I found the bottom of the cliff that rose sixty feet up to where I knew the old shelter was. I had appraised the cliff wall with interest when I had seen it the other day. It had been a long time since I had tried free climbing, but it hadn't looked like it would be a particularly difficult challenge the other day in the sun. A lot of things had looked less challenging the other day, in the sun.

Even under the best of conditions, there was no way I was hauling the Winchester up there with me. I could hang the rifle around my back, but the weight would throw my balance off. I laid it on the ground, under a patch of bushes, and checked the Glock was still tucked inside my belt. If everything went all right, it would be all I needed. The next time I laid eyes on Kurt Feldman, it would be at close range.

As if to reinforce the point, another two shots sounded from somewhere in the fog, followed by return fire from Green's rifle. Call and response. *Keep it up, Green.*

I remembered seeing the pile of gloves back in the armory and wasted a tenth of a second regretting not bringing them. And then I flexed my fingers, examined the wall for the first two handholds, and put my hands on the cliff face.

76

ISABELLA GREEN

Dentz hadn't made any sound for a minute or two. Isabella didn't think that was a good sign. She risked taking her eyes off the slope – not that she could see a whole lot through the fog – and saw McGregor. He still had a hand over Dentz's throat. There was blood all over both of them. Red on McGregor's hands, black on the blue of the uniforms. Dentz's head was lolling at an angle, his eyes wide open. McGregor caught Isabella's eye and shook his head. He took his hand off the body, and she knew then that Dentz was dead.

Feldman's last couple of shots had come from a position above and to the left of where he had originally fired on them. He was moving back up toward the plateau and the shelter. She couldn't let him get there. If Adeline was still alive, he might kill her, knowing there was nothing to lose. And if he worked out that Blake was coming after him, it would be like shooting fish in a barrel if he caught him halfway up the cliff.

McGregor and Isabella exchanged another glance. She indicated the last position Feldman had fired from and then pointed to herself to tell McGregor she was headed the same way. McGregor understood. He raised his rifle, moved out of cover and fired three shots at the spot she had shown him.

Isabella started to crawl up the slope. It was steep, but manageable as long as she kept her hands free to use roots and shrubs to steady herself.

She ignored the sounds of the shots passing back and forth as she moved up the slope, not daring to raise her head enough to bring her knees and elbows into play. It was tortuous. She kept going.

It felt like she had to have crawled a hundred miles by the time she glanced back and saw that it had been no more than twenty yards. She kept going and the next time she looked back, it was twice as far. She had to have come past Feldman's firing position with no sign of him. There hadn't been another exchange of gunfire in a couple of minutes. He must have retreated. There was a level patch of ground a little above her. She focused on the edge and dragged herself closer. And then she saw two size-twelve boots in front of her face. Slowly, she raised her head and saw the wide black circle of the muzzle of a rifle, and a little above that, Kurt Feldman's face, set into a stony mask.

"Drop it," he said quietly.

Isabella released her fingers on her own gun, and moved them gradually away from it.

"Are you going to kill me?"

"On your feet. Scream or say anything and I pull the trigger. Look at me. You know I'm not bluffing."

She did. He wasn't.

Getting to her feet wasn't easy, on the slope. Not wanting to make any kind of sudden movement that might attract a bullet between her eyes, Isabella brought her hands up, open palmed, and braced on her elbows. Then she got to her knees. She wondered if McGregor could see either of them, figured she had advanced too far for him to see anything. She just hoped he wouldn't pick now to take any blind shots. What about Blake? Could he have made it to the cabin by now?

Feldman took a step back, keeping the muzzle out of her reach, and then jutted his head up, wordlessly ordering her to her feet again. She did as requested.

He shook his head. "What are you doing, Isabella?"

"What am *I* doing? You killed all of those men. Wheeler too."

"And I did it for you!' he yelled.

Isabella flinched at the sudden change in him. He was coming apart, not worrying about drawing attention to his position anymore. She could see they were on the section of path above the one McGregor was on. She had crawled farther than she had thought. Feldman used the barrel of the gun to indicate their direction of travel. Up, toward the shelter. She only hoped Blake would be there to meet them.

"Where is Adeline?"

Feldman said nothing.

"Did you kill her?"

"Keep moving."

Isabella kept her voice low as they walked, remembering Feldman's instruction not to yell out. "Best thing you can do is give it up now, Feldman. You know it, I know it."

"Why are you talking like you're better than me? We both know that ain't so."

She felt a chill down her spine. She stopped in her tracks and slowly turned around to look at him. He just stared back at her. His eyes were blank, like he was daydreaming. It was deceptive, she knew that. She had seen that look in his eyes before, right before he sprang into action and broke an unruly drunk's nose, or pinned them down before they could hurt anyone. If she made a threatening move, he could drop her before she got within touching distance. Despite it all, she wondered if he could really do it.

"What do you mean?"

He stepped forward, the barrel of the gun not wavering from her belly. He got within arm's length and leaned forward.

"I know," he said. "I know what happened fifteen years ago."

She met his gaze. In the bottom of her vision, she could see the barrel of the gun, unwavering, six inches from her navel. At that range, she would be practically cut in half. All it would take would be a few ounces of pressure on the trigger.

"I waited so long to tell you about it. We're meant to be together, I know you can see that now, Isabella."

"Kurt, I ..." she began, her mind reeling with questions.

"I did it for you. Damn it, Isabella, can't you see that? All for you."

She blinked, and moistened her lips. She took a deep breath and said his name.

She heard someone cry out from behind them. It sounded like Adeline's voice. Instinctively he looked over Isabella's shoulder for a second, in the direction the cry had come from.

And then Isabella lunged for the gun.

77

CARTER BLAKE

I got about halfway up the cliff face before I met any serious challenge. Then I hit a stretch of smooth rock about ten feet high, with very few handholds. I maneuvered horizontally to where there was a little more purchase and managed to get to a break in the sheer wall, where it turned into a sloping shelf about three feet deep. I hadn't heard any gunfire in a couple of minutes. I hoped that didn't mean one of Feldman's shots had found its target.

I braced myself backwards against the wall, not looking over the drop, and then put my hand in a crack and gripped on so I could angle my body around to survey the rest of the climb. I had another twenty-five feet or so to climb. Two thirds of the way up, there was a stretch that looked like it would be tough. Not a lot to get purchase on, from what I could see. I just had to hope it would be passable.

My arms were out of practice. It felt as though I had been walking around for an hour carrying a couple of heavy suitcases. I hoped I would still have enough strength to get me to the top. After that? I would cross that bridge when I came to it. I examined the wall and planned out where my hands and feet would have to go, and then picked out the first handholds and started the climb.

It was tougher on this section, not just because the wall was more difficult, but because my arms were tired. I could hear my pulse thudding in my head, and my breathing seemed loud enough to be heard in the next state. I had gotten about halfway when I heard a scrabbling on the top of the cliff, only a few feet above and to the left of my position. I held my breath. If it was Feldman, I was a sitting duck. All he would have to do would be to look over the edge. There was nowhere to hide. I froze in place, holding on.

The sounds moved closer. Somebody was approaching the cliff-edge. And then I saw two shoes appear, and then ankles, and slender, jean-clad legs. Adeline. She had gotten loose somehow, and had decided to risk climbing down the cliff face. I didn't know if she had any climbing experience, but even if she did, it would be far riskier on the descent than the ascent.

I opened my mouth to call out, and then stopped myself. She was already scared enough to risk hanging off a cliff – a sudden noise from an unexpected direction at this moment could be a very bad thing indeed.

I risked a glance below me. I had climbed about fifteen feet above the sloping shelf. If I could get back down there without distracting her, I could be waiting when she made it that far. If she made it that far.

I made up my mind and started descending again. I retraced my route with relative ease, stopping to keep an eye on Adeline's progress. She made it down the first ten feet okay. I could hear her mumbling to herself. Whether she was uttering curses or prayers or self-motivation, I didn't know. And then she froze. She had encountered the difficult patch I had spotted. She clutched onto the rock, looking down at her feet. I could see her calculating, wondering if she could make it. She was close enough now that I could start to make out words. Curses interspersed with prayers.

I just held my breath and watched. She braced herself and let go with her right hand, stretching to reach the handhold, tantalizingly close. My reach would have been long enough to make it, but I wasn't sure hers was. She stretched farther, closing the gap a little more. Maybe two or three inches away. No more curses, no more prayers, not even grunts of effort. She stretched again, and I could see she was going to make it.

And then her right foot slipped from its hold.

For a second it was as though she was frozen in place. And then she pitched to her right and lost her grip on her left side and she was falling.

I didn't think. The whole time I had been watching, I had been willing her to succeed in her descent, not allowing myself to consider what would happen if she lost her grip. But that was simply a necessary self-deception. I had been watching her the way a power forward watches the arc of a basketball toward the hoop. Not consciously thinking anything, but allowing the brain space to make the mental calculations to predict exactly how the ball will rebound, and where to position himself. The good news was that Adeline Connor's position and angle of descent would be far more predictable than that of a rebounding basketball. The bad news was that she weighed a hell of a lot more than a ball, and I was standing on a narrow forty-five degree slope above a thirty-foot drop.

Dimly, I heard her scream as she fell. I held on with my left hand and swung out as she dropped, getting a solid grip around her waist, taking her weight as she hit the ledge and started to fall backwards. I felt the already-overworked muscles of my arm scream out as I took her full weight. For a second I felt the fingers of my left hand slip, and thought she was going to take me over the edge with her, and then they held, and I gripped her tightly, absorbing the momentum. I pulled us back in toward the ledge. I lowered her to the ground, keeping one hand on her arm in case she started falling again.

She looked at me in a daze.

"Are you okay?"

She said nothing.

"Anything broken?"

I examined her legs, they looked okay. I gave each of her ankles a light squeeze and she winced when I touched her left. I ran my hand over it gently, feeling for anything out of place. Clean break or a sprain, I guessed.

"How did you ..."

"We don't have time for that, do you think you can climb down?"

She flinched and shifted her weight closer to the wall of the cliff, away from the drop. I didn't blame her.

"I got away when he left me. There's an old hut up there. He told me there was nowhere to go. I thought I could ..."

"I have to keep going," I said. "Can you hold on here and wait until we can get help?"

She nodded. "I think so. He took me. That cop – he said he was going to finish the job. Is Deputy Green ...?"

"She's fine," I said, hoping that that was still true. It might not be if I couldn't get to Feldman. Adeline seemed a lot more alert now. I wasn't worried about her fainting and toppling over the edge anymore.

"Hold on and stay put," I said. "I'll be back."

I looked up at the cliff wall. It was the last thing in the world I felt like doing.

The close call with Adeline had given me a second wind. I made quick progress, ascending quickly, knowing that every second I hesitated was another second closer to using up the strength in my arms. I made the top quickly and hauled myself over the edge. The muscles in my upper arms sang out in pain. The shelter was dead ahead, in a wide clearing before the woods began. The fog was even thicker up here. I could see only the first row of trees in the gray.

I took my gun from its holster and moved toward the door of the shelter. I knew it was unlikely Feldman was there, since he would have seen Adeline had gone and would have looked over the edge, but I had to check it anyway.

But before I got there, I heard a shot.

78

ISABELLA GREEN

"Green."

Isabella looked up in the direction of the voice. Carter Blake emerged from the fog and paused between two thick trees, the muzzle of his gun pointed toward Kurt Feldman's body on the ground. He wouldn't be needing it.

When she didn't answer, Blake moved closer. He checked Feldman's hands and saw they were empty. Then he holstered his gun and knelt beside the body, putting his hand to Feldman's throat.

"He's dead," he said. His tone was flat, no relief, certainly no sorrow. He looked up at her. "What happened?"

She looked back down at Feldman's open eyes. He still seemed to be staring at her the way he had done a few minutes before. Death hadn't been able to remove that look.

"Green?"

Blake had stood up and was holding her arm, gently pushing the barrel of Feldman's rifle down.

"I got him," she said.

Blake seemed to consider this. "I guess you did."

She spoke slowly. It almost felt like someone else was doing the talking for her. She told Blake that Feldman had been distracted, and they struggled for the gun, and she had shot him.

Blake explained he had made it up to the shelter and had only gotten there in time to hear the shot that killed Feldman. He would have been here faster, but on the way up the cliff face, he had picked up some company. The two of them made their way back down to the trail, where they gave McGregor the news.

Dentz was dead. McGregor had taken his coat off and draped it over his face.

They followed the trail to the foot of the cliff. Adeline Connor was still on the ledge where Blake had left her. Isabella and McGregor kept her company while Blake went back down to the cars and got a length of rope. The trip took him a half hour. When he got back, the sky was dark, but the fog had thinned a little. Blake rigged up a pulley system with the thick branch of a nearby tree, and then climbed back up the cliff face to help Adeline down with the help of the rope.

McGregor filled Isabella in on what he and Blake had found at Feldman's house while they drove back down to Bethany. Materials from Haycox's investigation, Wheeler's notebook, even some files from the original Devil Mountain case.

"Do you think ..." Isabella stopped and thought about how to phrase it. "Do you think it could have been him, back then?"

Blake shook his head. "I don't know. We need to find out where he was back then. It's a possibility. But I don't know. That room, it wasn't like a trophy room. I think he was trying to find out who it was. And for some reason, he didn't want anyone else to be the one who did it. I think that's why he killed Wheeler and Haycox."

"He moved here in '07," McGregor said. "I guess that doesn't rule him out, though. We'll know more when we take a closer look at his place."

Isabella didn't say anything. McGregor and Blake fell silent, both men exhausted. She closed her eyes, focusing on the rocking of the car as it negotiated the turns on the slope back down to where the mountain road joined the north road. Without realizing it, she began humming the song again; the one from her dream. The words about going home.

I'm not scared.

It was a minute or two before she became conscious of Adeline staring at her. Isabella smiled back at her, wondering if she was worried about the blow to the head Feldman had given her. Adeline didn't return the smile. It took Isabella a while to work out why the other woman's gaze unnerved her so much. And then she had it.

It reminded her of the way Feldman had looked at her, at the end.

She stopped humming the tune and Adeline looked away from her. At that moment, she remembered where she had heard it first. On a dark, rainy night, coming from a car stereo.

They reached the station and Blake helped Adeline out of the car. Isabella got out and moved to the driver's door before McGregor could close it.

"I'm going up to Feldman's house. I need to—"

McGregor shook his head. "You've been through enough today, Isabella. Go home. I've got Carl out there sealing the place up for the feds. They may already be here." He sighed. "You know how this has to go now."

Isabella pretended to think about it. "Okay, you're right. Shift's over."

He looked at her, then glanced over at Blake, as though to get a second opinion.

"You want some company?" Blake asked.

Isabella shook her head. "I'll see you later."

She wanted to lean forward and kiss him hard. Instead, she just reached out and put a hand on the side of his chest, right over the place she knew the scar was. He looked a little confused, but didn't say anything.

Isabella got in the driver's seat and watched as Blake and McGregor helped the lost girl into the station. Both men glanced back at Isabella as they reached the door. Adeline didn't look at her at all. She backed up and pulled the car out onto the road.

Five minutes later, she pulled to a stop outside Feldman's house. There was crime scene tape across the door, and Carl Bianchi was standing outside. Isabella got out of the car and Carl looked like he couldn't decide how to react to seeing her.

"Are you okay? I heard."

She ignored the question. "Anyone been in there yet?"

"I'm not supposed to let anyone in."

Isabella started to protest, and he cut her off. "*Anyone*. The sheriff says we can't touch this, especially ..."

He tailed off. He didn't need to say the last part. Feldman's status as "one of us" meant that the department couldn't handle this investigation. And the person who had killed the suspect sure as hell wouldn't be getting in there.

Isabella looked beyond the sentry barring her way into the house and thought about what Blake had seen in there. All of the materials pilfered from the original DMK investigation. Everything Haycox had done. Wheeler's notebook. And any conclusions Feldman had come to, after putting it all together. And she knew he had put it all together.

"Fair enough, Carl," she said at last. She turned and walked back toward the car.

"I'll see you later?" Carl called after her. Isabella didn't answer.

She drove back toward town. The events of the past few hours replayed in her head like a movie. She knew she could deal with them, put them in the locked box with all the other unwanted memories, but she chose not to. She kept coming back to the look on Feldman's face after she pulled the trigger. Shock and disbelief, giving way to something like understanding before the light winked out of his eyes.

When she got to the crossroads at Main Street, she slowed down and stopped. A right turn would take her to the sheriff's office, where Adeline would be reuniting with her brother for the first time in fifteen years. Straight ahead would take her out of town and past the house where David Connor had lived above his dead father for a decade and a half, until his secret had been unearthed.

She took a look around Bethany's Main Street. There were knots of people here and there talking. Some of them pulled a double take when they saw her in the car: looked away, then tried to pretend not to stare. There were two women nearby. Through the open window, she heard a snippet of conversation.

"I heard it was her. She was the one who got him."

Isabella sat there for a couple of minutes with the engine running, knowing her time wasn't infinite. Bethany. A nice town.

She turned to look to her right, along the road to the sheriff's office. Then she looked straight ahead, at the road that would take her to Connor's place. Then she put the car into gear and turned left.

79

CARTER BLAKE

David Connor looked up as McGregor opened the cell door. He was sitting in the middle of the bench bolted to the back wall. He didn't say anything, just looked at me expectantly.

And then I stepped into the cell and Connor saw who was behind me. His eyes widened and his mouth dropped open.

Adeline waited for McGregor to go in first, and then stepped nervously into the cell. She looked at David.

"I'm sorry."

David stood up. I saw McGregor tense as he took three paces across the cell floor. He stopped and stared at Adeline. Then he put his arms around her and drew her in for a tight embrace. Adeline gasped, and then her own arms wrapped around her brother.

"I'm sorry," she said again. "I'm so sorry."

80

ISABELLA GREEN

Isabella stopped at the wide spot on the corner before the Mercer place. The house loomed out of the fog. It was full dark now, and the lights were on inside. Waylon Mercer's truck was in the driveway. She could see Swifty the dog sniffing around at the tires.

She took her phone out and called Blake, not knowing exactly what she would say if he answered. It was likely he would be busy right now, with Adeline and David. It went to voicemail, which was good. She left her message, and then got out of the car.

Sally Mercer opened the door. She had a fresh bruise, around her left eye this time. When she saw Isabella, she shook her head.

"I didn't call you."

"Your husband home, Sally?"

"I didn't call you," she said, raising her voice. Waylon Mercer appeared in the hall behind her. "I didn't call her!" she yelled again, turning to face her husband. His face was full of contempt. As though he wanted to get this formality out of the way so he could come back and talk to his wife about the importance of keeping family secrets. But Isabella was done with secrets.

"Get out of here," Mercer said. "You heard her. You have no reason to be here."

Isabella stepped across the threshold.

"Are you deaf? Get the fuck out of my house if you don't have a warrant."

"I don't need a warrant."

Mercer grabbed Sally by her upper arm and tugged her roughly behind him. "Kitchen," he ordered.

Sally did as she was told. Maybe that was for the best.

"Well, how about we see what my lawyer has to say about that, Deputy?"

"How about we don't?"

Isabella took her gun from its holster, and pointed it between Mercer's eyes. He had just enough time to smirk before she pulled the trigger, twice.

81

CARTER BLAKE

After a while, we had to leave David Connor in his cell. McGregor had taken a call from the deputy at Feldman's place to say that the advance contingent of the FBI had arrived and started going through the materials in his office. Adeline sipped a plastic cup of water in the main office while I spoke to Sheriff McGregor about her brother. He believed there was a better than even chance that the evidence found at Feldman's house would exonerate Connor of the murders committed in the past week, though he would still stand trial for his father's death.

For my part, I was slowly putting everything together. Feldman had developed a fixation on the Devil Mountain killings. For some reason, he didn't want anyone else looking into it. He had been rattled when David Connor made noises about the case, and somehow that had led to the deaths of six men, not counting Feldman himself.

But why? What had made him do it? His actions were those of a man obsessed: with the case or with something else. Something, or someone. With a shiver, I remembered the pictures of Isabella.

And there was something else niggling at me. Green had told me Feldman had been distracted by Adeline's scream, and that she had taken the chance to jump him and get the gun. In the heat of the moment, I hadn't questioned her account. It was only when I had time to think things over that I realized that left a time gap. Adeline had screamed when she fell from halfway down the cliff. I hadn't heard the shot that killed Feldman until I had reached the top. The time passing between the two events couldn't have been under three minutes.

So what? It didn't dispel Green's version of events. But it suggested she had left something out. What had happened in those three minutes between the scream and the shot?

McGregor's phone rang as he was reaching for it to call Connor's lawyer. I heard him exchanging updates and guessed he was talking to one of his men. He had a funny look on his face when he hung up.

"Everything okay?"

"I need to go up there. They've uh ... they found something. They want me to take a look."

"Was that Green calling?"

"No. Carl said she went out there, though. He turned her away."

McGregor kept his usual poker face, but there was a crack in his voice at the end of his sentence that gave him away. He cleared his throat. "Maybe she changed her mind."

"Maybe," I said. "You go, I'll head over to her place and check on her."

McGregor gave me a thankful nod. "Give me a call when you know."

I drove up the hill to Green's mother's house, keeping my eyes peeled for a sheriff's department car or Green's Chevy. When I got to the house, the lights were on but there was no Chevy parked outside. Mrs. Cregg opened the door as I got out of the car. She greeted me and told me Kathleen Green was in her bedroom.

"Is Isabella with her?"

"No, she called a half hour ago, though."

"What did she say?"

"She just wanted to check I was here tonight. Then she

345

asked to speak to her mom. I just gave the phone to Kathleen and ..." she paused. "Is Isabella all right? She just didn't sound like herself."

"Have you been watching TV? Listening to the radio?"

She shook her head. "Kathleen's watching *Columbo*."

A voice echoed from inside. "Who's there?"

"It's Isabella's friend," Mrs. Cregg called out. "Mr. Blake."

"Send him in."

Mrs. Cregg led me through the house to the small bedroom at the back. Kathleen Green was propped up on some pillows in the small single bed. The television was on, with the sound on mute. Peter Falk was conversing with Ricardo Montalban in silence. Kathleen looked smaller than she had a few nights before. Older, too. As I entered, she looked up. There was faint recognition in her eyes, and her features creased as she tried to recall who I was. I put my hand out and introduced myself again before she could feel awkward.

"I'm looking for Isabella. I need to talk to her about something. Mrs. Cregg said she spoke to you over the phone earlier?"

She seemed to think about it. "I don't know. I think so? Or perhaps not. Sometimes I get confused."

"We all do, sometimes. I'm sorry to have bothered you. I'll keep looking."

She smiled. I turned to go and stopped midstride as she spoke again.

"We worry about her, sometimes, Kurt. I told you that before, didn't I?"

I turned around. I didn't correct her, just waited for her to continue.

"Arlo always tells me not to be so silly, and I suppose you will too."

Arlo. Green's father, the last victim of the original Devil

346

Mountain Killer. My hand curled around the car key in my pocket. I knew time was of the essence. Green had disappeared, and I needed to get back on the road and look for her. All of a sudden, that look on her face before she drove off seemed like something more than the after-effects of the shock of almost being killed, and having to kill a man. I needed to find her. But something stopped me from walking away.

"Not at all. Why do you worry?"

She sat down on her chair and looked into the distance. "After what happened at our old house. Arlo told me all she needed was a change of scenery. And he was right, for a while. She seemed like a different girl at first. And then she got older and things changed."

I felt a cold sweat on the back of my neck. Mrs. Green kept talking. She didn't look at me. It was as though she was talking to herself. Her voice was stronger, clearer. Her eyes seem to have taken on a new focus.

"When the killings started, I didn't want to think— well, I mean, what kind of mother would think *that*? She went out at nights sometimes, and when she did ... That night when she came home in the rain I knew she had done something. She begged for my forgiveness. Maybe I shouldn't have done what I did, but I couldn't lose them both. We buried the gun under the tree, and we burned her raincoat and her clothes. Nobody ever came to ask us about anything. We never spoke of it again. She got better. I really believe that. You believe it, don't you? That I did the right thing?"

For the first time, she looked up at me. I heard a siren in the distance.

"I lost my husband that night. I couldn't lose my daughter too."

I ran back out to the car. A blue-and-white Bethany patrol car flashed by on the road outside as I got in. I started the engine and pulled out onto the road, following the car. It followed the main road for a mile before turning up toward the loop around the eastern edge of town. I followed until it pulled off the road in front of a wide house with a porch. There was a woman sitting on the porch steps, staring into space, absently stroking the fur of a slim black dog. Two deputies got out, guns drawn and approached the woman.

They wouldn't need the guns. The killer was already miles away. Now that the roadblocks were down, she would know exactly how to put the maximum distance between herself and Bethany without being stopped.

I looked down at my phone. One missed call, Green's number. The voicemail icon was lit up.

82

ISABELLA GREEN

Friday October 31st, 2003

It's coming down hard now, the raindrops hitting the hood of my raincoat so hard that it almost hurts. I could stand under the trees for a little more shelter, but I don't. In a way, the rain helps. Just like the cold air I'm breathing in through my nose, out through my mouth.

I go out almost every night, now. I don't even think about it anymore. Sometimes I just walk through town, other times I head out in the woods, or on the mountain. My dad made me take the gun when I started going out on my own, for protection.

Most nights I don't see anyone. Sometimes when I see people, I hide until they've gone. And sometimes . . .

I think about the fight before I left the house. I think they know. They're not ready to come right out and ask me yet, though. Maybe they're not even ready to admit it to themselves.

Tonight's going to be quiet. Nobody's going to be out in this weather who doesn't need to be. My plan is to hike the mountain. I've never tried to go all the way to the top at night, or in weather like this, but I don't want to go home until they go to bed.

And then I see a glint of light on the wet leaves ahead of me. I turn around and see a car approaching up the hill. Whoever it is has taken the wrong turn off the north road. Nobody else is crazy enough to be up here in the rain. I shrink back into the side of the road, hearing the rush of the swelled river down in the ravine behind me. He'll go past me, realize his mistake when he gets to the lot at the start of the trail, and turn back.

But even as I'm thinking it, I know that's not what's going to happen. The gun seems to gain weight in the holster on my hip, and I know what comes next. I step out into the road and hold my left hand up. My right hand is tucked under the raincoat, drawing the .38 from the holster and cocking it.

The car slows. It's a dark-colored Ford. The windshield wipers are working overtime. The windshield is a little more misted up than it would be with only one person in the car. The driver turns and pulls into the shoulder, drawing level with me. He buzzes down the window. I can hear a rock song playing on the radio. The singer's saying he's not scared. The driver is a bald, middle-aged guy, his expression amused for some reason. I wonder what the joke is. I can see there's someone in the back seat. Front passenger seat, too. From my angle I see only the skirt and bare legs of a girl in the front seat.

"You break down, man?"

An assumption I've heard before. I'm tall, and with the

raincoat ... well, who would expect a girl to be out here all alone in the middle of the night? No telling what could happen.

I ignore him, feeling the contours of the gun in my hand, and wondering if I'm just going to turn and walk away. I've done it before.

"Are you okay?"

Without thinking about it, I raise the gun. Bang. The inside of the car lights up in the muzzle flash. I see the legs of the girl in the passenger seat twitch in shock. Bang. The second shot at the driver sprays his blood over the passenger and she starts to scream. I'm aware of movement in the back. Whoever is there yells out a word that sounds familiar and tries to open the door. I put a bullet through the window. The girl in the front is screaming and trying to get out of her seatbelt. I swing the gun back around and shoot her, the angle a little difficult. I see her blood spatter the interior, mingling with the blood of the dead driver, but I don't lean in for the second shot. I'm distracted by the way the one in the back yelled. And then with a cold chill I realize what he was yelling, and what that means.

I reach out and open the back door. I see my father slumped in the seat. His dead eyes staring back at me.

My name. He was yelling my name.

After that, everything is a blur. I stuff the gun in my pocket and close my eyes. When I open them, the car is still there. The song on the radio is still playing. It feels like I've stumbled on the scene of a horrible accident, like somebody else other than me did this. I look around. The rain is still coming down hard. I know what I have to do.

I'm lucky that the ground at the edge of the road is on a slight slope. The hard part is getting the car moving. As it starts to roll I'm able to twist the wheel around and angle the car toward the drop. It starts picking up speed and I barely let go before it rolls over the edge and crashes down into the *darkness. And then it's quiet, except for the sound of the rain-drops falling through the trees and hammering off my hood.*

It takes me an hour to walk back home.

Mom is waiting for me at the door, a look on her face like I've never seen before. I mumble something about how sorry I am and collapse in front of her, holding the gun out in both hands like a sacrificial offering.

83

CARTER BLAKE

"By the time you hear this, you'll know, I guess. Adeline knows, I think, or she's working it out. Maybe she's told you already. Either way, Feldman knew, and he left all his notes. That means it's over. Did you suspect? Sometimes I wondered. Like when you talked about how Adeline made herself into a new person, how that was how she was able to fool you at first, because she fooled herself. That's exactly what I did too. What I said was true, the Devil Mountain Killer is dead. She died fifteen years ago."

Green's recorded voice spoke to me from the speaker of my phone as I sat in the driver's seat, looking straight ahead. The message was only a couple of minutes, but it felt longer. She laid it all out. How she had wanted to talk to someone about it forever. She said she didn't know why she killed those people, back then. She understood there was no explanation as to why some people were like her. Some of them have an excuse: childhood trauma, drugs, bad wiring.

She thought she was just born that way; born to kill. But she said she had it under control.

"One day at a time. That's all it takes. Sounds simple, doesn't it? Every day, you don't kill anyone. And I did that for fifteen years of days. But I already killed one person today, so I figure Waylon Mercer is a freebie. And I'm doing the world a favor."

As I listened, I saw one of the deputies come out of the front door of the house. He took his hat off and scratched his head, still lagging a long way behind events. I knew exactly how he felt.

"Under control". Little things came back to me. The running, the abstention from alcohol or cigarettes or even caffeine. Hints of a fiercely disciplined personality that had been holding a lot more in check than anyone had realized.

Green's voice kept talking to me, telling me that although she couldn't explain the urge to kill those people, she knew why she had stopped. Her mother and father had been concerned for a while. They didn't know for sure, but they were starting to piece things together. They had fought that night, and Green had gone out in the storm. She didn't learn until later that her father had gone out to look for her. A twist of fate and three people being in the wrong place at the wrong time had led to him being in a stranger's car with Adeline Connor.

She started talking about what happened afterwards that night, but I had already worked it out from what Kathleen Green had told me. Green had confessed and begged her mother's forgiveness. Kathleen had helped her, buried the gun and burned her clothes. She could have provided an alibi for her daughter too, but none was ever needed. No one ever suspected the young, beautiful, functional psychopath.

No one until Feldman worked it out.

I could fill in the rest of the blanks, now. Kathleen had told Feldman something as her control began to slip. Maybe the whole story, maybe just enough to put him on the right track. Feldman was in love with Green, so he had kept the knowledge secret, even from Green herself.

When David Connor had hired someone to look into his sister's disappearance, Feldman had seen to it that the trail went nowhere, by killing Wheeler and González in Atlanta, and then Haycox when he realized he was looking into it. When I appeared on the scene, he realized the problem was getting worse. It was no longer something that could be dealt with quietly. He killed more people; tried to frame me first, and then David Connor, using the Devil Mountain Killer's MO and hoping that people would buy the explanation that Connor was obsessed with the case.

Green's message was almost finished, now.

"Will the feds go public with this? I don't know. I think they'll keep it hush-hush. Whatever Feldman found, McGregor won't be able to truly believe it until he talks to me, and he's never going to talk to me. They'll look hard for me at first, but when they don't find me, they'll leave it be. Something else will come up for the FBI, and McGregor will be only too happy to put this back in the past. The Devil Mountain case has been dormant for fifteen years, because the killer has finished. But I want *you* to know, Blake. I want you to be sure, and to be sure that it really is over now.

"I know what you're thinking. Now I've started again, I won't be able to stop. I don't know, but it doesn't feel like it. I'm not that person anymore. I can control it. But if I'm wrong about that, then there will be a trail. And I'm counting on you to follow that trail, and stop me. But I don't think I'm wrong.

"If I do this right, no one will ever hear from me again."

The message ended and I was left alone in the car with the silence.

She sounded reasonable, reassuring. But perhaps that was why the end of Isabella Green's message chilled me more than any of the details that had come before. It wasn't her words so much as the way her voice sounded.

She sounded like the kind of person you absolutely want to believe.

ACKNOWLEDGEMENTS

Every year the task of writing a novel seems borderline impossible, but once again, it's somehow managed to happen. This is due in no small part to the support I get from an ever-expanding group of people.

Thanks as always to Laura and the kids for letting me disappear for hours on end to write. Special mention to Ava for making sure the BBC, *TIME* magazine and George Takei have heard of us – ice cream on me. Thanks to my editor Francesca Pathak for doing a fantastic job helping me knock this one into shape, and contributing some really great ideas along the way. Luigi Bonomi, my agent, and Alison Bonomi were brilliant as usual, and always available for ideas and advice. Thanks to everyone else at Orion, particularly Bethan Jones and Jon Wood for their enthusiasm and suggestions for this story, and Lauren Woosey and Laura Swainbank for making sure people know about me and the books. And the people who did the awesome cover – this one is my favourite.

My ace advance readers Mary Hays, James Stansfield, Liz Buchanan and Eve Short. All of my overseas publishers, especially Pegasus for a warm welcome in a wintry New York. The whole crime writing community, who never fail to support, boost and occasionally intimidate me (in a good way).

Finally, as always, a heartfelt thank you to all of the readers, bloggers, booksellers and librarians who read the books and tell the world about them. Ice cream for all of you, too.

Discover your next compulsive read from
Richard and Judy Book Club pick

MASON CROSS

*'Mason Cross is a thriller writer for the future who produces
the kind of fast-paced, high octane thrillers that I love to read'*
Simon Kernick

It was a simple instruction. And for six long years Carter
Blake kept his word and didn't search for the woman he
once loved. But now someone else is looking for her.

Trenton Gage is a hitman with a talent for finding people –
dead or alive. His next job is to track down a woman who's
on the run, who is harbouring a secret many will kill for.

Both men are hunting the same person. The question is,
who will find her first?

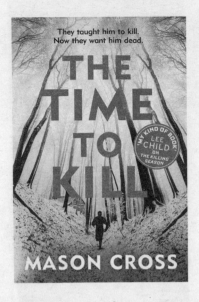

'One of the best new series characters since Jack Reacher'
Lisa Gardner

When Blake parted ways with top-secret government operation Winterlong, they brokered a deal: he'd keep quiet about what they were doing, and in return he'd be left alone.

But something has changed and now they're coming for him.

Blake may be the best there is at tracking people down, but Winterlong taught him everything he knows. If there's anyone who can find him – and kill him – it's them. It's time for Carter Blake to up his game.

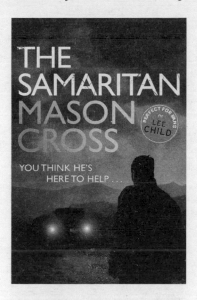

A serial killer dubbed 'The Samaritan' has been operating undetected for a decade, preying on lone female drivers who have broken down.

With no leads and the investigation grinding to a halt, Carter Blake volunteers his services. But he shares some uncomfortable similarities with the man he is tracking.

As the slaughter intensifies, Blake must find a way to stop it – even if it means bringing his own past crashing down on top of him.

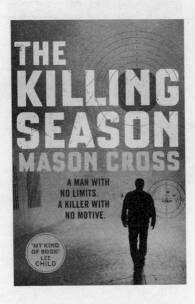